THE UNMADE WORLD

The Unmade World

STEVE YARBROUGH

UNBRIDLED BOOKS

This is a work of fiction. The names, characters, places and incidents are either the
product of the author's imagination or are used fictitiously, and any resemblance
to actual persons living or dead, business establishments, events,
or locales is entirely coincidental.

UNBRIDLED BOOKS

Library of Congress Cataloging-in-Publication Data

Names: Yarbrough, Steve, 1956- author.
Title: The unmade world : a novel / Steve Yarbrough.
Description: Lakewood, CO : Unbridled Books, [2018]
Identifiers: LCCN 2017034089| ISBN 9781609531430 (softcover) | ISBN
9781609531447 (e-isbn)
Subjects: LCSH: Life change events--Fiction. | Grief--Fiction. |
Guilt--Fiction.
Classification: LCC PS3575.A717 U56 2018 | DDC 813/.54--dc23
LC record available at https://lccn.loc.gov/2017034089

1 3 5 7 9 10 8 6 4 2

Book Design by SH • CV

First Printing

FOR JILL MCCORKLE

I have been so dislanguaged by what happened

I cannot speak the words that somewhere you

Maybe were speaking to others where you went.

Maybe they walk together where they are,

Restlessly wandering, along the shore

Waiting for a way to cross the river.

DAVID FERRY

CHRISTMAS IN

KRAKOW

2006

"You're lucky I love Ella Fitzgerald," his daughter says. She's standing on the chair he brought in from the kitchen, and she's just positioned the angel atop the tree. They bought that ornament this morning at a stall in the enormous Cloth Hall, which dominates the market square, and they bought the tree yesterday outside Galeria Krakowska, and then he dragged it ten blocks through the snow and up five flights of stairs. He was still jet-lagged, and though he goes to the gym twice a week and is in decent shape, he had to pause on each landing. Somewhere between the third and fourth floors, in the offhanded manner in which the most contented among us entertain such notions, he realized that his wife, who'd grown up here with her brother, had been right a few years back, warning that one day he'd wish they'd swapped it for a flat in a building with an elevator. He doesn't have that many regrets, but the lack of a lift may become one.

Anna cocks her head, looks hard at the angel, then reaches out and makes an adjustment. "We've listened to this same CD three times since we started decorating. Did you realize that?"

"It's a short disc."

"Not that short."

"And it's the greatest ballad album ever recorded."

She tosses her blonde bangs. "One could argue."

"If one did, what might one propose as an alternative?"

"Dexter Gordon's *Ballads. Clifford Brown with Strings. The Intimate Ellington*. Alternatives do exist."

He's having fun. He always looks forward to decorating the tree with her, but never more so than this year. They flew six thousand miles for the pleasure. "We started with Ella," he says, "so we're staying with her. It's important to maintain continuity when doing something as momentous as decorating your first Polish Christmas tree."

"This tree came from Norway."

"How do you know?"

"The sign above the booth where you paid for it said, 'Norwegian Wood.'"

"I didn't see that."

"You weren't looking." She puts out her hand, sticky from sap. "I'm finished," she says. "Help me down. I'm too mature now to jump."

He opens his arms. She steps into them, and as he lowers her to the floor, he gets a whiff of the scent she started wearing back in October after developing a crush on a kid who sits beside her in the string ensemble. She's no longer a child. She has breasts, for Christ's sake. "What do you weigh these days?" he wonders aloud.

"I would've hoped that by now you'd know not to ask a person of the feminine persuasion such a question. But I'll answer it anyway: a hundred and eight pounds, give or take an ounce." Gently, she pokes his stomach. "What do you weigh?"

"About a hundred and five kilos."

Like many musicians, she's also a proficient mathematician. "In other words, two hundred and thirty freaking *pounds*? Truly?"

"It sounds a lot better in kilos."

"You need to take it easy on the pierogi, Dad. Not to mention the goose-liver pâté."

A shade over six three, he's got broad shoulders that suggest he might have made a good linebacker in his youth, though the only competitive sport he ever played was baseball. He can carry a good bit of weight. Yet he can't deny that not long ago he had to let his belt out. He's been eating and drinking a little more than he should. The last few months have not exactly been stress-free.

He covers Central California for the *Los Angeles Times*. He's held that job for more than two decades, the only break coming seventeen years ago, when his Polish fluency brought him here to report on the revolutions sweeping Eastern Europe. Back in September, the *Times*'s publisher was ousted after protesting cuts proposed by the parent company. Then just last month, his editor-in-chief, a close personal friend, had also been forced out. What do you do if you can no longer do what you've done your entire adult life? Until recently, he hadn't thought he'd ever have to ask himself that question. Even now, he's not overly concerned. Still, when they return to Fresno in January, he'll send out a few feelers, just to stay on the safe side.

JULIA MIRECKA-BRENNAN: she's forty-six, a year younger than he is in December of 2006, her hair as dark as their daughter's is light. Her eyes are large, brown, and mildly convex, and they often roll out of focus when she's on top of him and an orgasm ripples through her. During their years together, she's taught Richard a great many things, one of which is to walk on her left, cantering along beside her like her personal Saint Bernard. If she decides to make a left turn, either to go around a corner or enter a shop where something has captured her attention, she drops her shoulder and nudges him in the proper direction. The single time he remarked upon it, she said, "What's a person my size to do when walking with someone like you?" He told her she could just say, "Hey, let's go in there," or "Why don't we walk down *that* street?" She responded that she liked how her approach was working, and he abandoned his inquiry because, basically, he did too.

Back in the '80s, when the country was under martial law, she had carried an extra toothbrush everywhere she went in case joining a demonstration led to her arrest. She has never been faint-hearted, nor has she ever been one to conceal her opinions. There's a particular way her mouth twists when she thinks you're full of shit. He doesn't see that expression very often these days, but it's definitely on display when she steps into the flat this evening, her cap and the shoulders of her sheepskin dusted with snow, and spots him and Anna standing there in the darkened living room, admiring the brightly lit tree, neither of them dressed for dinner. He's wearing slippers and an ancient pair of red Boston University warm-ups.

"Does either of you have the slightest idea what time it is?" she asks. She sets her shopping bag down in the hallway, then shrugs out of her coat.

He and Anna exchange glances. They had promised to be ready at a quarter till seven, and he knows it's at least six-thirty now. "I don't," he says.

"Me either," says Anna.

Julia lays her scarf aside, then bends to remove her boots. "It's six forty. The reservation's for seven thirty. You two are both hopeless."

"But what about our tree?" Anna asks.

Her mother pulls the boots off, stands them on the mat, then walks into the living room for a closer look. They await her assessment, pretending that it matters, even though all three of them know that this annual festive act belongs to him and Anna.

"The tree," she finally concedes, "is not hopeless. Unlike both of you, it appears to have a bright future, if only a very short one."

THE CAR is a '79 Mercedes diesel that they bought several summers ago. For much of each year it rests under a tarp. Until yesterday, he'd never driven it in cold weather. Mostly white, it features a beige rear quarter panel from a salvage shop and is missing its back bumper. The upholstery is a fungal shade of green, and at some point in the distant past, somebody had deemed the dashboard lighter the perfect tool for artistic expression, using it on the front passenger seat to burn little rings in the vinyl arranged to spell the name *Klaus*. Mercedes or not, it's a wreck, but it runs and is that rare European vehicle with an automatic transmission. He hates stick shifts. Truth be known, he can't drive one.

Julia and Anna climb in while he brushes snow off the windshield and the back glass. Five or six inches have fallen. It's coming down pretty hard now, but the forecast calls for it to quit by eight or nine o'clock.

He starts the car and pulls away from the curb, heading toward the Old Town. While he drives, Julia calls Monika, and from the conversation, he can tell that Stefan is still in the shower and that they'll be late too, something you can generally bank on. He thinks the world of his brother-in-law, but if he had to hold a real job, his life would be ruined. Fortunately, he doesn't need one. He's a successful crime novelist, his work published in more than thirty countries.

In Krakow, with the exception of approved vehicles, automobiles are banned in the Old Town. So they have to go around it rather than driving straight through. Traffic is surprisingly heavy. Everybody must be doing last-minute shopping. Stores will be open again tomorrow—Saturday—but virtually everything will remain closed on Sunday for Christmas Eve. He finds the country's transformation into a consumer culture both exhilarating and disquieting. Sometimes it seems that the profusion of color and the proliferation of choices have come at the cost of clarity.

"We're going to be pretty late," he says. "You better call the restaurant. The reservation's in my name. Ask for Mustafa and tell him who you are."

"Who am I?"

"The wife of the guy who wrote an article about his establishment for the *L.A. Times*. If Brad Pitt ever eats there, it'll be because of me."

She pulls out her cell, and from memory he rattles off the number. It used to amaze her that he could recall such minutiae, but she long ago accepted it as a by-product of his profession.

While she's on the phone, they pass the café where they met. It's called Bunkier and is attached to an art gallery that represents the purest example of Brutalist architecture in the city. Open to the air in warm weather, it's presently protected from the elements by clear plastic drop panels. The heaters must be turned up pretty high. Icicles hang from the eaves, and steam is rising off the roof. He's promised Anna they'll stop by for dessert tomorrow afternoon. They've logged many an hour beneath that canopy, whenever possible sitting at the table where he met her mom, whom he'd gone to interview for an article about women in the Solidarity movement. A couple of summers ago, while they waited there for their order, Anna rapped the tabletop. "So," she said, drawing the syllable out, "this is where the idea that resulted in me began to get a little traction. Right?" She told him later that he looked like a figure in a Renoir, with a scarlet splotch on each cheek.

Julia ends the call. "They'll hold our reservation," she says. "Your friend Mustafa's exact words were 'Please inform refulgent Mr. Richard that upon arrival he will receive supreme justice.' If I didn't know otherwise, I'd think he was threatening to execute you."

"You probably should've spoken English to him."

"Why? Is his English better?"

"No, but it's considerably less florid."

They cross the Vistula, then start west on Monte Cassino. Once they reach the outskirts, traffic begins to thin. Before long, they're traveling through the countryside on a two-lane highway. A lot of the *nouveau riche* have built villas along this route, many of them with four or even five stories. Interspersed among these new constructions are traditional Polish farmhouses.

Twenty kilometers from the city, he slows down. They turn onto the narrow blacktop and drive up the hill, where they finally see the sign. He takes a left onto an even narrower road and drives another half kilometer, and they find themselves in the snowy parking lot.

The popular dining spot is housed in a pseudo-alpine castle built by the Nazis, originally as a vacation site for Luftwaffe pilots. By the end of the war it had become a Wehrmacht hospital, and under the Communists it had served as the Institute of Forestry. Now it belongs to a wealthy Kurdish family who fled Saddam in the '90s, then bought and remodeled the rundown structure and established a Polish-Kurdish restaurant. The idea was disjunctive enough to make it wildly appealing, which explains why even on a night like this, the parking lot is jammed. He eventually locates a place between a Maserati and a Land Rover, the latter displaying a Croatian license plate. Someone else has come a long way for dinner.

Bogdan Baranowski is sitting on one of the checkout counters in the dimly lit grocery, watching it snow. The store occupies the ground floor of a dingy gray block that was purchased eighteen months ago by a young developer. So far he's succeeded in evicting over half the tenants from their flats. He plans to renovate the property and turn it into luxury condos.

Around a quarter past eight, a silver BMW pulls up to the curb and blinks its lights three times. At first, Bogdan can't believe it, so he doesn't move. Fifteen or twenty seconds pass. Then the lights blink again. "*O Jezu,*" he says. "*Matko boska.*"

He reaches under the counter and grabs the sack of kielbasa. Then he puts on his coat and sticks his hand in the pocket to make sure the balaclava is still there. It's black and made of wool and has holes for the eyes and mouth. When he tried it on in the bathroom, he immediately began to itch. He's always been allergic to wool, but this was the only one he could find. In the mirror he looked like a Chechen terrorist.

He steps outside, locks the front doors, lowers the security grating, and locks it too. Then he walks over to the gleaming sedan and opens the door. "Is this your brother-in-law's car?" he asks, lowering himself into the passenger seat.

Marek grins, his teeth white and perfect. Unlike Bogdan, he

still has a head full of dark hair only slightly shorter than it was in his teens. "Nice, huh?"

Bogdan reaches for the door but hears a faint whooshing sound as it slowly closes itself. "Did you tell him what you planned to do?" he asks. "If you did, admit it right now, and I'll get out. I'll probably get out anyway."

Marek throws the car into gear and pulls away from the curb. "Of course not. They flew to London to spend Christmas with their son and his family and asked me to feed their cats. I borrowed it for the evening." His wife's brother launched a small brewery around the time he and Bogdan founded their grocery chain. Five years ago Heineken bought it. Now his brother-in-law has a big house here, a smaller one in Zakopane, and a BMW.

It *does* happen. It just doesn't happen to Bogdan. "What model is this?" he asks.

"Seven sixty something. Under the hood, there's a V-12. If we need speed, we've got it. But we won't need it."

"How many of these cars do you suppose there are in the whole country?"

"More than *you'd* ever guess."

The emphasis doesn't pass unnoticed. Despite everything that's gone wrong for both of them, Marek has maintained his sunny outlook. He's been like that as long as Bogdan has known him, all the way back to elementary school. He's enough of a realist to admit he's never had a truly great idea but too much of an optimist not to think he'll have one eventually.

As a rule, Bogdan finds perpetual good cheer grating. But lately, the presence of a hopeful friend, no matter how deluded, may be the only thing stopping him from walking into the frozen-food locker, lying down, and closing his eyes. The truth, which he's incapable of admitting, is that he needs Marek. Almost every-body needs a Marek, if only to resent his existence.

"Since we're stealing your brother-in-law's car," he grumbles, "why don't we go over to their house and rob them instead of some stranger?"

THEIR BUSINESS losses can be traced to the arrival of heavyweight Western retailers like Carrefour and Tesco, with huge inventories and cutthroat prices. They owned four stores in '99, three in 2003, two in 2005. Now they're down to one, with a rent payment due on January 15 that they lack the funds for. They're in trouble with their suppliers too.

In all fairness, he and Marek aren't complete fools. Both of them have been to Western Europe, and Marek once visited relatives in the U.S. When they first started out, they knew what Western supermarkets looked like: bright colors splashed everywhere; countless versions of the same product, all packaged differently and positioned at various price points, the label on each item fronted with military precision; aisles as broad as the Champs-Elysées so shoppers can roll their carts past one another without toppling floor displays. They understood what was coming and believed they could counter it. They took over formerly state-run shops and made few if any cosmetic changes. They offered Polish products, kept prices low, and retained the employees who'd worked in the stores when they were owned by the state. This last practice produced the first hiccups.

In a country where nearly everything belonged to the govern-ment and nearly everybody viewed it as corrupt, cheating was tol-erated. Bogdan never did it, but back when he managed the warehouse, he knew that the guys who loaded and unloaded produce took a little bit home. A few apples here, a few pears there. As long as it didn't get out of hand, he looked the other way.

The people who worked the checkout stands in the first stores he and Marek opened were mostly women in their forties and fifties. They'd learned the appropriate survival tactics. Initially, they skimmed a few zlotys from the cash registers, but he put a stop to that by switching the drawers out several times a day. So they began overcharging the customers or shortchanging them, and complaints escalated. Finally, he called a meeting. "Listen," he told them, "things aren't like they used to be. You just can't keep cheating our customers. It has to stop."

A woman who reminded him of his grandmother asked, "Why do you care? It's not *your* money."

"If you steal from the customers, they'll quit shopping here. They'll go someplace where they don't get cheated. It's really pretty simple." Even as he made the statement, he knew it wasn't true. It wasn't simple for her, and it wasn't simple for lots of others. The world was changing faster than they could. Once people accept the notion that an old car ought to cost more than a new one because the old one is readily available but you can acquire the new one only by paying up front, putting your name on a list, and waiting ten years, it's hard to sell them the opposite reality. If you've lived your whole life upside down, living right-side up is like walking on the ceiling.

"I don't want to work here anymore," the woman said. He realized tears were on the way, and he prayed they wouldn't flow right there in front of him and the other employees. She pulled her apron off, flung it on the counter, grabbed her coat, and walked out. He stayed awake a long time that night, drinking vodka and feeling like a predator. Now he's become prey himself. And by this time tomorrow, if he's not dead, he'll be a thief as well.

MAREK HANGS a left, bound for the Grunwald Bridge. The snow is falling harder, in defiance of the forecast. "You know how this guy we're about to pay a visit to got started?" he asks.

"How?"

"Summer of '90, he begins hanging around the Auschwitz train station. This is before you had all those fancy tour buses ferrying visitors around from one concentration camp to another, giving them the Zyklon B tour. When he sees some Americans waiting on the platform for a train to Krakow, he ambles over and tells 'em the train'll take nearly three hours, that the bathrooms are filthy and smelly and there's no soap or toilet paper, and then he offers to deliver them in under an hour for fifty dollars. You know how impatient and finicky Americans are. A couple of times a day, all summer long, somebody accepts his offer. He converts the dollars on the black market, and come September he's got enough to start his construction business. Next thing you know, he's the go-to guy if you've made a bundle and want to build your own private swimming pool."

They're crossing the Vistula. Right in the middle there's a sheet of ice, though the water's still flowing on either side. "How rich can you get," Bogdan asks, "building private swimming pools in Poland?"

"Did it ever occur to you that if you've got enough money and a big enough house, you can put the swimming pool inside?" With a gloved finger Marek thumps the steering wheel. He can only stomach so much defeatism. Even if you think the world is shit, why not call it manure? It leaves a better odor. "No, it didn't," he says, shaking his head. "Besides, that's not all he does."

"So what else does he do?"

"Builds hot tubs, saunas, and heated doghouses. He's got branches in Warsaw, Gdansk, every major city. By the way, you didn't forget the kielbasa?"

"No, I didn't. Did you get your stuff?"

Marek pats his coat pocket. "Right here."

"I hope you've got the dose right."

"I guarantee you I do."

"I don't know how you can guarantee that when you've never laid eyes on the creature."

"The average weight of a German shepherd is thirty to forty kilos, and my cousin says this one's just regular-sized. To be on the safe side, I'm estimating forty."

"The safe side for who? Us or the dog?"

"We're people. It's a member of the animal kingdom. Besides, if it gets a little extra juice, all it'll do is sleep a bit longer."

Bogdan loves dogs. He's always loved them. As a boy, he wanted one more than anything, but his father said no. He and Krysia had to put down their chocolate Lab three years ago, and they've never gotten another one because they can't afford to take care of it. He'd rather starve to death than harm a dog. "You're sure about that?" he asks.

"Totally."

"How do you know?"

"I asked the vet."

"*What* vet?"

"The one who sold it to me."

This is not a good sign. "You said you were getting it from a farmer."

"I had to say that to keep you from backing out. See? You're scared now."

"Of *course* I'm scared. We're driving around in a snowstorm, in a stolen BMW, on our way to commit a crime. And you're telling me you bought a controlled substance from a vet . . . and asked his advice about how to tranquilize a guard dog? Stop this car right now. Let me out."

"Relax. The vet's in Rabka."

"In the mountains? What were you doing down there?"

"Going to see the vet."

"And telling him what?"

When you know Marek Ficowski as well as he does, you can tell when inspiration pays him one of its not infrequent visits. His face, young beyond its years, becomes even more boyish. In the greenish dashboard glow, the corners of his mouth have advanced with wide delight. He looks as happy as he did in fifth grade when they slipped away at recess with a bottle of vodka they'd stolen and drank it behind the wall of the Jewish cemetery. Bogdan got sick that day, and he's feeling sick right now. This night could end badly. It will end badly. He can all but guarantee it.

"The vet wasn't really a *he*," Marek announces. "It was a *she*."

"I don't care if it was a plow horse. What did you tell him, her, or it?"

"Funny you should mention a plow horse. Because the day I went to see this vet, her foot was in a cast. She'd been trying to vaccinate a horse the night before, and it stepped on her and crushed her instep. I told her I needed to knock my dog out for several hours because we were having our kitchen painted and a couple of years ago he'd bitten a plumber. This poor young woman was in terrific pain, and she just gave me what I needed, no questions asked. She was drugged herself and probably didn't remember the encounter an hour later. I felt pretty bad for her. I hugged her before I left, and the way she pressed herself against me . . . well, I'll be honest. If she'd offered to give me a rabies shot, I would've seized the chance to drop my drawers. You've got to take that first step somehow."

He probably walked into the closest veterinary office, greased the palm of some assistant with access to the medicine cabinet, and walked out with a syringe and a vial of liquid. Bogdan will just have to hope that he didn't say enough to become memorable. Because the truth is that if they don't come up with somewhere in the neighborhood of fifty thousand zlotys in the next few days, their last store will go the way of all the others. And then what?

He's forty-eight years old, with thinning hair and a potbelly. Sometimes in the morning, while they move around the kitchen making their separate breakfasts, he catches Krysia staring at him. She's quick to look away, but there's no mistaking her expression. It's not distaste, it's not disappointment, it isn't even pity. It's astonishment. How can someone who used to do so many things so well suddenly become incapable of doing even one thing right? When they were young, had almost nothing, and were still sleeping on the folding sofa in her parents' small flat, all he needed to do was lay his hand anywhere on her body—even someplace supposedly nonerogenous like her kneecap—to make her quiver. Now, if he touches her, she stiffens. He can't even recall the last time they kissed.

Marek turns off the highway, and they soon start to ascend, the road snaking past the occasional brightly lit villa that looks like it must've been transported here from Disneyland. When Bogdan was young, his grandmother lived out in this direction, in a two-room farmhouse that she'd once shared with his long-dead grandfather. Though there was always plenty to eat when he visited, Bogdan never quite understood where the food came from. For a while she owned a cow that she milked twice a day, had several chickens, and apparently sold eggs in a nearby village, though that was never talked about. At some point in the early '50s, as a result of remarks she'd made about the local collective farm, she'd been sent away for "reeducation." After that she kept her business to herself. She got by. That was all that mattered.

"You ever wonder who lives in these new houses?" he asks.

Marek shrugs. "Folks like our pool builder. He gets tired of the cold, so he and his young wife fly off to spend Christmas in Fiji. He has imagination. We've got imagination too, but so far we haven't tapped into it. When we get past this next little hurdle, we're going to have to innovate. Either innovate or deteriorate—that'll be our new slogan."

The snow falls harder, and they climb higher, finally cresting a big hill and then beginning their descent into a valley. You can see several clusters of lights down there, each one distant from the others, all of them gauzy, as if viewed through a layer of cheesecloth.

Leaning back, Stefan Mirecki pats his stomach. With his wild shock of salt-and-pepper hair and matching beard, he looks strikingly like Jerry Garcia and is, appropriately, a devotee of the Grateful Dead. "I just ate a meal," he announces, "worthy of a German field marshal. By the way, did you know one of them died upstairs, Rysiu? In '45, right before our liberators arrived."

Richard is still working on his duck. Roast duck with apples is his go-to dish in Polish restaurants, even one offering the potential for exotic fare. Stefan thinks that since his mother was a Polish immigrant, this must have been his favorite meal growing up and that he orders it in homage. Richard knows this is what his brother-in-law believes because he's read all his novels. In the most recent, a minor character clearly based on Richard appeared in a couple of scenes. When he ordered his duck, he was assigned a point of view for all of two paragraphs, solely so the reader could learn just how mawkishly sentimental a certain type of Polish American could be. The reality, at least in Richard's opinion, is more revealing than the fiction. His mother *never* cooked Polish food. His father, north-of-Boston Irish, doesn't like much of anything except roast beef, fried cod, lamb stew, and boiled potatoes. Richard never got to eat

roast duck until he came here back in '89, and the first time he
had it, he was with Julia. And now she won't cook it either, because she's worried about his cholesterol. He orders the goddamn
duck because he loves it. That's why most people choose one dish
over another.

"I guess I didn't know that about the field marshal," he says.
"Which one was it?"

His brother-in-law rolls his eyes toward the vaulted ceiling, admiring the inlaid crystals. The Jaziri family spared no expense
when it came to renovation. The enormous ivory chandeliers must
have cost many an elephant life. "Von Hötzendorf, I think."

Stefan has his own personal relationship with truth, and it seldom involves adherence to fact. Right now he's probably trying
out the field marshal business because he likes the atmosphere and
is thinking of setting a scene here. Generally, Richard lets these
moments glide by, but sometimes he can't resist calling him out.
"Von Hötzendorf's from the First War," he says. "He died eight or
nine years before Hitler took power."

"Well, then, it must have been some other *von*," Stefan says
cheerfully. He turns to Franek, who's laboring over his wild boar
and hasn't said two words since they sat down. "You better get
moving on that," he tells his son. "They've got some great desserts
here, and you'll be ineligible if you leave that much on your plate."

The boy's cheeks turn red. Looking at him now, Richard senses
that he feels very much alone. His mother plays viola in the Philharmonic and is often away at night, and his father makes frequent
jaunts to foreign countries as new books are released. The poor
kid's by himself too much, and puberty's on the way if it hasn't
already struck.

"Give him time, Uncle Stefan," Anna says. "I thought old people were supposed to be more patient than the young."

"Little lawyer!" To Richard: "I see she takes after my sister."

"Yeah," Richard agrees, "she's absorbed a few of her mom's character traits."

"You two are discussing them as if they weren't sitting at the same table," Monika says. "Like it's guys' night out. It's offensive."

To Richard, his sister-in-law has always been a mystery. A small, shapely woman who dyes her hair so black it's nearly blue, she usually doesn't say much. But when she does speak, she stares at you like you're the score of a concerto she's playing. This never fails to cause him discomfort, and he's occasionally had the feeling that she knows and enjoys it. Why that would be, he can't imagine. But she's the person who kindled Anna's interest in violin and gave her her first lessons, so he thinks maybe he should apologize, though he's not sure what for.

As though reading his mind, Stefan says, "I think maybe it's time for the guys to go have a smoke." He pulls a pair of cigars from inside his jacket. "Guess where these came from?"

"They're Cuban?"

His brother-in-law grins. "The benefits of being un-American."

Richard chews the last bit of duck and lays down his knife and fork. "The balcony?"

"Of course."

They excuse themselves and wind their way between tables. The other diners are all well dressed—a couple of women glitteringly so—and Richard hears a smattering of German, a phrase or two that he thinks might be Croatian, a fair amount of English. There's jazz on the sound system, "Someday My Prince Will Come." That's the only kind of music they seem to play here, and it's a big reason he loves this restaurant. His father ran a seedy jazz club in one of Boston's northern suburbs, and though it went out of business nearly thirty years ago, Richard thinks about it often, easily summoning the sight and smell of nineteen overflowing ashtrays, one on each table and three on the mahogany bar.

They step outside and light their cigars. The snow has slackened. Down below, they can see the lights of a few villas and farmhouses and, to the southwest, the airport's runway lights. It's cold but not that cold, especially because they're full of food and wine.

"Is it my imagination," he asks, "or is Monika on edge?"

"Rysiu, I've always felt you were wasted on journalism. With your sense of seismography, you ought to be a novelist." He looses a puff of loamy smoke. "I had this little thing going on locally. And Monika's not used to that."

The protagonist in his novels, a middle-aged detective in the Krakow police department, repeatedly cheats on his wife, often with three or four different women over the course of a three-hundred-page book. The twist is that he never pursues younger lovers. They're always at least his age and sometimes even older. His forte is highly atmospheric mature sex. He calls on them with weary eyelids, a bottle of Egri Bikaver, a tin of pasteurized roe, a chunk of smoked sheep cheese, cranberry relish. The world may be changing, but his actions affirm that in matters of the heart he adheres to the old ways: he kisses their hands coming and going.

"What kind of little thing?" Richard asks.

"She's twenty-two, works at that record store on Florianska."

He wouldn't be able to conceal his dismay if he tried. "Jesus. The blonde with that milky-white complexion?" The girl looks about as old as Anna.

"If you think what *you've* seen of her is milky white," Stefan says, "you ought to . . . Well, you don't like hearing this. Do you?"

"Not especially."

Stefan laughs and pats his shoulder. "I felt sure you wouldn't. But the setup's perfect, and I couldn't help but want to watch your reaction." He sucks hard on the cigar, the tip of it glowing bright orange. "Two brothers-in-law alone outdoors on a snowy night. One of them utterly, blindly infatuated with his wife. The other a hedonistic rake. Don't be surprised if this appears in a novel."

Richard won't be. "What surprises me is her age."

"Several of her predecessors were a year or two younger. Rysiu, our good detective's consorts are camouflage. They serve their purpose, though you should see some of the women who hit on me at book signings. The problem with this latest one's not her age. It's the fact that she lives in Krakow. I broke it off last week, but just yesterday I glanced out the window and saw her standing on the sidewalk watching our building. I suspect I may have fucked up."

"And Monika knows?"

"She does and she doesn't. In other words, she hasn't been told. I'm sure she has no idea who it is, at least not yet."

"Are you going to tell her?"

"Is that what you'd do if you were in my shoes?"

He's not about to say that he'd never be in Stefan's shoes. The only people who can truthfully say how they'd behave in any given situation are, by and large, people Richard Brennan does not want to know. "I think I probably would," he says.

"I think you probably would too. Of course, you'd never put yourself in this position to begin with." He gestures toward the dining room. "In there at that table, you've got everything you need. You've even got everything you want."

Why argue with the truth? In Richard's profession, you travel a good bit and see a lot of different people, a fair number of whom are women. He spends the occasional night in L.A., where he sometimes has dinner with a film producer in her early thirties, whose love life, he knows, is a disaster. The melting nature of her good-night hugs has led to the suspicion that if he wanted to, he could get himself invited back to her place or entice her to his room. It's not that he finds her unattractive or that her relative youth summons scruples an available woman closer to his own age might breach. It's just that he's already found what he spent his twenties looking for. How this came to be seems every bit as mysterious now as it did seventeen years ago. A geopolitical event got him sent halfway around the world, and he stumbled across the right person. That his domestic happiness is firmly grounded in happenstance sometimes unsettles him, but when he looks around at other contented couples, their stories are often similar. You can't say why fate smiles at some and sneers at others.

In a moment he and his brother-in-law, who writes fiction and lives it too, will go back inside and join their families for dessert. Mustafa will send over some cognac on the house, and Stefan will pronounce it the best he's ever tasted. Christmas plans made, they'll say their good-nights, and when Richard bends to hug his sister-in-law, she'll balance on her toes and whisper, "I'm sorry I snapped at you. Don't be angry." She will kiss him on the mouth, something she's never done before. It will surprise him, but he's going to forget it within the hour and will not think of it again for a long time.

Before any of that can occur, though, while they're still out there on the balcony, he asks Stefan the obligatory question: "What is it you want but haven't got?"

"I don't know. I have some of it—I just don't have all of it. And truthfully, Rysiu, if I were to find the missing element, you know what I suspect would happen?"

Richard takes a deep draft from his cigar, then blows out a cloud of smoke. He watches it disperse, the tiny particles spreading over the hillside, beyond the treetops, growing farther away from each other as they disappear into the night. "What?"

Stefan brushes a few snowflakes from his hair. "I feel all but certain that it would spell the end of me. With no need to hunt, I'd be a dead duck. One day I might show up on your plate."

HE'S HAD a good bit to drink, and his bladder's sending distress signals. So he asks Julia and Anna to wait in the foyer while he pays a visit to the bathroom.

To write news the way he does, you need to notice plenty of seemingly random details because life isn't just the big things, it's all the little ones too. For instance: a makeshift clock mounted on the wall in the bedroom of a boy killed by a stray bullet in Delano, California, in May of '93. The clock's hands were wooden skewers, one longer than the other, both of them glued to the hub of an electric motor that jutted through the spindle hole of a 33-rpm record which served as the clock face. The title of the record: *Internal Exile.* By the Chicano rock band Los Illegals. Where the boy came across the recording, which by then was more than ten years old, or what it might have meant to him, his grandmother who had raised him couldn't say, but she knew he'd built the clock for his seventh grade science project. Any good reporter notices a few things like that, but Richard likes to think he notices more than most.

Retained from his visit to the bathroom tonight: in the urinal there's a cherry deodorant cake.

The correct term for these items is "urinal deodorant block." They're also known as "piss pucks." If you look into the question more deeply, you'll find that in cities like Chicago, Detroit, and Cleveland, with their large concentrations of Polish immigrants, Polonophobes used to dub them "Polish mints." The thing is, you seldom see urinal deodorant cakes in Poland. Why this particular receptacle contains one is puzzling, yet there it is, lodged near the trap.

He finishes, zips up, washes his hands, and goes back to the foyer.

Julia's lips have officially pursed themselves, and her eyes somehow seem to have defied the laws of physiology and drawn closer together than they were three or four minutes ago. He calls this her *You fucked my sister* look, though she has no sister and what he thinks the look really means this evening is *You drank too much. Now I have to drive.* It will remain in place, he figures, until she pulls up outside their building and switches off the engine.

He's right about one thing: she hates driving and isn't happy to have to do it tonight. She never drove before she met him. He taught her himself, on long, empty stretches of Central Valley farm roads. Her car back home is a Honda Accord that she rarely drives farther than the grocery store. She dislikes the old Mercedes and has only driven it two or three times since they bought it.

That's not why she looks troubled, though. When Richard was out there on the balcony with her brother, Monika addressed her in the Russian every schoolchild of their mutual vintage had to learn: "You know what I appreciate about you, Julisia? If you think I'm a fool, you conceal it beautifully." Richard and Stefan returned before Julia managed to formulate a reply, which is fortunate. She doesn't know how she might've responded. What *can* you say when another woman, who happens to be your brother's wife, makes that kind of statement?

Anna, in contrast to her mother, could not possibly appear more radiant. Her golden hair brushes the shoulders of the white faux fur they bought her a few days ago at Macy's, and her face is flushed with excitement. She raises one hand and points at the ceiling. "It's *her*," she tells him. "It's like she's following us every-where we go."

At first he doesn't have the slightest idea what she's talking about. Then he hears that unmistakable voice wafting from the restaurant sound system. "Well," he says, "there are worse folks to be followed by than Miss Ella Fitzgerald." He puts one arm around her shoulders and the other around her mother's. Then he steers his family out the door.

When Bogdan climbs out of the car, more snow seeps into his shoes. Earlier, on their initial foray through the woods, his feet got soaked, and now his toes are numb. He has poor circulation anyway. "Let's hear the sequence again," he says.

Marek studies him across the roof. "Sure you wouldn't like a drink?" he asks, holding up the bottle. "Just to steady your jangling nerves?"

The bottle is small, and in the dark it looks almost empty. Earlier, when his partner first produced it, Bogdan came close to punching him, his fist rising as though it had a mind of its own. All evening he's been feeling like one of those drones the Americans are supposedly using. It seems as if some strange force has seized control of his body. "Give me the sequence," he repeats. "If you don't, you can count me out."

"I already told you four times."

"So tell me five."

Marek screws the cap off and takes another sip. "Four . . . two . . . one . . . six. Satisfied?"

"Not really. I won't be satisfied until I'm home in bed." Saying even that much represents wishful thinking. He'll never be satisfied again, whether they pull this off or not. Some places you can't come back from, and he's in one of them now.

"Time to do it." Marek crams the bottle into his coat pocket, grabs a crowbar from the backseat, and slips on his mask. It's black like Bogdan's, except above the eye slits there's an oddly shaped orange letter C and, next to that, the head of an orange bear.

Bogdan pulls on the balaclava and immediately begins to itch. His partner steps into the woods, and for the second time tonight he sets off behind him.

MAREK MADE the proposal a couple of weeks ago, the day after their produce supplier notified them that their account would soon be suspended. He would have suggested it earlier, he said, but he wanted to wait until his cousin had been in Ireland a while, to keep suspicion from falling on him.

When he recovered from the shock, Bogdan said, "You think this guy's smart enough to get rich but too fucking stupid to change the gate code after your cousin leaves to work in Ireland?"

"If somebody's in Ireland, why worry? He can't rob you from Dublin."

"No, but he can tell somebody the code, and they can rob you."

"He trusted my cousin."

"Well, that's an argument for his stupidity, I'll grant you. But he was still smart enough to install a burglar alarm—and smart enough not to give your cousin the code for that."

They were having this conversation in the meat locker, surrounded by carcasses suspended from hooks. Marek wore a blood-stained apron and was holding a cleaver. They'd had to let their butcher go last summer. "When the alarm's triggered," he said, "it sends a signal to the police station in Alwernia. We're talking about a town with a population of less than four thousand. On a typical Friday night, there are two cops on duty, and it's a safe bet at least one of them's drunk. Anyhow, it's nine kilometers away, on the other side of a mountain."

"What about the neighbors?"

"There aren't any. This guy bought everything nearby to guarantee his privacy."

"And the safe? How much does it weigh?"

"It's small, probably no more than forty kilos. You're telling me two healthy guys can't carry the damn thing a couple hundred meters?"

"I'm not healthy. I've got high blood pressure, and you've made it spike. Besides, you seem to be overlooking the guard dog."

"It's apparently pretty vicious," Marek admitted, "but we'll drug it. And you don't need to worry that it'll freeze to death, because it's got a fully heated doghouse. That animal lives better than we do."

He said absolutely not, hell no. Then he went home and found Krysia sitting at the kitchen table, and though her eyes were dry, he could see she'd been crying. The stove had just quit. She didn't complain or level any accusations, didn't tell him he was a loser or a fool, but the weight of their collapsed hopes was more than he could bear.

So now here he is, tromping through snowy woods right before Christmas. An hour or so ago, as they'd approached the back gate, the German shepherd had let out a growl that sounded like it was being amplified over a stadium PA and hurled himself at the gate so hard Bogdan thought it might rock off its hinges. The dog began to bark and snarl, and the noise continued even after Marek flung the medicated kielbasa over the wall. By the time they got back to the car, the barking had stopped. "Enjoy your dinner, you fucking Nazi," Marek muttered. Out came the vodka.

Bogdan stumbles over a fallen limb and staggers into a tree, banging his shoulder. "Shit," he groans.

"Quiet!"

"Quiet? You want me to be quiet?" He's almost shouting. "It'd be smarter to make as much racket as we can. Because if that dog's not out cold and we go through that gate, he may eat us for dessert."

"Don't be so goddamn dramatic."

"Don't *you* be so goddamn nonchalant."

At the edge of the woods, they pause. The clouds have parted, and they can see the house better than before. The wall is blocking their view of the grounds and the bottom floor, but you can tell the place is huge. It's got a couple of towers that make it look like something from the late Middle Ages or the Italian Renaissance, Bogdan isn't sure which.

There's plenty he doesn't know. He used to read a good bit, mostly popular history, books about the Second World War, the settling of the American West, polar exploration, the lives of various kings, queens, kaisers, and czars. But these last few years he hasn't read anything. He's worked ten-, twelve-, fourteen-hour days, and there's nothing to show for it except unpaid bills, unrealized dreams.

Inside that house, if Marek's cousin can be believed, stands a safe that always contains a couple hundred thousand zlotys. It supposedly rests in a concealed crevice on one side of the rock fireplace, behind a stack of logs. All they've got to do is bust in and, while the alarm is blaring and sending a signal to a police station, hurl the firewood aside, grab the safe, and carry it out the back door, across the lawn, through the woods, and to the car. When they return to Krakow, Marek will take it to his sister's empty house and go to work on it with a blowtorch. Bogdan will open the store tomorrow morning, and before they close the doors again their problems will be solved. The guy will miss the money. But he won't *miss* it.

"You know what bothers me?" he asks now.

Marek sighs. Most things bother Bogdan. But the main thing bothering him, his partner suspects, is that he hasn't gotten laid in the twenty-first century. If so, it must constitute excruciating torture, because his wife still has the kind of body that made God invent the fig tree. Marek has fantasized about her for years. "What bothers you?" he says to humor Bogdan and keep him moving in the proper direction.

"Somebody that builds swimming pools for a living must know everything there is to know about cement. Would you agree?"

"So what?"

"So when he's designing a secret compartment to hide his safe, why wouldn't he use cement to anchor it in place? Did you ever wonder about that?"

"No."

"Why not?"

"Because he didn't. And that's all that matters."

"You know what else bothers me?"

"What?"

"Why didn't your cousin rob the guy himself?"

"If he wanted that hotel job, he had to be in Dublin on a specific date. Besides . . ."

"Besides what?"

Marek pulls the bottle out and finishes it off, then drops it on the ground.

"He got bitten when he was little. He's terrified of dogs. Big or small, it doesn't matter."

The cousin clearly is not desperate enough to attempt anything this dangerous. Like most people, he probably just goes to work, gets paid, and accepts his lot. Whereas they convinced themselves they were destined to be tycoons.

Bogdan bends, picks up the bottle, and sticks it in his own pocket.

"Why'd you do that?" his partner asks.

"Because I'd bet that when you bought it, you weren't wearing gloves. Were you?"

Marek chucks him on the shoulder. "Good old Bogdan. We'll make a thief of you yet."

Without another word, they step out of the woods. Both of them served the military stint that used to be required of physically capable young Polish males, and they stride forward now in good order, as if a band that only they can hear has struck up "Dabrowski's Mazurka." *Cross the Vistula and the Warta, and Poles again we shall be. We've been shown by Bonaparte the way to victory.* He feels like he's marching to his own execution.

Without casualty they reach the wall. It's at least two meters tall. Trying to find out if the dog is ambulatory, Bogdan kicks the gate. This time Marek doesn't protest. His vodka-fueled bravado seems to have waned during their advance over open ground.

Nothing happens. He kicks it again. Still nothing.

"Well," he says, "if we're going to do it, now's the time." Operational command, he understands, has passed to him. He pulls a small flashlight from his pocket and shines it on the gate.

Above the steel handle there's a digital keypad. He suspects it allows a limited number of chances to enter the correct numerical sequence. He wonders if it might not also somehow be linked to the alarm, so that the final failure will set it off. A part of him would be relieved if that happened, because then they could turn and run before actually breaking the law. The other part knows how badly they need money. "Give me the code," he says.

Marek hesitates. "Four . . . four . . ."

"That's not what you've been saying all night. You've consistently said four two one six."

"Four two one six. That's right."

"You're sure?"

"Yes . . . Bogdan?"

"What?"

"You're feeling pretty good about the dog?"

"No," he says, bending and pressing the four key, "I don't feel good about the dog at all. But that doesn't matter. What matters is how the dog might be feeling about us." He punches the two key, then the one, then the six. Hearing a faint droning sound, he takes a deep breath, grasps the handle, turns it, and pushes the gate.

It budges but doesn't open wide enough for him to enter. "Too much snow's piled behind it," he says. Together they lean against it and finally manage to create barely enough space to step through. He goes first, and Marek follows.

No sound from the dog, and no sign of him either. About twenty meters ahead, on their left, is a small outbuilding that gives off an eerie blue light. Most likely the electrified doghouse. Bogdan hopes the animal got back inside before passing out, because if not he'll have to drag him in before they leave. Otherwise, he could easily freeze to death.

The big house itself is dark, not a light on anywhere as far as he can tell. He's thinking how strange that is when he takes another step and the night is suddenly ablaze.

Powerful spotlights are mounted on the roof and at various points along the security wall. For an instant, both of them are blinded. When he regains his vision, the first thing he notices is the kielbasa. It lies about two meters away, embedded in the snow, completely untouched.

A moment passes before the full import registers. "Oh, my," he says.

Marek, who to the best of Bogdan's knowledge has never attended mass in his life, crosses himself.

Simultaneously, they turn toward the gate. The dog stands before it, blocking their exit.

He's an impressive animal: his body is longer than it is tall, with powerful shoulders, straight forelegs, and a gently sloping back. He displays the classic wedge-shaped muzzle, oval eyes, and erect ears, and his nose is perfectly black. A showstopper for sure—and the show he's stopped tonight has two actors, each of whom will react to the threat in his own definitive manner.

For Bogdan, the event is simply the latest in a string of failures that started several years ago. Until then, he thought life was about addition: you worked hard for somebody else and saved a certain sum of money. Eventually you started your own business, and then you bought a place of your own. You and your wife had your own bedroom, with a bed that didn't have a crevice in the middle so it could be turned back into a couch the next morning. You had a new TV, a nice computer. Then one day, with little or no warning, you found yourself in the subtractive phase. Something went wrong, and that led to something else. You lost this, you lost that. And the next thing you know, you're standing in the snow, in the middle of the night, with a wall and a German shepherd separating you from your tomorrows. Only modest hopes remain. Maybe if they embrace their fates, conceding the dog's right to take a chunk out of their butts and make up for the kielbasa he's too smart to eat, they can get on with the business of living their shitty lives.

Marek, on the other hand, experiences the onslaught of terror, laced with no small amount of rage at the injustice. He's a person, yet he's been outfoxed by a dog. Before he can be cautioned to remain motionless, he brandishes the crowbar.

"You shouldn't have done that," Bogdan says.

As if to express agreement, the shepherd tilts his head to the right, studying Marek with those intelligent eyes.

"It's okay, boy," Bogdan whispers. "He wouldn't hurt you. He never hurts anyone but us."

The dog steps forward.

Marek yells, "Son of a bitch!" Then he hurls the crowbar at the animal, who drops his head. The crowbar sails right over him, clanging against the wall. Marek turns and runs toward the house, and the dog launches himself, halving the distance between them with a single graceful leap.

Bogdan is familiar with the concept of collective memory. Krysia, for instance, used to have a recurring dream in which she was pursued by German soldiers. Like him, she was born in '58, so she's unencumbered by recollections of life during the Occupation, yet that nightmare disturbed her sleep for years. One of his sisters has told him of a dream in which she's being force-marched through a frozen landscape, obviously bound for the Gulag. If he's ever experienced anything like that, he doesn't recall it. But when the dog bounded after his partner just now, he heard the thud of jackboots.

A few meters shy of the house, the shepherd takes Marek down. Within seconds he's on his back, flailing at his attacker, his high-pitched cries a pathetic counterpoint to the animal's basso profundo.

Later, usually when he's alone late at night and the vodka's all gone, Bogdan will try to convince himself that the instant he stepped through that gate, he lost the capacity to make rational decisions, and in a manner of speaking that's true. When you run out of good options, you just do what you do. In an altogether different sense, it will be a terrible lie, the worst one he's ever tried to tell himself, and he won't believe it for a minute.

The spotlights are still blazing. In the dark, he might not have found the crowbar. But there it lies against the wall, on top of a frozen drift.

Blood stains the snow. The dog has already bitten his partner numerous times: mostly on the hands and forearms. His claws have shredded the ski mask and made a mess of Marek's face. In a minute he'll go for the throat.

The big animal doesn't swerve from the task at hand. He maintains his focus. He must hear Bogdan's footsteps, the snow crunching beneath his inadequate shoes. But this is a diligent dog. His teeth remain embedded in Marek's flesh even as the crowbar shatters his skull.

"Let's hear your favorite Polish joke."

He looks away from the road long enough to see Marek's chest rise and fall. His eyes are closed, and the seatbelt appears to be the only thing holding him upright. He's definitely in shock. In the military Bogdan learned it's important to keep a shock victim conscious until he can receive medical attention; otherwise his brain may get too little oxygen. He knows a doctor he can trust. Anyhow, he hopes he can.

"Let's hear one," he says again. "Come on."

His partner groans but doesn't open his eyes. Both he and the car are covered in blood. "What?"

"You've been to the U.S. Don't they still tell Polish jokes there?"

"A few . . . But not to Poles."

Bogdan is breathing hard himself, sucking plenty of oxygen. His chest feels like it might burst. He's starting to wonder if he missed a turn a while back. There seems to be a lot more snow on the road than he remembers, and it doesn't look like anyone has come this way in the last couple hours.

"I bet you heard hundreds of them. Just tell me the best one."

"Two Poles . . ." Marek begins, then stops. His head lolls against the door post.

They crest a hill, and on the downslope Bogdan slows to avoid braking. At the bottom, next to a creek, he recognizes an abandoned farmhouse where a friend of his grandmother used to live, so he knows they're on the right road.

He picks up speed again, then reaches over and shakes his passenger. "Two Poles are doing what?"

"Walking."

"Walking where?"

"To California."

"And what happens?"

"In Arizona they get tired . . . so they buy . . ."

"They buy what, Marek?"

"A camel."

"And then?"

"I can't . . . I don't know."

He drives on. Before long, the road dead-ends at Route 780. They're no more than twenty kilometers from Krakow, and as he prepares to make a left, he thinks of calling the doctor to alert him that they're coming. The problem with that, though, is that he'd ask *why* they're coming.

He turns onto the highway. It's past eleven, the snow has quit falling, the road's in much better condition here, and as far as he can see, it's empty. So he lays his foot down on the accelerator. He's always wanted to drive a car like this one, and if he weren't terrified, he might be reveling in the BMW's response. He's never had such power at his disposal.

"You know what?" he says. "Don't take this the wrong way, Marek. But together, we've got the IQ of a hedgehog. That's why we believed we needed to rob somebody smart. Just cut out the thinking part and get what he's got. The problem is, one of the things he had was that poor German shepherd."

They top a slight rise. Ahead he sees the taillights of an old Mercedes.

"Compared to us, Marek, that dog was fucking Einstein. Are you with me?"

"Aah."

"Or maybe a better comparison would be to Rommel. Because the dog staged a *flanking* movement and took us from behind."

The Mercedes must be a diesel. It's belching soot from its tailpipe, needing a ring job as badly as any car he's ever seen. The oncoming lane is clear, so he darts into it. As they pass, he glances toward Marek and catches a glimpse of the other driver, a woman bending over the steering wheel, peering through the windshield as if she either can't see well or doesn't know the way.

He shoots back into the right lane. And that's when he hits the patch of ice.

He doesn't know that the BMW's iControl system has already sensed the skid and taken corrective action. So he reacts as he would have if driving his old Polish Fiat, slamming on the brakes.

In the rearview mirror, he sees the Mercedes swerve to avoid hitting them. It does a full three sixty, then disappears.

THE ROADBED is elevated a good three meters above the surrounding countryside. It's the kind of physical detail you can't fully appreciate just by driving through. Back when his grandmother was still alive, he traveled this stretch countless times, and if he ever noticed the raised roadbed, he doesn't recall it. His attention was never on the road itself but on the sights outside the window. Green fields and pastures, languid cows. The children of peasants frolicking barefoot, country dogs lapping at their heels. After he started school, he began to understand that terrible things had happened here. The Germans had used the road during their hasty retreat, the Red Army in its relentless pursuit. Plenty of people had suffered violent deaths in this bucolic setting. But for him, the highway represented escape from the tiny flat his family occupied in a Communist high-rise.

On the embankment, he loses his footing, falls, and slides to the bottom. He jumps up, pulls the flashlight from his pocket, and turns it on. The Mercedes is several meters away, its engine no longer running. It must have rolled over at least once. The roof has compressed like an accordion.

He runs to the driver's side. The glass is shattered, only fragments remaining in the frame. The woman's eyes, when he sees them, make him gasp. They're looking right at him—brown eyes, a little too convex, but they're pretty, those eyes, and completely unfocused. They don't see a thing.

He crosses himself, then touches her neck to check for a pulse. Immediately, his hand recoils. He shines his light into the rear seat, and after seeing the blonde hair and the arterial blood gushing onto the white coat, he bends over and retches into the snow.

Before clawing his way up the embankment, where he will climb into the BMW, put it in gear, and drive back to Krakow as fast as he dares, he stumbles around the front of the car to the passenger door and takes a look.

A FEW shards of glass have embedded themselves in Richard's cheeks and forehead. His mouth is full of salty fluid. His right arm and shoulder, though still attached to his body, don't respond when he tries to move them. He wants to push the light away, it's blinding him and he can't find Julia or Anna. As if the man with the flashlight understands that, he turns it off, and Richard gets a look at his face.

A pair of soft jaws that taper into a weak chin. A receding hairline, graying eyebrows, thin lips, a chipped tooth. Smallish eyes. To the left of an unremarkable nose, a large mole cleft in the middle, as if two separate growths have tried and failed to merge. It's a face destined to be forgotten by everyone who ever sees it, except the man who's seeing it right now.

ILL WIND

2009

If you walked across the yard this morning and peeked through the bay window, you might think you were seeing a man who's been banished from his matrimonial bed. Otherwise, why would he be balled up on the living room sofa, his long legs drawn toward his chest? It wouldn't be unreasonable to assume that he came home late last night with lipstick on his collar, reeking of sex and perfume, or that at the very least, he stayed out with his buddies and drank too much. Or maybe he simply sat there by himself and got shitfaced, though there's no bottle nearby, or a glass either. And since there's only one car in the driveway, odds are he's nobody's guest.

You'd all but have to believe he'd done something wrong to put himself where he is, this middle-aged man sleeping alone on the sofa in a three-bedroom house on a quiet California street.

THE DAY will begin and end with phone calls.

When the first one comes, he's still asleep. It's the landline, which he usually unplugs on his way to the bedroom, but it turns out he's not in the bedroom. At first, he doesn't know what he's doing on the couch. Then he remembers watching the Red Sox square off against the A's. At least this time he turned off the TV before curling up.

The closest phone is on the wall in the kitchen. When he lifts the receiver, he hears Monika clearing her throat. She does this at the beginning of every call. A couple of times he's thought about asking if she's aware of it.

"Richard?" she says, as if anyone else could possibly be answering the phone at his house.

"Hi, Monika."

"I know it's still early there, and I'm sorry if I woke you."

"That's okay. I needed to get up anyway."

"I'm by myself right now, and I just wanted to mention a couple of last-minute things."

He's standing in the breakfast alcove, where he seldom eats breakfast anymore. On the other side of the driveway, in the almost identical Tudor that belongs to Bob and Sue Lyons, he sees their daughter, Sandy, sitting at the kitchen table, staring at her laptop while she eats from a bowl of cereal. In the fall she'll be a senior. The other day her dad told him that while she's planning to apply to Berkeley and UCLA and a few other state schools, she'll choose Stanford if she gets in. He turns away from the window, steps over to the counter, and punches a button on the coffee maker. This time he's the one who needs to clear his throat. "Sure," he says, "go ahead."

She tells him that last week, Franek disappeared for more than twenty-four hours, during which he sent both her and Stefan numerous text messages, first begging them to let him remain in Krakow, then threatening not to come home unless they gave in. "Fortunately," she says, "Stefan's friend at the police department agreed to put a trace on his mobile, and they were able to locate him."

"Where was he?"

She's silent for a moment. "He was over at your place," she says. "I keep the keys on a peg in the pantry, and I didn't realize they were gone. I'm sorry."

"It's all right," he says, though it isn't quite.

"We went over everything with him again, and I think he finally understands that he's not being punished, that we're acting in his best interests, or at least trying to. But because he's always liked and trusted you, he may bring up the episode. So I wanted to let you know ahead of time."

"Okay," he says. "I appreciate it. If it does come up, I think I can handle it."

"The other thing is to just remind you to be careful with your computer. Banking, credit cards, and things like that. Because . . . well, you know what happened."

What happened is that Franek stole his parents' Bank Polski password and transferred several hundred zlotys to his weed source on a day when his mother happened to log in to one of their savings accounts and notice the debit. This led to the discovery of six previous transfers that had gone undetected because when you have as much money as they do, a few hundred here and there don't necessarily attract your attention. They're sending him a fifteen-year-old delinquent, hoping that a change in environment will help straighten him out. Richard's first inclination when they broached the possibility was to say no. It was swiftly superseded by the awareness that both Julia and Anna would have wanted him to say yes.

"I'll be careful," he tells her. "When I need to pay a bill, I usually just write a check. I'm fairly low-tech."

"Yes, I know, but he's not. By the way, I'm sure he looks at pornography too."

"Does that concern you?"

She laughs drily. "Not as long as he doesn't look at the wrong kind. How have you been, Richard?"

Over the past two and a half years, she's called him every few weeks to pose some version of that question. Sometimes Stefan talks to him too, sometimes not. Either way, hers is the voice he looks forward to. It has a soothing quality he was previously unaware of. "I'm hanging in there," he tells her.

Though he would not suspect it, she's standing in Franek's bedroom. Her son is at a café, having a going-away chat with his father. His bags are packed, and they're full of those things you can get with money: the latest MacBook Pro, the newest iPod, noise-canceling headphones that cost what some people earn in a month, numerous pairs of slacks and designer jeans, tailored shirts, a cashmere dressing gown that Stefan picked up for him in Copenhagen, as if it will ever be cold enough in California for Franek to put it on.

She sits down on his bed, which is twice the size of the one she used to share with her sister. Everything is bigger now, and there's so much more of it, so many different ways to anesthetize yourself. "Hanging in there is all any of us can do, isn't it?" she says.

"I guess so. Monika?"

She knows what he's about to ask her. The question is always the same, and so is her answer.

"Did you have a chance to drop by Rakowicki?"

"Yes, I did. Early last week. I left fresh roses in both vases."

There's a moment of transatlantic silence. Then he asks, "Was Stefan able to talk to Malinowski, see if he's turned up anything new?"

"To be honest, Richard, he hasn't. I reminded him of it, but he went to Denmark for the book release, and then Franek disappeared and he had to call Malinowski to help find him. But I will bring it up with him again soon. Now I need to get ready for this evening's performance. Please ring me the moment Franek comes off the plane. Will you do that for me?"

"Of course I will," he promises, then tells her not to worry.

After they've said good-bye, he finishes the first cup of coffee, then pours himself another and goes outside, where he sits on the steps for nearly an hour, staring at his lone sequoia.

HE PUTS on a pair of shorts, a tee shirt, and his Nikes and leaves the house on foot, walking up Maroa toward the gym. It's not yet nine o'clock, but already the temperature is close to 100, that dry, baking Valley heat that has never quite come to seem normal.

He spends forty-five minutes on the treadmill, working the speed up to six miles per hour, the fastest he can go without breaking into a jog. He's not supposed to run anymore. Twice over the last couple of years, his knees got so badly inflamed that he was forced to spend three or four days slugging back ibuprofen. On the treadmill he drives himself relentlessly, and as a result he's down to 185 pounds. It's not the weight loss he's after. It's the adrenaline.

When he's finished, he walks back home, takes a cool shower, gets dressed, and climbs into the car.

He drives out to a farm just east of Kingsburg, between Route 99 and the Sierra foothills. It's owned by a man named Jim Swenson. Eighteen years ago one of his three children, an eleven-year-old boy, died of cancer. Back then, Swenson was raising table grapes, using plenty of chemicals like almost everybody else. But after his son's death, he became a pioneer in clean farming. On the side, he's a landscape painter whose work has been exhibited in galleries and museums all over the state and even beyond. Richard wrote an article about him in '93, and for a while after that they kept in touch. He's going to talk to him today because last week he learned that the farm is being auctioned.

Swenson answers the door. He looks exactly as Richard remembers, a short, compact man whose smooth face is unusually pale, given how much time he spends outside. "Hi," he says. "Can I help you?"

This happens all the time. People he used to know no longer recognize him. "I'm Richard," he says, offering his hand.

Swenson recovers as best he can. "You're sure looking trim. Must've been working out."

"And trying not to be such a pig at the table. Thanks for agreeing to see me again, Jim."

Swenson leads him into the living room, which hasn't changed much either. He finds the same claw-and-ball-feet andirons before the same small fireplace; several overflowing bookcases, including a couple of shelves' worth of Wendell Berry; a pie chest that he had referred to in his article, noting that it had once belonged to Swenson's great-grandmother.

Two sofas face each other over the coffee table. His host gestures at one and takes a seat on the other. "So what can I tell you?" he asks.

Pulling out his notepad, Richard says that when he learned about the auction, he was both disturbed and surprised. "The last I heard, things were going really well for you. Mind if I ask what happened?"

Swenson locks his hands behind his head. "We're in the third straight year of drought. Priority water rights holders are still getting one hundred percent of their normal allotment. Last year we got thirty. This year we're getting ten. There's no more to be had, and even if there was, we wouldn't be able to afford it. But really,

that's just part of the problem." He says that he's had to borrow
more and more money to stay in business, and the only reason he
didn't reach this day a lot sooner is his income from painting. "I'm
not exactly Thomas Kinkade, but my stuff sells for decent sums.
It can probably continue to sustain my wife and me if we live
modestly enough, but it can't sustain this place."

"What do you think will happen to it?"

"The land? It'll be bought by an agribusiness conglomerate.
ConAg, Archer Daniels. One of those."

"Am I right thinking this must be costing you a lot of grief?"

"I wouldn't say it meets the grief standard. Grief's what you feel
when somebody you love dies." He says his failure to achieve long-
term success doesn't necessarily portend failure for anybody else,
that he still thinks clean farmers with know-how and commit-
ment can make a go of it. "Of course, they'll need a little luck," he
says. "Nobody can succeed in farming without that." For a man on
the verge of losing everything but his house and vehicle, he remains remarkably upbeat. He says he'll have a lot more time to
paint, that he wants to explore mixed-media techniques, that he's
developed enthusiasm for the works of newer artists like Soraya
French and Sera Knight.

Richard arranges for his photographer to visit the next day. Before he leaves, they stroll through a peach orchard. "I'm not going
to deny being sad about having to throw in the towel," Swenson
admits. "But all things considered, I'm pretty fortunate. I've still
got most of my family and friends, and I've still got my painting.
For a lot of people in my shoes, the end is just the end. What's left
of their lives turns into a long, dismal slog." He pulls a plump El-
berta off a branch, polishes it on his shirtfront, and hands it to
Richard.

AFTER THAT, he can't see going straight home. He drives up into the foothills, stopping on the roadside two or three times for no particular reason. Right now there's not a lot to look at except some sagebrush and honey mesquite. Whenever he and his family came up here together, Julia noted how dry and brown the landscape appeared, so different from southern Poland.

By midafternoon, he's at a quarter tank, so he turns and heads back down. In Fresno, he buys gas and stops at Subway to eat a sandwich. Then it's time to go home and perform the task he's been dreading.

The middle bedroom is his study, which he used to share with Julia, her desk facing the window so she could gaze at her garden, his facing the wall to avoid distraction. He considered turning it into Franek's bedroom and moving his work space into Anna's room. But he's been writing in the same place for nearly twenty years, and it's one thing that needs to remain unchanged. So he bought eight large plastic containers at Target, brought them home, and stacked them in the basement.

Now he carries them all into the hallway. He pulls the lid off the first one and opens the door to his daughter's bedroom.

He starts by removing the photos from the walls and bookshelves.

Anna hunkering before a toy refrigerator

Part of a kitchen set they gave her on her third birthday, when she was in what she would later refer to as "my 1950s housewife phase," the refrigerator was about three feet high, made of hard plastic, and lacking any source of electricity. She cracked four or five eggs, dumped them into a toy skillet, and left the skillet inside it while they went for a week to Yosemite. When they got back, you could smell rotten eggs from the driveway.

Anna onstage in Palo Alto at the Young Artist Competition, her face serene as she bows her way through the second movement of Szymanowski's First Violin Concerto

She won the bronze medal.

Anna cuddled up with his father on the couch in Massachusetts

She always called him "Dziadek." Never "Grandfather."

Anna wrapped tightly in a blanket, only her wizened face and one tiny fist visible as her mother holds her moments after giving birth

He doesn't even look at the last few photos, just removes them and places them in the container.

Next he goes to work on the books: Agatha Christie, Tove Jansson, Astrid Lindgren, and, though he once observed that they didn't jibe with her other choices, Larry McMurtry's *Lonesome Dove* novels. "Cowboys," she responded, "are my weakness." He thought the line was original, but it turns out there's a book of short stories on her shelf with that sentence for a title. A tidbit to savor when it seemed none were left.

The process ought to take days, weeks, months, years—a lifetime. Instead, it consumes less than three hours. He carries the containers, one by one, back into the basement. Then he returns to her room, where he puts fresh sheets on the bed for Franek, places a light comforter in a cover and a pair of pillows in their slip cases. By now it's eight thirty, and he knows he ought to eat but doesn't feel like preparing anything or going out for dinner, and anyhow he's not hungry. He crawls into bed with an Alan Furst novel that he's already read twice and manages thirty or forty pages before falling asleep.

WHEN HIS cell rings it's almost midnight. The name on the screen is that of his best local cop-shop contact, a detective in the Fresno PD named Joe Garcia.

"Brennan?"

He can hear out-of-sync sirens in the background. Then he realizes that at least one of them is actually close by, that it sounds like it's speeding south on Maroa. "Yeah. Hi, Joe."

"Listen, you need to hurry down to . . . What's the fucking address here again?" he hears the detective holler. Then, "Two thirty-six Paschal."

"That's near Calwa Elementary?"

"Not too far. It's behind a row of body shops. Which is kind of ironic, now that I think about it."

"What's up, Joe? What you got?"

Garcia makes a spitting sound. "A slaughterhouse," he says.

A boxy little prefab structure with a flat roof, iron bars over the windows and doors, it reminds him of houses he's seen in the Caribbean. At first, he thinks it's made of concrete, but Garcia says lath and stucco.

"No AC?" Richard asks.

"Just a fucking swamp cooler. But that's not even working."

The detective, who's about forty and nearly as tall as he is, wipes sweat off his forehead. His shirt is soaked. They're standing in the street, just outside the taped-off area, surrounded by police cars, ambulances, fire trucks, and a KSFN Action News van as well as thirty or forty neighbors whose toes and necks are being subjected to undue stress. More people are streaming onto the block from both ends. Some are wearing pajamas or nightgowns. One elderly man has ventured out in his boxers.

"We had to use a plasma cutter to get in," Garcia tells him. "It was around 120 degrees in there."

"Any idea how long ago it happened?"

"Not that long, and praise Jesus and Bill O'Reilly. 'Cause otherwise, in such heat . . ." He shakes his head.

"How many people are we talking about, Joe?"

The detective glances across the street and sees something

he doesn't like. Before turning away, he says, "Five, counting the one with the gun. But you didn't hear it from me."

"We're talking men? Women? Children?"

"We're talking I gotta go," he says over his shoulder, joining a gaggle of cops and crime-lab techs.

The woman he apparently left to avoid is tall and slim, a bit north of thirty, if Richard had to guess, with thick, reddish hair that sweeps across the shoulders of her burnt-orange blouse. He's never really met her, though he saw her a couple of weeks ago out at Corcoran State Prison after the news leaked that numerous inmates, including Charles Manson, had somehow acquired cell phones. She recently joined the staff of the *Fresno Sun*. Her hiring caught his attention because she used to work for the *Worcester Morning Journal*, where his former BU classmate is executive editor. He's read two or three of her pieces, and she knows what she's doing.

She puts her hand out. "We haven't been introduced," she says, "but I've been hoping to meet you. I'm Maria Cantrell."

Her palm is damp. On a night like this, whose wouldn't be? "Richard Brennan," he says.

"The *legendary* Richard Brennan. Alex said to tell you hello."

"How's he doing?"

"Ad revenue's drying up, circulation's plummeting. You know. But, hey, what're we gonna do?"

As soon as she opened her mouth at the Corcoran press conference, he knew she was not a native New Englander. Texas, he would guess. Probably the Hill Country.

"You don't sound like you're from Boston," he says.

She laughs. "You don't either, though I know you are. I grew up in Arkansas."

"Did you go to the University of Arkansas? A friend of mine teaches journalism there."

"Lake Village High. I never made it to college."

He senses she's waiting for a reaction to this last piece of information. If so, she'll be disappointed. "Was it my imagination," he asks, "or was Joe Garcia in a hurry to get away from you?"

"I interviewed him a few days ago about a cold case."

"Something he was involved in?"

"Yeah."

"Looks like your dredging may have caused a little discomfort."

"He actually brought the case to my attention."

"Oh. Well, Joe's his own private press agent. He can be useful, but I've got him marked 'handle with care.'"

"I told him I'm not seeing any story right now, and he acted pissed. Then the next morning he phoned and invited me out for a drink."

"Just so you know, he's married."

She laughs again. "Just so *you* know, I do know. And I said no."

The gurneys begin to roll out the front door. The lumps in the first couple of body bags are far too small.

"Oh, my God," she says. "Those are children."

The asphalt they're standing on is sticky. He lifts one foot and then the other, focusing on the suction—the tactile sense of it, the auditory. In another hour or so, when it cools down into the 80s, the surface of the streets will recover their firmness. There will be something solid and dependable to stand on.

The EMTs load the gurneys into the backs of ambulances, and they pull away from the curb, sirens ominously silent, flashers turned off.

An FPD spokesman faces the television lights and reads a prepared statement, which essentially says nothing. In the morning they'll hold a press conference, though when it will be, he doesn't yet know. Next the DA steps before the lights and says his own bit of nothing, and the crowd begins to straggle away. Richard tells Maria Cantrell good night, and she says that sometime soon she'd love to have coffee with him, let him bring her up to speed on the Central Valley, since Alex told her he knows more about it than anybody else. He says sure, instantly forgetting the promise as well as the person he made it to and moving off to accost as many neighbors as he can before they disappear inside their houses, turn out their lights, and bar their doors.

Family name: Aguilera. They'd lived there for two years.

The husband: Andres. In his midthirties. He worked at one of the nearby body shops.

The wife: nobody knows her first name or where she worked, or if they do, they're not saying, though everybody agrees she had a job of some sort and was often gone at night.

Three kids: one girl and two boys. The youngest a toddler, the oldest around seven.

An old lady came over most evenings, but nobody knows her name either, and descriptions of her differ.

Driving home, he turns the air on full blast.

In his study, he slams out twelve inches and e-mails the piece, then strips naked and climbs into the shower, turning it on as hot as he can tolerate, letting it pound his back and shoulders. Then he turns it all the way to cold, which isn't that cold, and stands there until the heat in his body starts to dissipate. He towels off, puts on a fresh pair of underwear, and steps into the backyard.

It's around three a.m., maybe a quarter past. His hands are balled into fists, and he's seeing that face looking in through the shattered window of the crumpled Mercedes.

Weak chin. Thin lips. Small eyes. Odd mole. It's as if nature chose not to waste time on the man's features, knowing something more essential was missing inside.

He sits down on the still-warm ground. Then he leans back, his knees raised, and looks at the sky. Despite the haze in the air, he can see a few points of light. Science was never his strong suit. He knows next to nothing about the constellations, can't recall more than a handful of names. Cassiopeia, Canis Major and Minor, Andromeda, Orion. At random he picks a pair of stars that look fairly close together, and though he knows they must be light years from each other and even farther from him, he stares at them until his hands and legs begin to relax and his pulse starts to slow. Like a patient prepped for surgery, he takes a final breath and falls asleep.

"Mr. Brennan? Mr. Brennan!"

At first, he doesn't know where he is or why Sandy Lyons would be bending over him in her nightgown, her hair down in her eyes. Nor does he know that he's not wearing anything but his underwear. Once this has all become clear, he masters the impulse to leap off the ground and cover as much of himself as he can. Instead, he slowly rises to a sitting position, holds it for a beat, then plants a hand and pushes himself up.

"I guess I gave you a fright, didn't I?" he asks, slapping dirt off his palms like he just slid into second.

"Well," she says, "I thought maybe you had a heart attack. You didn't, did you?"

"Not in the traditional sense."

"Did you maybe drink too much or something?"

"Not that either." There used to be a redwood fence between his house and hers, but because she and Anna were such close friends, he and Bob Lyons spent a Saturday afternoon nine or ten years ago sipping beer and knocking it down. He glances across the backyard and sees both Bob's and Sue's cars parked in the driveway. Neither has left for work yet and could well be watching while he stands here in his underwear talking to their teenaged daughter. As casually as circumstance allows, he asks, "What time is it, Sandy?"

"About a quarter after six."

"You're up kind of early, aren't you?"

"I went to get a drink of water and saw you through the window."

"It's sure sweet of you to check on me."

She looks at his compressor, which rests on a slab near the back door and is droning away. "Is your air conditioner okay?"

"Yeah, hon, it's fine. I had to go cover a really disturbing event last night, which I'm sure you can read about in this morning's *Sun*, and I just needed to lie down for a while and gaze at the sky. And I guess I got a little too comfortable."

"Isn't this the day your nephew's coming?"

"It sure is."

"What's his name again?"

"Franek. He may want to go by Frank here, I don't know."

"My mom said you asked if I could talk to him about school. I told her I'd be glad to, though several of the sophomore teachers are new and I never had classes with them."

"I appreciate that, Sandy," he says, "and I know he will as well."

"He's coming for the whole year? Or just the fall semester?"

"Probably just the fall. We'll have to wait and see. He'll actually be arriving right after lunch, and I've got a good bit to do before picking him up. So why don't you and I both go back inside before your folks wake and begin to wonder if I've lost my mind?"

"Okay," she says.

She turns and takes a couple of steps toward her back door, then

turns again. Before he knows what's happening, and perhaps before she does, she's thrown her arms around him, her breath tick-
ling his chest. She lets go of him as quickly as she grabbed him,
then slings her hair out of her eyes, walks across the yard, and disappears inside.

The building stands on Smolensk, not far from the Phil-harmonic. A five-story monument to Habsburg gloom, it still hasn't been renovated. The development company bought it six months ago. They've already done a couple of jobs here. They know this building well. "Call him," he tells Marek.

They're standing on the opposite side of the street. Marek whips out his mobile and punches in the number. He listens, his facial scars whitening from the tension. After a few seconds, he nods and presses the end-call button. "He's up there."

"Okay, let's go."

They cross the street, Marek carrying the boom box, Bogdan dragging the heavy burlap sack. It's midafternoon and swelter-ing, and he'd love to go someplace cool and drink a beer. He unlocks the front door and, once they're inside, hands the keys to his partner. "Go turn the power on to the elevator. This stuff's too heavy for me to lug it up five flights. I'll call when I get off."

"My mobile doesn't work down there," Marek reminds him. "You'll have to bang on the pipes. Do it hard." He turns and heads for the basement.

They do everything hard. If you look at it a certain way, they're avant-garde musicians, practitioners of the new urban art of percussive cleansing. The burlap sack contains their instruments.

The panel lights up, and he pushes a button and drags his load into the elevator. On the floor, in red paint, somebody has sprayed *go fuck a llama*. He knows it's English and understands the first three words but not the last. He used to have a Polish-English dictionary, and at one time he would not have been able to rest until he looked it up. But he's past the self-improvement phase. His self won't ever improve.

He steps out on the top floor, then drags the sack over to number eight and unlocks the door. The flat is in a shambles. Nobody has lived here since last spring, and it was a mess long before they left: wallpaper peeling off in every room, the toilet bowl tinged by the substances it's conveyed, the light fixtures broken or missing, the place reeking of cabbage and cigarette smoke. The only positive thing he could say about it is that it's not a lot worse than where he lives.

He drops his bundle and walks into the kitchen, where he opens the cabinet under the sink. He pulls a pipe wrench from his tool belt and hits the elbow joint five or six times, great ringing blows that on the floor below probably sound like gunshots.

A few minutes later, his partner knocks on the door. Once he's inside, they lock themselves in. Marek locates an outlet in the living room and plugs in the boom box, and within a few seconds some of the worst noise Bogdan has ever heard erupts. Pounding drums, belligerent bass. "What's the name of *this* shit?" he shouts into the din.

"It's a Swedish band named Steel Attack," Marek hollers back. "Fabian recommended them. The record's called *Diabolic Symphony*."

"Are they Satanists?"

Marek cups a hand to his ear. Over the last few months, both of them have lost a bit of hearing. "Are they *what?*"

"Never mind."

Together, they grab the sack and upend it, dumping the contents onto the floor. They've got a two-foot-high pile of broken bathroom tiles, bricks, and porcelain.

Bogdan tosses the sack aside. The cacophony is already giving him a headache. Every night when he gets home, his temples are pounding. "Well," he yells, "no point in putting it off." He picks up a bathroom tile and hurls it against the wall. Marek lifts a hunk of porcelain over his head and drops it on the floor.

AFTER THEY shut down back in 2007, he applied for jobs in the produce departments at all the big stores. The only response came from Alma, a Krakow-based chain that started the same year he and Marek incorporated and now had over forty shops nationwide. A high percentage of its products were luxury goods: Russian caviar, Italian coffee, French champagne.

The kid who interviewed him looked several years shy of thirty and called him "Pop." He informed him that there were presently no openings in either of the local produce departments and that even if there had been, most of the employees, including those who worked the bins, were college graduates. "It's a buyer's market," he said. "But our branch in Galeria Kazimierz does have a position available in custodial engineering."

"What would that involve?"

Seven days a week, from midnight until six a.m., he burned packaging left by the stock crew, then swept and mopped the floors and fronted the shelves. The good part of the job was that nobody watched him. He worked alone, locked into the store by the stock supervisor and set free the next morning by the assistant manager. The bad part was that because he worked alone, he had a lot of time to think. And he always thought about the same thing.

A few days after the accident, on the front of *Gazeta Krakowska*, he'd seen the face of the woman who'd been driving that night, along with those of her daughter and husband. Though he hadn't bought a paper for a couple of years, he fumbled through his pockets for change, then hurried into an alley to read it. He learned the names of all three people. Both the woman and her daughter were dead. The man, an American journalist, was said to be in serious condition, suffering from a broken leg and dislocated shoulder and the effects of hypothermia. The Mercedes had not been spotted until sunrise on the 23rd, and a hospital spokesman was quoted as saying the journalist could have frozen to death while unconscious, since all the car windows were shattered. An officer of the highway patrol, who requested anonymity, said police were investigating the possibility that another vehicle had been involved.

That evening, in the privacy of the bathroom, he opened his laptop to search for news of the wealthy pool builder, figuring that by now the dead guard dog would have been reported and that perhaps the authorities had already linked the two events. What he discovered was something else altogether: on the morning of the 23rd, during his Christmas vacation in the Fiji Islands, the pool builder went swimming off the Coral Coast. The last time his young wife glimpsed him, he was about two hundred meters from the beach, on a perfectly calm day. His body had not been found. It was a while before a troubling intuition made Bogdan check to see how many time zones separated Poland from Fiji, at which point he realized the guy must've drowned just as his dog was being bludgeoned to death. He again recalled how he'd felt as if he were doing someone else's bidding that night, as if his body were beyond his control.

For weeks that became months, he moved around in a fog, certain that at any moment there would be a knock on the door, a team of armed men waiting to escort him away. He read everything he could find online about the laws that pertained when you witnessed an accident. Even if you were not involved, it was illegal to leave the scene without notifying the police. And even if it hadn't been, his guilt was unquestionable. First he'd killed an animal, and then he'd caused the deaths of two human beings and in the process ruined the life of a third. He was missing some essential element. What it was, he didn't know. But he felt the absence as a void in his chest, and the void kept expanding, as though he were turning into absence itself.

After he got the job at Alma, he carried a small bottle with him to the store each time he reported for work. At first, he took care not to have a swig after three a.m. so the assistant manager would not witness the effects. But the analgesic wore off fast, and every time it did he'd return to that night on the side of the road, the lovely large eyes of the driver dead and unfocused, the blood gushing onto the blonde girl's white fur, the shock and confusion he saw on the face of the man he'd left alone to die beside his family. Three a.m. turned into four, and four turned into five. And when his own small bottle was empty, all the tall, glistening ones in the store's impressive liquor department began to beckon.

One cold morning a few days before Christmas, he felt a shoe prodding his rib cage. When he opened his eyes, he was looking straight up at the assistant manager, who held an empty bottle of Baczewski vodka, the least expensive brand sold by the store. "You know what I don't understand?" he asked, this young man who always wore the same pressed slacks, crisp white shirt, and neatly knotted green tie.

"No, sir."

"If you intended to drink yourself out of a job and shoplift too, why didn't you go for something better than this piss?"

"I guess I've just got poor taste."

He went home and told Krysia the truth, that he'd lost his job for drinking. She was in the kitchen when he gave her the bad news, and she didn't say much more than "Oh," just washed her hands and asked if he'd like some coffee.

Back in the '80s, she'd worked as a hairstylist, so the next day she signed up to retake the licensing exam. Though the personal upkeep industry could legally practice age discrimination, she landed a job at an upscale boutique owned by a guy in his thirties who affected a French accent and called himself Jean-Claude. His real name was Waldemar, and he came from Katowice.

Bogdan went on unemployment. They survived winter and spring by living off Krysia's wages and tips. He got up each morning and fixed their breakfast, which they ate in polite silence, and then while he washed dishes she went into the bathroom and prepared herself for the day. She had only three or four suitable sets of clothing, but she always left the building looking great, every hair in place, not a trace of gray. He suspected, though she'd never told him and he didn't dare ask, that she'd lied to "Jean-Claude" about her age. She could easily pass for forty or even younger.

For a while, he went out each morning and left applications at convenience stores, train-station kiosks, newsstands. But the gainfully employed were mostly in their twenties and thirties, occasionally their early forties. You might spot five new Lexus sedans rowed up waiting for a red light to turn green, but you almost never encountered a fifty-year-old man operating a checkout stand.

If you wanted to see guys his age in public, the best place to look was a park bench. You'd find plenty of them there, even in foul weather, their faces pasty, unshaven.

Before long, he joined their ranks, though he kept to himself, and if somebody else plopped down beside him, he'd leave and find another spot. He usually drank three or four beers with high alcohol content because they'd give him a quick buzz that would wear off before Krysia came home. He was sitting in the park one day around the beginning of summer, finishing his third one and thinking about the American whose life he'd destroyed, wondering where he was at that moment, whether he'd ever remarry, father another little girl, whether he could sleep, if he'd begun to drink too much, whether he recalled anything about the aftermath of the accident, if he remembered the man with the flashlight— when he looked up to find his wife standing before him.

The city has eight hundred thousand residents, but the old town is confined within the boundaries of a lush green band known as Planty, which follows the contours of the medieval moat. That she might happen across him one day had never crossed his mind, but when he saw her standing there he realized it should have. Yes, she worked in a different part of town, and Planty was not on her way home, but if Krakowians can find a reason to walk through there, they will. What her reason might be, he couldn't imagine. Wasn't this Wednesday, and didn't she work from nine till five on weekdays? It wasn't even noon yet.

She reached out and gently pulled the can from his hand. He thought she'd throw it in the nearby garbage receptacle, but instead, she raised it to her lips and took a swallow. He'd never seen her drink beer before. She used to drink red wine, a couple of shots of vodka from time to time, but in recent years very little except water and black tea.

"That's not bad," she said. She gestured at the brown sack on the bench beside him. "Do you have any more?"

He realized then what she was doing there at this particular time. Jean-Claude must have let her go. Maybe he'd discovered she was older than he thought and decided it was bad for business. He catered to a young clientele. Everyone did. "There's just one left," he said. Then, apologetically, "I never drink more than four. On a single day, I mean."

"Let's go home and split it." She patted her purse, which was large enough to conceal a small goose. "I've got a little something in here too."

What she had, he learned when they got back to their place, was a bottle of bison grass vodka. Stunned, he stood near the kitchen table and watched her stick it in the freezer. She found another beer in the back of the refrigerator and suggested that they carry it and the one he had planned to drink on the park bench into the living room. He followed her with a rising sense of unease. He couldn't imagine what had gotten into her. It scared him. He no longer believed she'd lost her job. If she had, she would've told him on the way home; he knew her well enough to say so with certainty. But instead she'd talked nonstop about a young woman she worked with who'd earned a degree in European studies at Jagiellonian University but now hoped to start her own salon.

She sat down on the couch, and he took his place beside her. She pulled both shoes off, leaned over and tapped the top of the beer can, then popped it.

"Why'd you do that?" he asked. For some reason, it bothered him.

"Why'd I do what?"

"Tap the top of the can before pulling the tab."

She lifted the beer—a Tyskie that he suddenly understood she must have bought, since he didn't like the taste of it and would never have bought it himself—and took a couple of big swallows. "You don't remember who used to do that before opening one?"

"No."

"My father. He did it every time."

Then he did remember. "That's right. He claimed it prevented the beer from spewing."

"He thought it was a terrible thing when they started putting it in cans."

"I remember that too."

"It's amazing what we forget," she said. "Little things and big ones too. You think you could never forget them, and then you do." She leaned against him. And then she let her head come to rest on his shoulder. "I've forgotten a lot of things I used to know about you. Things I always loved. The last few days, walking to and from work, I've made myself remember them. This may sound silly, but I even made a mental list. Want to know what's on it?"

Somewhere inside, the voice that kept losing the battle to govern his emotions warned him it might be best not to find out. "Sure," he said. "I mean, if you want to tell me."

She said that though at first it appalled her, she used to love it when they were still living with her parents and at the breakfast table he sometimes pulled a small square of milk chocolate from his robe and ate it with a slice of sausage. "You thought nobody noticed, but I did."

"Well, I used to love sugar and salt. Your mother, I guess, would've been appalled."

"No, my father would've been. As far as Mother was concerned, you could do no wrong. Remember how you used to eat ice cream?"

He hadn't thought about it for years. "I turned the spoon upside down right before it entered my mouth. The ones your folks had weren't silver, they were aluminum, and if they made contact with my tongue before the ice cream did, it spoiled the taste. I quit doing that when we moved out and could afford our own silverware."

"I know you did. You stopped doing a lot of things then, Bogdan."

The quitting, he might have pointed out, had occurred on both sides: it seemed that her interest in him had waned after they'd tried and failed to have children. She gave up her job and began to stay home, where she watched a lot of TV and filled out crossword puzzles, and he never protested because for a while, in the'90s, he really could do no wrong. They vacationed in Rome, renting an apartment near the Pantheon, eating lunch day after day at the same trattoria, drinking a liter of wine every time, paying no more than cursory attention to the amount on each check. They spent Christmas on the snowy slopes of Zakopane, where he bowled over a group of Japanese tourists who waited helplessly on their skis at the bottom of the course. She captured the collision on camera and thought it was the funniest thing she'd ever seen. She used to play it on the VCR when Marek and his wife came over for dinner.

"There's one thing I didn't quit," he said.

"I know. You never stopped loving me."

They finished their beers, and she said she'd go get the vodka. But when she left, she headed down the hallway rather than into the kitchen.

He lingered there on the couch for a few minutes until it became clear that she didn't intend to return. He finally rose and went to the sideboard where they kept porcelain and crystal. When he reached for the shot glasses, his fingers were trembling.

In the kitchen, he pulled the bottle from the freezer. It was coated by a layer of frost. He started for the hall, then stopped, screwed the cap off, and took a dainty swallow. Then he took a big one. In the hall he took another.

She'd closed the bedroom door. The icy bottle in one hand, the fragile shot glasses in the other, he pressed his forehead against the wood. The day was not that warm, yet in the last few moments his pores had opened, and he was damp from head to toe, perspiration trickling down his back and under his belt. He could see what she would see when he entered the room: a man turning to mush, melting from the inside out, as if his body was trying to purge itself of his poisoned essence. It took all his remaining strength to open the door.

The near side of the bed belonged to her. But she sat on the far side, her back to him. She wore a black negligee that was at least seventeen or eighteen years old. He hadn't known she still had it, but he recalled it well. She'd dubbed it the "Make-a-Baby Nightie" because of the ardor it always summoned when he watched her lift it over her head. No baby had ever been made, lust being an inadequate remedy for a low sperm count.

In the mirror on her dressing table, they established eye contact.

If she had been the daughter he'd never fathered, or either of his sisters, or Marek's wife, Inga, or any other woman he'd ever cared about, and he'd somehow come to witness this scene, he would've urged her to do whatever was necessary to stop him from laying a hand on her.

He turned the bottle up and took two or three swallows, then studied her image in the mirror. It was sliding in and out of focus. She stood and, without turning around, lifted off the garment and dropped it on the floor. Then she did turn, and as she walked toward him, he looked away, staring at the bedside table, where a small autographed photo of Lech Walesa had remained propped in its frame for many years. They'd met him a world ago in Zako-pane.

For the second time that day, she lifted a container of alcohol from his hands. When she turned it up to take a swallow, he allowed himself to look at her naked body, registering each detail: the shock of brown hair in her right armpit; her slightly asymmetrical breasts, the one on the left a little larger than its twin; her bold nipples; the dark thatch down below.

She stood the bottle on the nearby dresser. "It's not easy not to make love for so long, is it?" she asked.

"No. But I don't know if I can do it anymore. I got used to not doing it. Trying not to think about it. And in the meantime, I've become repulsive. Why would anybody want to do that with me?"

She didn't answer his question. And when he considered it later, his failure to insist that she do so seemed at best pathetic and at worst an act of aggression.

She closed the scant distance, pressing her heavy breasts against him, her breath hot against his neck. "You can do it," she murmured as she went to work on his belt. "I guarantee it." She took him roughly in hand, pulling, kneading, squeezing, then uttering the first of several obscenities. Soon she was on her back, her legs spread wide, her heels poised against the mattress.

Still wearing his shirt, he lowered himself onto her.

She drew him inside. "What'd I tell you, Bogdan?" she whispered. "Wasn't I right?"

As he began to move, he heard a plaintive cry, which he knew came from somewhere in his throat. Rather than study her face, like he always used to, he kept his eyes shut.

Her right arm lay stiffly at her side; her left hand gripped the corner post. Each time he moved into her, he heard her draw a shallow breath.

The lack of any other corresponding movement from her troubled and excited him. He sensed that she wanted it to be over, so he began to move faster. Suddenly, she wrapped her arms around his neck and pleaded, "Not yet. Not *yet*."

He felt the strength in her shoulders and with it a surge of confidence. He eased off, and they began to move in rhythm, just as they used to. Grace did what grace must do to be worthy of its label, conveying itself upon the blighted.

"My God," she cried near the end, her nails digging so deeply into his back that tomorrow he'd find his blood on the sheets. "Bogdan. Oh, Bogdan."

He buried his face in the cleft between her neck and shoulder. As the deepest sleep of his life overtook him, he decided that upon waking, before either of them left the bed, he would look her in the eye, tell her what had happened Christmas before last, and beg her to help him figure out how to live as decently as he could, given the terrible thing he'd done.

WHEN HE woke, it was nearly ten p.m. and already dark, and she was no longer there beside him. He reached into the wardrobe and pulled out his ragged bathrobe, shrugged into it, and carelessly tied the sash.

She sat at the kitchen table, her head in her hands. At first, though she must have been aware that he was there, she didn't look up. Then, finally, she did.

He stood no more than a meter away, so close that if he'd wanted to, he could have reached out and laid his hand on her shoulder. Yet even at this distance, her features faded to soft focus, her face and hair, her lips and eyes, the fine line of her jaw growing less and less distinct, turning into an assortment of pixels. He sensed that this was the final scene in a contemporary marital drama, and he was nothing more than a lens through which to view it. The presence of another person was implied, but the actor himself was invisible, and the scriptwriter had assigned him no lines. All he could do was listen.

"Bogdan," she said, "it isn't your fault, really it isn't. It's no one's fault but mine, and I hope one day you'll forgive me." She told him she'd be moving in with the young woman she'd met at work, the one who hoped to open her own salon. Agnieszka was the name he heard spoken. She said they'd become "partners."

MAREK AND Inga's sons were grown and on their own, so for several months he stayed in their old room. Unlike him, Marek bore visible reminders of their bungled burglary and under interrogation had revealed a creative version of it to his wife, omitting Bogdan's role and saying nothing about a wreck.

Before agreeing to let him live there, Inga made two stipulations. The first was that he had to shower every morning and go look for a job. The second was that as long as he slept beneath her roof he couldn't drink a drop. He tried to turn the latter into a joke, protesting that he seldom slept, but she'd never had much use for irony. She reached across the kitchen table and seized his forearm. "I'm not fooling with you, Bogdan," she told him. "It's nice out right now, but before long it'll be cold. Newspapers make shitty blankets."

She was a big blonde woman with broad hips and German blood, and though Marek often called her "the Brandenburg Gate," he also admitted that he would not trade her for anybody else. After the dog chewed him up, he said, he'd asked himself what really mattered, and the answer was family and friends and somehow finding just enough to get by.

Bogdan was being truthful when he told Inga he seldom slept. Most nights, he got only three or four hours before he woke, put his clothes back on, and let himself out to walk the streets. One rainy evening he crossed the Vistula twice on different bridges and walked all the way out to the western edge of the city before realizing he was retracing the route he and Marek had traveled eighteen months ago.

On those nocturnal meanderings, he avoided the part of town where his and Krysia's flat was located. He'd agreed to let her put it on the market, and agreed to a divorce too, and while he'd promised to come get his things sometime soon, there wasn't much he really wanted. He'd taken most of his clothes when he left as well as a couple boxes of books that would probably never be read again.

The place sold quickly. When she called to tell him, he didn't answer. In her voicemail, she sounded as if she was working hard to conceal her euphoria, thanking him again for his kindness and informing him when his share of the funds would be deposited into his bank account. She also reminded him that their belongings needed to be removed before the new owners took possession. He texted back, wished her well, and asked if she'd mind mailing him a few of his old family photos.

They'd gotten much less for the flat than they would have if it had been properly maintained. But his portion was still enough to pay rent and live on until he figured out what to do next. The problem was, he didn't care what he did next, or whether he did anything at all. "In the future" was a phrase he never used. The meaning of "tomorrow" had been radically reduced.

Once, around three a.m., a couple of weeks before he moved out of Marek and Inga's place, he found himself standing in the middle of the Grunwald Bridge. It wasn't really raining, not even sprinkling, but the air was full of mist. He stood with his back to the roadway, where every now and then a vehicle passed, setting off a small tremor. Ahead, to the northeast, Wawel Castle, brightly lit as always, loomed over the Vistula. Though spring had brought plenty of rain, the summer had been dry and hot, and the river was as low as he'd ever seen it. With no great sense of urgency, he wondered what it would feel like to hit the dark surface from this distance, whether the impact would knock you senseless, so that you were unaware when the water filled your lungs, or whether you'd flail your broken limbs as you sank into its depths.

He rented a studio in a smut-covered hulk on Blich, eye level with the elevated tracks. There was a balcony, barely large enough to accommodate a small stool, and that was where he sat and drank and smoked away much of the autumn. Trains clattered past all day and all night. Down below, on the sidewalk, people hustled along, most of them walking with their heads down, as Poles always do, even the happiest among them.

One afternoon, around the time people were getting off work, he saw Krysia. She'd just turned the corner. She wore a sheepskin that he'd never seen before, a green scarf knotted at her neck. She was gesturing with her hands while she talked to the woman walking along beside her, a much shorter blonde who carried a shopping bag and had a red purse suspended from one shoulder. The other woman kept nodding. As they drew closer he rose and leaned over the railing, hoping to catch a word, but just then yet another train rumbled by. He watched them all the way to the end of the block. There they paused, looked both ways, then crossed the street and disappeared under the viaduct.

Snow came, and when he could no longer sit on the balcony, he quietly began to go crazy. During a ten-day stretch in mid-December 2008, he didn't leave his room at all, not even after draining the final bottle of vodka and eating the last can of sardines. He had no television, no Internet connection either, so he tried to read an old biography of Pilsudski, but he kept having to go back and start over and finally gave up.

One day, he walked over to the snowy balcony, unlatched the door, and stepped outside. He looked down at the pedestrians hurrying along and understood that he had nothing in common with any of them and never would again. He considered jumping, but the sidewalk was not that far, and he estimated his chances of dying at no better than fifty-fifty. The thought of being confined to a hospital bed, facing questions from doctors and nurses, perhaps being catheterized and having his ass wiped by an orderly dissuaded him.

He hadn't looked at his phone for days and was not aware that the battery had long since died. So he didn't know that Marek had tried repeatedly to reach him, that Inga had too, as well as his sister in Zakopane. Nor did he know that Krysia had texted him holiday wishes. He'd lost track of time and could not have told you what day it was, though he'd heard a group of carolers one evening and understood it must be close to Christmas.

When the knock on the door came, it was dark outside. It was dark inside too, because he'd forgotten to turn on the lights. He'd fallen asleep sitting up and at first believed the knocking, insistent if not frantic, was just another element in the dreamscape where of late he resided. Dead eyes reigned there. Bloodstained fur.

"Bogdan? *Bogdan!*"

He stood. The room spun. He reached out and braced himself against the wall, then groped for the lamp on the table near the sofa bed and switched it on. Nothing happened. The bulb was gone.

"Please! Open the door, or I'm going to bash it in. I've got an ax. I swear it."

He moved in the direction of the voice, and his hand settled on the wall switch. He flipped it on and was instantly blinded, and as light illuminated the sorry space he began to sob. It was the dry kind of crying. Either it originated in a place too deep for tears, or he was so dehydrated that his body could not produce them.

When the door swung open, Marek saw him standing there heaving, his shirt incorrectly buttoned so that it bunched up under his throat and, at the bottom, left bare a patch of belly. The only furniture was the sofa bed and the table that stood beside it and over by the balcony door a small stool. The odor made Marek cough. His eyes began to water. Later, in the kitchenette, he'd discover that after the trash bin had filled up, his old friend had begun to leave his garbage on the counter and floor.

He hustled over to the balcony and threw open the door. A gust of icy air rushed in, taking his breath away and clearing, for the moment, his nostrils.

Bogdan had propped himself up against the wall. Otherwise, he would've collapsed.

"What in the world is going on here? Bogdan, what's happened? You've scared us all to death."

"Where's your ax?"

"What ax?"

"You said you had an ax. That's why I let you in. I didn't want to pay for a new door."

He spent Christmas back at their place. Inga insisted he shower every morning, and when she didn't think he'd eaten enough, she put more food on his plate and made him sit there and consume it while she watched. She let him have half a beer on Christmas Eve. One of her and Marek's grandchildren, a three-year-old girl, sat on the floor near his armchair while gifts were opened. Every time someone tore the wrapping off another one, she shrieked and clapped her hands. Marek and Inga had a lot less than they once did, but everybody got a present, and the children got two. His own was a pair of slippers.

As breakfast concluded on the 29th, Inga convened a meeting at the kitchen table. He had to go to work, she said. He couldn't just sit around wallowing in his own despair. He'd lose his mind. Anybody would.

"Go to work where?" he asked. "Get a job how? It's not as if I haven't tried."

She nodded at her husband.

"I've got one for you," Marek told him. "Fabian said he'd take you on."

For the past year or so, he'd been employed by the same development company that had evicted them from the building where they'd had their last store. He'd told Bogdan he was performing "maintenance," which seemed a little unusual because he'd never been able to fix or maintain much of anything. The developer himself hadn't hired him, he'd been approached by an underling whose first name and last were the same: Fabian Fabian. That alone invested the guy with sinister properties, at least in Bogdan's mind.

But Inga was right. He couldn't keep spending his days caged in the room near the tracks. If he did, he'd eventually throw himself off the balcony or walk across the street, climb the embankment, lie down on the rails, and wait for the next train.

Since sobering up and regaining a bit of strength, he'd had a strange feeling: somebody somewhere would one day need his help. Who that person was or why he or she might require the assistance of a man like him, he couldn't imagine. But he knew, as surely as he'd ever known anything, that the only honor left lay in being ready when the moment came. "All right," he said. "When do I start?"

"A week from today. I'll take you in to meet Fabian tomorrow."

It was a couple of minutes before he thought to ask, "By the way, what exactly does the job involve?"

Marek glanced at Inga, then rose and stepped over to the counter, where he poured himself more tea. With his back to the table, he said, "A little of this. A little of that."

THEY HAVEN'T been at it long before someone starts pounding on the door. Marek drops a brick on the floor, then turns to open it.

Bogdan grabs him by the sleeve. He has to shout in his ear so he can be heard over the satanic racket. "Not yet. Let him simmer." Back in January, when they began working together, his partner was nominally in charge. Now he is.

His Christmas awakening is only a distant memory, much like his marriage, the grocery chain he cofounded, the flat he was once so proud of. No one needs him, and no one ever will. Sometimes it seems that if he was put on the earth for any reason at all, it was to wreck the hopes of others. He rises each morning, drinks a pot of coffee, and goes out to do harm. He's not like Marek, who views this work as a prelude to something better—namely, superintending a group of renovated buildings, just as soon as they get rid of the remaining tenants in these recently purchased properties. That's what Fabian promised them. But Fabian's a liar and a hoodlum. There won't be a clean job at the end of this dirty job. There will just be more dirt.

The pounding doesn't stop. Bogdan turns off the boom box, steps over, and opens the door.

One look at the old man tells him plenty. He's in his eighties, slim and erect, with chiseled features and iron-gray hair, the collar of his powder-blue shirt stiffly starched, his bronze cufflinks untarnished. He almost certainly hails from what used to be called the intelligentsia. The Nazis seldom managed to rob men like him of their dignity, and neither did the Communists.

"May I ask," he begins, "what you think you are doing? I'm downstairs trying to work."

"We're just preparing the flat for renovation. I'm sure you've received several notices from the new owner."

"I know what you're doing."

"Well, then," Bogdan says, starting to close the door, "you don't need to ask."

The old man shoves his palm against it. His strength takes Bogdan by surprise. "If you think hooligans, riffraff, and peasant rabble frighten me, you are dead wrong. I fought in the Home Army. I've taken the lives of better men than you."

This is something new. All they've been told is that the last remaining resident used to be a professor at Jagiellonian University. His wife has been dead for many years. He's probably lived in this building since sometime in the '50s. He thinks it's his home, but he's wrong.

"I thought you were retired," Bogdan says. He's aware that Marek has stepped into the hallway behind him, that he's looking over his shoulder at the old man. This is the first time they've laid eyes on him, which is odd when you think about it, because a couple of months ago they spent a good bit of time in the building. Normally, they clear the stubborn ones from the top down, but

Fabian knew the occupant in number six would be especially troublesome, so they started from the bottom up.

"I am retired from the university where I used to teach," the old
man says. "I am not retired from work."

"What's the difference?"

"I remain a scholar. I am composing an article about a great
poet."

"Which one?"

"One you will not have heard of."

"Try me."

"I will not speak her name to so foul a presence." He tilts his
chin up, and his cold blue eyes look directly into Bogdan's. It
comes to him that he would not have wanted to encounter this
man in a forest at night. "I am warning you," the professor says,
"that I will not be driven from my home. I shared it with my wife,
and within those walls we raised three children. I have told your
Mr. Fabian"—he pronounces the name with disdain—"that I intend to expire in my own bed, beneath my own roof, in my own
good time. Unfortunately, I can't prevent his 'renovations,' but I
can and will file harassment complaints. The city code prevents
you from engaging in any activity that purposely creates a hostile
environment for legal residents, of which I am one. If that hideous
excuse for music disturbs my work again, of if you continue hurl-
ing missiles at the walls and dropping boulders on the floor, I
promise you that you will come to regret it. If you think the scum
that employs you will protect you from prosecution, you are every
bit as stupid as you look. Now, good-bye."

He turns and starts back downstairs. That's when Bogdan notices that one of his legs is shorter than the other. He walks with a
twisting motion that's painful to observe. It looks as if his right
hip might pop loose from his body.

He shuts the door and locks it. He's perspiring badly, his armpits soaked.

"Well," Marek asks, "what comes next?"

"What do you think?"

"Do we do it tomorrow?"

"No. We'll hit the building in Mistrzejowice in the morning and then move on to one of the others. Give this guy a little breathing room, let him think he scared us off. For all we know, he'll reconsider and move out. But if we eventually have to do it, one thing's going to be different."

"What?"

He mops the sweat off his forehead. He never drinks on the job anymore, but he could stand a drink now. "This time, we'll let Fabian go get the fucking acid."

They leave everything behind but the boom box.

On the sidewalk, Bogdan asks Marek if he wants to have a beer, but Marek says he promised to take his granddaughter out for ice cream this evening, so he'd better hurry home and clean up. He usually gives that sort of answer when Bogdan invites him for a drink. It's not that he's become abstemious, or that he's trying to distance himself from his friend. It's just that he has a life and everything that goes with it: a wife, kids, grandkids. A while back he and Inga even acquired a cat, and though he was never an animal lover before, he talks about the creature all the time now and takes great pleasure in the weight it's gained since they took it in off the street.

They agree to meet at the building in Mistrzejowice the next morning and tell each other good-bye. On his way home, Bogdan passes the Philharmonic, then crosses the street. He's trying to decide if he wants to sit in a café in Planty and sip a beer and watch people for a while or if he ought to just buy one and take it home. The problem with the former is that if he orders one, he might order two, and if he orders two, he will almost certainly order four. Whereas if he carries one home to drink, lethargy will usually stop him from going back downstairs and walking to the end of the block to buy more. He'll just sit on the balcony till the evening cools off, and then he'll go to bed.

He's decided against the café when he sees the woman hurrying toward him with her instrument case. She's short and dark-haired, nicely shaped, probably in her late forties, though you might think she was younger until you get close enough to observe the well-concealed lines at the corners of her mouth. He's still some distance away, but he's noticed this woman before, usually right around this time of day. The fact that she's always carrying the instrument and is dressed in black, even on a sizzling afternoon, has led him to draw the obvious conclusion that she's a member of the Krakow Philharmonic. There's nothing extraordinary about her appearance, yet once or twice after they've passed each other, he's allowed himself to imagine what she might be doing when she's not heading toward the concert hall to rehearse or perform. For some reason he wouldn't be able to specify, he suspects she lives alone, and since he's never gotten a good look at her ring finger and has no contradictory information, that's the fate he's assigned her. After performances, he sees her returning to her small apartment, where she puts on a Beethoven quartet and sips wine. It's always red.

Today, when she's within a couple of meters, he almost says hello. What prevents him is not his sense of decorum, which normally precludes such unsolicited greetings. It's the expression in her eyes. She's looking straight ahead, almost directly at him, he thinks, though later he will wonder if she wasn't gazing past him at the Philharmonic.

He was right the first time: it's him she's looking at. An instant earlier her thoughts were elsewhere, wondering what her son's first day in a foreign school would be like, whether they had made the right decision in sending him away or just shifted their problem onto someone else's shoulders. That was what was on her mind when she raised her gaze and saw the man with that strange mole split down the middle, as if each of the halves had a will of its own.

"You know what I can't remember?" his uncle asks.

They're sitting in the breakfast alcove, and he's just finished his second frosted Pop-Tart. During the last couple of weeks, he's gone through ten or twelve packages. At home, he never ate anything sweet for breakfast, but the sugar seems to satisfy some baffling new urge. "What?"

His uncle takes another sip of coffee, then sets his mug down. "The Polish name for Xanax," he says, speaking English as they always do at the table. "Is it the same, or is it called something else over there?"

Franek studies the brown stain at the bottom of his empty teacup. He can't stop himself. He does it whenever someone confronts him at the dining table with evidence of wrongdoing. He only became aware of the telltale gesture after reading his dad's last novel, in which a sullen young man with latent criminal tendencies did something similar. "Xanax is just Xanax," he says.

"Did you enjoy the ones you took from the bottle in my nightstand?"

If his dad had asked him the same question, his jaws would have locked themselves so tightly that he couldn't have responded even if he'd wanted to. His uncle has failed to produce that effect, maybe because he's smiling and it sounds like he actually wants to hear the answer. "I'd rather have some weed," he admits.

"Now, that never agreed with me. I haven't touched it since I was about twenty. It made me horribly paranoid, and looking back, I think it probably also depressed me. Sounds like it affects you differently." His uncle picks up the last of his toast and pushes it into his mouth. You can see he doesn't enjoy food very much anymore, that he only eats because he has to.

"Weed makes me feel a lot lighter," Franek says.

"Lighter how?"

"It's hard to describe."

"Why don't you try it in Polish?"

So Richard's nephew tells him that the lightness first manifests itself as a loss of sensation around the base of his spine, which then spreads upward into his back and shoulders, his neck and his head. He loses feeling in his ears, he says, and his nose too. "And as for my legs, it's like they don't have much of anything to do. They're still there, and I can feel them, but I don't need them. I know it's a biochemical-induced illusion, but it *seems* as if a lot more is possible, that if I chose to I could fly."

His scholarly tone might have made Richard laugh but for the suspicion that his nephew has too often been viewed with ironic detachment. "Well," he says, "I guess I can see why you enjoy it. I will point out, though, that it might be dangerous to think you can fly. Because you can't."

"Yeah, I know. And there *is* one thing about it I don't like."

"What's that?"

"A couple times when I was high . . ." Franek begins, then falters.

His uncle sees that his cheeks are turning pink. "Go on," he says. "What happened?"

"It made me use the bathroom on myself."

IT'S MONDAY, one of his mornings to drive. The sky is overcast, and the air smells like smoke. There's a fire in King's Canyon, another in Sequoyah.

Waiting near the car, Sandy waves hello. His nephew mumbles a greeting before climbing in beside him. She parks herself in the middle of the backseat, just as she used to during the years when he drove her and Anna to school. He never expected to have her in his car again, but her parents both work all the way downtown, and when Bob proposed that they carpool, he could think of no good reason to refuse.

Today, while he drives, he tries to draw them into mutual conversation, but it fails as it did on previous days. Sandy responds at length, her smooth face visible in his rearview mirror. Franek either says nothing at all, or if he does reply, it's usually no more than a word or two. Within a few minutes Richard gives up and turns on KFCC, where the morning jazz show is in progress, breathy Ben Webster caressing each note of "Danny Boy."

The high school on the University of Central California campus is housed in a collection of temporary modules and resembles nothing so much as a trailer park. He lingers just long enough to let them out. Though their eight o'clock classes meet in the same unit, they head for opposite entrances.

He plans to do a little work and take a shower before his lunch date. Most days, he takes the freeway, but this morning he's not pressed for time, so he drives back on surface streets. According to the dashboard display, it's already 88 degrees, with highs above 100 forecast for the remainder of the week. He recalls how badly the Valley heat affected Julia in their early years together. That first fall they experienced hundred-degree temperatures into mid-October, and it was 94 on Thanksgiving Day. They left town almost every weekend, driving over to the Central Coast or up to Yosemite or the Bay Area.

"Every time I leave Fresno," she once said on their way back from Carmel, "I fall in love with California. In Fresno, I only love you."

He laughed, because that didn't seem like such a bad state of affairs then, and it doesn't seem bad now.

This is what he's thinking about as he waits at a stoplight behind a black F-150 pickup with a University of Central California Cowboys bumper sticker. On some level he's aware that in the lane beside him, there's a silver BMW convertible with the top down, and that the driver, whom he can see out of the corner of his eye, appears to be talking on a Bluetooth device. Perhaps because he's taking in all of this as well as thinking about his wife and those couple of years before Anna came along to absorb them, he's oblivious to the sound coming from the speakers in the doors and dash. But gradually his awareness of all other sensory data—the odor of smoke, the bronco-busting UCC mascot depicted on the bumper sticker, the driver beside him in the BMW—subsides. That familiar, velvety voice captures his attention and assumes control of his body. It's Ella. Somebody told her goodbye and took her heart away, and from now on she'll be travelin' light.

The pickup pulls into the intersection and the BMW blurs past. As horns began to blow, he finally reaches over and, as calmly as he can, given how hard his hand is shaking, he shuts off the music before releasing the brake.

Chicken Liver's is about as downscale as downscale gets. It stands on Olive Avenue in the heart of the Tower District, Fresno's answer to the Haight. There's a U-shaped counter in the middle of the dingy room and along two walls a series of booths, all of them covered in forest-green vinyl except for the large lime-colored V's halfway across each backrest. He once interviewed a registered sex offender here. A group of residents was up in arms because he'd moved in nearby.

"This has become my favorite spot in town," Maria Cantrell says when he takes his place across from her. "Reminds me of where I come from."

"And where was that again?"

"Pine Bluff, Arkansas."

"I thought you said Lake something or other."

"Lake Village? I lived there too. We moved around."

He lifts the plastic menu from the holder and eyes the lunch specials. Country Fried Steak 'n Gravy. Honey Ham Steak. Fried Chicken Livers. Pot Roast. A tremor runs through his stomach.

She smiles. "Lighter fare's on the back."

He flips it over and studies it, then sticks it in the holder. "I think I might order the grilled-cheese sandwich. I ate a pretty good-sized breakfast."

"You know what I can't figure out?" she asks.

"What's that?"

"What the *V* on each of these backrests is supposed to indicate."

"*V* as in Valley—in other words, the San Joaquin."

"Oh, of course. And one other thing. Why'd they put the apostrophe in Chicken Liver's?"

"You tell me and we'll both know. Tell them and they will too."

The waitress is a hard-looking blonde who wears a green smock and could be anywhere between forty-five and sixty. She calls Maria by name but refers to him as "honey." After she's taken their orders and disappeared into the kitchen, Maria says, "Her folks came from eastern Oklahoma, though she was born down in Oildale. Merle Haggard's her cousin by marriage."

"Which marriage? He's had quite a few."

"She didn't say. I actually had a beer with her a week or two ago. She's a real nice lady."

Sitting across the table from her in the clear light of day, he notices a few things he missed the night of the shootings. The first is the thickness of her eyelids, which might suggest Slavic ancestry, though her last name points in a different direction. The second is her complexion: she uses a fair amount of concealer and probably had some issues with acne when she was younger. The third is that when she was younger might be a little bit farther back than he originally thought.

"So what can I tell you about the Valley?" he asks.

"Well, for starters, when will it cool off?"

"It ought to be fairly comfortable by Christmas."

"You're joking, right?"

"Sort of. Christmas probably will be nice, unless we're fogbound, which is always possible."

"This is the tule fog I've been hearing about?"

"Yeah. It's laced with agricultural pollutants as well as exhaust from cars in the Bay Area that's drifted down and gotten trapped. There will be some nights in December and January when the stuff's so thick you can't see ten feet. And by the way, when you go rushing out to cover a pileup, as you inevitably will, be careful, or you'll end up part of it." He tells her February is usually the most pleasant month of the year, that it's often warm enough for shorts and tee shirts and you don't yet have the March winds that'll coat your car in a thick layer of dust or the pollen that will clog your throat and nose in April.

"I've just got one more question," she says. "Why in God's name do you stay here?"

She's being facetious, but he's been asked this question before. His father is living alone in Massachusetts, in a house that's too big for him now, and he recently wondered aloud why somebody with Richard's credentials couldn't get a job at the *Globe* or the *Herald* or maybe even the *New York Times*. He suggested that a change of scenery might do his son good. Richard doubts it would, but from his father's point of view there's not much holding him here except that he agreed to take his nephew in for some unspecified period of time. He could pick up and go if he wanted to.

"Well," he tells Maria Cantrell, "this is where we raised our daughter. It feels as much like home as anyplace I know."

In time, he will learn that her frequent recourse to banter, which her accent renders more inane than it might otherwise seem, is her own personal screen saver. When she's ready to reveal something deeper, she will, often in a manner so direct it jars. "I heard what happened to your family," she says. "I'd never get over it, and I doubt you will either."

His throat feels constricted, like it used to when he was a kid and suffered an allergy attack. "You might be right. Probably are."

She locks her fingers together. "I don't know you well enough to have said what I just did," she tells him. "I'm very familiar with the taste of my own foot."

"It's okay. Don't worry about it."

The waitress returns with his grilled-cheese sandwich and Diet Coke, Maria's Cobb salad and iced tea. For the next couple of minutes they busy themselves eating. Then his lunch companion asks if he's ever been to the Golden Palomino.

It's a North Fresno restaurant and bar. There's a rearing horse in front of the low-slung building, but the entrance is in the back. He went there once years ago to have a drink with a guy that the FPD detective Joe Garcia told him knew some interesting facts about local chop shops. All the windows were about seven feet from the floor, narrow slits that let in almost no light, and the establishment featured not one but four different bars. The waitresses were barely clothed, even though it was midafternoon. "Yeah, I've been there," he says. "But it was probably ten or twelve years ago. Why?"

She spears a chunk of boiled egg, puts it in her mouth, and chews it. When she's finished, she says, "Jacinta Aguilera worked there as a hostess. Did you know that?"

It's news to him. The FPD held a second press conference two days after the shootings and announced that Andres Aguilera had taken the lives of his wife and three children before turning the 9-mm handgun on himself. No foul play was involved.

He's been trying to put the event out of his mind, just as he's tried to banish so many others: instances of domestic abuse, gang killings, multicar pileups. He's written a lot of fluff lately, something he hasn't really acknowledged to himself until now. A couple of weeks ago he wrote a piece about a former Fish and Wildlife agent who was training a three-hundred-pound Duroc-Jersey hog to break the world record for pulling Volkswagen Beetles. Fortunately, that one never made it into the paper. "No," he says, "I didn't know she worked there. Want to tell me why it's important?"

"Maybe it isn't."

"In other words, you think it is."

"She called in sick the night she was murdered." She pokes around in her salad, like she's looking for something in particular. "Are you a football fan?"

"Not especially. If the Pats are on, I'll watch them."

"What about UCC?"

"What about it?"

"The football team. Ever watch them?"

"Once or twice. But I'm not crazy about their coach."

She lays her fork aside, though at least half of the salad remains. "Why's that?"

He's not sure where she's going, but the means by which she hopes to get there has become intriguing. Supposedly a social engagement, their lunch has an agenda. He's got nothing better to do than play along. "I'll tell you why," he says, "but first, why don't you tell me what you know about Nick Major."

She shrugs. "I don't know much at all."

"'Much' is a relative term."

"Okay. He grew up in Visalia, played quarterback for San Diego State in the late '80s, bounced around the NFL for a while without ever starting a game, then held a series of assistant coaching positions at third-tier football schools like Northern Iowa and Montana State before becoming offensive coordinator at New Mexico. After they pulped Central a couple of times, he got hired here as head coach. He beat Oregon last year and Texas the year before that, and everybody thinks he's going to somehow turn this upstart little state school that doesn't even play in a major confer-ence into the national champion. He's got blond hair and a baby face and a trophy wife with big tits, and they have a thirteen-year-old daughter and a ten-year-old son." She crosses her arms and cocks her head. "So why aren't you crazy about him?"

Ten or fifteen seconds pass. During this brief time span, she searches his face for an indication of how her recitation went over. She's still angry at herself for the clumsy comment about the loss of his family. He didn't need to hear that, and she didn't need to say it. He's probably thinking, as so many men have, that she spends too much time alone in left field.

What he's actually thinking is that she possesses an attribute he's lost, though he hasn't admitted it's gone until now. It's impos-sible to assign a single word to it. "Relentlessness" comes closest but is too cold for his taste. "Doggedness" could work, but it im-plies lack of talent, whereas he doubts she's operating at a deficit. Later, he'll remember this moment as evidence that at least as of today he still understood a thing or two about character and moti-vation.

"After Central beat Texas down in Austin," he tells her, "an edi-tor at a nationally circulated general-interest magazine contacted me to see if I'd be interested in writing an article about Major. He'd beaten Washington the week before the Texas game, and though it turned out they weren't half as good as people thought and would finish the season with six losses, UCC suddenly had wins over two teams that were in the top twenty-five when they whipped them. The guy who got in touch with me was interested in how quickly an entire region with a very diverse population had coalesced behind a coach and a football team."

He tells her that the proposal was not without appeal, so he asked for a little time to think it over. Then one evening a few

days after the conversation, he pulled into the Whole Foods parking lot, and there was Nick Major climbing out of a black Jaguar.

"I trailed him into the store and kept an eye on him while I did
my own shopping. You didn't have to watch very long to see that
he loved attention. He signed an autograph while waiting for the
butcher to carve him a couple of forty- or fifty-dollar steaks, posed
for a photo with a young woman and her daughters, and threw an
imaginary pass to a chubby kid in a UCC Cowboys tee shirt.

"I introduced myself to him in the wine section. I told him
which magazine had asked me to write about him and said I'd
love to chat if he could find a little time over the next few days,
because I was trying to find an angle for the story. I have to admit
I figured he'd be plenty eager, since this was not a sports publica-
tion but a pretty tony outlet. So he pulls a bottle from the rack
and examines it for an inordinately long time, then informs me
that if I don't know what I'm doing, I probably ought to let somebody else write the piece."

"Jesus Christ," she says. "Are you serious? What'd you say?"

"I assured him I'd heed his advice and wished him good-night.
They were upset the following Saturday by Utah State. I considered getting drunk to celebrate."

He picks up the remaining half of his grilled cheese, handling
it carefully because it's dripping butter. He sticks a corner of it in
his mouth, takes a bite, and starts to chew. He will not say another
word, he decides, until she tells him what link she's found, if any,
between Nick Major, the Golden Palomino, and Jacinta Aguilera.

As if she's read his mind, she says, "I guess you're wondering
why I brought up Nick Major. So here's the answer, insofar as I've
got one."

She tells him that something about the second FPD press conference, where the chief and Joe Garcia responded to questions

about the Aguilera shootings, just didn't sit right. The chief, it seemed to her, was acting nervous, whereas Garcia exuded confidence, and the disparity began to trouble her. "The night of the shootings, I remember, you went one way talking to neighbors," she says, "and I went the other. Did you speak with the woman two houses east of the Aguileras, on the opposite side of the street?"

He calls up an image of the residence: beige stucco and something he'd never encountered before, a carport where the driveway ran straight to the front door. One of the oldest International pickups he'd ever seen was parked right there, the grill nearly touching the doorknob. He didn't even attempt to reach the bell. "No," he says. "Did you?"

"Not that night. But after the FPD press conference, I went back."

She tells him that a family from El Salvador lives there, and if she had to guess, she'd bet not everyone is legal. The woman who opened the door is named Ascension, and she's probably about sixty, a small, gray-haired lady whose relationship to the rest of the family is unclear. "The first time I went there," she says, "she was home alone, and we talked for close to an hour. The second time, a man of about forty opened the door, and when I asked to speak to her again, he said nobody with that name lived there and shut it in my face. I've been back twice with no luck."

She says that on her initial visit, Ascension told her she didn't know the Aguileras but that their children used to play in the yard, and sometimes she saw their father playing with them, acting like he was a kid too. She never noticed anything unusual over there, she said, except for a few times when a fancy car stopped and the woman climbed out and went inside. "'What woman?' I asked. She said she thought it was the one who got shot. So I asked her if she could describe the car, and she said she couldn't, that she didn't know a lot about cars. And then, if you can believe this, she said, 'But I make picture,' and while I sit there dumbfounded, she pulls out a cell phone and shows me the photo."

She reaches under the table for a leather shoulder bag he didn't know was there. She unzips it, pulls a manila envelope out, and undoes the clasp. She's enjoying the moment, and he can't blame her. He used to enjoy this kind of thing himself.

"Does this look familiar?" she asks, handing him the glossy eight-by-eleven.

It's a black Jag. In the photo you can see the back of the woman who's walking away from it. She has dark, shoulder-length hair and is wearing a black blouse beneath some kind of gold vest. It's a sunny day, and the gold is so glittery that it must have sequins on it. You can't see the driver from this angle. What you can see is the rear bumper with the California license plate.

He can't make out the entire number, but it begins *4RQW.*

"*KRK*," he told Stefan's friend from the Krakow police department, Malinowski, when the detective came to see him in the hospital two and a half years ago. "I don't remember the numbers. Just the letters."

The detective was about his own age, maybe a little older. With a long, sad face, large ears, and a wispy mustache, he resembled Charles de Gaulle, which was exactly how Stefan described the philandering hero of his crime novels. Discovering the real-life version might have proved mildly entertaining had he been there for a different reason.

"*KRK* would indicate a Krakow license plate," Malinowski said from his seat near the foot of the bed.

"I know."

"Except that the *KR* would be at the top, followed by a set of numbers below, usually five, at the end of which would come another *K*. So are you saying you saw the letters *KRK* at the top of the plate?"

"I don't know where I saw them. I just know those letters were somewhere on it."

"And you don't recall any of the numbers, not even the first?"

"No. I only saw it for what, maybe two or three seconds?"

The detective sighed while Stefan stood near the head of the bed with his hand on Richard's undamaged shoulder, patting it every now and then in a touching but futile effort to offer comfort. His brother-in-law wore a black jacket that would look just fine on Sunday at St. Mary's. Underneath it, a psychedelic tee shirt, Jerry Garcia with rattlesnake hair. The grave and the grotesque.

"It's amazing that you can recall anything whatsoever," Malinowski said. "But if you were able to remember even the first of the five numbers, it'd make our task a lot easier. That would rule out at least ninety percent of the registrations, if not more."

"It was a 7-series BMW. There can't be that many in Krakow. And it was either gray or silver. Wouldn't that narrow the field?"

"You might be surprised," the detective said, offering a prophecy that would not prove true.

There were, Richard learned a few days later, exactly three. The first belonged to a retired brewer, whose passport proved that he'd been in London with his family on the 22nd. The second was owned by the city president, but he was spending Christmas with his wife in a Zakopane B&B, and because the storm was especially severe in the Tatras, the roads had been closed all day. Malinowski made it clear that he had acquired this information at no small personal peril. The inquiry hadn't sat well with his superiors. For one thing, since the wreck had occurred beyond the city limits, it didn't fall within his jurisdiction—though this being Poland, everyone understood that when friends requested your help, you gave it, and Stefan had been his friend for quite a while.

The third car presented a more interesting possibility. The registered owner was twenty-eight years old. He lived in a six-room apartment near Planty, a prime location. He held no job and didn't seem to have worked anywhere in his entire adult life. His income, he told police, came from "investments," but it appeared insufficient to support his opulent lifestyle. Over the last year he'd visited Turkey twice, gone to Russia three times, and taken so many trips to Sweden that they weren't worth enumerating. The curious thing about the BMW, however, was that he'd purchased it new in Krakow on December 19th, and when the police examined it on the morning of January 3rd, the odometer read 33 kilometers. Insufficient to drive to the site of the accident and back.

Richard was sitting in an armchair when the detective gave him this news. It was late afternoon, already pitch-dark outside, snow falling again. An hour or so earlier, a doctor had informed him that he was well enough to leave the hospital. *And go where?* he wondered. *And see whom? Meet somebody for a drink?* If he hadn't drunk too much two weeks ago, he would have been behind the wheel that night, and by now he'd be in California with his wife and daughter. Reentry, he knew, was going to burn him to a crisp.

"The odometer reading can be rolled back," he told Malinowski. "In the U.S., when you drive a new car away from the dealer's, it usually has at least a hundred miles on it."

"I agree. The reading is extremely suspicious. But I'm afraid there's another matter we have to deal with." The detective said that the BMW had stood in a guarded parking lot on Karmelicka from three fifty-one a.m. on December 21 through one sixteen a.m. on December 27th. Footage from three security cameras confirmed its presence.

"Who buys himself a new car," Richard asked, "and parks it for a week?"

"I wouldn't. But he did."

"And what was he doing the whole time?"

"Celebrating the holidays with his girlfriend, he says. And she confirms it."

"And you believe him?"

"I didn't say that."

"But you think he's innocent."

"I didn't say that either. I strongly suspect he's involved in criminal activity—most likely the opium trade—and now that we're aware of it, I'm hopeful we can make his life unpleasant. But with respect to the accident, we have no case. And by the way, he looks nothing like the man you describe."

As far as Richard could remember, the last time he'd succumbed to rage was after getting bounced off a seesaw on his elementary school playground. He'd picked himself up, chased down the guilty playmate, and punched him in the stomach. He'd been given detention every day for a week.

He couldn't punch the driver of the BMW because Malinowski couldn't find him. And he couldn't punch Malinowski without ripping an IV from his arm. So he vented the only way he could, and if anything it was even more childish than cornering his friend and socking him in the gut. "Why don't you just get out of here," he said, "and go fuck somebody you're not married to, like the guy in Stefan's novels?"

The other man sighed, crossed his arms, and rolled his eyes toward the ceiling. "I'm not married to anyone, Mr. Brennan. My wife died four years ago. Breast cancer. It runs in her family."

In that moment, before he rose from his chair and dragged his cast and the IV stand a few feet so he could offer the detective his hand and ask forgiveness, he understood what he would become: a lost man who went quietly about his job, doing the best he could, though he didn't care very much about any of the things that remained for him to do.

HE STUDIES the photo a moment longer. "There's no time stamp on here," he tells Maria Cantrell.

"No, but there was a time stamp just above it, in her camera roll. It was taken on Thursday, July 30th, at eight twenty-three a.m."

He hands the photo back. "You checked the registration, I assume?"

"I don't need to. A black Jaguar with the license plate *4RQW150* is parked outside the University of Central California athletic building every day in the spot labeled 'Head Football Coach.'"

"What made you look there?"

"I learned that Major likes to have a drink at the Palomino. There are a couple of private rooms there, and anytime he wants one, he gets it. Once I found that out, I decided to see what kind of car he drove and discovered it was the one in the photo."

"So what do you think that picture proves?"

She pushes her salad to the side of the table so she can prop her elbows there, then brings her hands together and rests her chin on her knuckles. "Honestly?"

She's not that much younger than he is—ten or twelve years, he would guess, though he will learn it's only nine—but he feels the need to play devil's advocate, to protect her from whatever impulse made her ask him here to look at the photo. She hasn't been in town long enough to understand that the tree she's barking up has some gnarly roots. Fresno and the Valley don't have a whole lot going for them: they're dirty, hot, poverty-stricken and crime-ridden, with an inferiority complex the size of El Capitan. But one thing they do have is that football team. "Yes, honestly," he says. "Because I can't see how it proves much of anything."

She glances around the diner, which has gotten a lot busier than it was half an hour ago. "Well, for starters," she says, "it proves the good coach brought Jacinta Aguilera home very early one morning."

"You can't see the driver in that photo. It could be Major's wife."

"But it wasn't. Ascension told me that every time she saw the car, a man was driving."

"Yes, but she won't talk to you anymore, and for all you know she could be in Ilopango."

"Where the fuck is that?"

Her crudity surprises him, but he's still as adept as anybody when it's time to look impassive. "A city in El Salvador. INS catches undocumented aliens in the Valley every day. This is not central Massachusetts."

"It also proves that when he brought her home, she had on her hostess clothes. That's what they wear at the Palomino: gold vests over black blouses that reveal plenty of cleavage, black miniskirts that barely cover the South Pole. She spent the night with him somewhere."

"Maybe she babysat on the side and took care of their kids the previous night."

"Would you have hired a babysitter who dressed like that?"

"No. But I also wouldn't have bought that kind of car, even if I could afford it. And I wouldn't coach football for all the money in Fresno—and there's more money here, by the way, than you may think. There are a lot of things I wouldn't do that other guys might."

"She spent the night with him."

"So what if she did?"

"And a short time after they spent a night together, her husband supposedly shot her and his kids, though everybody I talked to said he doted on those children, that he tried to take them somewhere every weekend. His boss at the body shop said nothing had ever stunned him more than to hear he'd shot his family."

"That's usually how people react to tragedy," he says quietly. "They have a hard time believing it. Partly because they don't want to."

There's movement beneath the table. He feels pressure in his toes, and it increases almost to the point of pain. One of her feet is on top of one of his. She's pushing down as hard as she can.

"What in the *world* are you doing?"

"Trying to wake you up." The pressure eases off. "Your friend Joe Garcia likes to drink at the Palomino too."

"Quite a few people do."

"Did you know he sometimes handles security for private gatherings?"

"No."

"Well, he does. And he's done several events at Major's house."

He's in no rush to speak. He takes a little time to process the info and factor in her need to share it with someone who works for another paper. Then the dots begin to connect. Sometimes they do that on their own. Sometimes they don't.

He mentions the name of her editor, a man he's known for twenty years and one who has never impressed him. "Have you discussed this with him?"

"Of course, I did. Would you care to guess his response?"

"If he was having a good day, he probably pointed out the circumstantial nature of your 'evidence,' emphasizing the unreliability of a possibly undocumented immigrant who can no longer be found and most likely wouldn't talk to you again if you did find her. And then I imagine he administered a gentle lecture, explaining what the football team means to Fresno and the Valley, how important it is to both their economy and their morale."

"He wasn't having a good day."

"So he told you to fuck off."

"Lyrically speaking."

"And now, since you feel certain you've got a story, which he's warned you not to pursue, you hope to pull me in, on the theory that if I break it in some form or fashion, he'll have no choice but to let you off the leash."

She tosses her bangs out of her eyes, exactly like Anna used to. The only thing different is the color of her hair and the fact that she's about twenty-five years older than his daughter will ever be. "Want to go to a football game?" she asks.

When he gets home, it's nearly four o'clock. He enters the house through the side door, which leads directly into the dining room, and the instant he steps inside he hears their voices. They're coming from Anna's bedroom. He'll never think of it as anything else.

Rather than barging in on them, he stops to listen.

"That's the talk among the sophomores," he hears Sandy say. "I'm telling you for your own good. If you keep acting like you're not interested in anybody else, why should they be interested in you?"

"Maybe they shouldn't be."

"See? That's what I mean. It's like you're doing *this*—"

Richard wishes he could see the gesture she's using to illustrate.

"—to the rest of the world."

"It's just that people act so strange here."

"Strange how?"

"Like when Mrs. Maldonado calls names off the roaster—"

"*Roster*," she corrects.

"—rooster—"

"Not *rooster*. Roster. *Rah*-ster."

"*Raw*-stuh," he says, sounding for all the world like he was born in South Boston. "When she calls the names off it, everyone acts like they're waiting to learn if they'll be sent to the gas chambers."

"What gas chambers?"

"I mean they behave as if it's a matter of life or death. And it isn't. Why don't they . . ."

"Why don't they what? Finish your thought."

"I don't know how to say it in English. *Mogliby poluzowac.*" Apparently, he uses some body language of his own to convey the term, drawing a burst of laughter.

"Why don't they loosen up?" she says. "Is that what you mean?"

"Loosen up. That's right. American students need to loosen up."

"What's the Polish word for 'arrogant'? Or is that not a concept you have over there?"

It seems like the right time to let them know they're no longer alone. "Hey," he hollers, "just so you know, I'm home."

There's a moment of silence. Then the bedroom door opens, and they emerge into the dining room, where he's rifling through the mail.

"I was just offering Francis X a little unsolicited advice," Sandy says.

"Francis X?"

"That's how Mrs. Maldonado mispronounces 'Franciszek,'" Franek says.

"Yeah? I asked them to put 'Franek' on your student records. But maybe they had to go with the name on your passport."

"I prefer 'Francis X,'" Sandy says. "It adds a touch of mystery. Like he's been sent here to infiltrate and undermine our most cherished institutions."

Franek's cheeks, Richard notices, are problematically red, about the same color as the soccer jersey he's wearing. He knows Sandy means well, that she's trying to help the poor kid crawl out of his shell. He also knows, because her father told him, that she recently got dumped by her boyfriend. Maybe she views his maladjusted nephew as a worthwhile distraction, even though he's two years younger.

"Aren't you a football fan, Sandy?" he asks, pretending to study his PG&E bill.

"I watch games sometimes with my dad. Why?"

"A friend of mine and I are planning to go see UCC play a week from Saturday. It's a pretty important intersectional contest. Wisconsin's ranked number five nationally. I'll be up in the press box, but if the two of you wanted to come along, you could sit with my friend and keep her company. Afterwards, maybe we'll go out and grab a pizza or eat Chinese. Interested?"

"Sounds fine to me," she says. She turns to his nephew. "What about it, Francis X? Are you ready for some football?"

It's clear that he doesn't want to say yes but equally clear that he doesn't know how to say no. So he stands there with his hands in his pockets, his cheeks aflame. As if it's being dragged out of him, he finally whispers, "Okay."

Richard excuses himself, carries the mail into his study, and shuts the door. It will be a while before he thinks back to the scene in the dining room and understands that for each of them, today marked the start of reengagement.

From where Stefan Mirecki is sitting, the views are excellent. The trees in Planty wear their fall colors, red and gold and burnt orange, and the air has that crisp quality that makes him love autumn, which is technically still one day away. Of even greater interest than the foliage are the young women who stroll past, talking on their mobiles or chatting with friends. The university is nearby, and a lot of them look like students, though those typically are not the ones he's drawn to. They look a little too fresh, too innocent. He doesn't mind smooth skin, he actually admires it, but there's a certain kind of funkiness he prizes above all else, a hint of decadence. You generally don't find it in young women who spend their days studying metaphysics or Polish prosody. You're much more likely to discover it behind the counter of a shoe store or a chocolate shop, or waiting tables in a place like this.

He's been here before, though not for several years. It's the café where his late sister met his poor brother-in-law, and he's here to soak up some of the atmosphere that together they might have experienced. He decides to take a few photos, since he often forgets details that are purely descriptive and has never excelled at making them up.

The chairs are unusually rickety, so he snaps a shot of one, and as soon as he examines it he notices something he missed when looking at the thing itself: about five centimeters from the floor, its front legs curve coquettishly to the outside. He checks to see if the legs on the other chairs are similar, and indeed they are. On his laptop he opens a file titled "Notes on X" and types *chair-legs at Bunkier Café = women's feet poised against bed, toes angling out. Use somewhere.* He snaps two or three photos of menu pages and a photo of the weathered floorboards and another of the ceiling rafters, which look like they're made of cast iron. He takes a photo of a waitress—a dishwater blonde a little more solid than he prefers—whose breasts, he discovered when she leaned over to place a pot of tea on an adjacent table, are full and lovely. She's not his waitress, but he's been watching her for some time, and no smile has graced her face. Something has made her unhappy. But what?

She's about twenty, maybe a little older. *Three or four years out of high school. How long has she been working here? Already two years. Name: Jolanta. Grew up in the city but no place nice. Podgorze, let's say, before they began to spiff it up. One of five children, father waited tables at Hawelka, mother was a bathroom attendant, lived in a building not far from Schindler's factory, gray crumbling façade, somebody on the ground floor kept leaving the front door open, a good thing because often the odor of cooking—cabbage, fried cutlets—merged with the smell of vomit, sickening scent that robbed you of your appetite, the old man in the flat below theirs kept throwing up on the landing after his wife, Mrs. Grebkowska, let's say, locked him out, she was an unpleasant old woman with peasant features, in winter she wore two or three skirts at the same time and never spoke to any of the children in the building. She sometimes growled at them and you could hear her calling her husband names—piss pot, puke kettle—and her father said stay away from her, she's the kind of crazy that might rub off.*

She can't see any future for herself except right here, right in this café, working eight or ten hours a day. She has a boyfriend, but it won't last, she already knows it. He's a student . . . a black American, let's say, he's from an upper-middle-class family—East Coast but not New York, somewhere in the suburbs . . . Connecticut . . . went someplace good for college but not Harvard, that's where his parents went (same time as Obama, they knew him but considered him aloof), look up the name of a private college that's okay not great, someplace not too big, studies international relations but isn't that serious, his name is Alfred, he came here on semester abroad, joined a band, a couple of Canadians and a South African drummer . . . some kind of blues band that wouldn't sound like blues anywhere but here . . . and he continues to hang around rather than go home, because people think he's a rock star and he's had his pick of various women, and she's the latest. She's pregnant! That's it! Pregnant with a black child in alabaster Krakow! And then somebody kills her, and Nowakowski is summoned, forming yet another link to this mysterious café.

His own waitress holds no interest for him. She's a petite brunette with a well-adjusted smile affixed to her face. He catches her eye and raises a finger, signaling for another beer. Then he closes his laptop and puts his mobile away, finished with today's research.

The Supreme Darth Vader mask and helmet, according to the label, is constructed of "heavy injection molded ABS material, cast from the original Lucas Studios molds." It belongs to Marek's grandson, but he's at school and won't miss it unless something goes wrong.

Eventually, it's bound to. Maybe not today or tomorrow. But it's coming. An article ran in *Gazeta Krakowska* last week. Titled "'Cleaners' Harass Residents but Developers Deny Knowledge," it detailed the actions of "hooligans" who were driving mostly poor and often elderly residents from their apartments in recently sold buildings. As long as the tenants had a lease and were paying their rent, the article said, they couldn't legally be forced out, though those who stayed impeded developers' plans to renovate the properties and turn them into luxury condos. The piece ended by quoting an official in the police department who urged anyone with knowledge of such activities to immediately contact the authorities.

"How am I supposed to get this goddamn thing on?" he asks.

They're crouching in the attic of the building on Smolensk. The retired professor has refused to leave, and they've been told to get him out by the end of the week, or else. Neither of them is certain what *or else* might mean. Marek thinks they could lose their jobs, which Bogdan takes as a given. A more momentous question is what the professor might lose, since he would not appear to have much left beyond himself.

"You've got to detach the helmet from the mask," Marek says, pulling it free. "See? There's Velcro on both sides."

Bogdan dons the mask, and then Marek helps him with the helmet.

"It's pinching my fucking ears."

"Sorry."

His partner adjusts it, then squirms backward as far as the sloping ceiling will allow and studies the results. His lips start to twitch, like he's trying to suppress laughter.

"If you snicker at me," Bogdan says, "you can climb your ass out there instead." Marek's got the world's worst case of acrophobia. He can get dizzy looking out the window.

"Sorry. It's just . . . it's just . . ."

"I'm warning you."

". . . it's just that you really look like you come from the Dark Side."

Bogdan reaches for the handle on the roof hatch. "That's because I do."

THE AFTERNOON is not that warm, but it's sunny, and he expects the tiles to be hot. He's wearing gloves, and he's got on a harness they rigged up, with a long, heavy-duty nylon rope like mountain climbers use to tackle Everest. They've anchored the other end of it to the kitchen radiator in the flat below. The bottle Fabian gave them is stowed in a pouch secured to his harness.

He's been on top of buildings before, but they weren't that tall, and they all had flat roofs. This one slopes steeply. He thought he was prepared for the sight he'd confront when he got up here, but he was wrong. From his sitting position beside the yawning hatch, he can see all the way to the Vistula and even beyond. The scale of everything has been dramatically reduced. The Grunwald Bridge looks like something from an Erector Set. The houses are Lilliputian, the people about as big as good-sized roaches.

He holds his place, transfixed. It occurs to him that this is not a bad vantage point from which to observe the world. It affords a perspective that's unavailable when you're down there in it, rushing along to work, hoping to resuscitate your business, rejuvenate your marriage, retain your dignity. From up here, no one is invested with any dignity to lose. "This is quite a view," he says.

"Please, Bogdan. Let's get this over with. Knowing you're up there's making me light-headed."

He doesn't answer. With no terrible sense of concern, he wonders what will happen to the rope if he slips and begins to slide toward the eaves. The tiles around the hatch opening are rough and jagged, and it's not impossible that they might fray or even cut his lifeline. If he falls, it won't solve the professor's problems but would at least spell the end of his own.

"Come on, Bogdan. Let's put this behind us."

The vent pipe is farther away than he thought, a good three meters to the right of where he's sitting and a bit higher. The best way to access it, he decides, is from the ridge.

He plants his foot in the gully between a couple of tiles, then begins to move backward, a few centimeters at a time, Marek paying out rope, which he keeps between his legs. Finally, his hand feels the flat surface at the top. Twisting his torso to the left, he throws his right leg over the ridge.

It's broader than he anticipated: about a meter wide, coated in tar and pigeon shit. On hands and knees, he creeps toward a point directly above the vent pipe. When he gets there, he lowers himself onto his stomach. He reaches down with his left hand, groping, but he can't feel anything except air.

The Vader helmet isn't helping matters. It's hot inside the damn thing, and it's obstructing his peripheral vision. He thinks of removing it, throwing it off the roof, but the longer he's up here, the more likely he is to be spotted and photographed.

He grips the back side of the ridge with his right hand and swings his left leg out over the edge. He braces his foot against a tile, reaches down a little farther than he'd like, and finally feels the vent pipe. Lying there precariously, he pulls his hand back and withdraws the bottle from the pouch.

The principal element in many a stink bomb, butyric acid draws its name from the Greek word for "butter." It's present in goat milk, Parmesan cheese, and human vomit and lends the last of these its characteristic odor. Inhaling it, while decidedly unpleasant, can also cause respiratory troubles. Its presence in the air irritates the eyes and in extreme cases may result in loss of vision. They had to use it once before, about three months ago, in a building near Radio Krakow. That time, they simply drilled a hole through the floor and poured the acid into the flat below, on a weekday when the adults were at work and the kids had gone to school. A photo of the damaged ceiling appeared in the *Gazeta Krakowska* article. Fabian told them if they did anything that stupid again, they were on their own.

It feels very much like they're on their own now, like they've been on their own since they stepped through that gate into the pool king's estate. "Marek?" he calls. "Can you hear me?"

"Yes. What's going on up there?"

"Marek, you're the best friend I ever had."

"Bogdan, you're frightening me. Are you planning to throw yourself off? Jesus, Bogdan, please!"

"No, I'm not going to jump. I'll wait till all my bad choices do me in. Here goes the big stink." He inhales deeply, then holds his breath.

The acid is in a large plastic squeeze bottle. With his thumb, he manages to flip off the safety cap. He upends the bottle, reaches out and jams it into the pipe, and squeezes. Within about half a minute, it's empty.

This is when things begin to go wrong. No matter how hard he pulls on the bottle, he can't get it out. They intended to plug the pipe anyway so that the odor would have no means of escape. He brought a hunk of modeling clay for that purpose. But now the bottle is stuck there, and it will have both his and Marek's fingerprints on it, as well as Fabian's, should anyone figure out how the odor entered the building. And he suspects someone will. "Marek?"

"Yeah?"

"We have a little problem."

"What kind of little problem?"

"The kind that could become bigger."

"Bigger how?"

"The bottle's stuck in the vent pipe."

"So leave it."

"Our fingerprints are all over it." He's no sooner said that than a gust of wind hits the roof and dislodges the bottle. It bounces two or three times, then disappears over the eaves.

He nearly lost his grip on the ridge. He waits to see if the microburst, or whatever it was, will be followed by another, but the afternoon is again still, with scarcely a breeze. So he pulls the hunk of clay from the pouch where the bottle was and crams it into the vent pipe.

"I'm done up here."

"What about the bottle?"

"The wind blew it off."

"I thought I heard something hit the roof. We better try to find it when we get outside."

He crawls backward until he's directly above the hatch.

"Okay. I'm about to start down. Move away from the opening, because if I slip, I'm going to fall right in on top of you." He swings his legs off the ridge, once more assuming a sitting position.

Down below, on the other side of the street, in a nicely renovated Bauhaus with gingerbread trim, a woman stands watching him from an open window. She has grayish hair with just enough of a tinge to suggest it used to be red. She's wearing a black blouse with white polka dots, and a teacup is resting on the windowsill. She must have put it there when she pulled out her mobile, which she's holding against her ear. He can read her lips as she recites the address.

THEY DIDN'T turn on power to the lift, and anyhow it would be too slow. They bound down the stairs two at a time. The building is already beginning to reek.

When they reach the ground floor, he realizes he's still wearing the Darth Vader helmet. So he rips it off, and the mask comes with it. He's the first one through the door. He's carrying the helmet when he steps outside.

There's a saying in Krakow: if you're having an affair, meet in the main market square. You won't see anyone else you know there, and no one you know will see you.

They're both in bad need of a drink, and it makes sense to them to get it in a place where they stand a good chance of remaining anonymous. Late afternoon finds them parked at a café table on the north side of the world's largest medieval square, surrounded by tourists luxuriating in the crisp air of early autumn. He hears plenty of German, some Italian and Japanese, a little English that he suspects is of the American variety. A line of horse-drawn carriages stands between them and the massive Cloth Hall. Near the entrance to the market stalls, a band decked out in Krakowian folk costumes has struck up "The Vistula Is Flowing." It sounds horrible.

The only thing that might call attention to them is the Darth Vader headgear. He pleaded with his partner to drop it in a garbage bin, even offering to buy his grandson a new one, but Marek claimed they were virtually impossible to find, not to mention overpriced, and anyway the kid would know the difference. So they've placed it under the table and turned it upside down.

Marek has just ordered his second beer and a brandy to go

with it. In some ways it's sad to see how easily rattled he is these days, his once ravenous ambition, his bravado and optimism all gone. He only wants to get along, and right now he's scared they won't. He keeps cutting his eyes from side to side, like he expects the police to descend on them.

"Do you ever think about it?" Bogdan asks.

"About what?"

"You know what."

His old friend wraps his hands around the sweating beer glass. "Yeah. But I imagine it's worse for you, because you saw them."

"How do you feel when you think about it?"

"Mostly, I try not to."

"But sometimes you do. You just said so."

"I got some help dealing with it."

Now the beer glass is not the only thing sweating. "You didn't tell Inga, did you? About the wreck? For Christ's sake."

Marek gazes past him in the direction of St. Mary's, the Gothic basilica in the corner of the square. "I went to see a priest," he says.

The image of his partner kneeling in the confessional is so ludicrous that at first, Bogdan assumes he's kidding. Unlike his own parents, Marek's were not churchgoers, and well into adulthood he was a walking catalog of jokes about priests and their sheep. But all you've got to do to see that he's serious is look at him. "Does Inga know you went?"

"No. She wouldn't understand."

"Why wouldn't she understand? She attends mass herself."

"She attends mass, but it doesn't really mean much to her. It's just something she's always done. I don't go to mass, but church means a lot to me."

"What's the difference?"

"I go to church when no one's there. That's what the priest sug-

gested after I'd told him what happened and then admitted I
didn't believe in God. He said to just come in and sit down and
maybe God would speak to me, or maybe He wouldn't, but that
even if He didn't, I'd feel better while I was there."

"And has God spoken to you?"

"No. But I feel better every time I go."

Bogdan lifts his glass and finishes the beer in a single swallow,
then turns and looks over his shoulder at their waitress, who is
propped against the building, her tray resting against her knee.
He signals for another.

By the time he gives Marek his attention again, the bitterness
has overcome him. "It's that easy for you, is it?"

"What's easy?"

"Just walk into the fucking church of a god you've never believed in, plop down in the pew, and have a Saul of Tarsus moment. You're such a simple bastard. You always have been."

His partner runs his finger over the white marks on his face, a
gesture that Bogdan has noticed him resorting to with greater and
greater frequency, as if the scars prove he's paid a price for all the
wrong they've done. "You're right," he says. "I've always been a
simple bastard. Did you know I was often unfaithful to Inga? I
didn't appreciate what I had."

Bogdan has long suspected that he slept with other women, but
he'd felt certain he'd never confess it. For Marek to do it now, after
revealing that he slinks around churches seeking respite from his
guilt, further fuels his outrage. "What will you tell me next?" he
asks. He knows he's speaking louder than he should, but there's a
group of Asian tourists on their right, and the table on the left's
empty. "That you like to put your finger up your ass and take a
sniff? We caused the deaths of two people, ruined the life of at
least one other, and probably added to the grief of the pool tycoon's

wife when she came home and found the frozen corpse of her dog, whose brains had been hacked out. We've spent a few months driving folks from their flats—for the very same shithook that turned us out of our last store—and you've found help *dealing* with it?"

The waitress brings his beer just as a guy sits down at the empty table. Bogdan glances at him. He's got a wild shock of salt-and-pepper hair and a beard that matches, and he's wearing a black blazer over a ridiculous-looking tee shirt that depicts some fellow with snakes coming out of his head. He takes a laptop from his shoulder bag, places it on the table, and opens it. They hear him order a shot of Irish whiskey.

Marek observes the new guest for a moment, then leans closer. "If we need to discuss this particular subject, could it wait till later?"

Bogdan takes a sip of beer. His anger has subsided as quickly as it surged. "We don't need to discuss it. I meant what I said when I was out there on . . . when I was where we just came from."

"I know you did. And I feel the same about you."

The guy at the next table doesn't look their way, but Bogdan knows the remark registered. So he changes the subject, asking his partner if he's planning to take his grandson to the Saturday football match. As soon as they've finished their drinks, they pay and stand up.

"Oh, my," his partner says. "Look what we're about to forget." Before Bogdan can stop him, he reaches under the table and grabs the Vader helmet.

The guy at the next table glances up, sees what's he's holding, then looks back at the open laptop. Walking away, Bogdan hears him pecking the keys.

THEY PART at the edge of Planty, each promising to let the other know if he hears from Fabian, who hasn't responded to their messages. Bogdan waits until his partner has disappeared, then strolls back into the Old Town, stops at the first liquor store he sees, and buys another beer. He returns to the park, finds an empty bench near the Slowacki Theater, and opens the can. He takes his time, drinking slowly.

Before long, it begins to grow dark, and the spotlights that ring the theater finally come on. The Baroque structure modeled on the Paris Opera House is suddenly aglow like an enormous nugget. He's lived in this city his entire life, yet the only time he entered the Slowacki was in grade school, when they took his class through. He can't recall anything about the interior. Nor can he imagine how it would be to watch a play in there, or an opera, or what it would be like to go listen to a symphony at the Philharmonic or visit one of the many jazz clubs around town. He's never been to any of the big new cinemas to see a movie, and he hasn't visited a bookstore or checked a title out of the library in nine or ten years. He never holds a real conversation with anyone anymore except Marek or Inga, or occasionally his sister in Zakopane. He can't even remember when he last heard from his other sister. There's not much left of his life and not much that could be made of what remains. The simplest thing would be to bring down the curtain.

It seems unlikely that the American journalist saw him long enough to retain an image. But Bogdan knows he did, that someplace on the far side of North America, his otherwise forgettable face is the locus of grief. Tonight, he can feel it more strongly than ever. Somewhere in California he takes center stage in another man's nightmare.

IF YOU live in Krakow but are not devout—and maybe even if you are—you seldom notice churches, though they're everywhere, particularly in the older parts of the city. By the time he reaches his street, he wouldn't be able to tell you how many he's walked past since getting up off the park bench. There's another one up ahead. He knows it's a Jesuit church but can't recall the name. Instead of turning onto his street, he crosses it, then crosses to the other side of Kopernika.

It's past seven now, and most churches will be closed. But the main doors of this one—the Sacred Heart Basilica, says the plaque—are unlocked. For some inexplicable reason, he steps inside.

The nave is dimly lit, but it doesn't require a lot of light to constitute an impressive sight. Enormous frescoes. The controlling colors magenta and gold, the central aisle white marble, with a series of black concentric circles running down the middle, each except the last connected to its predecessor by an oversized comma. He walks toward the altar, the echoes of his footsteps overlapping.

The benches are hard and uncomfortable, designed, no doubt, to keep the numb awake. He takes a seat in one on the right-hand side, then crosses his arms over his stomach.

There's a presence here: no question about it. Whether it's godly, he can't say, but he considers that doubtful. What seems plausible is that all those who ever sat in this pew left something of themselves behind. The physics that might be involved will lie forever beyond his ken. Maybe he's aware of people who attended mass here last Sunday. Or those who came ten years ago, or forty or fifty. It's one of those things that his father, a tram driver with little education but a lot of sense, used to call "the imponderables." He once asked what the word meant, since it seemed like he heard it every few days, most often after his father finished reading the paper. "It means," he was told, "that if you think about it too long, it'll make your head hurt, so you might as well save yourself the trouble. Better go play with Marek." At the time, he found the answer maddening, just another example of something the adults knew but refused to reveal.

Now, almost everything that matters is in the realm of the imponderable. Why did a man who'd never stolen anything in his entire life decide to go rob a complete stranger? He'd had money troubles before and never stooped to theft. Why did he slam the BMW's brakes at precisely that instant? He'd been driving since he was seventeen and never had an accident or caused one either. Why did the pool builder drown at almost exactly the same time as two people were dying in the old Mercedes?

Imponderables everywhere, no answers to be found.

He doesn't know he's fallen asleep until his neck starts to hurt. When he opens his eyes, he sees the bearded figure in the nearest fresco wagging a finger at him. "Too late, Jesus," he says. He rises, works out a few kinks, and walks home.

Morning brings a text from Fabian ordering him to lie low. A while later, he receives a call from Marek. The old professor, he learns, taught the city president's wife at Jagiellonian. A time-tested Polish civic tradition—the Dictatorship of the Acquaintance—has been powerfully invoked. The building on Smolensk is being deodorized, and in the meantime the professor is staying at the Radisson Blu on the developer's tab.

"Fabian said the old man gave the police descriptions of us," Marek informs him. "He told them I had white scars on my face, and he mentioned that mole of yours. Did you ever think of having that thing removed? At least you could do something about it. I can't get rid of these scars."

Bogdan looks around his room. It's no longer as squalid as it was last winter, but there are no pictures on the walls, no TV or stereo, no quirky possessions that would identify it as his rather than someone else's. "I am my face," he says.

"Bogdan, I'm serious."

"So am I. Every now and then, I see it in a mirror, or it's reflected back at me from a dirty windowpane, and I think, 'Hell, I know that guy. He's what I turned into.'" He tells his partner not to worry, that he has no intention of going anywhere.

And for most of the day, he doesn't. He drinks a few beers in the afternoon and falls asleep for a couple hours, then sits on the balcony for a while and watches trains pass. But there's not much to eat: some stale rye bread he bought day before yesterday, a tub of herring salad that isn't yet out of date but smells dangerous, a few frozen Ruskie pierogi. His appetite is oddly robust. And, as is usually the case when he's truly hungry, he craves kielbasa.

THE BLUE van is a Nyska, readily identifiable as a former police vehicle. Six nights a week, from eight until three in the morning, it's parked near the Hala Targowa tram stop. No matter how foul the weather, two guys clad in white smocks grill large kielbasas over a wood fire and sell them, along with a roll, for eight zlotys. They're both in their early sixties and sport gray goatees. He once heard that they were brothers, but some years ago a rumor circulated that they were unrelated, hated each other, and no longer spoke. He's never heard either of them say a word. They've supposedly gotten rich.

Tonight the line already has forty or fifty people in it, all but a handful of them male, more than a few drinking beer while they wait. He wishes he'd had the foresight to bring one and, for a moment, contemplates leaving the line long enough to buy a can at the liquor store next to Hala Targowa. But it's starting to sprinkle, so he decides to maintain his spot. When he reaches the front of the queue, it's raining in earnest, and one of the entrepreneurs has extended an awning over the grill. Bogdan orders two sausages to go, then tucks the hot sack under his arm and hurries home.

He eats the blackened kielbasa with mustard, taking his time, biting a hunk out of a roll every now and then, washing everything down with cold beer. The sausage seems especially juicy tonight, the mustard nice and tangy. The rolls are light and fluffy, not soggy, as if they were baked within the last couple of hours. He will remember it as one of the most satisfying meals he's ever eaten. It might even be the best.

He's in the kitchen opening another beer when someone knocks on the door. It's strange, since he doesn't know any of his neighbors and no one is supposed to get in without buzzing, though Marek did last winter. Maybe it's him again. He pops the cap off the beer, takes a good swig, and goes to the door.

It's not Marek. One of the men is in his late thirties, short and bald, and he's wearing beige cords and a brown leather jacket that's flaking badly. His companion is younger, taller, and better dressed, in a light gray suit, crisp shirt, and tie.

"Mr. Baranowski?" the older one asks.

He's as calm as he's ever been, with no unusual physiological response except a faint tingling near his tailbone. He wonders if they've also grabbed Marek. Hopefully not. There's Inga, his sons, those grandkids. He'd be missed by many, whereas nobody will miss Bogdan except Marek himself. "That's me," he says.

"You'll have to come with us," the older man tells him.

He cocks his head toward his companion, who delves into the pocket of that immaculate gray jacket and pulls out a set of black handcuffs. Bogdan offers his wrists. As the younger man clamps on the cuffs, he asks if they've got time for him to finish his beer.

The room is a mess: mug shots tacked on the walls alongside a poster advertising *X-Men II.* Three-ring binders piled on top of the filing cabinets, Styrofoam cups littering the floor, an overflowing ashtray. A half-eaten container of low-fat apricot yoghurt stands on the desk, the plastic spoon perfectly erect. The older officer's feet are propped beside it. The soles of both shoes are in bad shape.

They've taken the handcuffs off and given him some coffee, though they wouldn't let him finish his beer. Spread out before him on the desk, not far from the officer's feet, are three large color photos. In the first, he's sliding down the roof toward the hatch, sunlight glinting off his Vader helmet. In the second, he's emerging from the building, carrying the helmet under his arm. In the third, he's just rounded the corner onto Smolensk— you can see part of one leg and all of his shoe—and Marek is about to reach the corner, too. But you can't tell it's Marek because his head is turned away from the camera.

"We've got your partner," the officer says. "He's the one who told us how to find you. What he won't tell us is his name. And apparently, he thinks you're such a loyal friend that you won't tell us who he is either, even though he was pretty eager to point a finger at you. He says he didn't even know you went onto the roof, by the way, that he was working in number eight and happened to leave the building when you did."

Bogdan doesn't believe they've got Marek. It's certainly possible that he could have been identified by any officer who'd read a description of his face, but if he'd been arrested, there is not one chance in a thousand that he'd refuse to tell them his own name. He would've been too frightened to withhold that information. The only facts he wouldn't have divulged are the name of his partner and his address. Bogdan knows this as surely as he's ever known anything.

"I don't have any partner," he tells the pudgy officer.

The younger man has been standing behind him and hasn't said a word since he handed him his coffee. "Do you know how long you can go to jail for harassing a legal resident?" he asks.

Five years from now, this officer, who is only twenty-six, will be the highest-ranking detective in the department, the superior of colleagues with thirty years' more experience. He earned a degree in public safety management from the University of Zielona Gora, where among other subjects he studied psychology. But he's made several incorrect assumptions about the man he's standing behind. The first is that he's terrified. The second is that there's almost nothing he wouldn't say or do if he thought it would get him back on the street in the least amount of time. The third is that he has something to lose. Most people, even if they're wrong, think they do.

One assumption that he's made is right: Bogdan is running some options through his mind, along with the outcomes they might lead to. He could offer up Fabian, and even the developer himself, in hopes that whatever penalty he's about to incur would be reduced. But Fabian would finger Marek, and odds are the developer can buy his way out of trouble, because that's how things work in this country. More importantly—though this kind of thinking runs counter to everything the officer learned in his psych class at the University of Zielona Gora—Bogdan has drunk enough beer to achieve a degree of clarity he might be denied if he were sober: he deserves to do penance. So what if he serves time to pay for a lesser crime? "I don't have any partner," he says again.

"You just run around," the older detective says, "trying to drive helpless people out of their homes?"

"That's the size of it."

"Somebody gave you a key to the building. Who was it?"

"I stole it."

"From who?"

"I don't know his name."

"Why'd you do it?"

"I'm a shell of a person, and I'm drawn to old buildings that remind me of myself."

The older officer swings his feet off the desk. "Slap the cuffs back on him," he tells the other guy. "I guess his bosses have paid him to take the fall. Too bad the money'll be worth a lot less when he gets to use it."

WALKING DOWN the hall between the two officers, he sees another man coming toward them. It stands to reason that he must be a detective too, since he's wearing not a uniform but a pair of dark pants and a herringbone jacket. He has long ears, a high forehead, and a thin mustache, and he trudges along studying the floor, a sheaf of papers dangling from one hand. He reminds Bogdan of someone else, a figure from history, maybe, or some disgraced politician. Right before they pass him, he raises his head, and his heavy-lidded gaze lights on Bogdan. He pauses for a moment, then nods at his colleagues and continues on his way.

The zoom lens on his new Swarovski digital imaging binoculars affords him a perfect view all the way across the playing field to section 31. He watches from the press box while Maria, Franek, and Sandy step over one set of feet after another, Maria mouthing *Excuse us please excuse us* until they finally reach their seats. They're way up high, under the skyboxes, but right on the fifty-yard line. Franek keeps his head down as if it's embarrassing to be where he is, or maybe just embarrassing to be himself.

Richard bought the binoculars online earlier in the week for the princely sum of seventeen hundred dollars. He was looking for a cheap pair, but these popped up under "related products," and he liked what he read about them and thought, *Why the hell not?* He hadn't bought anything expensive in years. Since they're capable of shooting video and taking still photos, he snaps one of Franek and Sandy sitting side by side, thinking maybe he'll e-mail it to Monika. As an afterthought, he snaps another one of Maria just as she takes a bite out of her hotdog. She's gathered her tresses into a ponytail and is wearing a New England Patriots cap.

The Wisconsin team runs onto the field, drawing a few thousand boos. Then a cowboy on horseback emerges from the opposite end of the stadium. As the crowd roars, he waves a lasso in the air and spurs his mount, and the home team bursts out of the tunnel, following the horseman toward their sideline. The coaches jog along behind them, Nick Major's blond hair shimmering beneath the lights.

For most of two quarters, it looks like Major and his fans are in for a long evening. The visitors are bigger and stronger, and they keep handing the ball to a pair of bruising tailbacks who find huge holes to run through and, when they reach the secondary, punish the Central California safeties. It's 17-0 with three minutes to go in the half. Then the UCC quarterback hits his fastest receiver for a sixty-yard touchdown, and on the second play after the kickoff the Wisconsin running back loses the ball and the Cowboys recover. They add another touchdown and go back to the locker room trailing by three.

The second half is all UCC. What the team lacks in brawn, they make up for with speed. They score on another deep pass and add another touchdown on a screen. When Wisconsin falls behind and has to start throwing, their quarterback is picked off twice, and the second interception gets returned for a score. They manage nothing but a field goal, losing 35-20. The fans storm the field, tearing down one of the goalposts while Major, soaked in Gatorade, rides off on his players' shoulders.

Before heading down for the postgame press conference, Richard again checks to see what's happening in section 31. They're still there, though the seats around them are mostly empty. To his surprise, Franek and Sandy are now deep in conversation, and while he watches she casually pulls a large soft-drink container out of his nephew's hand and treats herself to a big swallow. Franek doesn't protest, just takes it when she hands it back and keeps talking. Maria is scribbling on a notepad, but as if on cue she puts it away, then looks toward the press box and waves.

Aside from local media and a few Wisconsin sportswriters, the press conference is not much of a draw, even though the visitors came in ranked fifth in the country and the game was on ESPN. Central California still flies under the radar, which is what Major has on his mind. After praising tonight's opponent—"the best team in the Big Ten and one of the best, period"—he tears into the pollsters. "At kickoff," he says, his surprisingly small hands resting confidently on either side of the podium, "we were ranked, what? Twenty-three, twenty-four? I don't pay much attention to it, but you all do. So tell me."

"Twenty-three, Coach," one of the *Sun* writers obliges.

"Twenty-three." Major looks down and slowly shakes his head. When he raises his gaze, you can tell he intends for those assembled to note that there's fire in his eyes, or whatever cliché springs instantly into the mind of a sportswriter with a looming deadline. "If you think my guys are the twenty-third-best team in the country," he says, "you need to buy yourself one of those books . . . what do they call 'em? *Football for Dummies*, or something like that? I'm not trying to insult anybody, though, because I doubt anybody here thinks that, especially not after what we all saw tonight."

He expresses disdain for the East Coast media—"I guess after two or three martinis, they need to go to bed, so they probably aren't up for a seven o'clock West Coast kickoff"—the PAC 10—"We'd gladly play 'em every week, but they won't let us in"—and the UCC faculty—"They complain about all the attention paid to our football program, but I don't see them pulling down any Nobel Prizes." Then he gets in a dig at the administration, pointing out that unless the stadium is expanded, people won't be seeing many top teams like Wisconsin at home games, since the school can't offer a big enough payout.

Long before he takes the final question, says a curt good-night, and leaves the room, he's made Richard despise him. He doubts the coach has done anything worse than spending a night or two with a Golden Palomino hostess. He doesn't condone that, but it's probably not any more blameworthy than what his brother-in-law's been doing for most of his life. It's also probably not newsworthy. But the link to Joe Garcia continues to bother him. A woman and her family are dead, and until now nobody but Maria Cantrell has tried very hard to find out why. His own reporting was perfunctory.

As the other reporters depart, he introduces himself to the Sports Information Director, a small man in a garish green jacket with a Cowboy pin on his lapel. The guy has a sweaty handshake. "I was glad to get the request from you for credentials," he says. "Your paper tends to ignore us unless we're playing UCLA or USC. I notice you didn't ask any questions, though."

"No, I didn't. What I'm working on's not about the game, per se."

"Want to tell me about it?"

So Richard does what people in his profession often do when pursuing a story: he doesn't exactly lie, but he doesn't exactly tell the truth either. He mentions the name of the magazine that asked him to write about Major but says that at the time he didn't feel like he knew enough about the coach or the football program to go through with it. It's clear to him from the SID's excited expression that Major did not mention the magazine proposal or their prior encounter at Whole Foods. "I've been watching the growth of the program over the last couple years," he continues, "and I'm starting to feel like maybe I see an angle for a piece about the coach and the way he's energized the Central Valley." He waves his hand in an all-encompassing gesture. "I'd love to pose a question or two tonight, but I didn't want to detract from the conversation about the game itself, since it was such a huge win. Any chance I could get a minute with him this evening?"

"Well, normally, I'd say that needed to be scheduled in advance. Believe it or not, Coach is probably already over there in his office starting to get ready for next week's Colorado State game. But if you'll hold on, I'll see what I can do."

Richard trails him into the hallway, where a thick green-and-gold carpet covers the floor. While he waits, he sends Maria a text: *Looks like we might get a bite. Why don't you take the kids to Spagnola's and I'll meet you there later.*

He stands around for nearly half an hour before the SID returns. "Like I figured," he says, "he already has a staff meeting in progress, but if you'll follow me, I can get you a few minutes."

The guy leads him around a couple of corners, past pictures of former Cowboy stars, past several offices with the names of assistant coaches on the doors, and into what appears to be a small lounge: a few round tables, a couch, a coffee urn, a refrigerator. Major sits in a metal folding chair, his elbow resting on one of the tables. He's changed out of his Gatorade-soaked game attire and is wearing a pair of slacks and a short-sleeved pullover. He doesn't stand or offer to shake hands but gestures at an empty chair. "I think we met once before, didn't we?" he asks.

"Just briefly."

"So what can I do for you?"

Richard was afraid the SID would remain in the room, but he hears the door close discreetly and realizes they're alone. He sits down at the table, whips out his pad, and tells Major he finds it fascinating that he's been able to stimulate fervor from Bakersfield to Sacramento and all points in between as the most ethnically diverse region in the country unites behind a college football team. How, he wonders, has the coach gone about it?

It's a question Major has probably answered a couple of hundred times, if not more. He offers up a few platitudes about making people feel like the team represents the entire Central Valley rather than just a segment. He's got Hispanic players, Asian American players, black players, white players. And so on. Near the end of his spiel he yawns but makes a perfunctory attempt to hide it behind a raised palm.

Richard scribbles a note on his pad, nodding as if this is groundbreaking stuff. Then he looks into the coach's powder-blue eyes and says, "Given how much is riding on you and the team, you must feel a lot of pressure. What do you do to relax?"

"Sleep. Play with my kids. Spend time with my wife. Go for a swim. Same as everybody else."

"What about when you want to kick back, let off a little steam? Where does Nick Major go to do that?"

The coach looks at his watch. It's clear that he's not used to masking irritation. "If I want to kick back? I put my feet up on my recliner."

"Ever have a drink at the Golden Palomino?"

Later tonight, when he describes this moment to Maria Cantrell, he will admit he enjoyed watching the color drain from Major's smug face. What he won't tell her is that immediately afterward, he experienced the familiar sinking sensation that always follows even the smallest pleasure: a drink of cold water on a hot Valley day, the taste of robust coffee in the morning. He struggles to remain in the here-and-now. He never leaves the there-and-then for very long.

"I don't allow my players to visit bars," Major says. "So I don't go to them either."

"Never?"

"Never."

"I actually heard otherwise."

The coach stares at him. "You know what? I think you missed your calling. You should've been on *NYPD Blue*."

"Since you mention the police, I believe maybe you know Joe Garcia, from the FPD?"

Major rises.

Richard stands up too. He's taller than the coach by a couple inches, and he can tell the younger man would love to punch him and might be pondering the advisability. "I heard Garcia handled private security," he says, "for some parties at your place."

"I've got a meeting to conduct," Major tells him. "Show yourself out. And do it pretty fast." He walks toward the door.

"Ever heard of a woman named Jacinta Aguilera?"

The coach never breaks stride. He wrenches the door open, and it slams into the wall with a plaster-cracking thunk.

Monika lifts the electric kettle and fills the stainless-steel mixing bowl with boiling water. She adds a few drops of cold, then carries the bowl over to the kitchen table and sets it down beside her laptop. From the living room she hears the painters moving a stepladder, the metal legs banging against yet another piece of furniture, one of them starting to call either the ladder or whatever it hit a fucking whore but breaking off midsyllable. Yesterday she asked that they curtail the cursing when they're in the flat. "If I've got something really terrible to say," she told the youngest one, "I usually say it in my head. Most of the time, though not always, that satisfies the urge."

She sits down, plunges her bowing hand and wrist into the hot water, then rereads Richard's e-mail. In it, he explains how he shot the grainy attached photo of Franek and the neighbors' daughter, then tells her a little bit about the girl, how she was Anna's best friend for many years, that she's now a high school senior, a sweet, bright kid with a "sassy" sense of humor. He says he's formed the impression that she and Franek might be taking a liking to each other, despite their age difference. He and another reporter went out for pizza with them after the ball game, and they elected to sit at their own table rather than joining him and his friend. Because he writes in Polish, where nouns indicate gender, she can tell that the other journalist is a woman.

In the photo from the football game, just to the right of Franek's knee you can see another knee, and since the neighbor's daughter is completely visible on his left, she assumes it belongs to the female reporter. Without being told anything about her, she makes a second assumption: the woman is younger than her late sister-in-law, probably quite a bit so. She no doubt looks up to Richard, who is probably what she hopes to become. You can take that kind of ambition and run with it, if you'd like to. Or you can give yourself to those who harbor it and let them run with you.

Her son might soon have a girlfriend, the first of his life, and he's on the other side of the world. When Monika left Krakow for the music academy in Katowice, she was nineteen years old. The train ride lasted little more than an hour, but she pressed her face to the window in the second-class compartment, hiding her tears from the other passengers. She was glad to leave her family behind—her parents drank too much and quarreled all the time, and her sister was a slob—so she would not have been able to say what made her cry. Now it's obvious: she was afraid of the unknown, which in her case meant a city eighty kilometers away.

The longer her hand remains in the water, the looser her wrist feels. If she were to guess, she would say she's capable of holding her orchestra seat for at least a couple more years, perhaps even three or four. Her physician has told her he can't administer another cortisone shot until next March and that he will only do it then against his better judgment. The principal cellist had to leave the Philharmonic this past spring after multiple operations failed to correct ligament damage in his elbow. Carpal tunnel forced the concert master into retirement last year at the ripe age of fifty-one. Every occupation carries its own set of hazards: repetitive motion injuries haunt hers. In certain pieces she bows at the rate of 350 strokes per minute. But as Stefan often reminds her, they don't need her income. Six months ago they bought a garden flat in Berlin, where he stays when he visits his German publisher, and they're checking out villas in Zakopane.

Her bowing hand still in the water, she becomes aware of a presence. She looks over her shoulder to see the youngest of the three workmen. He's standing just inside the kitchen in his paint-spattered overalls, disheveled hair in his eyes. The instant she looks at him, he begins to blush, just as he did yesterday when she admonished him about cursing.

"My boss said to ask if you're sure you want the crown moldings painted the same color as the walls."

"We already covered that."

"Well, but he just called and said to ask one last time. Because, you know, if they're the same color, it makes the ceiling look lower."

"I was certain yesterday, and I'm still certain today."

"Yes, ma'am," he says but fails to leave.

"Is there something else?" she asks.

"Have you . . . did you hurt your hand?"

His impertinence is mitigated by the blushing. "I'm a musician," she tells him. "We have a lot of problems with our wrists, forearms, and elbows."

"I've had some troubles like that." He raises his right hand above his shoulder, mimicking the back-and-forth motion of a brush or roller. "Could I show you something that might help?"

Why she accedes to his request will remain a mystery to her

long after he and the others have finished their work and left the flat. For months, whenever she sees a team of painters climbing out of an old van, carrying paint buckets into a building, or teetering above the sidewalk on scaffolding, she will check to see if he's among them. He never seems to be, though next winter, at Galeria Krakowska, she will think she sees him riding down on an escalator as she's riding up. It will happen so fast that she'll never know if she was right. When she turns to look, she will briefly lose her balance and be prevented from falling by the man on the step below, who will grab her elbow. Later, she'll have a drink with him in the bar at the Europejski.

The young housepainter approaches the table, wipes his palms on his overalls, then gently lifts her hand out of the bowl. "You always want to do this right after soaking it in warm water." Letting it rest in his left hand, he begins moving his right thumb and index finger over her carpals in a circular pattern, constantly varying the pressure. "You can do this for yourself, but it's better if someone else does it. You can't really relax if you're having to move your other hand. My girlfriend does it for me. Unless she's pissed . . . Sorry, I meant mad. If she's mad, I'm on my own." Once or twice, when he bears down hard, she feels darts of discomfort, but the overall sensation is anything but unpleasant. At some point she closes her eyes. Though her sense of timing is impeccable, she loses all temporal awareness. She smells the paint that spatters his clothing, the odor of male sweat, and something else too, some strange scent she once knew but had forgotten.

She jumps when someone cries, "Leszek! Are you eating dinner in there?"

"Shut up!" He doesn't stop, but the spell is shattered.

She clears her throat, like Richard has so often heard her do, and says, "Thank you." As gently as he lifted her hand from the water, she pushes his thumb and finger aside.

He stands there for another moment during which she stares at her spice rack, at the bottles of coriander and thyme, cumin and rosemary, dill seed and curry powder, each in its designated place.

The night he interviewed Nick Major, he stayed up till five a.m. Maria Cantrell had driven over to his house, and though he assumed that after saying good-bye to Sandy, Franek would just go to bed and let them talk, his nephew instead asked if he could have a beer with them. "Sure, you can," Maria said before Richard could respond. So he surrendered the bottle he'd opened for himself and went to get another.

The kid sat there with them for nearly an hour. The transformation was startling. He asked one question after another—about American football, the state of Arkansas, the different varieties of pizza crust, the correct plural of the word "stadium"—and only went to bed when his request for a second Sierra Nevada was declined.

After he left, Richard gestured toward the kitchen. She followed him in there, he opened two more beers, and they sat down at the table. "What's gotten into him?" he asked. "If I didn't know better, I'd think he'd been smoking weed all night."

She shrugged. "Lights. Color. Action. He asked Sandy a question or two about the game, and that got them talking. The next thing I know he's telling her about some Renaissance-era building in Krakow. I'm probably mispronouncing it, but it sounded like Suck-a-Knee—"

"Sukiennice. The Cloth Hall."

"And then she's saying she'd love to see it, and he's telling her that maybe she'll come visit next summer, that his folks have a huge place in the best part of town. Stuff happens faster when you're young."

"I guess so."

They went back over his conversation with Nick Major. She wanted him to call Garcia first thing in the morning and request an interview. He said absolutely not. For better or worse, he told her, she'd handed off this story to him, at least for now. "And my guess," he said, "is that tomorrow or the next day, Garcia'll be on the phone to me. Or show up at my door."

"And if that doesn't happen?"

"Then in a week or so, I might call him."

"You're joking. Right?"

"No, I'm not. For one thing, if Major's at all worried, he's probably already called Joe."

She slapped the table hard enough to rattle her beer bottle. "But what if he's not worried? What if the slime ball just figures he's immune, that fuck-all will happen to him because of who he is? I mean, Jesus. He spent God knows how many nights with a woman who was murdered alongside her kids, and then he denied knowing her *or* the detective who investigated their deaths. And we're gonna sit here and let whether or not he's worried dictate what *we* do?"

"You're a good writer," he said. "Better than good. A lot better. But you didn't listen to what I told you back at Spagnola's. You just heard what you wanted to. I didn't say he denied knowing Jacinta Aguilera or Joe Garcia. I said that after I asked him if he knew them, he got up and walked out."

She leaned over the table. She was wearing a low-cut blouse, and he could see the tops of her breasts. To his embarrassment, his eyes remained there a bit too long, but she was so agitated that she apparently either didn't notice or didn't care. "What's the fucking difference?" she asked.

"You do know there's a difference. Don't you?"

He'd posed the question as a mild rebuke, and she accepted it in that spirit, sitting back in her chair and crossing her arms. "All right," she said, "there's a difference. He could be taking care to avoid having to admit a little farther down the road that he lied to you when you asked. And that might mean he's smarter than you think I'm giving him credit for."

"It could also mean that while he slept with her any number of times and knows somebody suspects it and may even have something close to photographic proof, he's not guilty of anything worse than hoping to keep it quiet. And while that's immoral, it's not illegal, unless of course he paid her, and maybe he did. At this point, I'm not sure what I think the story is. I won't know until I see whether he calls Joe and how Joe reacts if and when that happens. I may not even know then. So we're going to wait. Or at least I am. What you do is up to you."

He thought she might get up and walk out. Later, she'd tell him she considered it. Instead, she said, "I think I want to sit here and get shitfaced."

He studied his beer bottle. The first time he offered Julia a Sierra Nevada, she protested that she could see a layer of sediment at the bottom. He explained that this particular pale ale was bottle conditioned, that they added yeast and sugar after filtering, which accounted for the residue. She didn't really like beer that much, but after she tasted this one, it became her favorite. In hot weather, she sometimes preferred it to white wine.

For the past two and a half years, he hadn't drunk alcohol at all, believing that if he hadn't had too much that night, he would've been behind the wheel and everything that did happen wouldn't have. He'd bought a twelve-pack last week. Who'd want him to keep living like he'd been living, if living was what you could call it? Not Julia. Not Anna.

"Well," he said, "I'd be happy to sit here and get shitfaced with you. But only on one condition?"

"Yeah? And what's that?"

He gestured toward the living room. "You'll have to sleep on my couch. I've seen enough wrecks for three lifetimes."

NOW IT's Thursday morning, four and a half days since he walked into the coaches' lounge and spoke with Nick Major. Garcia hasn't visited or called. The UCC Cowboys are presently ranked number nine in the Associated Press poll, having jumped fourteen spots after dismantling Wisconsin. Last night on ESPN, Mark May predicted they'd finish the year unbeaten, that in a worst-case scenario they'd play in a BCS bowl and, if a couple more heavyweights lost, might even compete for the national title. A brief interview with Major followed, and he acted as self-assured as ever, claiming that the only thing on his mind was Colorado State, his cocked chin suggesting exactly the opposite.

Maria has become increasingly insistent, sending several texts a day asking if there's anything new. Last night, after he went to bed, she left a voicemail that he listened to at breakfast. "Hey," she said, "have you ever heard of an 'orange Coke'? I had a cousin from Little Rock who used that term. Took me a while to figure out she meant a Fanta. To her, 'Coke' was just generic for 'soft drink.'" She paused, and he heard liquid being poured. "You know what I have a problem with, Richard? I don't wait well. Never have. But I guess you're asleep. I probably ought to be too. Call me tomorrow?"

He will, but not until later. His car's due for service, so after letting Franek and Sandy out at school, he drops it off at the Toyota dealership, where they tell him it'll be ready by noon. This is a nice day for early October—a little overcast, temperature around 70—and he decides to walk home. It's about two miles, straight down Maroa through old Fig Garden, so called because once upon a time it was an orchard. About half the shade trees in Fresno stand here, mostly ash and eucalyptus. They used to talk about trying to buy in the neighborhood but never found the right house at the right price.

There are no sidewalks, but since the speed limit is 25, with a stop sign at the end of every block, it's safe to walk on the pavement, stepping off into someone's yard if you hear a car approaching from the rear. He's just done that when a maroon Buick pulls up beside him. The glass slides down, and Joe Garcia says, "Want a ride?"

There are several reasons to deem this encounter unlikely. The first is that the detective lives way out north, in Woodward Park. The second is that the police department is miles south of here and more easily reached via the 41 freeway. The third is that while "Old Fig," as locals call it, is surrounded by the city of Fresno, it's technically not part of it. Administered by the county, it falls under the jurisdiction of the sheriff's department. The FPD stays away.

He steps over to the car. "Hey, Joe. What are you up to this morning?"

Garcia observes him for a moment. "What am I up to? Well, let's see. Oh, I know. I'm driving down Maroa."

"It's unusual to run into the FPD in Old Fig."

"Think so?"

"This is the sheriff's turf, right?"

"Who says I'm on duty?"

He squats beside the Buick. "I thought you were always on duty."

"I am unless I'm not. I pretty much control my own schedule. Know what I mean?"

"Actually, I do. Because I pretty much control mine too."

"I know you do. Most people, when they go to a football game, they're there to have fun. But some people go on business. Coaches, refs, the folks that sell hotdogs. Sportswriters. Which I didn't know you were one of. Why don't you climb in? We'll drive around for a few, and I'll tell you what I've been musing about."

He's dealing with a different Joe now—though, in retrospect, it's a Joe he always knew existed. Julia only met him once, but she disliked everything she'd heard about the detective and was never happy to learn they'd had another conversation. One day, she maintained, Garcia would cause a big problem. "Tell you what," Richard says. "I'm taking this walk in lieu of the gym, just trying to get my exercise. So why don't I keep going, and you meet me back at my place? Shouldn't be more than another ten, twelve minutes."

Garcia sighs and turns his gaze to the street. "I need to gas up. See you in fifteen."

As soon as the Buick disappears, he calls Maria and tells her about the encounter.

"That's kind of spooky," she says. "You think he's dangerous?"

A few years ago, after he wrote an article on Valley gangs, somebody slashed his tires, sprayed graffiti all over his car, and left a mutilated cat near the front door. A piece he wrote about eco-terrorists led to death threats, and for a while the FPD placed his house under twenty-four-hour surveillance. You sign on for certain risks. They troubled him when he still had the safety of his family to worry about. "I never thought he was dangerous," he says. "I always just thought he looked out for Joe. In the past, that meant working extra hard to get his name in the paper. Now it might mean keeping it out."

"Want me to come over?"

"And do what?"

"Hide in the basement or the bedroom. Just in case."

The other night, when he got drunk with her, a subtle shift occurred. Not a quake, just a tremor. At one moment they were talking about Nick Major and Joe Garcia and the Aguileras and the FPD, and the next she was asking him if he'd been back to Krakow since the accident. "No," he'd said, "though I'm sure I'll go back one day."

"Because you feel like you have to face up to it?"

"I faced up to it before I left. It happened. It's final."

"I don't guess you're religious, are you?"

"I don't go to church."

"But do you believe?"

"Intelligent design makes a certain amount of sense to me. What about you?"

"I was raised Southern Baptist. I have no doubt God exists. And there's another thing I don't doubt."

"What's that?"

"That He's a great big son of a bitch."

He rolled his eyes toward the ceiling.

"Am I making you uncomfortable?"

"Not at all. I'm just checking to see if the sky's about to fall."

"It fell on me a long time ago."

One look at her, and he decided she wished she hadn't said that. In an effort to ease her discomfort, he offered the blandest response he could come up with on short notice. "Oh, it falls on everybody from time to time."

"You know what I've been wondering?"

"What?"

"After you lost your wife and daughter," she said, "did you ever . . . well, did you ever consider suicide?"

It took a moment or two to recover from the shock of being asked. "No," he said, "I can't say that I did. But I would've been perfectly happy if I could've rolled back the tape and died alongside them."

After that, she steered the conversation into inanity. The alleged sharpness of razorback hackles. The stupidity of style sheets, which once led a copy editor at the *Sun* to change a robbery suspect's vehicle from "black Ford Taurus" to "African-American Ford Taurus." The merits of Texas barbecue. The decline of the apostrophe. When all the beer was gone, he went to bed and she went to the couch. The next morning he woke to the sound of voices and the odor of fried bacon. She was in the kitchen with Franek. Though hungover, she'd made herself at home and was wearing one of Julia's old bathrobes. "Hope it's all right to borrow this," she said. "I found it in the bathroom closet." She must not have noticed the effect on him, because she continued to wear it until she finally got dressed and left. That night he dreamed he was back in the crashed Mercedes, waking to find the sun in his eyes, Julia's head turned away, her body still, one cold hand locked around the wheel.

"I'm not scared of Joe Garcia," he says now as he walks on down Maroa toward his meeting with the detective. What he doesn't say is that the reason he's not scared of him is he's not scared of anybody or anything. Along with so much else, he's lost the capacity to feel fear. The worst that could happen already did.

WHEN HE gets home, Garcia is sitting in the driveway. "You're not quite as swift as you thought," the detective observes, climbing out of his car. "Took you twenty-one minutes."

"Really?"

"Give or take."

Richard steps onto the porch. "You put a stopwatch on me?" he asks as he pulls the house key from his pocket.

"Time's money, money's time. Mine is anyway. I'm looking to retire the second my social security kicks in."

"Retire and do what?"

"Kick back. Let off a little steam."

The front door has six glass panes, and in one of them he can see the other man's reflection. He's not smiling, or scowling, or doing anything else that it's easy to find a name for. His face is expressionless and stiff, as if a layer of sealant has been applied.

SEATED ON the couch, Garcia lets his eyes roam the room, taking in the ailing rubber plant in the corner, the pile of magazines on the coffee table, the photos of Julia and Anna that stand above the fireplace. He's been here before, though the last time was years ago. He picks up a copy of the *New Yorker*, flips through it, then lays it back on the table. "In some parts of town," he says, "you see this thing on everybody's coffee table. It and *New York Magazine* and the *New York Times*. Why are so many people in Fresno, California, so goddamn fascinated by New York?"

It's a rhetorical question, Richard understands, part of some process they'll have to go through before they discuss what Joe came to discuss, so he doesn't point out that while he probably enters at least as many homes as Garcia does, he almost never sees any of those publications on people's coffee tables or anywhere else except Borders or Barnes and Noble. "Well, New York's the media and entertainment center," he says. "That's probably a big part of it."

"Other day," Garcia tells him, "I went to the doctor. Fucking prostate's got me wanting to climb Half Dome. So I'm sitting there in the waiting room with needles shooting up my ass, and there's this professorial-looking fellow who's reading guess what? The *New York Times*. This scruffy kid's in there with us, and he's got a plaster cast on his arm that somebody's drawn a king-sized cock on, and he says to the guy with the paper, polite as can be, 'Excuse me, sir. If you're not reading them right now, could I get the want ads?' Can you fucking beat that? The want ads?"

"No," Richard says, as if this is all great fun, "I guess not."

"Hating New York's probably in my DNA."

"Yeah? How come?"

"'Cause I was born in L.A." He crosses his thick thighs, then locks his hands around his knee. "So what's your problem with Coach Major?"

"Nick Major? I didn't know I had one."

Garcia shakes his head, then looks out the window as if he can't bear to make eye contact. It occurs to Richard that the detective honestly, and justly, feels betrayed. This little epiphany is followed swiftly by another: until Saturday night, when he stepped into the coaches' lounge, it had been a long time since anything he'd done or said had caused this kind of discomfort. When he was doing his job the way it's supposed to be done, he caused it all the time. There's not much bite to him anymore. His edge has been rounded off.

"If I made a list," Joe says, looking at him now, "of all the times I helped you with a story, it'd be pretty lengthy, wouldn't it?"

"It sure would, Joe."

"Talked to you when I wouldn't talk to folks from the *Sun*, though since they're a local outfit, it might've been to my advantage to cuddle favor there."

He means "curry favor," of course, but when Richard thinks back on it, he will decide that "cuddle" is closer to the truth, not to mention more poetic.

"And what thanks do I get? You go give the coach the third degree and start making insinuations about me. What's behind this, Brennan? It's that new redheaded Okie at the *Sun*, isn't it?" Problematically, he glances at Julia's photo.

Whatever residual gratitude Richard might have harbored for the information Garcia has fed him over the years is washed out to sea. "Maria Cantrell, you mean? She's actually from Arkansas."

"Arkie, Okie, whatever. She's got a nice can trailing behind her, I'll give her that. So I guess we could say she's well named. She's been buzzing around the Palomino, asking questions about who drinks with who . . . is it 'who drinks with who' or 'who drinks with whom'?"

"Depends on how correct you want to sound when quoted. Or is this conversation off the record?"

Garcia uncrosses his legs and leans forward, a hand on each knee. "This conversation is being conducted between you and me. Like all the other conversations we've had over the last however many years. Either you call me up with a question and I tell you as much as I can afford to and then some, or I call you up and make sure you get dibs on a story. I don't know why you didn't do that this time. But here I am, Richard, for you to ask me whatever you want to know. If I can tell you, I will."

It sounds perfectly reasonable, and it would be if Maria hadn't shown him the photo of Major letting Jacinta Aguilera out of his car, if she hadn't found a bartender at the Golden Palomino who said Major liked to drink there and was often served by Jacinta, if she hadn't learned that Garcia handled security for private parties at the coach's house. This last bit of info is the main thing that gives him pause: she says she can't tell him how she came by it, that her source was scared and she promised to protect his or her identity. He mostly believes her, and the coach's reaction seemed to confirm his ties with Garcia. But since Joe is sitting here asking him what he'd like to know, that seems like a good place to start.

"Did you handle security for a private party at Major's?" he asks.

"Several times. I've also done it for the UCC basketball coach. You may recall—or maybe not—that I got four kids. Unlike me, they're all gonna go to college. Two of 'em are there right now, another one'll start next year and the last one a couple years later. So I don't turn down work. I'm like most joes walking around out there."

"Are you and Major friends?"

"A guy like me doesn't get to be friends with guys like him. I *work* for him sometimes. He's bought me the occasional drink."

"Are you aware of any link between Major and Jacinta Aguilera?"

Garcia had to know the question was coming, that he wouldn't be here otherwise, yet he takes a while before answering. Finally, he says, "You met my wife once, didn't you?"

More than once. Her name is Cloris, and she's a nurse at Valley Children's Hospital. Years ago, one afternoon when Anna and Sandy were riding their bikes around the neighborhood, they

somehow contrived to crash into each other. Sandy emerged un-
scathed, but Anna fell flat on her face, and when he saw the bloody
mess it made of her mouth and nose, he threw her in the car and
broke every traffic law driving her to the hospital. Garcia's wife
immediately got her in to see the doctor, and within the hour she
was stitched up and on her way home with a promise that she'd
heal just fine, which she did. He hugged Cloris that afternoon,
thanking her profusely. The following day he returned with the
biggest box of See's Candy he could find. His choice of gift was not
accidental, though when he told Julia about it, she voiced dismay.
Cloris was and is an enormous woman. The clinical word would be
"obese."

"You know perfectly well that I've met her," he says. "But what's
that got to do with Coach Major and Jacinta Aguilera?"

"Cloris, God love her . . ." Garcia shakes his head. "Great
woman. Totally. But she's not exactly Marilyn Monroe. You ever
seen Coach Major's wife?"

"I'm afraid not."

"Well, she kind of *is* Marilyn Monroe. You know what I'm
saying?"

He knows what he's saying. And he also knows what he's not
saying. "You didn't really answer my question, Joe."

With his tongue, Garcia probes his jaw, as if he's having second,
third, and fourth thoughts about Richard's intelligence. "What's
your favorite pie?" he asks.

"Apple."

"Like it a lot?"

"Actually, I do."

"So, loving your good old deep-dish apple pie, you're walking
by a bakery one evening after closing time, and there sits a pecan
pie in the window. Well, that looks kind of good, you think. So

what do you do? Bash the window out to get it? Or go home and eat some more of that good apple?"

"I go home and eat more apple. But that doesn't answer my question either."

"I always heard Massachusetts offered excellent education. But I'm starting to wonder."

He decides to return the sarcasm, fully aware he's taking a calculated risk that could result in combustion. "Oh, it most definitely does, Joe. But I was not the brightest student in that storied state. So I'm afraid you'll need to walk me through this. My devotion to apple pie means what with respect to whether there was a link between Nick Major and Jacinta Aguilera?"

While he watches, Garcia gets up and disappears into the dining room. He hears him walk through there and into the hall, and then he hears the door to Anna's old bedroom open and close. More footsteps, and the bathroom door opens and closes. Then the door to his study, followed by the bedroom door and the door to the basement. After that, the kitchen. A moment later, the detective reappears, his face now purple. Breathing hard, he stands beside Richard's chair so that there's little choice but to look up at him.

"You want me to tell you he fucked her?" he asks. "Well, I can't. You want to know why?"

"Sure, Joe. Why?

"Because if it happened, sad as this may be, they didn't invite me to watch. I don't say what I don't know. But there's a few things I do know, and I'm gonna relate 'em before I go to work.

"Here's the first. When we entered the Aguileras' house that night, we found the woman sitting in the kitchen slumped over the table. Her right hand's wrapped around a nearly empty bottle of Chihuahua, and she's got a hole in the back of her head. The two boys were in bunk beds. He shot the one in the upper bunk in the side of his head, and there were brains and blood all over the wall. The one in the lower bunk must have woken up and tried to get out of bed, because he was shot in the face. The toddler was in her crib and probably never did wake up, thank God and Joseph and Mary. I'll spare you the details about her condition, except to say that when a kid's that small, a 9-millimeter slug might as well be a hand grenade. He probably shot her last, since his own body was right beside her crib. The motherfucker just snapped. Why he snapped is anybody's guess. Maybe his wife knew the answer. Maybe she didn't.

"I could walk you through all the ballistics reports, tell you about powder burns and all that shit, but what's the point? If you and your girlfriend or whatever she is wanted to know any of this, the time to ask was at the press conference. You didn't even attend, but she did, and I never heard a peep out of her. You got anything else you want to know, ask me now. Or forever leave me be, as I intend to do unto you from this fine morning forth."

"Move away from my chair, Joe."

"Why?"

"Because I want to stand up. And I'd like a little space in which to do it."

"'In which to do it.'" Garcia shakes his head. "Who in the world says shit like that?"

He backs up, but only a couple feet. Richard watches him for a moment until he moves a little farther.

Then he stands. Eye to eye with the detective, he can see a shred of meat caught between his incisors. Ham or bacon, it's hard to say which. "Andres Aguilera didn't leave a suicide note, right?"

"Like we announced at the press conference you didn't go to, no, he most certainly did not."

He doesn't know why he asks the next question, though when he tells Maria about it tomorrow evening, he will realize he asked simply because it made sense. He was just doing his job better than he had for a while. "Did you happen to find Jacinta Aguilera's cell phone?"

Some people can cover it up when you hit home. Some people can't. Garcia is quick to say no. But not quick enough.

She lives on a quiet street bisected by a canal. Like his house, hers is a Tudor and though a good bit smaller has many of the same features: rounded arches, wooden floors, in the foyer a stained-glass window. "This is the first place I've ever owned," she says as she shows him around. She opens the bathroom door to reveal black-and-white art-deco tile and a pedestal sink. "You've got the same tile in your bathroom, I noticed."

"Most of these Tudors were built in the early to mid-'20s, when there were only about three construction companies in town. You'll see a lot of similarity from one to the next."

She tosses her hair, which he has come to recognize as her trademark gesture. "Want a beer?"

"Sure."

He follows her into the kitchen. It's neat, dishes put away, no cartons or cans left standing around. He looks over her shoulder as she opens the fridge. There's not much inside: just a couple six-packs of Sam Adams, a quart of milk, some Trader Joe's lasagna.

She hands him a Sam, grabs one for herself, then pulls an opener out of a drawer and pops off the caps. "Cheers," she says and clinks his bottle. "Want to go sit out back?"

"Sure."

She leads him into the fenced-off yard. At the rear of it,

there's a deck with a Jacuzzi and next to that a glass-topped table shaded by a beach umbrella. He pulls a chair out for her, then one for himself.

"Know what I drank when I lived in 'Wistuh'?" she asks. "Three guesses."

"Harpoon?"

"You're amazing. I've looked for it out here, but nobody's ever heard of it."

"I doubt it's sold beyond New England."

"Well, you're wrong about that, partner. I once slurped down a whole bunch of 'em in a Miami bar."

"Yeah?"

"Fuckin' A, as they say at the corner packie."

In the text he sent late last night, he told her he'd had an interesting talk with Garcia and that if she had time for a beer this evening, he'd be more specific. Now he takes her through their conversation word by word. When he's finished, she says, "Goddamn. So you're thinking the son of a bitch found her cell phone and concealed the evidence."

"Given what else we know, it wouldn't surprise me."

"You think anybody else is involved in the cover-up?"

"Like who?"

For the second time in the last thirty-six hours, someone looks at him as if he were an unusually dense child. "Duh?" she says. "Like the other officers who entered the house that night. Like the fucking police chief. Like the DA. Maybe even a judge. Like, who do *you* think?"

He downs the last of his beer, then with the bottle gestures at the Jacuzzi, which is covered by a fiberglass lid. "You use the hot tub much?" he asks.

"Yes, I do. I get in it when I feel tense. And I'm feeling tense now. But I didn't have the foresight to turn on the heater. You're fixing to tell me we need to proceed with caution, aren't you? Just chill for the next . . . oh, I don't know, the next month or two. Or maybe wait till sometime in January, after the national championship game?"

"May I ask you a question, Maria?"

"Might as well. I mean, since it sounds like you're not planning to ask the police any."

"When you went to that press conference where the FPD announced its findings, I was covering a Modesto city council meeting. Garcia said that during the Q&A, you didn't say a word. Is that true?"

"I can't remember. It could be."

"Maria?"

She's looking at her fence, as if redwood boards are the most interesting sight in town. "Okay. I didn't."

"Yet you told me that you were bothered by the chief's apparent nervousness as well as Garcia's cockiness."

"Are we having a Malcolm-McGuiness moment?"

"I'm sorry?"

"You know, where one journalist interviews another one to expose his—or in this case *her*—foibles?"

Yesterday afternoon, when he got his car out of the shop, he did something he should've done sooner, paying a visit to both the police department and the office of the superior court clerk. After that, he went home and placed a phone call, which lasted over an hour. Then he made a big pot of coffee, and by sunrise this morning he'd read every piece she'd written for the Worcester paper. As far as he can tell, her reporting there was flawless. She covered her share of fires and wrecks as well as numerous assaults and a handful of murders. He searched for retractions or corrections but couldn't find a single one. He thought of calling his former BU classmate but decided against it. It wouldn't be necessary.

"Let's make it both his foibles and hers," he says. "We'll start with mine. For the last couple years, I've been going through the motions. That's what you detected when we were at Chicken Liver's and you pinned my foot to the floor. I used to work a lot harder. For the record—"

"Oh, so now we're on the record."

He ignores the barb. "For the record, I still believe what we do's crucial. But there's a right way to do it and a wrong way. The right way nearly always takes longer. I've already made one bad mistake."

She doesn't ask what that bad mistake was. She's receded into herself, to the place of inner darkness he knows all too well.

"I shouldn't have interviewed Major before I'd taken some other steps. Of course, you're the one who suggested it, but I should've known better. For one thing, I should've talked to Joe before that, though it probably wouldn't have gone any better than it did yesterday. More importantly, I should have read the police report, then driven down to superior court and taken a look at the search warrant."

He gives her a moment to respond. But she's not going to.

"After all," he says, "that's what you did."

"Okay. That's what I did."

"And since you've examined lots of search warrants, when you looked at the one executed during the Aguilera investigation, you would've noticed immediately that no mobile phones were listed among the items retrieved from the house. And that would've struck you as strange because these days, who doesn't have a cell phone? My guess is that this is when you went to see your editor."

"I waited a week."

"And did what?"

"A little more digging. Followed Major around town, spent some more time at the Palomino. And found out about Garcia handling security for his parties."

"Speaking of that," he begins.

"I'm still not going to tell you who I learned it from."

"Eventually, you may have to."

"No. I'll tell you how and when, if you insist. But not his name."

He's silent for a moment, during which he decides to let that one go, at least for now. "I don't suppose you'd like another beer?"

She says sure but doesn't get up. She's still staring at the fence. She hasn't looked at him even once since he started asking questions.

He takes their empty bottles back to the house, drops them in the recycling bin, and grabs a couple more. When he pulls out the drawer where the opener is, he notices a neatly rolled joint. It's lying in the tray that holds kitchen utensils, almost but not quite concealed beneath the spoons. He pops the caps and goes back outside.

Now she does look at him, watching him all the way across the yard. "That was quick. If it had been me, I would've probably seized the opportunity to look around, paw through a closet or two while claiming I took a big piss."

"I'm sure you would have," he says, handing her the beer. "I did find your joint, though I wasn't looking for it."

"No, that wouldn't be your style, I guess. Was it ever?"

"Not really."

"Of course not. You went to journalism school and made the right connections and got a job with a big paper when you were still in your twenties."

He sits down and crosses his legs. "One connection I made was with a guy from your home state. Remember, I told you I had a friend who teaches at the University of Arkansas?" He mentions the name. "He's from some small town up in the Ozarks. I don't suppose you know him?"

She shrugs. "I know who he is. Used to be a foreign correspondent for the *Washington Post*, and when he retired he moved back home and accepted some kind of fancy chair or whatever you call it at the university. I never met him, though. I don't travel in those circles. Never have."

"He and I met in Poland," he tells her. "In the fall of '89. At the time, he was the *Post*'s regular Eastern Europe correspondent. His Polish was serviceable at best, but I found it easier to understand him in that language than I did when he spoke English. We used to laugh about it. His accent was really thick. Still is. I talked to him last night. He's got the most amazing memory of just about anybody I ever met."

He pauses again, leaving her a blank to fill in, should she choose. His kindness, if only he knew it, is grating. That's a word she learned in the cotton gin her father used to run.

When she first heard it, the word was a noun rather than an adjective, and it had no *g* at the end. She'd asked why there was a hole in the gin's concrete floor and why that hole was covered by four or five rusty iron bars. And her daddy said, *We're so close to that old grudge ditch that we get flooded sometimes. When the water comes in, it runs through this gratin' into the drain, and the drain carries it right back out. We can't let the machinery get wet. That'd foul it up bad.*

That's another word that means one thing sometimes and something else at others. Water can *foul* up gin machinery. You can commit a personal *foul* in a football game like the one she went to with her friend Grace Ann's family one Friday night in the fall of '81. Which is why she was not at home when someone whose face she'll never see, whose name she'll never know, induced her father to open the door. He'd just finished ginning the last scrap picking. He was too tired for a ball game. *Angel, your old daddy needs some rest.*

The house stood on a badly maintained blacktop road about halfway between McGehee and Dermott. She and her parents lived there three years. For a few months, her older brother did too, but then he enlisted in the Marines. It wasn't a big house, it wasn't a nice house, it was cold in the winter because they only had space heaters, and there were stains on the ceiling where the roof leaked. Why anybody would think there was anything in that house worth so much trouble was never explained. All they got was a wallet, a purse, and a metal box that couldn't have had more than a few hundred dollars in it, if that. They tore her room up, but nothing went missing.

Foul play, the article said, as though you could make everything right by throwing a flag and blowing a whistle. It was news for quite a while, and the sheriff appeared on the Little Rock stations as well as the one in El Dorado. He'd get to the bottom of it, he promised, but he never did, though the following year his tough-on-crime campaign won him a seat in the state legislature. By then, she was living with her aunt. Later, a different aunt took her in, and then she went back to the first one. They handed her off as if she were a football. That game again.

"So your friend served up my backstory," she says.

"He was working for the *Arkansas Gazette* at the time. He didn't cover the story. But he remembered it when I said your last name. They've got a pretty good archive, so I paid for online access and found the articles. Is this what you would have told me the other night if I hadn't turned into a stuffed shirt?"

She wraps her arms around herself and her lips jut out. She's fighting tears, and it's clear that doing it is making her angry and that at least some of the anger, if not all of it, is directed at him.

He rises from his chair, bends over, and puts his arms around her. Her hair smells like orange peel. There's also a hint of feminine perspiration. Some people might not think it smells that different. But it does. It's one of the things he used to know and had all but forgotten, in the way you forget certain sensations when the sources of them are long gone.

"My folks didn't matter much," she says. "My daddy was just somebody who ginned other people's cotton. If he'd owned a plantation, they would've busted ass to catch whoever did it. Nobody gives a shit what happened to the Aguileras either. They all just crave their goddamn championship. They don't want their golden boy fucked with."

"I have a feeling you're right about that," he says. He stands and looks at her, surveying the damage. Her cheeks are damp, but her eyes are clear. "Why don't we take a walk? It's such a nice evening."

"All right," she says. While he watches, she turns the beer up. It wouldn't be accurate to say she chugs it, but it wouldn't be that far off the mark either. He takes a few sips of his, just to be polite.

They walk around for an hour or more on narrow streets in her neighborhood. It's getting dark, but there are quite a few kids out playing, many of them Hispanic. The cars and trucks parked in the driveways aren't fancy, and a few look pretty old, but this neighborhood is a lot more stable than the one where the Aguileras lived. These folks have been here longer. Most are probably native-born.

"Was it all black and white where you grew up?" he asks.

"You mean racially? Or morally?"

He laughs. "Racially."

"Pretty much. During the Mariel boatlift, some Cuban refugees were housed at Fort Chafee, but they weren't there long. It's different now, so I hear. I haven't set foot in the state for fifteen years. If you want the current demographics, I guess you'll have to ask your friend who told you all about my tragic past."

"If you met him, by the way, you'd like him."

"I have no doubt. I've liked a lot of guys I shouldn't have."

He decides to let that one go too.

If she's disappointed by the lack of response, it doesn't show. "You know what puzzles me about the Aguilera investigation?" she asks. "They didn't even have to request a search warrant. They had probable cause. But they did it anyway."

"The more high-profile it is—and five dead people are plenty high-profile—the likelier they are to dot the *i*'s and cross the *t*'s."

"Or make it look like they did."

They're back on her block now, and he's been smelling Mexican food for the last hour. He's thinking they should climb in his car and drive down to a little hole-in-the wall that he used to go to with his family. Their *chile verde* is the best around.

But before inviting her to dinner, he tells her that since he now knows the names of the officers who responded that night, he's going to get in touch with one whose son used to play in the string ensemble with Anna. "A guy named Danny Scanlon. I don't know if he'll discuss it with me or not, but it's worth a try." Then he recalls something else he intended to bring up. "When you talked to the guy at the body shop," he says, "did you think to ask him if Andres had a cell phone? If he did, his boss would surely know it. And he'd probably still have the number."

She stops in front of her house, so he does too. "No," she says. "I didn't do that."

"Then I think tomorrow, I'll pay him a visit and see what he says."

"There's no need."

It's the finality he hears in her voice, rather than anything he sees in her eyes, that alerts him. "There's something else you haven't told me," he says. "What is it? Don't bullshit me anymore, Maria."

Rather than answer, she turns and heads for her front door. With a rising sense of alarm, he follows. Once inside, she disappears into her bedroom, then returns a moment later with an envelope. In the upper left-hand corner, he sees the familiar blue-and-white striped logo of AT&T Wireless. It's a phone bill addressed to Andres Aguilera.

The Palace of Culture and Science looms over the city of Warsaw like a giant soot-stained wedding cake. Two hundred thirty meters high, with forty-two stories and a total floor space of 125,000 square meters, it's one of Europe's tallest buildings as well as one of the ugliest. For more than half a century, it's been the butt of jokes.

Q: Where do you go for the best views in Warsaw?

A: The observation deck at the Palace of Culture and Science. That's the only place in town where you don't have to look at the building.

She and Stefan are here for the Polish Festival of Books. Today also happens to be their twenty-fifth anniversary. They're staying at the Bristol for three thousand zlotys a night. This evening, they will have dinner at a restaurant called the Great Unknown, which is in a secret location and has only one table. Dining is by invitation only. The chef is a fan of Stefan's novels.

Her husband doesn't know that she decided to visit the festival. She said she preferred to stay at the hotel and read. But she grew tired of their suite, has never been inside the Palace, and started to feel curious.

The book exhibition consumes three floors. For half an hour, she strolls around the lowest level, passing booth after booth.

Most of them have few if any guests, and many of the publishers look depressed, especially the purveyors of poetry. There is, however, a huge crowd waiting for autographs from a famous actress who starred in films by Wajda and Kieslowski. She doesn't look at the autograph seekers, just scrawls her name and pushes her memoir back across the table.

Spotting an information desk, Monika picks up a schedule and discovers that her husband is signing on the floor above. She climbs a marble staircase, steps into a colonnaded hall that was probably designed for party gatherings, and scans the aisle markers.

He's drawn quite a crowd. Unlike the actress, he looks his fans in the eye and chats with them. If they happen to be women—and most of them are—he pats them on the hand before saying goodbye. A couple of times, he rises and gives them a hug and a peck on the cheek. Two women ask to have their photo taken with him, and he obliges, standing between them, an arm around each. You'd have to be watching closely to notice when one of them slips him a scrap of paper.

"Do you like his work?" someone asks in English.

The person who spoke to her is a tall man of about sixty, with a finely chiseled chin and silver hair. He's wearing a gray suit and a silk shirt and tie. She has the feeling that if she glanced down at his shoes, she'd see her reflection.

"Not particularly," she says. "What about you?"

"I find it always predictable, frequently pretentious, and occasionally disgusting. He probably thinks he's writing literature." He offers his hand. "Enrico," he says.

She returns the gesture. "Monika."

"I'm from Rome. And you?"

"Krakow."

"Now, that's a lovely city. My late wife and I went there twice. The last time was probably at least ten years ago."

"It's changed a good bit since then."

"No doubt. But I'm sure it's still beautiful."

He asks if she's here in an official capacity, and she says no, that she just wanted to see what this building looked like on the inside. Then she asks if he is. He says yes, that he owns a small publishing house. "Nothing very sexy, I'm afraid. We specialize in cuisine and travel. Right now, our best-selling title is a history of the olive."

"Well, olives could be sexy. Hasn't their oil sometimes been put to amorous use?"

He laughs. "I think maybe you and I should have a drink."

Why say no? It's two thirty, and Stefan told her not to expect him back at the Bristol until seven, though his signing is supposed to conclude at three.

On the other hand, why say yes?

She thanks him but politely declines, and he accepts her decision with grace, then bids her good-day and wanders away.

SHE DECIDES to have a drink anyhow, in a small bar in the Old Town. She orders an eighteen-year-old Glenlivet on the rocks, then calls the waitress back and asks for it neat. She never drinks whisky. Except when she does.

She sips it, enjoying the chocolatey aftertaste as she watches people walk by on the cobblestone street. For every person who passes alone, she sees ten or twelve pairs. Most are young, in their late teens or early twenties. One couple goes by seven or eight times, heading north, then south, then north again. The girl talks with her hands, as if she were a mime. The boy, whose sandy hair laps over his collar, looks captivated. He could be watching a total lunar eclipse, a blood moon, the kind of thing you might get a look at every couple of years. But now it's all his. Block after block.

The bar is empty except for a couple who sit in a distant corner, beneath a poster of Joel Grey strutting with his cane in *Cabaret*. Their fingers are intertwined. He's drinking beer. She's having white wine. Two or three times, Monika hears the word "baby." Hears "temp job," "budget," "brainstorm," "masseuse." She orders another Glenlivet. She seldom drinks whisky except when she wants it.

She pulls out her mobile, which has been on silent all afternoon. There's a text from Stefan:

> lets meetin the lobbya t sven twenty five as the car is due to be there to pickyps upat svenetythirty looking for ward to a special evening with thelove of my life

Whatever else one might say about his novels, they are impeccably punctuated. As a rule, his texts are too. The sloppiness of this one could be due to the urge to escape an adoring crowd, the eagerness to escape with an adoring member of that crowd, or both. What it can't be attributed to is a lack of regard for the recipient. She doesn't doubt for an instant that she's the love of his life. He's probably never loved any other woman except his mother and his sister. What being the love of his life means is open to question. If she had to guess, she'd say it means she's his best female friend, the one he feels he can say anything to. Except for one thing.

She also has a couple of e-mails. The first is from Franek, asking if it's all right for him to go to Disneyland the first weekend in November with his "friend" Sandy and her parents, as he's never been there and Sandy says it's something every kid should see and it's a shame he didn't get to. The second is from Richard, posing the same question and assuring her that he's known the girl's parents for many years and that her dad is an excellent driver. He also tells her that he's pretty busy these days, working on a story that has become more and more absorbing. She suspects he's working on it with the female journalist. She sends him a quick note telling him that it's fine for Franek to accompany his friend's family and that she'll reply to her son tomorrow. Rather than closing with *Love, Monika*, as has been her practice for the last couple of years, she writes, *Best, M.*

She puts her phone back in her bag, takes another sip of whisky, then notices that there's a newspaper on a nearby table. To give herself something to do besides looking out the window or listening to the couple in the corner, she goes and gets it.

The lead article announces that Barack Obama has won the Nobel Peace Prize. Beneath that, there's one about inflation. Idly, she begins to flip through.

"'Cleaners' Becoming Nationwide Problem," a headline says. "Harassed Residents Often Elderly, Infirm." The report has a Krakow dateline. It takes up an entire page and is accompanied by two photos. In the first, a figure perches on top of a steep roof, wearing a Darth Vader helmet. The second is a close-up of a man with thinning gray hair, flaccid cheeks, small but intelligent eyes, and a strange-looking mole.

She stares at his face for a while. She's sure she's seen him before, though she doesn't know where or when. He could be anybody, really, just one of those hapless people you walk right past in Planty or the Market Square and never give another thought to. Wherever she saw him, he probably hadn't given her another thought either. Why would he? She's just a small, dark-haired woman on the brink of fifty.

The day they release him to await trial, he goes for a long walk in Planty, making three complete circuits. The afternoon air has some bite in it, the temperature a few degrees above freezing, a strong breeze raking dead leaves across the paved footpaths. The cafés have fired up their space heaters and lowered clear plastic drop panels to break the wind. Most people are wearing coats, scarves, and gloves. He has only the nylon jacket he wore the night of his arrest, but he's not uncomfortable.

The police have returned his mobile phone along with his belt and wallet. He assumed they'd subject the mobile to forensic analysis, going through his text messages and voicemails, but they evidently didn't. After turning it on a couple of hours ago, he found several unread texts from Marek, the final one sent the same day Bogdan's face hit both the local papers and *Gazeta Wyborcza*, where it would've been seen all over the country. There were numerous texts from his sister in Zakopane and two from Krysia. Also, a new voicemail left just this morning from a number marked *Unavailable*. "If you've squealed," whoever it was said, "you better ask for life in prison. Meantime, watch your ass. Try to keep it clear of everything but your own shit."

He's infamous, yet no one he meets appears to notice. When he stops to buy a pretzel, the old woman behind the stand looks right at him and behaves as if he's worth exactly one zloty, no more and no less. When he sits down at Bunkier Café and orders a beer, the tall, dishwater-blonde waitress treats him just as brusquely as he saw her treat those at the table nearby. None of the other patrons pays him the slightest mind. He's every bit as invisible as before his crimes came to light.

That a lesson should be derived from his continuing anonymity seems obvious, and he resolves to think more about it soon, just not today. He liked both of the men who'd been in the cell with him—one a pickpocket, the other a hacker who maintained that cybercrime was the only way to go, so much easier on the body, he said, as long as you got up from your chair occasionally and did some exercises for the back and neck—but he hated the cell itself. It was in the basement, damp and poorly lit, and the toilet emitted an odor that only fresh air could make you forget.

When he finishes his beer, it's growing dark, and the street-lights have come on. He pays the check and strolls toward the Market Square.

The stalls in the Cloth Hall are closing, but the shops and restaurants that line the Square are brightly lit and busy. In autumn, it used to present a gloomy, colorless sight, mostly deserted at sundown or shortly after. This evening there are still plenty of people out and about. Close to the Town Hall Tower, a man and two boys are examining the large sculpture known as the Head. Cast from bronze, it lies on its side, the eyeholes big enough to accommodate a child's body. While Bogdan watches, the man lifts the smaller of the two boys and lets him peek in.

Normally, he wouldn't engage a complete stranger. But there's nothing normal about being released from jail or knowing that before long, you'll be back behind bars for a lengthier visit. "I've always wondered whose head that's supposed to be," he says.

The other man shrugs and hoists the bigger boy so he can see inside too. "Some Greek god, I think. Or maybe it's a Roman."

"I can't even remember when they put it here."

"Three or four years ago. It was supposed to go in front of Galeria Krakowska. But the sculptor objected."

"Yeah?"

"Yeah. He said he didn't want his work commercialized." The man sets his son back down. "I mean, I understand that artists are different from the rest of us. But what did he think he was doing when he sold the sculpture to the city? That's not commercial activity?" With his knuckles, he raps the bronze nose. "I build cabinets for a living. I build them as nice as I know how, but then I sell them and they go where they go. If somebody wants to stuff them full of old clothes, that's their business. The way I look at it, when you write *Paid* on the invoice, it's the end of the story."

His younger son is tugging at his coat sleeve. So he says goodnight, and the three of them head off across the Square, one boy on each side clinging to his hand.

Bogdan's eyes are watery, and in the cold air they sting. How simple and clear and easy it sounds. An invoice marked *Paid*, the end of the story. He steps over to the sculpture and runs his hand over the cold surface, feeling the furrowed contours of the forehead, the wavy ridges that simulate hair. He looks over his shoulder, then turns and sticks his head through one of the sockets.

HE BUYS a kebab and a sack of fries and sits down to eat them on a bench near the Florian Gate. By the time he finishes, it's nearly

THE UNMADE WORLD | 181

seven, and he's starting to shiver. Pulling out his mobile, he checks to see how much of a charge is left, then phones his old partner.

At the other end, the call produces consternation. Marek and Inga are in their bedroom, listening to Frank Sinatra. He's sitting on the side of the bed, and she's opposite him in the armchair. Both are naked. They've been staring at each other for the last few minutes, neither of them saying a word while they gently touch themselves. This kind of behavior started the day Marek learned of his friend's arrest. Sex between him and his wife had gone the way of his grocery chain, but now he can't get enough of her body. He wants her in the morning and again when she returns from work. At first, she acted surprised, put off, and embarrassed, but she quickly entered into the spirit of the endeavor. Last night, he licked Moldavian champagne off her nipples.

"It's Bogdan," he says after glancing at his phone, with which he was about to take a close-up of her navel. "What should I do?"

"Answer it."

"What if it's being taped?"

She's quit touching herself. "He's our friend," she says. "Besides, if they were going to arrest you, they would've done it before now. I'm pretty glad they didn't."

So he takes the call. "Bogdan? Where are you?"

"Marek, how have you been?"

"Well, to be perfectly honest, I've been kind of scared. The police . . . are you with them now, Bogdan?"

"No, they turned me loose."

"For good?"

"Just until my trial. They appointed an attorney to represent me."

"Does he think he can get you off?"

"Not a chance."

"*O, Jezu.*"

"It's all right, Marek."

He hears Inga's voice in the background, then Marek whispering back.

"Bogdan, Inga says why don't you come over? You could have supper with us. Maybe even stay here tonight. You don't want to be alone on your first free evening."

Until his friend issued the invitation, he thought he did want to be alone, but he was lying to himself. The reason jail was not nearly as onerous as he'd expected, even with the toilet discharging its foul perfume, was that for the first time in forever, he had company. "Are you sure?" he asks, already on his feet and heading their way.

"SO THE pickpocket—his name is Pawel, and he's got one of those faces where all the features have been compressed, making him remind you of a bulldog—he and his new partner run along the platform toward the far end of the first-class car, the partner pulling an empty suitcase. They jump on and start down the aisle just as the couple enters from the opposite end. The Australian guy's big, well over two meters, probably about 110 kilos, and he's dragging a pretty good-sized suitcase himself. You can see a string around his neck, so his passport's probably in one of those security pouches, and for all they know his credit cards are too. But in his right front pocket there's a bulge, and they're sure it's his wallet. His wife's behind him, and she's got a huge purse, but the strap is wrapped around her neck, so you'd nearly have to kill her to get it off. 'Watch out for pickpockets,' she warns when she sees Pawel and his partner. Her husband rolls his eyes like he's heard the same thing twice a day for two weeks, or however long it's been since they left Emu Park, Queensland."

"How do you know this is where they were from?" Inga asks. She's taking up two-thirds of the couch, one arm on the backrest, her big, bare feet drawn up beneath her. She's wearing a green bathrobe, and her toenails are painted deep purple. You would not normally associate bright colors with Inga. She's had a bit more to drink than usual too, though Bogdan did see her sloshed once back around 1990, on New Year's Eve.

"I'll get to how we know where they were from in a minute. The Australians start down the corridor, looking into each compartment, trying to find their seats. Keep in mind, this is the first-class car—"

"So it's almost empty," Marek interjects. He leans toward the coffee table and spears another morsel of pickled herring.

"Completely. Pawel and his partner meet them about halfway down the aisle. He starts by on the right, his partner on the left. 'Excuse, excuse,' he says, 'sorry, sorry.' The guy's face is turning red and his nose has wrinkled up like he's smelling a horrible odor, which he is. They wear really bad-smelling clothes on purpose, to add another level of distraction.

"Pawel's got his fingers in the guy's pocket, he can feel the wallet, but he's having a hard time pulling it free. So what does the big Australian do? With one hand, he lifts that heavy suitcase into the air so he can turn sideways and let them pass, and when his hip moves, that wallet comes right out and he never notices. Pawel and his partner are on the platform within seconds."

"And then what happens?"

"The police are waiting for them. Turns out the new partner was an undercover officer. It's Pawel's third arrest, so he's probably going to get more than a brief vacation."

"And what about you?" Inga asks.

"What about me?"

"How long are you likely to be in jail?" She reaches for the vodka bottle, and when she leans over, he realizes she's wearing nothing beneath the green robe. Then he looks at Marek, who's in his pajamas. When he got to their place, it was only seven thirty, and it seemed a little odd that they were already dressed for bed. But the three of them had several drinks in rapid succession, and this prevented him from putting two and two together.

When he phoned them, they were fucking. They might even have been making love.

His friend used to sleep around, whereas Bogdan didn't. Marek still has his wife's affection, whereas he doesn't. At a different time, the disparity might have held a lot more interest. It could even have resulted in the kind of bitterness that makes your throat burn. But which is more worthy of consideration—inequity or mystery? He'll bow before the latter, not the former.

A certain tightness has announced itself in his groin, and heat is rising into his neck and cheeks and ears. Until this moment, he never felt one milligram of lust for big-boned Inga, with her broad hips and manly shoulders, and this now seems to him grossly unfair. Controlling your urges is both decent and necessary. Deficiency of desire, on the other hand, is like anemia, a condition to overcome.

When he thinks he can look at her without revealing his burgeoning lust, he tells her his lawyer informed him that the maximum penalty for his offense is a year in prison. "But at least while I'm in there," he says, "I won't have to pay rent."

This news provides Marek more than enough impetus to finish getting drunk. He downs shot after shot, and when the bottle is empty, he staggers into the bathroom, where he leans over the toilet and offers up the contents of his stomach. As soon as he's finished, he promises himself that when his friend is in jail, he will visit him weekly, no matter where he's incarcerated. It's the least he can do, and more often than not the least he can do is what he has done. He ought to be in jail himself. Why he's been spared is a puzzle, the kind of thing he'll ponder the next time he steps into a deserted church or visits the cemetery where the woman and her daughter lie buried.

He brushes his teeth, gargles with some antiseptic mouthwash, and takes himself off to bed.

Back in the living room, Bogdan and Inga have broken out the cherry cordial, the only thing left to drink besides water and tea. Time passes fast, as it often does when you're on the glorious side of drunk. Eventually, the clock strikes three, and they drink a final toast to Pawel the pickpocket. What they've talked about, if they've talked about anything at all, Bogdan will not recall.

What he will remember is following Inga down the hallway past her bedroom, where Marek lies snoring, each release of air ending in a faint, almost dainty whistle. She opens the hallway closet, pulls out a towel, then steps into their sons' old room and switches on a lamp. She's saying something about breakfast, how he'll have to fend for himself, that she'll be gone when he wakes. She turns to hand him the towel, and that's when she sees that she was right several hours ago in believing she knew what was on his mind.

So there they stand, the Brandenburg Gate and a felonious man. Let the moon shine down on this town of kings and dragons.

The house they're watching is an airplane bungalow off Huntington Boulevard. Several roof shingles are gone, the gas grill on the porch is missing a wheel, and the front steps are rotting.

"Makes me feel right at home," she says. "Stack some old tires up in the yard, and I could be back on the wrong side of Eudora, Arkansas."

"Are you aware the town you claim to come from keeps changing?"

"Certain habits die hard."

She insisted on coming with him today in case he ran into trouble. They're sitting in her car. Given the neatness of her house, the old Honda is comically messy. Starbucks cups and Diet Dr. Pepper cans litter the floor alongside countless Bic ballpoints, a Pizza Hut carry-out box that reeks of mozzarella, and at least two umbrellas with broken spokes. CDs are everywhere, most of the cases damaged, many of them empty. She has horrific taste in music. The 1910 Fruitgum Company. Peppermint Rainbow. Tommy James and the Shondells.

"What year were you born?" he asks.

"Nineteen seventy. Not that you should ever pose that question to a woman. Why?"

"This music is all before your time."

"I got a thing for sunshine pop."

Nearly three weeks' worth of sustained efforts, his as well as her own, have brought them to this house in southeast Fresno, which might or might not be the right place. It's a cold, rainy day: the first rain to fall on the Valley since last February. The streets are slick, the oil deposited on them starting to run after lying there undisturbed for more than eight months. She still uses a pager, and it keeps beeping. All over town, people are crashing into one another. A lot of wrecks are going uncovered.

"Ever wonder," he asks, "what'd happen if your boss finds out how you're spending your time?"

She's wearing a red leather jacket that looks good with her black jeans, though it clashes with her hair. These days, he can tell, she's putting a little more thought into her appearance. She's started applying lipstick and a touch of eyeliner, and he last saw a ponytail when they went to the ball game. At dinner the other night, she told him there was a period in Worcester when she wore nothing but warm-ups, even on the job—his old BU classmate finally spoke to her about it. Winter was getting to her. Turned out she had seasonal depression as well as the regular kind. That's the main reason she's here instead of there.

"I don't have to wonder what my boss would do," she says. "He'd send me packing. But hey, I been sent packing before."

"But not from a job?"

"Not from a job. That's a lesser kind of loss. Right?"

"Compared to what?"

She never takes her eyes off the bungalow. "When I was thirty-one," she says, "I seduced a nineteen-year-old. Well, tried to anyway. He was hanging around the pool at the apartment complex. A total virgin, which I didn't know at the time. Just as sweet as he could be but scared half to death, and that scared me too. So we're sitting on the couch, beating around the bush, and I finally just blurted, 'Let's do it.' And this poor child said, 'Do what?' I went all Lauren Bacall on him, graveling out '*You* know what.'"

"In other words, I should know the answer to my question?"

"In other words."

"Have you read a lot of Faulkner?"

"Not a single sentence. Why?"

"Never mind."

A couple of cars crawl by. It's a quiet street, and this is late morning, kids at school, the gainfully employed at work. The neighborhood isn't upscale, but it's still predominately white. Huntington Boulevard, at one time one of the better streets in town, is only a block away. You might find the occasional CPA living nearby, a teacher or two, a smattering of city, state, and county employees, and no small number of attorneys, mostly public defenders and specialists in immigration law. You could also find people who successfully operate at the margins. One of the more memorable individuals he interviewed in years past was a Nova Scotian who'd taken up residence about three blocks from here and reputedly did a good business selling refurbished assault rifles. He spoke on condition of anonymity, and while he was coy about his supplier, his hints indicated a source in the Israeli defense forces.

"You eat much clam chowder growing up?" she asks.

"Not at home. We had it at school sometimes."

"I ate a lot of 'chowduh' when I was living back there."

"It's good on a cold day."

"I ate it with cornbread. Made myself a big skillet of it and ate chowder twice a day till the cornbread ran out, and then I baked some more." She glances at her rearview mirror. "Don't turn around, but I think this may be our guy."

A maroon Dodge Ram passes them and turns into the driveway.

"Was there somebody in the passenger seat?" she asks.

"I couldn't tell for sure, but I believe so."

"How old you reckon that truck is?"

"Oh-seven, '08."

"Joe Bob must be doing all right."

His name is not Joe Bob. It's Rupert. Until about three years ago, as far as they've been able to determine, he lived in northern California, close to Clear Lake, where it's not uncommon to see Confederate flag decals displayed on the rear bumpers of vehicles or suspended from the eaves of houses. It's an area where you find a fair number of survivalists and white supremacists living in close proximity to aging Deadheads and assorted hippies. Sometimes they see eye to eye. Sometimes they don't. Disappearances have occurred.

The driver climbs out. He's a skinny guy with dark hair, and he's wearing khakis and a blue windbreaker. While they watch, he walks around the front of the truck to the passenger side, opens the door, and lifts something out. When he steps back into their line of sight, they see that what he's carrying is nearly as big as he is, that it's white and has hot-pink paws.

"What the fuck is that?" she asks.

"Looks to me like a stuffed bear."

Skirting puddles, he totes it across the yard. When he mounts the steps, she says, "Hadn't you better get going?"

He lays his hand on her right arm. "There's no rush. I'll give him a few minutes."

She sighs, then looks down at where he's still touching her. He thinks he knows what she's going to say: that for somebody so big, he has small, delicate hands that would look just fine on a woman.

His wife said that the first time they made love. He wills Maria not to. She's already worn Julia's bathrobe.

"I've always loved stuffed animals," she tells him. "The bigger they are, the better."

A FEW weeks ago, he did something he thought he could never do again, attending a performance of the high school chamber orchestra Anna used to play in. It took place in the main concert hall in the UCC Music Building, and the program consisted of works by Beethoven, Berg, and Mahler, concluding with the Adagio from the last composer's unfinished Tenth Symphony. Richard has only a rudimentary knowledge of classical music, but he recalled that this particular Adagio was among the most mournful pieces ever written. He wasn't looking forward to it.

When you're pursuing a story, there are times when you want the person you're interviewing to be back on his or her heels, worried, unsettled, confused, or just plain frightened. There are other times when you prefer exactly the opposite, which was why he'd decided to attend the concert. He wanted to talk to Danny Scanlon when he was comfortable, and he knew he'd be there and that in all likelihood he'd be by himself.

Scanlon was the father of the boy Anna had had a crush on in the fall of 2006. The kid would be a senior this year, and he'd casually gleaned a few facts about him through conversations with Sandy Lyons: he now had a girlfriend named Janette, who supposedly hated her parents because they were Mormon; his own parents had gotten divorced about eighteen months ago, and his mother had moved to the Bay Area; his sisters were living with her, but he'd elected to remain with his father, who never missed one of his performances, even if he had to take sick leave.

Richard used to talk to Danny from time to time, usually during intermission, or sometimes when he was waiting to pick Anna up from school. If Danny wasn't wearing his uniform, the last thing in the world you'd take him for was a cop. He wore old-fashioned black-rimmed glasses and was average-sized, soft-spoken, polite to a fault. He was also deeply religious, though Richard couldn't recall what denomination he belonged to.

The entrance was at the rear of the hall, the seats laid out below in tiered rows. He arrived about two minutes before eight and immediately spotted Scanlon, who'd taken an aisle seat halfway down. Fortunately, no one was directly behind him, so Richard waited until the lights began to dim, then walked down the aisle and grabbed the spot.

Being there nearly killed him. He recognized Danny's son, who'd filled out since the last time he'd seen him, and he found it impossible not to wonder what he might have come to mean to Anna. Maybe nothing. Maybe everything. Maybe they'd be trying to coordinate college applications now. Maybe they'd be sitting side by side onstage. He would never know.

He shut his eyes and let the music envelop him. The Berg was dissonant, at times even violent, and he kept thinking of the face that had looked at him that night as he sat strapped into the old Mercedes. His wife and daughter were either dead or dying, and the person that face belonged to must have known it. And knowing it, he walked away. He never called the police, never called a hospital, just left them there to bleed and freeze.

For many years, Richard Brennan had been a man about whom many things could be said. That he was a father and husband, a lover and companion. That he was good at what he did. That when he couldn't get out of wearing a tie, he chose a clip-on. That he loved a rich cassoulet. That he hated Pepsi but could tolerate Coke.

That he knew the music of Bud Powell like the letters of his own name and could list the personnel on every cut the great pianist had ever recorded. Now there was only one thing worth saying about him: that he was trying hard but mostly failing to overcome his loss.

By the time the lights went on for intermission, he was damp all over. He knew he must look terrible. He also knew he'd better act then, if he intended to, because there was no way he'd make it through the Mahler. When Danny placed his hand on the armrest to rise, he did the same. The other man looked right at him, nodded, then stepped into the aisle. He didn't have a clue who he was.

"Danny?"

Scanlon looked at him again. "Richard? Sorry, I didn't . . . I mean, well, it's been a while." He offered his hand. There was nothing to do but shake it and hope Danny didn't notice the moisture.

Richard decided to drop any pretense. "Can we step out for a minute?" he said. "There's something I'd like to ask you."

"Well . . . I mean, yeah. Sure. Okay."

Once outside, they stood on the sidewalk in front of the music building, students streaming by, many of them wearing green-and-gold UCC Cowboys paraphernalia.

"This place has gone football crazy," Danny said, probably because he was puzzled and felt the need to say something. Later, Richard would realize he had no idea what was coming, that he might not even have remembered Richard was a journalist, if in fact he'd ever known it. Not that many people read the *L.A. Times* in Fresno. Home delivery north of Bakersfield had stopped fifteen years ago.

Danny was four or five inches shorter, so Richard was careful not to crowd his space. "Forgive me, but I'll get straight to the point. You were one of the officers who responded to the Aguilera shootings back in August."

It was a statement, not a question. But Scanlon treated it otherwise. "Yes, I was. But what's this about, Richard? Why are you asking?"

"To be blunt, I've been looking into the investigation."

"Looking into it? Looking how?"

Richard pulled out his wallet, extracted a business card, and handed it to him. "I work for a newspaper. I thought you knew."

The other man stared at the card for a long time. Then he stuck it in his shirt pocket and raised his gaze. "You know, you really should contact Public Affairs. That'd be the normal way to arrange an interview. But I'm not the one you need to talk to. That'd be Joe Garcia. He's—"

"I know who he is. I also know that contacting Public Affairs would do neither me nor you any good."

"Me? What are you getting at, Richard? I haven't seen you in years. Not since . . . not since, like, two or three years ago."

"Did you or any of the other officers who entered the Aguilera residence that night find a cell phone? Before you answer, let me tell you what I know. You guys requested and were granted a search warrant. When the warrant was returned, it didn't list a cell phone among the recovered items. Both Jacinta Aguilera and Andres Aguilera had mobile phones, and I know the numbers of each one."

By that time, Danny was looking pretty bad himself. Sweat beads had popped out on his forehead, and his glasses were starting to fog up. "I don't have anything to tell you, Richard," he said. "Except that you should call Public Affairs. That's the proper way to approach something like this. Now, before long, the second half of the concert'll start, and I need to use the bathroom. So I'll ask you to excuse me." He turned toward the building.

"The last thing I have to tell *you*," Richard said, "is that if I don't get an answer to my question, I'm prepared to contact the grand jury. That's what you do when you suspect misconduct during an investigation."

Scanlon kept going.

"My cell number's on the card. The conversation would just be between you and me. Your name wouldn't appear in any story I might write."

Danny entered the building, the glass door swinging shut behind him.

Richard walked to the parking lot and climbed into his car. He sat there for a good while, losing track of time, as he so often had these last couple of years. The less you cared how you spent it, the less a minute meant. He thought of time as a substance to be burned.

Nothing he did would resurrect Jacinta Aguilera or her three children. Whatever he uncovered could only lead to more trouble: perhaps for Danny and his son, for Garcia and his family, for Nick Major and his family. Once again, the temptation to walk away from the story and write a piece about classic roadside diners or the freaks who hung around the spot where James Dean crashed his car arose. About the only thing preventing him was a woman who reminded him of his daughter every time she tossed her hair.

He finally started the car and drove home, where he took a long shower. He'd just walked into the kitchen and opened a Sierra Nevada when his cell began to vibrate. He didn't recognize the number, but it was local.

Scanlon wasted no time on hellos. "Richard, it's Danny. I need you to swear on the Bible you'll keep my name out of this."

"For me to swear on a Bible wouldn't mean much, Danny. And

anyway, I haven't got one." He was already reaching for a notepad. "But I give you my word I won't reveal you as a source."

"Even if you go to jail. I got my son to think about, Richard."

"I know you do, Danny."

"He and I don't have anybody but each other."

He started to tell the other man he knew that and that each of them was lucky to have the other. "I'll keep my promise," he said.

"All right," Scanlon said. "So I know there was at least one cell phone in the house that night."

"Where was it?"

"On the kitchen table."

"Near the woman's body?"

"About . . . about a few inches from her hand."

"Which hand?"

"Her right hand."

"So her right hand was on the table?"

"Yeah."

"What else was there?"

"Salt and pepper shakers. An avocado. Stack of white napkins."

"No beer bottle?"

"What?"

"Was there a beer bottle on the table?"

"No. Why?"

"No particular reason. You think maybe she'd recently taken a phone call?"

"I have no idea. When you walk into a situation like that, you're not wondering if somebody took a call."

"Was the phone turned on?"

"I don't know."

"Did you touch it?"

"Of course not."

"What happened to it?"

"I don't know."

"Was Garcia on the scene when you saw it?"

"Not yet. He got there a couple minutes later. My partner and I were already in the bedroom."

"Had your partner seen the phone?"

"I don't know. We never talked about it."

"So you went into the bedroom."

"Yeah."

"And then what happened?"

"What do you mean what happened, Richard? Do you have any idea what we saw in there?"

"Actually, I do." The coolness he heard in his own voice reassured him. There were still things worth doing. And maybe he could still do them. "I read the police report. The boys in bunk beds. The toddler in her crib. Andres Aguilera on the floor. Blood everywhere. I assume that's right?"

"Yeah. Your assumption's correct."

"So where did Garcia go when he entered?"

"He went . . . he went to the kitchen, I guess. That's where he was when I stepped out of the bedroom."

"And was the phone still on the table?"

"I'm not sure."

"Really?"

"Yeah."

"That's strange."

"Well, I'm sorry."

"Because, you know, I've seen some traumatic sights myself, Danny. Mostly in the line of work. But not exclusively. And things like whether or not the phone was still lying there . . . I tend to remember them. Just like you remember there were salt and pepper shakers on the table, and an avocado, and a stack of white napkins, and no beer bottle. I'm a person, but I'm also a professional. And so are you."

Silence on the other end. Then Danny Scanlon said, "The phone was gone."

SOMETHING ALWAYS happened to him when he knew he'd found his story. A moment came when it seemed as if it would write itself as long as he kept putting one foot in front of the other and didn't complain about lack of sleep, difficulties that threw themselves before him, people who either lied or paid out the truth like fishing line.

"So we know Joe took the phone himself," he said that same evening, on the couch in Maria's living room. She'd thrown a fake log in her fireplace, and it was flickering nicely but producing no heat. Which was fortunate, since the temperature outside was about sixty-five.

She wore velour pajamas that landed on the color spectrum somewhere between maroon and purple. She also had on a pair of furry pink sleepers. She must be cold-natured, he decided.

"Not that it was ever in much doubt," she said and sipped her pinot noir. "We knew he took it. We just didn't *know* it."

"The question is what he did with it."

For once, she deferred. "You know him a lot better than I do. What does your sense of Joe Garcia tell you he'd do?"

"Try to turn it to his advantage. But in order to do that, he'd have to first find out what was on the phone. And that'd be dif-

ficult if she set a passcode. You still have that little item you
stole?"

"No. I kept my promise." She gestured at the fireplace. "It went
up in smoke."

"I suspect you made a copy."

"Your suspicions are well founded. Would you like to see it?"

"No, because I hope to die without becoming a felon. But I
wouldn't mind if you went and got it."

She rose and disappeared down the hallway, then returned a
moment later with a manila folder labeled *W-2 Forms*.

She'd already told him that the cut-off date on the bill she'd
stolen from the overflowing mailbox was thirteen days past the
shootings. Both phones were registered to Andres Aguilera. One of
them never called anybody except the other number and the body
shop where Andres worked and an all-night gas station on West
Jensen, where they knew he sometimes picked up a few hours. The
second phone got a lot more use. Before her boss ordered her not to
rock the boat, Maria had phoned every number it had called or
texted or received a call or text from in the month of August. One
number was in Mexico, and it belonged to Jacinta's mother, who
burst into tears when Maria said she was calling about her daughter. Her mother couldn't speak English, and Maria spoke only a
few words of Spanish, so the only thing her call accomplished was
to cause the poor woman more grief. One number, in Brooklyn,
belonged to Jacinta's sister, who immediately hung up when Maria
said she worked for the *Sun*. Another number belonged to the elementary school the older boy attended, another to a day care center, yet another to the Golden Palomino. Everybody who picked
up at any of the other numbers either answered in Spanish or
sounded Hispanic, and no one would tell her anything about Jacinta Aguilera. One number with the local area code was no longer

in service, and she'd done reverse lookups online without finding it. It had sent forty-one texts to Jacinta in the seventeen days before she was murdered, the last of these arriving the evening she died.

"The disconnected number," he said, "what was it again?"

She read it off.

"That's a mobile phone, of course," he said. "So the number tells us nothing about where in the area code it might have been located. It still could prove useful, though. A few years ago—I'm guessing back in 2005, but it could have been either late 2004 or early 2006—there were three or four articles in the *Sun* about excessive cellular charges for several UCC employees. One was actually the former campus police chief. My recollection is that he was making non-school-related use of a state-owned phone—nothing particularly juicy, if I remember right, just lots of calls to department stores, liquor stores, the gym, his kids' babysitter, his wife, carry-out places, and so on. Somebody at the *Sun*—I'm thinking maybe it was Jim Concannon, who accepted a buyout before you were hired—got wind of it and filed a FOIA request and was able to access the charges that way. It's mostly administrators who get assigned school-owned mobile devices. Deans, vice presidents, fund-raisers, etc. Professors and department chairs are too lowly. But I wouldn't be surprised if every single Athletic Department employee has one."

"But why wouldn't it show up in a reverse-number search? I went through two different sites, and it didn't come up on either one. And they've got lots of government-owned phones listed there, as well as the names and addresses assigned to numbers that were disconnected years ago. For instance . . ."

"For instance what?"

She stood in front of the fireplace, staring at the floor as if she wished she were beneath it. It must have cost her a considerable sum in emotional currency to look at him, but she finally paid it. "Well, I think I found the numbers that belonged to your wife and daughter."

"Oh."

"You probably didn't need to know that."

"You're probably right."

"I'm sorry."

"Let's forget it."

"I'd love to."

He told her that if need be, he'd file a FOIA request and attempt to learn if the disconnected number was a state-owned phone assigned to a UCC employee. "In the meantime," he said, "the bill probably tells you what kinds of devices the Aguileras were using. Right?"

She shuffled the pages until she found what she was looking for. "One of them was a Nokia 6085. That's one of those older flip-top phones. The other was an iPhone 3G."

"Let me guess. The one with all the calls on it was the iPhone."

"Yep."

"So that's the one Jacinta was using. And for our purposes, that might be a good thing."

"How come?"

"What kind of phone do you use?"

"A BlackBerry Curve. I'm surprised you didn't notice."

"I did. The question was rhetorical. That's what I use too."

"I know you do. The other night at the Mexican restaurant, when you went to the bathroom, I picked it up and tried to see what was on it. But you'd set a passcode."

"I set it earlier that day," he said, "since I knew you'd check it out the first time you got a chance. Until you entered my life, Maria, I didn't bother."

"I'm honored."

"Don't be. When you went to the bathroom, I took yours out of your purse and tried the same thing. But of course you'd set a passcode too."

"I *thought* you'd looked through my purse," she said. "But I discounted the possibility, figuring you were just too damn forthright. It's nice to know I'm the impetus for character change."

He let that one slide as well. Anyhow, he'd lied to her about going through her purse. He'd worry about why he'd lied later. It was a troublesome sign. "An iPhone costs about twice what a BlackBerry does," he said. "From what I know, it can do everything our phones do and a lot of things they can't. And every kid, as well as every adult who hasn't quite grown up, wants one." Last year, he told her, he'd gone to Massachusetts at Christmas to see his father. While there, he'd read a piece in the *Globe* about a guy in Watertown who was making a killing repairing damaged iPhones. "Because obviously, if a kid with a seven-hundred-dollar toy drops it in the toilet, the warranty's no good."

"I actually remember that article—I was still in Worcester. The guy called himself iPhone Ed, right?"

"iPhone Art. It didn't sound like what he was doing was illegal. It mostly involved drying phones out or replacing cracked screens or whatever. But I guarantee you there's somebody in Fresno who specializes in fixing those devices. And whoever it is probably knows how to do a number of other things to the phone too. So I'm thinking what we need to do, starting tomorrow morning, is locate that person, or those persons, and see if Joe Garcia's made their acquaintance."

As it turned out, there were several. She found the first one before breakfast, an ad for local iPhone repairs on Craigslist. No address was provided, so she gave him the phone number. As soon as he dropped the kids off at school, he called.

The voice that answered could have belonged to either a man or a woman. It did not sound particularly young. That surprised him more than its androgynous timbre. He told the person on the other end his name, said he was not calling with a repair request but that he was a newspaper reporter researching an article about how new technologies spawned the need for new services, like the one the individual on the other end was advertising. Would he or she perhaps consent to an interview?

"Sure. In my situation, I'll take all the pub I can get."

He was given an address in Woodward Park. When he looked it up on a street map, he discovered it was no more than three blocks from where the Garcias lived, in a solidly middle-class area of newer homes. An unlikely location, it seemed to him, for someone in a fly-by-night business.

The house was one of the more modest in the neighborhood. It stood on the corner. He drove by, continued to the end of the next block, hung a left, and came back up the side street. The backyard was fenced, but through a gap in the boards, he could see a blue expanse. Whoever lived there had a pool. He turned the corner and parked near a large boulder that had no doubt been trucked in by a landscaping service to keep the shrubs company.

The person who opened the door told him her name was S. J. She was only slightly shorter than Richard. She wore a light blue shift with a padded apron that had pictures of birds all over it, most of them perched on branches. Her handshake was bone-crunchingly robust. The house smelled like a freshly baked cookie.

She led him into the living room. Bookshelves lined the walls. No light reading fare for S. J. Her shelves fairly sagged beneath Russell and Whitehead's *Principia Mathematica*, Dreben and Goldfarb's *The Decision Problem: Solvable Classes of Quantificational Formulas*, Tarski's *Logic, Semantics, Metamathematics*. "Can I offer you coffee?"

"Oh, no, thanks, I've already had three cups."

She gestured at the couch, then seated herself in an adjacent armchair. "So what can I tell you," she asked, "about my new profession?"

"So you're new at this?"

"I'm new at almost everything. So far, you're the only one to call about phone repair. I have another job in the evenings, but I'm even new at that." She waved at the window. "Did you pass the 7-Eleven on your way?"

"The one near Von's?"

"I've been working there since mid-August."

She'd been turned down for tenure in the Philosophy Department at UCC. She was suing them, of course. Wouldn't he rather write about that than iPhones? iPhones were trinkets, she informed him, superficial, transient objects based on technology that was all but obsolete before they developed it. She could build a better phone if she chose to, but the real problem was the notion of the cell phone itself. Did he realize it? Cell phones were already obsolete, though the average person lacked the necessary information to understand that. How much, for instance, did *he* know about implanted circuitry or open-source technology?

Nothing, he admitted.

"Because they don't want you to," she said. "And Microsoft and Apple represent only the tip of the conspiracy."

For the sake of politeness, he remained nearly an hour, during which he might have spoken all of five words. When he rose to leave, she asked for his card. Would he like her to keep him abreast of developments in her lawsuit? Oh, most definitely.

At the door, a thought came to him. "Speaking of technology," he said, "while I was in the shower this morning, I got a call from a mobile number that looked familiar, but whoever it was chose not to leave a message. As luck would have it, I've also been working on a story about some possible financial irregularities at UCC—forgive me for not being more specific—and I have reasons for thinking maybe it was in regard to that. I generally don't like to return calls without knowing who's likely to answer. You wouldn't have any kind of cellular directory for the school, would you?"

"Not exactly. But what's the number?"

He pulled his phone out and pretended to look at his call list. Then he recited the disconnected number from the Aguileras' bill.

"Give me a second," she said.

She left him standing there. From somewhere down the hallway came the sound of rapid keystrokes. It was three or four minutes before she returned.

"Sorry it took me so long," she said. "They actually do a halfway decent job with their protected databases. Most of their cellular numbers have names listed by them. But for that one, it just says 'HFC.' And I can't find anyone at the school with those three initials."

Head Football Coach.

"You know what else is odd?"

"What?"

"That you'd be receiving a call from that number. Apparently, it was disconnected two months ago."

He shrugged and shook his head. "Technology," he said.

ARMED WITH the knowledge that Nick Major's phone was the disconnected number, they spent a couple of weeks going nowhere. A computer repair shop in Clovis worked on all kinds of damaged cell phones but shied away from iPhones because, according to the proprietor, the people they belonged to wanted them fixed immediately, whereas he was of the old school: first come, first served. You hand it over and wait your turn. "You ask me," he told Richard, "we've created a couple of extremely impatient generations." He had a protruding eye, the result, he said, of Graves' Disease, and the longer he talked, the harder he was to watch.

While protective parents looked on, Richard spoke with a fourteen-year-old computer whiz from Edison Computech, who told him, as if it were an everyday occurrence, that he'd graduate from high school in December and enroll at Cal Tech in January. He hadn't worked on iPhones for about half a year, he said. It just hadn't proved that lucrative. He gave Richard the number of his Cal Tech sponsor, who he said was a security specialist in Sunnyvale and might be able to help.

Richard left several messages, invoking the name of his young "friend," and after a few days, the guy called him back. "I can't talk to journalists for attribution," he said, "but I happen to know there's a person down there who—let's just put it this way—is doing some fairly creative things to certain of our products. Are you familiar with an establishment called Garabedian's Bakery?"

"Absolutely. It's on Van Ness."

"The individual I've got in mind lives in a studio apartment above the bakery. I've got a feeling he might be the guy you need to talk to. And maybe you'll let me know if you learn anything interesting?"

"I'd be happy to."

The young woman behind the bakery counter recalled Richard from the days when he used to come in with Anna, who loved their little pastry horns filled with sweet cream. She told him the tenant wasn't around much during the morning or afternoon, but they usually heard him up there after five. "Sometimes," she said, "he can be kind of noisy." She said the stairs were accessible from the alley.

Richard returned around six, walked into the alley, and saw a mud-spattered Harley parked near the steps. Mud being in short supply at the moment, this detail seemed worth remembering. Nobody answered his knock, though he was sure he heard somebody moving around inside. He went back again at nine, but the Harley was gone, the apartment dark.

He finally caught up with him a couple of days later. The guy who opened the door wore frayed jeans, no shoes, no shirt.

On his right biceps, several tattoos: an iron cross, a swastika, the legend *White Pride*, a coiled serpent.

On his left: the Stars and Stripes, billowing as if struck by a forty-mph gust.

Stringy hair more gray than black, a mustache that didn't quite match. It had some red in it.

"Yeah?"

"A friend of mine told me you repair iPhones."

"So?"

"I'm a newspaper reporter, and I'm working on an article—"

"Fuck you and your article," the guy said and started to close the door.

"—about Apple's plans," he continued, changing course, "to prosecute people who are illegally altering their products."

The progress of the door was thus arrested.

Over the guy's shoulder, he could see into the apartment. It called to mind junk shops he used to visit with his father in his periodic searches for old 78s by musicians like Gene Krupa. Motorcycle parts and stereo equipment, circuit boards, laptops, desktops, TVs, LED monitors, and pile upon pile of cell phones mingled with empty bottles. How could anybody live in these surroundings?

"You stay right here," the man said. "Let me get some more clothes on."

He returned to the landing wearing a long-sleeved green tee shirt and a pair of unlaced boots. Closing the door, he said, "I don't know who told you I'm doin' anything illegal, but it's a bald-faced lie. I've been where illegal can take you, and I don't intend to go back."

"Where's that?"

"Corcoran."

"You feel like a cup of coffee?"

"Not really."

"Beer?"

They walked down Van Ness to a bar/pool hall. The Dead were playing "Ripple" when they entered. He bought his companion, who said his name was Bradley, a Bud Lite, and they sat at a table up front, where the guy's nervous eyes could survey the street.

"I'm going to level with you," Richard said, triggering twitches near both corners of the other man's mouth. "I've got reason to suspect that a pretty streetwise individual has in his possession an iPhone that he wanted to get some information from. He wouldn't know the passcode. I've had some contacts with security specialists up in Sunnyvale, and they told me exactly where to find you. They also asked me to let them know what I learned when we talked. By telling you that, I'm giving you some information that might be of use. Would you agree?"

"It could be. I'm not sayin' it is or it ain't."

"So what I need you to tell me is whether this hypothetical individual, with this hypothetical iPhone, came to see you sometime between about mid-August and right now."

Bradley took three or four swallows of his beer, then set it back down. "You payin' anything for the info?"

"I just did."

Bradley accorded himself a little time to consider that response. You could tell he understood that he'd acted too quickly too often, that even he was aware his first impulse was nearly always the wrong one. He took another couple of swallows of his Bud Lite. "What would that hypothetical person look like?"

Richard called upon his descriptive powers to evoke the presence of Joe Garcia.

A little puff of air left Bradley. He didn't bother to conceal his intense happiness. "Ain't nobody like that been to see me. I guaranfuckin'-tee it."

"So since the individual I just described didn't come to see you, who might he have gone to see? Hypothetically, I mean."

Slowly, Bradley said, "There's this fellow moved to town a while back. I'm not exactly sure when. Coulda been as long as two or three years ago. I don't know his last name. First name's Rupert. He drives a red pickup."

"What's he look like?"

A shrug. "He don't look that different from me. Good bit younger, though."

"How old would you say?"

"Thirty-two. Thirty-three."

"And?"

"And what?"

"What else can you tell me?"

"This guy . . . this fuckin' guy, he's like . . . See, you come lookin' for me. You don't go lookin' for him. You see what I'm sayin'?"

"Not entirely."

"Life just ain't fair."

"That's an indisputable observation, Bradley. Say more."

"This guy, he's got a house. His truck ain't that old. He's got a wife and kids. Regular job, with health benefits? He's got that too. Works in the tire shop at Costco. You have any idea what it's like tryin' to find respectable employment when you been where I have? Whole fuckin' system's designed to make sure you go back to gettin' mail through Write-a-prisoner dot com."

"I understand, Bradley."

"Naw, you don't. How could you?"

"I understand in the way you can understand things that didn't happen to you directly. If I told you I'd lost my wife and daughter, for instance, you could imagine how I might feel about that, couldn't you? Even if it didn't happen to you?"

"I never had a wife and daughter. But yeah, I can appreciate somebody dealin' with divorce. You fuck around on your old lady or what?"

"No, they both died, Bradley. And generally speaking, I prefer not to discuss it. I'm just mentioning it now as a means of noting that we've all dealt with loss in one way or another. Some of us lose our freedom like you did. Some of us lose our loved ones. You know what I mean?"

"Yeah. I see what you're sayin'. And, man, I sure am sorry about your folks. My momma died while I was in Corcoran. I didn't even get to attend her funeral. But don't get me wrong, I ain't sayin' I didn't learn anything in there. My cellmate was in for doin' stuff that involved cell phones and computers. And it wasn't very nice stuff, either, but I liked him, and I learned a lot from him. When I went in there, I couldn't do nothin' but write an e-mail. He taught me some pretty amazing skills. Wasn't for him, I don't know what I'd be doin' now. Livin' under an overpass, I guess, and eatin' out of the Dumpster."

"What else can you tell me about this guy Rupert? Confidentially, of course."

"Meanin' you ain't gonna write my name?"

"Or say it, either. The first article of the California state constitution contains a shield law."

"Yeah, well, when you say 'shield,' I see a badge." Nevertheless, he said that while he didn't know Rupert's actual address, word was he lived somewhere on East Balch, "closer to Cedar than First."

Richard ordered them two more Bud Lights and let Bradley tell him a little more about his life, a tale of hopes dashed and dreams extinguished. Before saying good-bye, he reminded him that for the time being, he probably ought to shut down any Apple-related operations.

HE WAITS until the guy with the big stuffed bear has been inside his house for ten minutes, during which time he and Maria say very little. Her beeper goes off again. Body shops around town are going to get some new business. In Fresno, after the first rain, they always do.

"Okay," he finally says, "I'm going to see what's what. If he's not our man, we may have hit a dead end."

"Dead ends only exist if you believe in them. I don't."

He climbs out, opens his umbrella, and walks across the street. On the porch, he hears a radio voice: "KPFA. Listener supported, community powered." In an effort to combat AIDS, he learns, the Kenyan government has announced it will conduct the first census of its gay population, though homosexuality is a criminal offense. There's a doorbell, so he presses it. The radio, which was plenty loud a second ago, suddenly falls silent. A moment later, the door opens.

Up close, Rupert really doesn't resemble Bradley. His hair's much shorter and free of gray. He's got a well-kept mustache. He's wearing a white short-sleeved shirt with the Costco logo on the left side of the buttons and his first name on the right. "Hey," he says. "What can I do for you?"

Richard hands him his business card. He glances at it. Then, before Richard can tell him why he's there, he says, "Okay. Come on in."

He leads him into the living room. It's got a matching couch and loveseat, and there are toys on the floor: a Zagonauts launch pad, a house play set, lots of crayons and markers. "Sorry the place is a mess," he says. He gestures at the loveseat, one-half of which is occupied by the white bear.

"Looks neater than my place," Richard says and sits down beside the stuffed animal.

"Can I offer you something to drink?"

"No, thanks. I'm fine."

The guy acts neither disturbed nor surprised to find himself facing a journalist who didn't bother to get in touch ahead of time. That could mean a number of things. One possibility is that Bradley has alerted him, but given the animosity he expressed toward him, this seems unlikely. Another is that Garcia has indeed been here and that he's warned Rupert a reporter might pay him a visit. Regardless of what the reason might be, it calls for certain adjustments.

Rupert places himself on the couch. He lays one hand on each knee. He's not wearing a wedding ring.

"I've heard you can do some amazing things with iPhones," Richard says.

"It's not really amazing if you know what you're doing. Are you interviewing me?"

"I'd like to."

"Could the interview be off the record?"

"It sure can."

"So why don't you go ahead and tell me what you want to know?"

"All right." Richard says he has reason to believe that somebody in Fresno might recently have taken possession of someone else's cell phone and that this person could, for reasons of his own, want to find out what was on it. "Things like text messages, voicemails, e-mails, call logs."

"Or maybe photos?" Rupert says. "And videos?"

"Those too. Certainly."

"It happens a lot, actually."

"Really?"

"Say some guy thinks his wife's screwing around on him. He swipes her phone, but he doesn't know the passcode, so he takes it to somebody that's got the right equipment. And that person needs about two minutes to copy everything that's on it. He puts it on a memory stick, hands it to the aggrieved spouse, and out he walks."

"After paying a fee, of course."

Rupert spreads his hands, palms up. "Everything costs."

"What kind of equipment might be required?"

"Your basic UFED."

He asks what "UFED" means, though he already knows. Lately, he's gone back to doing his homework.

"Universal Forensic Extraction Device," Rupert says.

"Have you got one?"

"I might."

"Is it legal to use it?"

"Depends who's doing it."

"Let's say somebody like you's doing it. Would that be legal?"

"Probably not."

"What would happen if you did it and the police found out?"

"That'd probably depend on the circumstances. If somebody brought his wife's phone in here and asked me to access her data for him, about the only folks that would most likely care would be her and her husband and whoever she was messing around with, if she was messing around at all. If she was, she probably wouldn't ask a lot of questions about how her data came to light, because she'd most likely have worse things to worry about. And if she did ask, he most likely wouldn't tell. Now, would he?"

"Probably not."

"And even if he did tell her, and she raised a fuss, in that situation the police wouldn't give a damn. For one thing, if the couple were on a family plan, which most married folks are, both the phones are probably registered to the husband. So technically, and legally, he'd be asking me to copy stuff off his own phone. And anyway, the police have got worse things to worry about too. Rapes . . . murders . . . extortion."

He seems like a guy who chooses his words carefully, and the last one resonates. "For the sake of discussion," Richard says, "let's suppose that somebody came across a cell phone that belonged to someone who died violently. And this person brought the phone to you. My guess is they probably would tell you some bogus story about who the phone belonged to and why they needed the data off it. Something fairly run-of-the-mill. Regardless, let's say you did what they asked you to do. And then the police found out about it. What would happen then?"

"That could cause me some serious trouble. But if it was brought to me under false pretenses, it'd probably mitigate in my favor. Especially if I then cooperated with the police, and I probably would. I've got a couple of kids that depend on me."

"And a wife, I assume?"

"We're separated. My kids live with her. I get 'em every other weekend. Want to cut the bullshit and give me a description of this individual who might've gotten their hands on the violently dead person's phone?"

"Happy to oblige. He'd be about my height. Six three or six four. Heavier than I am, probably two twenty-five, two thirty. Dark complexion, dark hair cut short, not much gray in it. Around fifty years old. If I had to guess, I'd say this person might've rung your doorbell sometime in mid- to late August."

"I can categorically assure you that nobody anywhere close to that description has asked me to do anything to a wireless device that belonged to someone who suffered a violent death. Not in August . . . not in September . . . not in October. Not ever, actually."

Richard's intuition tells him he's looking at the man who knows what was on Jacinta Aguilera's cell phone. It also tells him that this man wishes he *didn't* know, that there's one job he wishes to God he hadn't accepted. Furthermore, it's clear to him, perhaps from the expectant expression on Rupert's face, that the younger man's last statement was not an attempt to end the conversation, that it was instead an invitation to pose another question. What the right question might be he can't imagine.

And then, as used to happen with such regularity that it seemed commonplace, the kind of thing that would fall into your lap if you were smart and worked hard and listened to people and showed them you were willing to walk the proverbial mile in their shoes, it presents itself to him. Even as he asks it, he suspects that sooner rather than later, he's going to wish he hadn't recognized the opening for what it was. "Has somebody who doesn't fit that description approached you with such a request?"

"Yeah."

"Recently?"

"The nineteenth of August."

The day after the Aguilera shootings. "Could you tell me what he looked like?"

Rupert crosses his legs and locks his hands behind his head. "It wasn't a 'he,'" he says. "The person who asked was very much a 'she.'"

SHE WATCHES him descend the rickety steps and head for her car. He's carrying his umbrella, but it's rolled up, even though if anything it's raining harder than it was when he entered the house an hour and twenty-two minutes ago. He walks with his head down, studying the ground as if at any moment it might open beneath his feet. He doesn't even look before crossing the street.

She knows, much better than most, when a man is about to lie to her. And as impossible as it would've seemed when she woke up this morning, he's about to lie to her now. Why he will lie is of greater interest than what he will lie about. She will eventually learn the answer to the latter question, but she suspects she may never know the answer to the former. He must not have a clue how she feels about him. He'd probably be stunned to know that she thinks of him as Sluggo. This is partly due to the deliberate manner in which he goes about his business. But it's also because that was the name of the dog she had when she was a child. He moved slowly too, especially as he grew older. He lay around a lot. If you dropped down next to him, he would let you rest your head on his broad back. She went to sleep like that many nights, and her father picked her up and carried her to bed.

Or maybe, after all, Richard Brennan knows exactly how she feels about him. In which case his lie will mean many things at once.

He opens the door, gets in but doesn't speak.

"Well?" she finally asks, a little more loudly than planned.

He won't look at her. "Another dead end."

Now she can't look at him either. She glances at the house. A gap in the blinds disappears. "So he's not our guy?"

"I'm afraid not."

"What were you talking about so long?"

"He was explaining how somebody might go about doing what he swears he didn't."

She turns back to him just as he's rubbing his eyes. In that instant, he looks like a man who hasn't had a good night's sleep in years. He could be sixty. He could be seventy. "Are you saying you believe him?"

"Yes. That's what I'm saying."

She starts the car and pulls into the street.

He tells her that after school the next day, Franek is going to L.A. with Sandy and her parents. They'll be down there for the entire weekend—Bob and Sue plan to take them to Disneyland and show his nephew what's left of Hollywood—and he thinks he'll seize the opportunity to drive down there himself and catch up with his editor. There are several other things he needs to discuss with him, and he might well possess some insight into what they ought to do next.

She doesn't bother to ask if he'd like company. He's a truthful man. Why make him lie twice?

The Magic Kingdom is right across the freeway. But from Franek's window, about all you can see is the hotel parking lot and, beyond that, a wrought-iron fence and another parking lot where fifty or sixty U-Haul trucks stand waiting to be stuffed with people's household belongings.

The phone rings, so he lets the curtains fall shut, steps over to the bedside table, and lifts the receiver.

"Francis X," Sandy says, "here's the deal." She tells him her parents are feeling nostalgic and have decided to drive down to San Clemente, where they spent their honeymoon, and eat dinner on the pier. "Now, officially, we're invited to tag along. Unofficially, I suspect they'd be positively euphoric if we remained behind and either ate in that café off the lobby or at the taqueria."

"Where is the taqueria?"

"On the other side of U-Haul. Didn't you see it coming in? We can walk to it, but they don't want us to go any further than that. What's your preference?"

He's sitting on the side of the bed. A few moments ago, while paging through the loose-leaf binder about the hotel, he discovered you can watch "adult films" on the TV. You have to pay extra for them, though, and he wonders if they would show up on the bill as a specific charge or if it would just say that he watched some movies and not what kind. The free stuff he can view online is getting old. "I don't know," he says. "What's *your* preference?"

She lowers her voice. "My preference," she says, "is for you to act like a man. Be decisive. If you were an American, in two or three years you'd be able to vote for president and die in Iraq. You can't even decide whether you want to eat a taco or a croissant?"

The other day, she debuted new hair. Rather than reddish-brown, it's now silver with a few darker streaks, and the effect is to make her look older. Last night, for the first time, he let himself fantasize about her. Previously, his conjuring was limited to teachers at his former school. In his favorite scenario, each male in the class is assigned a day and time to appear at a room on the third floor, overlooking Planty. When the door opens, one of the teachers is standing there, dressed all in white like a nurse, and the room has a hospital bed in it as well as an IV stand. She tells you that she's been assigned as your personal sexual clinician. Unbuttoning her blouse, she says not to worry about making too much noise, because the door and the walls are padded. He usually cycles through two or three teachers per session, but he almost always finishes up with his Information Sciences instructor, Mrs. Jarzynka, who's about thirty-eight and has hair that looks exactly like this crazy girl's since she dyed it. It's uncanny. Last night, he submitted himself to Nurse Sandy.

"*Doprowadzasz mnie do szalenstwa,*" he says now.

"What in the name of Lady Gaga does *that* mean?"

It means "You're leading me to madness," but he's not about to translate. Instead, he says, "I want to eat the tacos."

"All right."

"But I want to bring them back and eat them here."

"Now you're talking."

"And I want to smoke a joint."

"I don't have one."

"I've got four."

"Where'd you get them?"

"I can't tell you."

She drops her voice even lower. "I don't suppose you had the foresight to bring along a lighter?"

He hadn't thought about that. Frantically, he looks around, hoping to see one of those little matchbooks like you'd find in almost any Polish hotel, but there's not one. They've stuck him in a nonsmoking room.

"It's all right," she says, as though she's read his mind. "I saw a 7-Eleven next to the taqueria. We can pick up something there."

"There is one other thing I want to do," he says.

"And what's that, X? Just say it."

"While we smoke the joints, I want to watch a dirty movie."

The silence on the other end tells him that he's gone too far and made a complete fool of himself.

"I will *not* watch a dirty movie with you," she finally says, a strange little growl in her voice, "until after I've had my dinner. You can mark my words, Francis X. They're written in red."

WHEN BOB and Sue Lyons return from San Clemente, all the lights in their suite are on, but Sandy's not there. He calls her cell but gets no answer.

"She must be with Franek," his wife says. "But why doesn't she pick up?"

Dread announces itself in the pit of Bob's stomach, where space is already at a premium, due to the surf 'n' turf special, a massive slab of mud pie, and more wine than he should have drunk before driving. Thank God he asked for an extra key. "I'll check up on them," he tells Sue. "You go ahead and get ready for bed."

The room is on the same floor as theirs but about two-thirds of the way down the corridor. When he gets there, he presses his ear to the door but can't hear a thing. He knocks two or three times, but nothing happens. Finally, he takes a deep breath, inserts the card in the lock, and turns the handle.

The bathroom door is open, and the light above the sink is on. There's a funny smell in the air, but he can't identify it because he's allergic to red wine and his nose is partially plugged. From where he's standing, the bed isn't visible. He takes a couple more steps.

His daughter and Franek are lying fully clothed on top of the covers. They're sound asleep. Her left foot, still shod, rests on his right shin, but other than that they aren't touching. The boy has a remote control in his hand, but whatever movie they were watching must have long since ended. The set is still on, and a screen icon asks *Buy Again?*

Gently, he pulls the control out of the kid's hand and switches off the TV. He wonders if he shouldn't pick his daughter up, carry her to their suite, and put her to bed. But they'd have to make the sofa down, and she might wake. She looks so peaceful lying there. And anyway, he wouldn't mind having some fun with Sue.

He tiptoes toward the door and, before leaving, reaches into the bathroom and switches off the light.

Saturday morning finds Richard in San Francisco rather than L.A., in a corner room at the Marriott–Union Square. He drove up here yesterday afternoon to clear his mind before taking the next step, and he chose this particular hotel because it's the last one he ever stayed in with his family. Back then, it was called the Crown Plaza. They'd driven up to see a Chagall exhibition. November 2006.

He makes a cup of coffee and drinks it while scanning the paper on his laptop. When he finishes, he looks at his phone and discovers a text sent a couple of hours ago by Monika, wondering if he's communicated with Franek since he left for southern California. He sends her a reply saying he heard from Bob last night, that they'd checked into their hotel and everything was fine. To his relief, there's no message from Maria.

He showers, then goes out to have breakfast at Lori's Diner, a place Julia hated but tolerated because Anna loved the retro motifs, especially the '59 Edsel parked opposite the counter. The booth closest to the old lime-colored hardtop is taken, but he finds one not too far away and orders another cup of coffee and the seasonal fruit salad. He didn't really come for the food per se.

While he waits for his salad, he sips his coffee and observes the other patrons. It's late enough that the young couple in one booth, who have chosen to sit on the same side, holding hands and whispering to each other and even exchanging a couple of R-rated kisses, have probably spent two or three morning hours having sex in one of the nearby hotels. But it's early enough that the couple in another booth are dealing with two ravenous, querulous kids. He can't see the children's mother—she's got her back to him—but the father looks like he woke up wondering exactly what crimes he committed to merit the punishment his life has turned into. Every time one of the kids shrieks, his face tightens. Finally, he leans across the table, and though Richard can't hear him over the juke-box, he can read his lips: *Shut the fuck up.*

"Love me tender," Elvis pleads, "love me sweet."

He eats his soggy fruit, has a second cup of coffee, and pays the check. On the way out, he has to pass the booth where the family is sitting. The kids—a four- or five-year-old boy with tousled red hair and his strawberry-blonde sister, who's about a year younger—are happy now, both of them working on stacks of pancakes. But he can tell that their parents are unlikely to ut-ter pleasant words to each other for hours, if not days. Their mother is picking at her poached egg, her eyes narrowed into a look of concentration that neither this egg nor any other could ever warrant. Her husband is shoveling omelet into his mouth, which is probably wise since from the look of things, he's going to need a certain amount of strength to survive the ordeal that lies ahead.

Decorum calls for Richard to walk past their table and out the door, but his legs have quit moving, though he's attuned to his surroundings. The Big Bopper is singing "Chantilly Lace," and a waitress has just stepped away from the counter with two platters balanced on each arm. Through the plate-glass window, he can see a cable car blocking the intersection of Sutter and Powell.

The children pay him no mind. But before long, he's drawn their mother's attention away from her poached egg, and that alerts her husband, who is now staring at him too, another hunk of omelet speared on the tines, poised between plate and mouth. The guy's about thirty, a redhead like his son. He wears glasses with black plastic rims, a long-sleeved polo shirt, and a nice watch—a Tissot, Richard would guess, not one of the flashiest, just a well-crafted timepiece that might last the rest of his life. Some people look stupid, but this man is not among them. He has an intelligent face. He's smart enough to know a good watch when he sees one, tasteful enough not to value shiny objects with lots of bells and whistles.

Husband and wife finally quit looking at Richard long enough to exchange glances. This is their family that's arrayed around the table, and a strange man is standing over them. You never know what kind of crazy person you might meet in San Francisco. He could be about to flash himself, right there in front of the kids. Things like that do happen. He could be about to ask them if they're saved, or to try to hand them some kind of cult literature. In San Francisco, the fact that he looks like a solid, middle-class citizen might be deceiving. This is not the hinterland. It's not even San Jose.

Perhaps for the first time since they woke this morning, the children's parents have reached agreement. Something will have to be said.

The guy lays his fork down. "Do we know you?" he asks.

"No," Richard tells him. "I was just thinking what a great-looking family you've got. I guess it stopped me in my tracks." He gestures at the intersection, where the cable car is pulling away. "It's a gorgeous morning. Hope you all enjoy yourselves." Within seconds, he's outside, shielding his eyes from the blinding sun.

HE RETURNS to the hotel, picks up his digital imaging binoculars, puts on a fleece jacket, and heads for Fisherman's Wharf.

It's a cloudless day, not even a wisp of fog, and he's struck, once again, by the constant smell of food. He can't think of another city where so many scents ought to seem enticing. Certainly not New York, which to his mind always reeks of the subway, as if the entire city were one big tunnel crying out to be deodorized. L.A. has no identifiable smell. How much of a city can you smell from your car? There's too much wind to give Boston a characteristic aroma unless you're within shouting distance of the Union Oyster House. Dublin? Lamb and mint jelly. London? The Thames. Dortmund smells like hops. Why wouldn't it, with a brewery on every block?

Krakow? Better not go there.

When he reaches Fisherman's Wharf, he can't help but wish he were hungry, but he's not. The last time he was here, he had a bread bowl and a huge shellfish platter, washed down with a couple mugs of Anchor. He also consumed a Blondie Sundae, which was loaded with chunks of brownies and walnuts and ice cream and topped by a Biscoff drizzle. There's much to be said for maintaining a healthy appetite. Hunger isn't always a negative. He wishes there were something, anything, that he could honestly say he desires to put in his mouth, no matter how bad it might be for his health. But today there isn't. Most days there's not.

He continues on to Ghirardelli Square and along the pier, then up the hill to Great Meadow Park. From there, he has a superb view of the Golden Gate. He pulls out his binoculars and trains them on it. He recalls the first time he ever drove across it, a year or so before the paper sent him to Poland. He was traveling up the coast with an extremely attractive young woman named Kay. She was about his age, twenty-six or twenty-seven, a lifelong resident of Fresno, the daughter of an almond grower. She'd graduated from Mills—art history—and was working at the museum when they'd met. He'd asked her to dinner because he admired her looks and hoped to sleep with her. They quickly wound up in bed, and it went very well, and when they drove across the bridge that day, they were on the way to a wine-tasting weekend in Napa Valley.

He can't remember much about any of the wineries, though he does recall that when they were escorted into the tank room at one of the larger ones, they simultaneously turned to each other and referenced the *I Love Lucy* episode in which Lucy stomps grapes. They laughed, locked hands, and pronounced themselves made for each other. The relationship lasted another month or so, by which time the only thing binding them was sex. And as she noted, not unkindly, "Either of us could find that pretty much anywhere, you know?"

She moved away years ago, and he forgot about her. But lately, she has reappeared in his recollections, if only because she accompanied him on that initial drive across the bridge. Like everyone else, he'd seen pictures of it and had visited San Francisco several times and observed it from a distance. But when they drove across it that day, he was surprised to discover that the real thing was burnt-orange rather than gold and the road surface was in poor condition. Rather than sunny, the afternoon was cloudy, though free of fog, and as they crossed the south viaduct, he was thinking that whereas Yosemite exceeded its reputation for grandeur, the Golden Gate underwhelmed. He was about to voice his disappointment when the shoreline disappeared beneath them and a powerful crosswind struck the car. As he clenched the wheel, vast depths opened on both sides, and in all that yawning emptiness, the world came unmade. Anything seemed possible.

The following autumn, a tidal wave of dissatisfaction hit Eastern Europe, and he was dispatched to record its effects. He took a seat in a colorless café. A woman with dark hair and oversized eyes entered, examined the few patrons, then walked over to his table and said, "I'm Julia. Are you by any chance Richard?"

Yes, by chance, he was. And then, by chance, he wasn't any longer.

Now about all he can do anymore, even on a perfect fall day with the most beautiful bay in the world at his back and an ocean stretching endlessly before him, is put one foot in front of the other. So that's what he does, turning and retracing his route to the hotel. On the way, he steps into a liquor store and buys himself a bottle of Bushmills.

When he gets back to his room, it's midafternoon. He pours a water glass half full of whiskey and carries it over to the armchair near the window. He draws the curtains closed and turns on the reading lamp. Then he sits down with his laptop and props his feet on the divan. He takes a big swallow of Bushmills, turns on the computer, and pops in the memory stick he got from Rupert.

OVER THE next few hours, a couple of things happen. The level in the bottle drops, and a picture of the woman whom until now he has known only by name begins to emerge. At first in words, almost all of them Spanish. There are text exchanges between her and her mother. Her father became ill back in June and couldn't go to work. Her mother appreciates the money sent by Jacinta and Andres, as she suspects that contrary to what she's been told, they struggle to survive in *el norte*. There are exchanges with her sister in Brooklyn, who repeatedly calls attention to the cost of living in New York. How does Jacinta think she can possibly send their parents more? How much does she think you can earn, even in

Manhattan, scrubbing toilets? There are exchanges between Jacinta and her husband, each of them concerned with the mundane:
who will pick the kids up, who will take the sitter home, who will
cook tonight, who will pick up a can of *chiles poblanos*, a bottle of
Tajin Clásico, which bills can be left until next month and which
can't, the possibility that Andres might be laid off by the body
shop, since a lot of people who are involved in wrecks are out of
work themselves and can't afford to fix their damaged cars. There
are countless exchanges with someone who has a local number and
has been entered in her contacts only as *Tia*, though it's clear she's
not a real aunt and is instead the "old lady" neighbors told him
about, who often came over in the evenings. In several of these, the
woman complains about what she's being paid and in a couple of
exchanges warns Jacinta that she may need to find someone else,
that she can't keep working late hours for *los centavos*.

And beginning in early July and ending at ten forty-three p.m.
on the evening she was murdered, there are numerous exchanges
between her and the person the disconnected mobile number belonged to. That individual is entered in her list of contacts as *El
Entrenador*. The coach.

The first thing that surprises Richard about Nick Major's messages to Jacinta Aguilera is that they are also written in Spanish.
Unlike her responses, which are fragmented and filled with typos
or English words that the autocorrect function has inserted in
place of whatever she was trying to say, they are delivered in impeccably correct, perfectly punctuated prose. No txt-speak from *El
Entrenador*. He always begins with a term of endearment: *Mi
Querida, Preciosa, Dulzura, Mi Vida*. In his initial message, he tells
her he appreciates her willingness to share her number with him
and promises not to become a nuisance. The conversation they had

after the bar closed last night, he says, is the best he's had with anyone except his daughter in months, if not years. He said things he didn't even know he was feeling until he said them. That just doesn't happen to him. He's in the public eye a lot, and he has to think before he speaks, but last night he didn't, and this morning he feels a hundred kilos lighter. And he only weighs about a hundred kilos, he jokes, to begin with.

She doesn't respond. Over the next ten days, she receives more than eighty texts from her mother and has several increasingly heated exchanges with her sister. Their father is close to death, he needs surgery, the wait may be too long. There's only one way to move him ahead. Everything has a price, *ya sabes, querida, ya sabes como es.*

On July 14th, another text from Major. He's glad they talked again last night, that she trusted him enough to share her troubles. He has a few himself, not like hers, but troubles nevertheless, and he wouldn't mind sharing those sometime, if she's open to hearing about them. As for her mother's problems, he'd be happy to help solve them. Do her parents have a bank account? And does she know the number?

Evidently, the answer to both questions was yes. Three days later, there's an ardent text from her mother, her gratitude hard to behold when you already know the ultimate cost. A few days later, her father undergoes surgery, the nature of which is impossible to discover from the texts. Subsequent messages from her mother indicate he's recovering, though still unable to work.

Jacinta begins to reply to Major's lengthy texts, but usually in just a few words. The contrast between what she writes to him and what he writes to her is stark and jarring. She has given him back his life, he tells her on the 22nd of July. Some people think he's the best in the country at what he does; he's already received feelers from two NFL teams whose coaches will be let go if they fail to make the playoffs, but what is that kind of success worth if you feel like you're suffocating each morning when you wake up? Her replies concern logistics. He's to park at the back of the lot, please, away from the big light. They must go someplace else next time. Please do not do that again with the phone. It scared her, because once you make something like that, it exists forever. No, she can't, not tonight, her husband will be pumping gas at his other job, and there is no one to stay with the children. She does not wish to wound him. Her husband is a good man; he works hard for their family but is also gripped by fierce pride. This cannot continue.

He understands, he does, *Sirenita, Florecita,* but just once. Just once all night. There's a place they could go, one of the rich men who supports the program owns it, a lodge in the foothills, no one will know, he will pay the woman who looks after her children, she can say her friend from work suffered a loss in her family, that she's mad with grief, she has to help her through it, she can't be left alone. Hasn't he helped her mother? Hasn't he helped her and Andres? He doesn't know him, but he respects him; he wouldn't hurt her and her family for the world. One night. One night all night long. The season will start soon, and then he'll leave her alone. So help him God—and yes, he does believe in God. He knows what they're doing is wrong.

Tomorrow morning, when Richard wakes with a hangover the likes of which he has not known since his twenties, he will not be able to recall if this is the point at which he quit reading through the texts for a while and looked at the handful of photos Jacinta had on her phone the night she died, of if he read all the way through the last few exchanges between her and Nick Major and perhaps even watched the lone video before looking at the photos. It will all run together, just as so many things must have run together in the mind of her husband the night he took their lives.

She has long, dark hair with plenty of natural wave. Her eyes, like Julia's, are hazel-toned. Her oldest son has a burr cut; he's standing in front of their house, grinning at the camera, spinning a soccer ball. The younger boy is missing two front teeth. The toddler is captured in the act of eating what looks like a Twinkie. Cream filling smeared on her chin. Andres? One assumes he took the photos using her phone, since he appears in none of them and she appears in several. Given what was on that phone, she should have guarded it with her life. How unskilled she must have been at dissembling.

The other thing he will not be able to say with any certainty tomorrow morning is when he rose from the armchair and turned on the TV. UCC versus Boise State on the blue field where so many confused birds plummet to their death. He won't recall the score, and he won't be able to say how long he watched before turning his attention back to the laptop, or how he retained enough clarity to tap out his reconstruction of that August evening, the last of the Aguileras' lives. What he will remember about the football game is a single play and its aftermath. On a pitch-out toward the UCC bench, one of the Boise receivers delivers a crushing blind-side block on a Cowboy linebacker, driving hard and low at his knee. The player goes one way, his knee the other. He lies on the ground, writhing. For an instant and an instant only, as if even the camera operator is embarrassed by the absence his lens has captured, there's a close-up of Nick Major, who calmly sips Gatorade, betraying no reaction to his player's pain. He could leave the scene of an accident and never glance back.

Tuesday, August 18th

4:17 p.m.

Andres sends Jacinta a text telling her they've called from the gas station where he's been working part time. They can use him again tonight for four or five hours, so she will need to get the old woman to stay with the kids. Between then and 5:15, Jacinta places three calls to the number of the woman listed as Tia. *The first couple last only five seconds, indicating that she reached voicemail and hung up. The third lasts twenty-four seconds: long enough for her to have listened to the greeting and left a message.*

5:21 p.m.

The sitter sends a text saying that as she has repeatedly told Jacinta, she cannot continue to work late hours for so little. Por favor no me llame de nuevo.

5:23 p.m.

Jacinta calls Andres. The call lasts thirty-one seconds.

5:25 p.m.

Another call to Andres. Eight seconds. Either it went to voicemail and she hung up, or he answered and she hung up on him after an unpleasant exchange, or he hung up on her.

5:27 p.m.

Another call to Tia. *Ten seconds. Nobody has a good word tonight for Jacinta Aguilera.*

5:29 p.m.

She places a call to the Golden Palomino. It lasts a minute, sixteen seconds. This is when she phones in sick.

After that, what does she do? The evaporative cooler isn't working, and it's miserably hot. But she's got three children to feed, so she fixes dinner. (The police report noted that part of a badly burned casserole was found in the oven, which was still set at 375 when the officers arrived, and that this contributed to the stifling heat alluded to by J. G. when he and I talked on the street that night.) Maybe after feeding the kids, she reads to them for a while, or maybe she parks them in front of the TV.

8:18 p.m.

She sends her mother a text asking how her father is doing. Her mother will not reply until the following morning, by which time her daughter will be dead.

8: 26 p.m.

She sends a text to her sister in Brooklyn apologizing for some of the things she recently said to her. We know her sister never replied, but of course, she would have found out within a day or two that Jacinta was no longer alive.

10: 30 p.m.

According to what the manager of the all-night gas station on West Jensen told Maria, Andres leaves work.

10:36 p.m.

A phone call from Andres. Nine seconds. He's probably calling to ask her to warm up some dinner.

10:43 p.m.

The text comes with a twenty-one-second video file attached. El Entrenador most likely thinks she's at work. She last answered him nine days ago, begging him not to write to her again. He doesn't know that the phone is lying on the kitchen counter when the text tone sounds, or that her husband, who's worn out, stressed, and suspicious, is standing nearby.

Nick Major clearly appreciates the power of technology. He just doesn't appreciate it enough.

MOST AMERICANS of a certain age recall the sitcom *Hogan's Heroes.* Set in a fictional German POW camp during World War II, it chronicles the adventures of the American prisoner of war Captain

Robert Hogan and his merry band of saboteurs. They are surrounded by a cast of bumbling Germans, chief among them Ser-
geant Schultz and Colonel Klink. As a child, Richard loved the
show, though his mother hated it. For her, Nazi Germany could
never be a source of laughter.

Richard remembers when the actor who played Hogan—Bob
Crane—was murdered. The man eventually brought to trial and
acquitted was a video specialist who had taught Crane how to sur-
reptitiously film himself having sex with countless women. The
AV equipment required at the time was apparently elaborate.

Whereas all Nick Major needed was his cell phone.

The text that came with the video he sent Jacinta shortly before
she died said *No me digas que no lo ama.* Don't tell me you didn't
love it.

We see only her face, aglow from perspiration. Her eyes are
closed, her dark hair spread out on a white pillow. She's breathing
rapidly, lips parted, teeth clenched.

"Oh, baby," a male voice grunts. "Oh, yeah, baby, yeah. You're
my own little personal porn star."

On Monday morning, Bogdan's sister Teresa appears at his door with a guy named Roman, who smells strongly of cologne. His silver hair rises into a gravity-defying pompadour. When he removes his leather jacket, revealing a white shirt unbuttoned about halfway to the navel, Bogdan sees a gold cross glistening amid wiry chest hair.

Teresa offers a critical appraisal of her brother, whom she last saw several years ago: "Cheeks a little sallow, belly appears to have a load of concrete in it, and you still haven't gotten rid of that mole. Overall, not too bad."

"Don't let your sister get to you," Roman urges. "She has a huge mole herself on the inside of her right thigh. They probably run in your family."

"Beats the hell out of the toe funguses that run in yours," Teresa says.

She walks around the room as if she's considering purchasing it. If she chose, she could probably buy the entire building. In 1990, she and her late husband acquired and restored a decrepit Zakopane pension. Last week Bogdan learned that she now owns three others. The second is also in Zakopane, the third is in Krynica, and the fourth is halfway across the country, in the Sudeten Mountains. Until they spoke at length, he had no idea how well-off she'd become. On the other hand, she seemed to know exactly how far he'd fallen, probably because she's had a few conversations with Krysia. "It doesn't look like there's a whole lot here for us to do," she says, gesturing at the small pile of clothes he's laid out on the daybed alongside a few stacks of books. "Is that it?"

"Yes, that's about all I add up to."

"Whose furniture?"

"It came with the place."

"Okay, then, let's make it happen, guys."

Roman has brought several flattened boxes, and they pack them and tape them while she stands on the balcony and smokes. When they've finished, she asks if he'd like her to take a photo of the place to serve as a reminder, and he tells her no, that he'll remember it the rest of his life. They grab the clothes and the boxes, and he switches off the light and leaves the key in the door, as instructed by the slumlord.

He and Roman trail her down the sidewalk. She's always walked as if she were contesting a race. That's probably what keeps her looking so athletic. The other day, she told him she had exactly two bad habits: men and cigarettes. She said the second was harder to control than the first.

While they walk, he asks Roman how long they've been together.

The other man laughs. "We aren't really together," he says.

"No?"

"I work for her. For a good while now, I've also been sharing her bed. But I begin each day with the assumption that come evening, I might be looking for lodging. Understand, I'm not complaining. She's a special woman. Her husband was a lucky man."

A lucky man who dropped dead at forty-six, most likely from

trying to keep up with her. By the end of the second block, Bogdan is puffing hard. Nothing in either of the boxes he's carrying is worth this much exertion.

She parked half a kilometer from his building, in the lot near the Hala Targowa tram stop, where he bought kielbasa the night he was arrested. When they finally get there, she pulls a keyless remote from her bag and aims it at a Lexus SUV.

Slowly, silently, without human touch, the cargo door begins to rise, its progress occurring independent of time. Bogdan sees himself rutting away between Krysia's splayed legs as she whispers obscenities to hasten her relief, sees himself sitting alone on a park bench, a beer can balanced on his thigh. A young man with a perfectly knotted green tie shakes his head at the besotted figure laid out before him on the floor of a store someone else owns, a young woman with a pageboy cut and a small red purse walks down the street beside her new partner. Red snow, Marek's mangled face, the dull thud of steel crushing the cranium of a diligent dog. Shattered glass, dead eyes, white fur turning scarlet.

"What's wrong, Bogdan?" his sister asks. "Better hurry. You want to be late for your own trial?"

"I'm already on trial," he says, prompting her to roll her eyes at Roman, who shakes his head and puts his arm around her brother's shoulders.

THE PROCEEDINGS take place in a small room where all the furniture looks like it came from Ikea. The desk he and his court-appointed attorney sit behind has a fiberboard top with walnut veneer, and the arms of their chairs match. The prosecutor, who could not have left law school more than two or three years ago, sits across the room at an identical desk, and the court reporter sits at a smaller one adjacent to the bench. To Bogdan's left, there are eight or ten chairs like those he and his attorney are sitting in, but the only observers are Teresa and Roman. He made Marek and Inga promise to stay away.

An officer of the court announces his case, and the judge walks in and takes her seat on the bench. He recognizes her immediately. She used to shop at one of his stores. She typically bought only a few items, suggesting that she cooked for no one but herself. He recalls that she frequently purchased red wine, though mostly on the weekend, and he also remembers that on more than one occasion, she came to the office to complain about being cheated.

She puts on her glasses, opens the folder she brought with her, reads for a moment, then asks if either side has preliminary motions. Bogdan's attorney stands and tells the judge that since his client does not dispute his guilt and will present no defense, he moves that the hearing proceed to judgment.

The judge turns to the prosecutor and asks if he agrees to the motion. The young lawyer stands and says what Bogdan's attorney predicted. "No, your honor. Given the defendant's refusal to cooperate in the investigation, we prefer to make our case."

"Very well," she says. "The motion is denied."

Over the next three-quarters of an hour, during which the prosecutor offers an opening statement and calls three witnesses, Bogdan is reduced to a set of despicable acts. Though he did everything alleged, as well as worse things that the prosecution and witnesses are not aware of, he does not recognize the individual they're talking about. The man they describe is bold and brassy, untroubled by fear or scruple, above all decisive and in control of the situation. To hear them tell it, one might conclude he's been wasted on crime, that he really ought to be president or prime minister, or at least commander of the nation's armed forces. NATO could use a man like him too. He'd quell every heart in Al-Qaeda.

"Hour after hour, day after day," says the old professor from the building on Smolensk, "he and his accomplice tormented my neighbors and me. This man"—pointing an accusatory finger—"drove everyone else from their homes. Mrs. Kotkowska? She moved there in 1960, when she was no more than thirty. Forty-nine years she lived in that building. As a teenager, she risked her life delivering messages for the underground. For more than two decades, she worked at the Wawel chocolate factory, starting as a chocolatier and rising to a managerial position—which she lost in 1980, I wish to note, after being labeled an 'antisocialist element' due to her activities on behalf of Solidarity. When I urged her to resist their efforts to dislodge her from her home, this woman, whom neither of our most recent Occupation forces *ever* cowed, broke down and wept. Only *that* diabolical creature"—the finger again—"was able to break her spirit."

The woman who took the photos of him and phoned the police comes next. In her account, he becomes an accomplished high-altitude athlete, a dark lord of dance pirouetting across the perilous roof. If he'd been around in 1953, the world might not have heard of Hillary and Tenzing. She's never seen a more audacious sight. "My heart nearly stopped when I looked out the window and spotted him up there," she says. "Though given what he was doing to innocent people, I wish he'd gone over the edge."

The final witness is the older of the two officers who arrested him. Today, he's dressed in a black suit, and he's slicked his remaining hair over his bald spot. He tells the court that the defendant is as recalcitrant a criminal as he's ever encountered. "We gave him numerous chances to cooperate, and he rebuffed every one of them."

"When you say that he 'rebuffed' them," the prosecutor asks, "exactly what do you mean?"

Though they are on the same side, it's apparent that the detective finds the question irksome. "I just mean what I said. He rebuffed them."

The young lawyer's face turns red. Bogdan can't help but feel sorry for him. Like everybody else, he'll be given a limited number of chances to make his mark on the world, and this is one of them. "Yes, but *how* did he do it? Did he simply sit there, for instance, with downcast eyes and remain silent? Or was the rebuffing accomplished in an activist manner?"

"It was active."

"Could you explain?"

"He more or less sneered at us."

"Verbally? Facially?"

"Verbal and facial."

"Could you give the court a specific example?"

"Well, when we showed him the photo of him running out of the building with the other guy, he said he didn't have a partner, that he did it all on his own."

"And he sneered as he said it?"

"Yes, sir, he did."

"Could you demonstrate for the court, please?"

The officer sighs. Bogdan suspects he wouldn't be a bad guy to watch a football match with, that you could stake out space with him at Pilsudski Stadium, drink a few beers, and analyze the shortcomings of Cracovia's midfielders. The guy would probably rather be there than here. Still, he does what he's been asked to do, puffing out his chest, the corner of his mouth curling up in a Cagneyesque smirk. "'I don't have any *partner,*'" he growls.

"And how did he explain getting a key to the building?"

"He said he stole it."

"Did he say who he stole it from?"

"He said he forgot."

"But you didn't believe him?"

"Of course not."

"And what did he say when you asked why he had gone there in the first place?"

"He said he went there because he was a shell of a person."

"Those were his exact words?"

The policeman nods. "That he was a shell of a person and was drawn to old buildings that reminded him of himself."

"But you didn't believe this either?"

"I believed he was a shell of a person."

The defense attorney starts to rise, probably to object on some ground or another, but Bogdan lays his hand on his forearm, and he remains seated. The attorney is not that interested in the proceedings anyway. His present client, like almost all the ones he's assigned, is guilty beyond doubt. Furthermore, the attorney's tooth is killing him. He suspects he needs a root canal, which theoretically the state health care system can handle. But the last time he went there, he learned the limits of theory. And because prices at private practices are low by Western standards, so many Brits, Germans, and Swedes come here for endodontic treatment that he'll probably have to wait weeks for an appointment. His client is the least of his problems.

"I'm suggesting that you didn't believe the defendant went there," the prosecutor says, "simply because he was a shell of a person."

"I believed only a shell of a person would do what he had done."

Bogdan wishes he could help the foundering prosecutor. It would be best for both of them if this ended quickly.

"I *mean* you didn't believe he went there and harassed the residents for any reason other than remuneration."

"No, sir, I did not."

"Could you tell the court why?"

"Because he didn't impress me as someone with enough initiative to take action on his own. I felt certain he'd been paid by somebody else to do what he did and that whoever it was also paid him to keep his mouth shut if he got caught."

"And you gave him plenty of opportunity to tell you who had paid him and who his partner was?"

"Yes, sir. I most certainly did."

"Thank you," the prosecutor says, then tells the judge he rests his case.

With the exception of his own attorney, who has trouble remembering if his last name is Baranowski, Baranski, or Baranek, everyone in the small courtroom is directing his or her attention at Bogdan. He feels the warmth of their interest. It's as if someone has rubbed analgesic into his chest. The sensation is not unpleasant. With humility, he bows before their concern.

Each of them is using him as a measuring stick. The prosecutor is thinking that if the window of opportunity opens for you, you had better hurl yourself through it, because it will close quickly, just as it did for the defendant and his own father, who is also an attorney. In the '80s he defended dissidents, always without success and always to his detriment, as the secret police subjected him and his family to constant harassment. Several of those dissidents are now powerful. A few are rich. Rather than court their favor, his father assumed they would knock on his door, just as they did before. Those knocks never came. He scrapes by drawing up wills for people who, unlike him, have things worth disposing of.

Teresa is remembering what a docile baby her brother was. Their mother told her that she suffered from colic, that she hardly ever slept, that her face was always red and angry, her hands balled into fists. Whereas her baby brother lay in his bed smiling at the mobile that spun overhead. Such happiness! She recalls how he rolled a yellow dump truck across the floor when he was three or four, how he kept saying that the truck was driving to the U.S.A., though he hadn't a clue where the U.S.A. was and her parents were always warning him not to say that kind of thing around strangers. Her brother never learned to ball his hands into fists, never learned to cry and turn red on behalf of his own cause. All he learned to do was get himself into trouble in the service of others. He's had more than his share of bad luck.

The judge does not believe in luck, though she used to. She has a forgettable face, forgettable hair that she let go iron gray in her forties, a forgettable body. No one made love to her until she was nearly thirty. The man who did it was a Czech doctor she met at a resort in Montenegro. When it started, she didn't even know what was happening. When she finally caught on, her first thought was to stop it—he was breathing hard and pushing himself against her, and she wasn't sure she appreciated that—but then she made the decision to go ahead and see what it was like. She expected it to hurt more than it did, and afterward she expected him to be more surprised than he was that she'd never done it before. It happened at least once a day for the rest of her stay, and when she came home, she took a little time to decide whether to pursue that kind of experience again. In the end, she elected to try it for a while. Over the next few years, she cut a broad swath, sleeping with more than forty men, including the prosecutor's father. She closed that chapter with no regrets. She's glad she did it and glad she's not doing it anymore.

She lives in a nicer flat than she ever expected to own. A few years ago, after a vacation in Tunis, she became fascinated with African and Middle Eastern cuisine and taught herself to prepare it. On Friday evenings, when she's finished with her week's work, she opens a bottle of wine and cooks a good meal, and afterward she sits on the couch and finishes the wine while listening to music or watching a movie. Once or twice a month, before she climbs into bed, she removes her nightgown. On those occasions, she never imagines being in bed with a man. Instead, she envisions what she would see if she were watching the scene: a woman with certain tastes and predilections enjoying her own body, able to satisfy herself.

If this makes it sound like she's a solitary person, with few if any friends, that couldn't be farther from the truth. She's got more friends than she knows what to do with. Most of them would tell you she's one of the kindest people they know, the type of person who will bring you food when you're sick or offer to drive an elderly neighbor shopping. When it comes to dinner parties, she's at the top of the list. She turns down twice as many invitations as she accepts. When she would have welcomed more of them, they were seldom forthcoming. She understands why. Without realizing it, she had presented herself as an insecure, lonely woman who might need more from you than you were ready to give. Now she needs nobody. And almost everybody senses it.

Bogdan does. The black robe, her gray hair, her expressionless face—everything about her suggests that she's a strong woman with few failings who can be expected to administer stern justice.

There's no indication that she recalls their earlier encounters, how polite and considerate he was when she appeared in his office to complain. The sums she'd been cheated of were tiny, not worth arguing over. Handing her the money, he apologized and assured her that he and his partner were committed to preventing this from happening. On one of these occasions, he recalls, she asked why he didn't simply walk over to the clerk, whom she would gladly point out, and fire her? He told her he hoped to solve the problem without cutting people loose, that most of them had worked there for years and had families that depended on them. "Undependable people," she responded, "can't be depended on by anybody." Just as she would not have cut his clerks any slack, she's not likely to cut him any. He can imagine what's going through her mind: the man who comes before me is one of the dregs, a person of poor character, with weak will and no concern for others. A man who probably can't be reformed, who can only be taken off the street for however long the law allows. Mercy is not her forte.

He's wrong in thinking she doesn't recognize him. She knows she's had prior dealings with him. But she can't recall when or where. This in itself is unusual, as anyone who knows her would tell you. Her memory is the stuff of stories. She can recite entire passages of the most obscure case law. She knows the names and faces of everyone she's ever sat in judgment of, who sang lead on every one of the Beatles' tunes, which ones were composed by Lennon and McCartney and which ones weren't, what time trains leave Krakow for Warsaw, Wroclaw, Gdansk, Berlin, Vienna, or any other city you care to name. But who this man is, what he did before he committed the crime in question, has escaped her. And she finds it troubling.

"Mr. Baranowski," she says, "will you please rise and approach the bench?"

What she intends, when making this request, is that he step into the center of the small courtroom, stopping three or four meters away so that she can render her decision and he can respond if he chooses. Instead, he walks all the way up to the bench, halting only when he's so close she can smell his aftershave. She can also see the ugly mole, in all its divided particulars, and that allows her to place him in the proper context. He used to run a grocery store that went out of business years ago. She recalls the two visits she made to his office, how he returned the money his clerks had stolen. She remembers thinking that he was a nice man, that since he wore a wedding ring, he had probably made someone a very good husband, someone for whom his disfigurement did not matter, because whoever she was, she could see beyond it. She also remembers thinking that his store would probably not last, that he did not have the heart of a businessman. She remembers the morning she went there to buy a half liter of milk and discovered she'd been correct. For a while, she wondered what had happened to him. Now she knows. She experiences the onslaught of a sorrow so profound that it robs her of speech.

That evening, when the prosecutor describes this uncomfortable moment to his father, he will say that for an instant or two, he considered the possibility that she was suffering a stroke. "She was trying to get her lips to move, but it was like she couldn't. She had a strange look on her face too."

"Strange, how?" his father will ask, treading carefully, for of course neither his son nor his wife is aware of what happened between the judge and him twenty years ago. It didn't last long—six weeks—and while for her, it was nothing more than a brief affair, he fell deeply in love. He's never gotten over it. If he sees her coming toward him in Planty or glimpses her at a sidewalk café or in Galeria Krakowska, he turns and heads the other way. He wants to spare her the longing she will not fail to recognize if she has to look into his eyes. It's a good thing his son cannot see him, that their conversation takes place over the phone.

"As if . . . It was almost as if she were about to cry or something. I thought maybe she'd lost a family member, but the court reporter told me she has no family. She said she thought it was strange too, that she's never seen anything like it. It was . . . I'll go ahead and say it. It was *unseemly*."

He'll be right when he says that, and the judge realizes it herself, even as it's happening. Bogdan understands it as well and believes he can guess the source of her discomfort and confusion. She has recognized him. She remembers how she came to his office, how he returned the money. She cannot understand how *that* man became *this* man who stands before her awaiting judgment. If he could tell her how it happened, he would. But he doesn't know himself. He could tell her how one thing led to another, but each of them could just as easily have led somewhere else.

He's unaware that in contrast to her, he has succeeded in forming words and that he's spoken them under his breath, so quietly, so quickly that she can't hear them, though she can read his lips.

Please help her.

Those words, spoken to no one in particular, have their effect. They will get through this together, the two of them. "Mr. Baranowski," she says, "you *do* understand that the actions you engaged in were both legally and morally wrong. Is that correct?"

"Yes, ma'am."

"The penalty for harassment of tenants can be anywhere from three months to one year in jail. Has your attorney explained this to you?"

"Yes, ma'am."

"Has he also explained that failure to cooperate in the investigation—refusing, for instance, to divulge the names of others who might have been involved in this activity—is likely to result in the maximum sentence?"

"Yes, ma'am."

"Is there anything you'd like to tell the court before I pass judgment?"

He came prepared to say several things. First, that he's sorry. Then, that he'll do nothing like this again. That in the future, he'll work hard to make up for the harm he's caused. But the only one of these statements that would be true is the first. He can't say what he might do in five years, because he doesn't know what troubles might be headed his way. And his worst crimes can't be atoned for.

What's about to emerge from his mouth will appall his sister.

Upon hearing his statement, the prosecutor will marvel that people like the defendant can't even imagine how a contrite individual might behave.

The defense attorney will wish, as he so often does, that he'd studied corporate law or intellectual property law or maritime law, anything that would keep him from having to sit at the table, day after day, with sociopaths.

"When I'm released from jail," Bogdan says, "I'm going to get a dog. That's one thing I can promise."

The only people in the courtroom who find this a reasonable response are Roman and the judge. Each of them, on more than one occasion, has considered getting a dog too, though the judge eventually opted for a cat. A few days from now, after her leaking blood vessel finally bursts, triggering a hemorrhagic stroke, it will be the cat's persistent yowling that alerts the building superintendent, who will enter her flat and find her naked body.

Right now the judge has only a mild headache. She pronounces Bogdan guilty, sentences him to a year in prison, rises, and retires to her chambers, where she lingers alone until well past dark.

The coals have turned white. Sitting on the back steps, Richard tells Franek how each spring, when he took the grill out for the first time since the previous fall, he used to burn dinner. "It never failed," he says. "Anna dubbed it 'Pizza Night.' I'd burn whatever I put on, and then we'd call for carry-out. After a few years, your aunt learned not to let me start with steaks, because they're expensive. She'd hand me a plate of hamburger patties, say, 'Go ahead and get it over with,' and I'd burn 'em to a crisp. It's harder to do it right than you might think. I guess it's like anything else. It takes practice, and doing it right one time doesn't mean you'll do it right the next." He pauses. "I haven't grilled in ages. Nevertheless, we're having steaks. How would you prefer yours?"

An objective witness would probably conclude from looking at his nephew's face that he knows something is up and is waiting to find out what, it being a given that the adult is not going to enlighten him quickly. His uncle has already handed him a beer. He's never done that before without being asked, and in all but a couple of instances, when he was asked, he said no, pleading the necessity for Franek to do his schoolwork with a clear head or making a joke about not wanting to participate in the corruption of a minor. Speculation has led to the suspicion that despite the affability Sandy's parents displayed while driving back yesterday, they've learned the entire story: about the porn film he watched with their daughter, the joints they smoked, what happened between them Saturday morning around four o'clock. "Thank God I'm still just seventeen," she remarked before slipping down the hallway to their suite. "Otherwise, I'd be guilty of statutory crime."

He tells his uncle he would like his steak medium.

"Which side of medium?"

"Rare."

"Good. That's the safer side for me to aim at."

He goes into the house, picks up the platter with the steaks on it, and grabs himself a second beer. He'll be driving later this evening, but he needs another drink.

He throws the steaks on. "You know," he says as they sizzle, "when I think about it, my dad was inept with a grill too. I believe maybe I inherited a little bit of his attitude toward cooking and food in general. That's almost always the case with fathers and sons. You take on aspects of their personality without realizing it until you get to be a certain age yourself. The way my dad looks at it, eating's something you have to do, so he does it. But I don't think he's ever viewed it as a source of pleasure. As long as he can get a piece of meat down his throat, he doesn't care if it's burned."

Franek recognizes this as the sort of verbal foreplay an adult engages in before moving on to serious business. You have to put up with it when you're a child. You mostly have to put up with it when you're an adolescent. But he's entered the magic kingdom. In this elevated state, it seems important, even necessary, to adopt a proactive attitude.

Be a man, Francis X.

Switching to Polish, he says, "Uncle Richard, why don't we cut to the chase?"

He's a sensitive boy—Richard has always understood that. God knows what he thinks they're about to discuss. The likeliest possibility would be weed, which he's almost certainly found a source for. If so, he may fear that a search has been conducted, his stash located. Another strong possibility would be Sandy. Yesterday, when the two of them said good-bye after returning from Disneyland, they exchanged a glance the likes of which Richard hadn't seen before, and this morning, without explanation, Franek climbed into the backseat beside her rather than riding up front like he used to.

He leans over and flips the steaks, then says, "After dinner, there's something I need to go do. It's probably going to take a while. It may even . . . I may not make it home till really late. It's possible I might not be here by the time you wake. So if that happens, go next door, and Mrs. Lyons will fix you breakfast. And then either she or Mr. Lyons will take you and Sandy to school. I already checked with them. So I hope it's okay with you."

His nephew says nothing, just stares at the smoke rising from the grate. Richard suspects he's upset. Who knows what he's learned about his father, what he thinks Stefan does all those nights he's away from home, when he leaves Franek's mother alone.

In fact, Franek has never felt more manly. It's as if, over the past three days, the contract the adult world dictated between itself and him has somehow been altered to his own advantage. How this came to be is mysterious, if not miraculous. He understands that along with new privileges, certain additional responsibilities have been conferred upon him and that one of these is the necessity to suspend childish needs. Who gives a shit who prepares his breakfast as long as he eats? Even if nobody fixed it, he'd survive.

He turns his beer up and finishes it off. Then sets the bottle down, rises from the stoop, and, grinning, chucks his uncle on the shoulder. "Go for it," he advises. "I believe I'll get myself another beer."

She answers the door in warm-ups and furry pink slippers. Her hair's back in the ponytail. She looks at the bottle he's carrying—Black Bush—then turns and walks into the living room without bothering to say hello, leaving it up to him whether to follow or go home.

He steps inside, shuts the door, and heads for the kitchen, where he has to open three cabinets before finding a set of rocks glasses. They've got the Flying Elvis logo on them. "Hey," he calls, "did you buy these Pats glasses at Gillette?"

She doesn't answer.

He carries them into the living room. She's seated on the couch, one leg crossed over the other in a pose he's never seen her strike before. A fake log lies on the grate in its wrapper, but it hasn't been lit.

He stands the bottle and the glasses on the coffee table. "It's crisp out," he says. "You mind if I start a fire?"

"Suit yourself."

He takes the box of matches off the mantel, pulls the screen aside, strikes one, and lights the log.

"How was San Francisco?" she asks. "Or was it Berkeley? Or someplace else up there?"

"I told you I was going to L.A."

"Yeah, I know you did. But that was a lie."

"What'd you do? Stake out my house and tail me?"

"I drove by a few times. Finally saw you pulling away from the curb. I only followed you as far as 99 North."

He twists the cap off the bottle. "You're really something. You know that?"

"What makes you think I like Black Bush?"

"Just a guess."

She picks up one of the glasses and holds it out. He pours about an inch into it.

"More."

So he pours another inch, then the same for himself. "Cheers," he says.

"Fuck you."

He takes a sip, sits down next to her, and waits.

She watches the fireplace for a while. Then she uncrosses her legs and draws them onto the couch, squirming sideways to face him. "Why'd you lie to me?"

"I needed a little time to think."

"About what?"

"Several things."

"So why didn't you just say so?"

"Would you have accepted it?"

"Not for a minute."

"Well. See my point?"

"Has it ever occurred to you," she asks, "that you don't actually like me?"

He lifts the glass, starts to down the whiskey but thinks better of it. He has a small sip, then returns his glass to the table. "No, Maria, it hasn't. I like you enormously."

"Well, I'll be goddamn!" she cries, her face bright with joy that he figures is not entirely feigned. "Truly? You're not shittin' me, are you?

"No, I'm not shitting you, Maria. You're attractive, smart, full of energy, you're on the right side and determined to make things happen. You bring a lot to the table. Much more than I do. All I'm bringing, I'm afraid, is that Black Bush. And this." He reaches into his pocket, pulls out the memory stick, and lays it next to the bottle.

Idly, she scratches her shoulder through the fabric of her sweatshirt, then shoves her hand inside and scratches harder. He can see her collarbone.

"Is that what I think it is?" she asks.

"Everything that was on her phone the night she died."

"And you got it from that last guy you talked to the other day?"

"Let's just say I got it from somebody."

He takes her through it, starting with the photos of Jacinta and her children, then offering a lengthy summary of the phone calls and text exchanges, sometimes quoting the latter word for word, referencing dates and times. Once or twice, she asks a question, but otherwise she just listens. A couple of times he refills their glasses. A couple of times she does.

He leaves the information about the final message and the attached video for last. He hasn't forgotten how to craft a narrative or how much satisfaction lies in telling a good story, no matter how sad or disturbing the outcome. The more trouble, the better the tale. That's one of two rules you live by when you do what he does. The other is that you don't make things up. She lives by those rules too.

"Major filmed her face while he was having sex with her," he says, then relates the coach's line about Jacinta being his own personal porn star. "The chronology makes it all but certain that when the text and the attachment came, Andres Aguilera was already at home. My guess is he saw the message and the video and then lost it. How he could do what he did, I don't pretend to understand. It'd take my brother-in-law to tell that part of the story."

"Why your brother-in-law?"

"He's a novelist. I'm not. And neither are you."

She tosses back the last of her whiskey and holds out her glass. He finishes his, reaches for the bottle, and pours the remainder, giving her a little less than he gives himself.

She takes a good-sized swallow. "So our friend Joe Garcia carried Jacinta's phone over to . . . Well, let's say he carried her phone *somewhere*, to *somebody*, who downloaded what was on it and saved it on a memory stick like this one, which he handed to Garcia—for a nice fee, of course. But Garcia didn't realize the guy had also copied the info onto his hard drive, because he's a sleaze too. And then this *somebody* reads the newspaper or turns on the TV and realizes that the phone belonged to a murder victim—at which point it dawns on him that he's got a little time bomb on his hands."

"That's about the size of it," he says. "Except for one important discrepancy."

"What's that?"

"The person who carried the phone to him?"

"Yeah?"

"It wasn't Joe Garcia."

STEAM CLOUDS rise from the Jacuzzi. She's been using it every night, she tells him. "Stress, backache, whatever. I just kind of like hot water. I may have thrown a little too much chlorine in it the other day, though, because I've been itching a good bit." She's standing on the other side of the tub as she says this.

She turns her back, pulls the sweatshirt over her head, and tosses it onto the glass-topped table. When she starts to lower the warm-up bottoms, he turns his back to her, bends, and unlaces his shoes. He pulls them off and sets them on the deck, then unbuttons his shirt. He hears her step into the water. He tosses the shirt onto the table near her warm-ups, steps out of his jeans and briefs, and throws them on the table. Then he turns and steps into the water, still without looking at her.

"Feels good," he says, his gaze settling on her face. She's turned her hair loose, letting it fall to her shoulders. "As much alcohol as we've got in us," he observes, "we better not sit here too long. You're not old enough to have a heart attack. But I might be."

"Anybody with a heart," she says, "can have an attack. And boy, have I got one." She picks up the whiskey glass, which is filled now with cheap brandy, and raises it for a toast. "To our aortas," she says. "Long may they remain unclogged."

"I left mine on the table."

"Your aorta? *That's* a new one."

He smiles. "My glass."

"No prob. I'll fetch."

Before he can protest, she stands, water streaming over her small, perfectly shaped breasts. He doesn't even try to look away. When she turns to climb out, he admires her smooth back, her white hips. She picks his glass up, steps back into the water, and hands it to him. Then she reaches for her own glass and, when she has it, sits down beside him. Her leg and hip are touching his.

He puts his arm around her shoulders, which feel thinner than he expected.

"You can't drive," she says. "You've had too much Irish."

"I don't intend to."

"All *right.*" She rests her head against his chest. "So, Ricardo. Tell me. What do you think?"

He hadn't planned to drink any more, but he buys time with a sip of brandy. After the whiskey, it tastes like cough syrup. "About what?"

"Oh, I don't know. The moon. The stars. Nick Major. Joe Garcia. You. Me."

He knows the moon and the stars are up there somewhere, hidden by a layer of smog. About them he has no opinion, other than relief that tonight they aren't providing a whole lot of light. What he thinks about Nick Major is unprintable. But this is okay because, though he hasn't yet said so, he will not be committing the coach's name to the printed page. What he thinks of Joe Garcia would be more complicated to express. But this is okay too, since he won't be writing his name anywhere either.

So that leaves her. And him. "I said what I think about you in the living room. You're really something."

"Well, so are you. Any chance you might possibly, just maybe, like to kiss me? On a strictly voluntary basis, understand."

"I'd love to."

Everything blurs: her face meeting his, the taste of a mouth other than his own for the first time in so long, her hand stroking his cheek, then grasping his own hand and pulling it toward her breast. He leaves it there for a moment, then runs it over her neck and face and into her hair.

How long their kiss lasts, he wouldn't be able to say. He likes how it feels to hold her, to feel her heart beating, not racing, just maintaining a strong, steady rhythm as her chest presses against him. He doesn't protest when she slides her leg over his, then straddles him, the water rolling off her shoulders.

She cups her right breast and leans closer. He takes her nipple in his mouth. She tastes of salt and chlorine.

"Oh, man," she murmurs. "Man alive." She shudders, tosses her hair, and tilts her head back. Her desire is palpable and rich, and he wishes he could meet it with a full measure of his own.

Gradually, a whirring sound intrudes. It's coming from above. He looks into the sky. She does the same.

It's the FPD helicopter, flying a tight circle a couple of blocks south of them. "Must be a wreck," he says.

"Either that, or somebody done somebody else wrong."

"One doesn't preclude the other."

She leans over and kisses him again. "Let's go inside," she says. "I'm itching pretty bad."

Neither of them thought to bring a towel, and the night is nippy. At first, he can't find his shoes. Then he sees them, and when he leans down to pick them up, he realizes just how much he's had to drink.

He tucks them under one arm, then grabs his clothes as she gathers hers. In the manner in which you register sound when you're drunk, he understands that the copter is somewhere else now, much closer than it was only seconds before. It has lift at its disposal, drag and thrust. It can do things people can't.

Maybe the accident, if there was one, has been satisfactorily dealt with by the police. Or maybe they caught whoever staged a break-in, stole a car, committed assault, rape, or murder. Or maybe miscreants are loose nearby.

"Hurry," he says.

She giggles, and they make a dash for her back door. They're halfway across the yard when the spotlight blinds them. He ducks his head, so he doesn't see her turn her face to the sky. But he hears her over the noise of the blades: "It's biblical!" she cries. "We're naked in the garden!"

HER BED is a wrought-iron affair that he expects to creak beneath his weight, but it doesn't. The mattress feels artificially lush, like those in every Marriott he's ever stayed at. The covers smell faintly of vanilla, the scent of her shampoo.

She switches off the light and backs up against him. For one unrealistic moment, he thinks maybe she wants to go to sleep. That's what he would like, to lie here holding her all night, listening to the sound of her breathing. He doubts he will sleep much himself. He never used to when he had too much to drink, and he didn't the other night in San Francisco.

"Fondle my tits?" she says.

He works his right arm underneath her so he can caress both at once.

"Ah. Pull on my nipples, will ya? Draw 'em out."

He does as she asked, and in a matter of minutes, or maybe it's only seconds, she's shivering. She stops his hands, waits till her tremor subsides, then says, "Lil' more." She comes at least three times, the last aftershocks accompanied by a sound that falls somewhere on the spectrum between a laugh and a sob.

"Jesus Christ," she whispers, "that was so fucking nice."

She rolls over, her face inches from his. Stealthily, like she's about to lift his wallet, she reaches between his legs.

The easiest thing would be to blame it on drink. But morning will arrive, and so will another night. "It's not you, Maria," he says.

She pulls her hand back and studies it. "Looks like me." Sniffs it. "Smells like me." Licks her forefinger. "Tastes like me." Then she pushes the covers aside and begins working her way down his body, kissing his chest and stomach before taking him in her mouth.

He closes his eyes.

Along with most other Poles he's ever met, his wife hated the film *Sophie's Choice*, considering it a self-indulgent, romanticized American take on her nation's tragedy. Lying here in this strange bed, he calls upon the dissolve at the end, when Meryl Streep's face fades into pixels and the strings coax out every canned emotion the male heart can harbor. Only now it's the face of his wife he sees, the dark hair in soft focus, the large eyes alight.

How would what's happening look to her? Might she wish him quick gratification, since little else is possible? Would she sympathize with Maria, who's giving so much more than she'll receive and, on some level, must know it? Julia used to tell him that if she died first, she hoped he would soon find someone else. He said the same thing. You can toss platitudes into the air like confetti when you're young and the eventuality seems far away, if not inconceivable. You don't think that day will come, but then it does. And here it is.

And here he is.

Maria is nothing if not tenacious. She works hard to make it happen, and they are finally both rewarded, his hips arching off the bed. It would be difficult to say which of them labored more.

"Oh, man." She reaches toward the floor, for a glass of water artfully placed. She takes a swallow, wipes her mouth, then crawls the length of his body, planting kisses on the way up as she did on her way down, until she's lying on top of him, her damp hair spread out on both sides of his chest. She falls asleep like that, and he lets her lie there for a long time, stroking her thin shoulders before gently shifting her onto her side.

She wakes happier than she's been in a long time—happier, maybe, than at any time since the first weeks of her marriage, nearly twenty years ago in Arkansas. Richard, of course, has no idea she was ever married. He didn't ask, and she didn't volunteer. Her husband was a wonderful man, sixteen years older, owner of a lumber company in Hot Springs. He had countless good traits. He was solicitous, soft-spoken, generous to a fault. He also had one very bad habit that she wasn't aware of until they'd been married for a month: every week or two, he visited the racetrack at nearby Oaklawn Park. He'd been doing it for years and was in debt up to his neck. She learned that the morning a guy she'd never seen before approached her in the dairy aisle at the grocery store.

She can hear Richard moving around in her kitchen, and she can smell coffee and hear the Mr. Coffee chugging away, hissing and gurgling. It needs to be cleaned. Making a mental note to buy white vinegar, she shrugs into her bathrobe. She can't locate her house slippers, so she walks in barefoot.

She's thinking how nice it is to wake up and find someone in the house, somebody who's taken the time to make coffee so you won't have to. If he hasn't already fixed breakfast, maybe they'll go eat at the French bakery in Fig Garden Village. She's an early riser and has dropped by there a few times to pick up croissants or fresh rolls. You see a lot of older couples in there, re-tired people, probably, who have nothing pressing to do and can go out to enjoy breakfast together and sit there all day if they choose.

He's fully dressed. And he's having trouble looking at her. He studies the level in the coffee pot as if he's involved in a lab exper-iment that will go up in flames after one drop too many.

In an instant, she lowers her expectations. If you told her that five years from now, she'll be covering crime and immigration for the *Washington Post*, living in Bethesda, Maryland, happily married to a high school principal and with a daughter whom they adopted from Thailand, not only would she not believe you, she might also slap your face. She has a good mind, right now, to slap his. "What is it?" she says.

He removes the pot from the coffee maker and fills two cups. Then he finally does look at her. He's not just embarrassed. What she sees in his eyes is mortification—of which, she would grant you, embarrassment is a subsidiary property, at least in her experience.

"Can we sit down?" he asks.

"Sure. We can sit down, we can lie down, we can roll over and play dead. Whatever you choose."

"This is not what you think, Maria."

He tries to hand her the coffee. She won't take it.

"How the hell," she asks, "do you know what I think?"

"You're right. I don't. Would you agree to tell me?"

"Okay. To start with, I hate your fucking wounded nobility. You wear it like a motorcycle helmet. Get over it."

"I'd love to."

"Then do."

"I'd love to. But I'd be doing you a disservice to pretend I have when I haven't."

He realizes immediately how poorly he chose his words. Still, he's unprepared for the speed with which she eliminates the distance, grabs his shirt collar, and twists it. "I am not an automobile," she says, so close now that he feels a blast of hot breath. "I don't need service. If anybody got serviced last night, it was you."

She clenches his collar for a few more seconds, during which she decides the best way to move past where they are right now is for her to go ahead and slap him. She lets go and whacks him on the side of the head, a halfhearted blow that nevertheless stings her palm and leaves his left ear red.

"Now what are you supposed to say?" she asks.

"'Thanks, I needed that'?"

"Good boy. I had high hopes for you. You know it, don't you?"

He carries his coffee over to the kitchen table and sits down. "What can I say, Maria?"

She picks up the cup he filled for her and sits down opposite him. "Whatever it is," she advises, "you better avoid mechanical imagery."

So he tells her that when he woke up in Krakow and learned he'd lost his wife and daughter, he understood he was ruined for anybody else. Why it's so, he doesn't know. Plenty of people transcend their losses and go on to make second lives, sometimes even third lives. Whereas he returned nearly three years ago and began to go through the motions, slogging from one day to the next without caring too much whether the next one ever came. "When we had lunch a couple months ago at Chicken Liver's and you stomped on my foot, you said you wanted to wake me up. You did that. And I'm grateful—really, I am—for the chance to remember what being awake feels like. I hope you'll forgive me for saying this, but I think the best thing for me would be to go back to sleep."

She's heard all kinds of exit lines and delivered a fair number herself. He's the first man she's ever slapped. And now, in the wake of being dumped by him, he's become the first one she feels the need to look after. He's many times worse off than she will ever be. He no longer believes in possibility. A small part of her can't give up on that belief. It needs to be watered daily, kept alive until conditions improve. They're bound to.

"About the story we've been working on?" he says.

"Yeah?"

"It's no longer ours. It never really was. It's all yours."

"I've just accepted a whole lot from you, Richard. But *that* I don't understand."

"I can't write it."

"*Why?*"

"I just can't. I don't have what it takes anymore. It's related to everything else I don't have."

"You know I was ordered not to pursue it."

"Of course I do. That's why the two of us spent the last couple months doing what you were told not to."

"So what are you suggesting? That we just let the story die along with those poor people while that fucking sleaze continues to chase his championship?"

"Not at all. Take what's on that memory stick and lay it on your editor's desk. Inform him that if he won't let you write the story, I will write it instead, and that a big part of *my* story will be how *he* put the lid on your efforts. What do you think his response will be?"

With greater calm than she feels, she takes a sip of coffee. It will be a couple of months before she wonders if this was a gift of sorts, a present in lieu of other responses she could not inspire. She'll entertain that line of thought for only moments before rejecting it. That's not who he is. Those kinds of calculations are beneath him.

She sets down her cup. "That cowardly bastard?" she says. "He'll be on his knees begging me to write it."

HE PULLS into a parking lot at City College to check his phone. There's a text from Monika, telling him Stefan just had to have emergency gall bladder surgery but that he'll be okay. A text from Stefan, striking a jocular tone, noting that since the Polish word for "death" is feminine, if he dies, at least it will be at the hands of a woman. In no mood for dark humor, Richard presses the escape key, leaving the rest of it for later. There's also one from Franek, sent late last night, saying he's in love with Sandy, that he wants to remain in America and marry her rather than go home, because he doesn't love his parents and never did.

What a lovely day.

He pulls back into traffic. When Rupert said the person who brought Jacinta's phone to him was a "she" rather than a "he," his disbelief had lasted only a few seconds. The picture came into focus, as it does when you're looking at a pointillist painting and you locate the optimum viewing distance. He knew immediately who "she" was, and when he described her, Rupert confirmed it.

If your son's welfare is at stake, you do whatever you have to. If he's hanging around the wrong kinds of people, smoking too much pot, and revealing a proclivity for cybercrime, you send him elsewhere, hoping that a change of scenery will solve the problem. Maybe it will, maybe it won't. Maybe it will lead to other problems, which might be worse. You won't know until you try.

If your daughter falls off her bike and busts up her beautiful face, you throw her in the car and head for the children's hospital as fast as you can, hoping that your worst fears will not be realized, that she'll be treated quickly and expertly, that her scars will heal, that she won't have to live with a face that looks like a road map. Right then, you can't imagine anything worse, even though you know that worse things do in fact happen to people. You're just convinced they won't ever happen to her.

If you didn't get to attend college because your folks were first-generation Mexican immigrants and you lived in a shitty house on a dangerous street in East L.A., it stands to reason that you'd like to give your own kids the chance you never got. So you and your wife work your asses off. She pulls extra shifts and eats too much candy, and you pull extra ones too. Like most joes, you don't turn down work. As the tuition bills come due, you lie awake at night, wondering how you're going to pull it off. Four kids times a hundred thousand dollars or even more if they're accepted by private schools that don't offer a ton of aid. How much overtime can the two of you stand? If you're never home, they may get into trouble. That's what unattended kids do.

Then an opportunity falls into your hands. And you've got the one piece of knowledge you need to capitalize on it, because your eyes and your ears are your currency and you've kept them open. You didn't kill anybody. No matter what you do or don't do, you can't bring them back. You see that phone lying there on the table, so you pick it up and put it in your pocket.

You know, because you keep your eyes and ears open, that there are folks around who can tell you what's on the phone. They will have their price. It's a gamble. It might not reveal anything at all. But it's a risk worth taking. The thing is, your face is known. It occasionally shows up on TV, usually in the background, as one of those guys standing around behind the chief or his designated spokesman. You can't take the step yourself, though you will take the necessary subsequent steps if anything of use turns up on that phone. In a good marriage, the partners pull together. You both do what you have to for those you love the most.

Richard understands this. He remembers how it was. That's the truest thing he could say to Cloris Garcia, the woman who once made certain his daughter went right to the front of the line, that she got the best care in the least time.

SAFE

SPACE

2016

When Bogdan wakes after another poor night's sleep, he looks at the clock. It stands on his bedside table, less than a meter away, but he still can't quite decipher the glowing green numbers. In the last few years, he's developed blepharitis. Lately, perhaps because he lies awake at night listening to the sounds coming from the room above his, it seems to be getting worse. This morning, it takes a couple of minutes for his vision to clear. Even after it does, his eyes keep burning.

He swings his legs out of bed, his bare feet recoiling when they touch the floor, which feels like a sheet of ice. He reaches for the radiator, wondering if the boiler is again on the blink, but the surface is hot. It must be really cold out. His sister will be pleased. Having little to fret over, she worries about the cancellations warmer temperatures bring. You can't ski without snow.

He rises, flips on the overhead light, then pulls off the long underwear that he's been sleeping in and steps into the small bathroom, where he turns on the shower. He lets the water run for a moment before entering the stall. Until recently, he got up each morning, washed his face, put his clothes on, and went to breakfast, saving the shower for the evening. He only changed his routine after Teresa hired the Ukrainian refugee.

Elena is blonde like Krysia, but her hair has a few gray streaks, and her face looks tense. It's impossible to say how old she is. His best guess would be forty-five. Around the pension, she always seems to wear the same clothes: a pair of pleated jeans, a green sweater that needs depilling, black shoes of the type that are usually called "sensible."

He has seen her wearing something different exactly twice. The first time was about a month ago, on a Saturday night when he was strolling down Krupowki, Zakopane's steeply sloping main street, which is lined on both sides by shops, restaurants, hotels, and bars. She emerged from one of the latter. It was snowing, and she had on what he assumed was a fake sheepskin but no scarf or cap. The lampposts on Krupowki curl into the shape of a bass clef in honor of the composer Szymanowski, and when she reached out to steady herself against one of them, he thought she'd lost her footing. Then he realized she was drunk. He took a step in her direction, but she shook her head, as if to say, *No, I don't need or welcome your help*, so he continued on his way to meet Roman for a beer. He didn't mention what he'd seen.

The other time was last week when the boiler quit. He was down in the basement with two repairmen all afternoon and most of the evening, and once they finally got it working, they asked him to go into each room and make sure the release of hot water hadn't caused any leaks. The last room was the one above his. When he knocked, she didn't answer. So he knocked again. This time he heard familiar footsteps. The door opened a crack, but she left the night latch engaged. "What?" she said.

He could see just a sliver of her face: her right eye, the corner of her mouth, part of her jaw. The effect was jarring, as if the rest of her head had been sheared away.

"I need to check the radiator," he said.

"It works."

"I know that. But they're worried about leaks. I'd just be a minute."
The door closed again. The latch clicked, and she let him in.

She was wearing a plaid flannel shirt that must have belonged to a very large man: it hung halfway down her otherwise bare thighs, and though she'd rolled up the cuffs, they still covered her wrists and part of each hand. She gestured toward the window. "There," she said, like he might not know a radiator when he saw one.

He moved past her bed, his eyes taking in what they could. She'd mounted a couple of icons on the wall: Madonna and Child, the Archangel Michael. At the foot of her bed lay a magazine, the title in Cyrillic. An orange duffel bag was open on the floor, still only partially unpacked.

He checked for leaks, found none, then turned to go.

"I was rude," she said. She hadn't moved since he entered.

"It's all right. Nobody likes being disturbed late at night."

"That Saturday. I was scared."

He wasn't sure what she was referring to, then realized she must mean the night he'd seen her coming out of the bar.

"Your sister," she said. "She told me not to big drink."

He laughed, though not at the grammatical slip. Her Polish is more than serviceable. "Oh. Well, she tells me not to drink big too. But sometimes I do it anyway."

"Different," she said. She shook her head. "Very different."

"That's true. After all, we're relatives."

"It's good to have relatives," she said. She glanced toward the alarm clock on her bedside table.

He took the hint. "Well, good night. See you in the morning."

In the shower now, he turns his back to the nozzle, letting the spray pepper his neck and shoulders, loosening muscles grown tense from lack of sleep. Last night, around eleven, he again heard her praying. He caught a word here, a word there, but he couldn't understand whom or what she was praying for. It lasted five or ten minutes. Then the floor began to creak, as he had known it would. She started walking back and forth, from one side of the room to the other. Four steps west, four steps east, the ceiling giving an extra little shudder each time she reversed direction. She's not a large woman, just average-sized, and she was probably trying to be quiet. But he heard every step. Her pace is metronomic. Around seventy steps per minute, night after night.

The first time it happened, he thought that, like Teresa, she must be an exercise fanatic, but weeks ago, he discarded that notion. For one thing, she does it for no set period. One night, it will last an hour and eighteen minutes, the next night an hour and thirty-two minutes, the night after that an hour and ten minutes. People who are simply out for exercise usually have a goal in mind that can be measured in time or distance, but she appears to have neither. One night she kept it up for nearly two hours.

He could put an end to it by telling his sister about it or by simply climbing the stairs, knocking on her door, and either asking or demanding that she stop. But he can't bring himself to do it. He doesn't know her story, but he knows she's trying to walk away from something big.

HE SHOWERS, dresses, and heads downstairs. It's Saturday again, and for the first time in three days the sky is clear, the forecast good, so he decides to make the trip to Krakow that he's been putting off due to the weather. Every couple of weeks, he drives the van into the city for provisions. His sister buys in bulk from Tesco, placing her order online. By the time he gets there, it will be waiting. All he has to do is drive up to the loading dock and give them the number. It's a wonder he and Marek remained in the grocery business as long as they did. If only they'd given up sooner.

He borrows a copy of *Gazeta Wyborcza* from the young woman at the front desk, then steps into the dining room. The pension is booked to capacity right now, and most of the tables are already taken, everyone eager to get caffeinated and fed and head for the slopes. He chooses the table nearest the kitchen and opens the paper.

The lead item, predictably, concerns the new government's release of documents purporting to prove that back in the '70s, Lech Walesa collaborated with the secret police. Maybe he did, maybe he didn't. Either way, Bogdan can't bring himself to read it. Let the merchants of unforgiveness hawk their wares to those who will buy. Plenty of willing customers are out there. He flips to the sports.

He looks up to find Elena holding a coffee pot. She turns his cup right-side up and fills it. She seldom speaks when serving breakfast, not even a good-morning to him or the guests, but today she says, "You're going to Krakow?"

"Actually, I am." He wonders how she could know that.

"Your sister told me," she says, as though his mind were a browser accidently left open. Later, he will realize she was giving him a chance to lie to her in case he anticipated the coming request and wanted to squelch it. "She said maybe I might go with you? I have this business I need to do."

He's not sure he wants her company. Though he used to dread the trips, fearing that he couldn't keep himself from driving by his old building, or that he might see Krysia on the street with the other woman, or that returning to the scene of his crimes might shatter the fragile peace he'd found, he long ago began to savor them. He likes the drive down from the mountains, how the countryside spreads out before him: green in summer, white in winter, an impressionist landscape in spring and fall. Along the way, he listens to audiobooks. The novels of Sienkiewicz and Hugo and Dumas, *Pan Tadeusz*, John Grisham, Harry Potter, all sorts of things. On most trips, he meets Marek for a beer and once or twice has eaten supper with him and Inga.

Neither is he certain that he doesn't want Elena's company. The last time he tended to what's left of his sexual needs, he imagined making love to her instead of Krysia. It puzzled him that he felt the urge to do that. She's not especially attractive, and she's never been pleasant. But she's intriguing, and he knows she gets Saturday nights off.

"Sure," he says. "You can go with me. Can I ask where you want me to take you, though? That'll determine which route into the city we use."

"The Ukrainian Consulate. On Beliny-Prażmowskiego."

"But this is Saturday. All the consulates are closed."

"For me, it won't be."

"Okay," he says. "Could you be ready in an hour?" There's a chance of snow again tonight, and he'd rather not be driving through bad weather in the dark.

She nods and returns to the kitchen. Later, when she brings a basket of rolls and again when she brings his eggs and fruit, she doesn't say a word.

He finishes breakfast and steps into the office to see his sister. Roman says she drove over to her other local property but that she sent her order to Tesco before leaving. So he climbs the stairs, grabs his coat, iPad, and earbuds and goes back to the deserted living room, where he seats himself beside the fire.

While waiting for Elena, he puts the buds in, opens iTunes, and clicks on Arvo Pärt's *Tabula Rasa*. He started listening to what he now thinks of as "serious" music after visiting Szymanowski's villa, which is only a few blocks away and has been turned into a museum. Like almost everyone else, he hated this kind of music when it was inflicted on him in school, but he has grown to enjoy it and likes reading about how mountain string bands inspired such composers as Bartók and Ligeti. He would never have thought that people who spent their days herding sheep and their nights drunkenly playing the fiddle could influence what was being performed in concert halls in Paris, London, New York, or Los Angeles. But they did. The poor and the dirty inform the divine.

Thinking about Los Angeles leads him to open Safari and type the words "Richard Brennan."

ONE DAY in late 2010, near the end of his jail term, he'd visited the prison library. To call it a library was misleading, as it had only four shelves of books, at least two-thirds of them geared toward the vocational: *Fundamentals of Plumbing, Eternal Principles of the Internal Combustion Engine.* What it did have plenty of was computers. You had to log in with an assigned password, and they'd all been warned that porn sites were forbidden and that their browsing history would be retained and checked, but the word was that in reality, nobody gave a damn what you did online unless you initiated a correspondence with Osama bin Laden. Still, he hadn't wanted to take too many risks.

That day, he visited the Los Angeles newspaper's website for the first time in more than a year. Until he went to jail, he'd made a habit of checking the paper every month or two to see if the American journalist's articles were still appearing there, as they had since the summer of 2007, when he must have regained enough of his health to go back to work. He couldn't read any of the pieces or even tell for certain what they were about. Nevertheless, it gave him comfort to see them. He hoped the man would recover more than just physical health, that he'd find someone else to love, maybe even start another family.

There was nothing in the paper by him that day or three days later, when he checked again. He checked the following week. Nothing. He checked off and on until the day he was released, never finding a piece with Brennan's name on it.

As agreed with the probation officer, he moved into the pension and went to work for his sister. Here, he had daily access to the Internet, and over the next year, he visited the newspaper's site every day, sometimes more than once. He never saw the name "Richard Brennan" there again. He did a Google search, thinking that maybe Brennan had changed jobs and gone to work for a different paper. To his chagrin, more than thirty-five million items came up, and while some of them were archived newspaper articles written by his Richard Brennan, all of those pieces were old, the last one dated March 2010. Most of what he found concerned other people with that apparently common name.

This morning, he again does what he's been doing off and on for many years, checking a few Richard Brennans to see if he can find the one who never leaves his mind for very long. There are several he can't rule out. Without being able to read the language, he can't tell a whole lot. But none of the images he examines resembles the face he recalls from that night nearly ten years ago. He's beginning to wonder if the man he thinks of as "my Richard Brennan" is now dead. Maybe he's been dead a long time.

He becomes aware, in the diminished way that we all do when staring at our mobile devices and listening to music, that a set of arms and legs and the torso they're attached to is moving toward him. As the physical presence draws closer, he realizes that a black-and-white wool skirt is involved, as are black leggings. For those reasons, he does not look up until they stop right in front of him. It never occurred to him that the body might belong to Elena.

She's wearing a black blouse and the faux sheepskin he saw her in before. She's also wearing lipstick—if he had to name the color, he'd say it's purple—and her pale complexion makes it look even brighter and more daring than it otherwise might. She's done something to her hair too, and whatever it was has revealed more of her face, where the lines he's used to seeing have either been hidden or somehow disappeared, though the second possibility seems unlikely.

He pulls the earbuds out. "Ready to go?"

"Yes. They expect me early afternoon."

"Okay." He switches off the iPad and grabs his coat.

The van is parked behind the pension. It was still snowing yesterday afternoon when he left it there, and it's covered. He climbs in and starts it, then reaches under the seat for the ice scraper.

In the meantime, she has begun clearing the passenger-side windows using only her gloved right hand, and he notices that she's sweeping the white power aside forcefully, as if its presence were an affront. "I'll take care of it," he says, but she pays him no mind and keeps swatting snow.

For the first forty-five minutes, they're both silent. He doesn't know what to say to her, and she appears to have no interest in saying anything to him. He turns the radio on, but reception is not that good, and all he can hear is the crackly voice of the new justice minister, who's intoning about "the worst sort of Poles," meaning any of those whose views don't jibe with the government's. Forty-five years of Communism, twenty-five of Capitalism, and now an era that he doesn't know a name for. Too bad "Vindictivism" isn't a word. He reaches over and switches it off.

By the time they reach Rabka, he's in physical distress. He can't hold liquids like he once did. He pulls into a gas station and asks if she needs to visit the restroom, but she shakes her head.

The men's is taken, so he waits four or five minutes. When it's finally free, he has to stand in front of the urinal a good while before anything happens. He probably ought to see a urologist, but he hates going to the doctor, and the obligatory medical exams at the correctional facility didn't improve his attitude.

When he climbs back into the van and apologizes for taking so long, his passenger remains silent. He starts the engine, looks both ways, and pulls out of the parking lot.

He drives on a few more kilometers, his dissatisfaction building. There's such a thing as basic courtesy. He doesn't deserve a lot from life, but it seems to him that he deserves that, at least as long as he extends it to others. Finally, he says, "Do you mind if I ask you something?"

"I might," she replies. "It depend."

In front of them, he sees a tractor. It's driving right down the middle of the road, putting along at about fifteen kilometers an hour, loosing clouds of smoke. There are two people on it: the driver and a woman who's perched on the fender. As they get closer, he can see that she's laughing and talking with her hands, like she's on the biggest lark of her life. Why anybody would be taking his girlfriend joy-riding on a tractor, on a mountain road in the middle of winter, is not just puzzling, it's outrageous. When he's within about fifty meters, he slams the horn.

The sound startles the woman. She flinches, turns, and nearly loses her balance, reaching out to grab the arm of the driver, who swerves to the right. For an instant, Bogdan fears he will steer the tractor off the road. The drop would not be precipitous, but the hillside is strewn with boulders.

As he starts around them, he hears the woman yell something, then gets a look at her face: she's probably no more than twenty, a farm girl with long blonde hair that sweeps out from under her cap. The driver has a thick red beard and a red face to go with it, and there's a large object in his right hand: a hatchet, it looks like, though they will never know for sure because when he throws it, aiming at the window in the cargo door, he misses. It strikes the van's roof, prompting Elena to scream, lurch forward, and cover her head. Bogdan floors it.

THE CONSULATE is a whitewashed villa on a residential street, not far from one of the last blocks he and Marek "cleansed." She hasn't spoken since the incident on the road, but then neither has he. It left him shaken, and he needs a beer. When he asks her what time she wants to be picked up, she simply shakes her head.

He's had enough of this behavior. "I'll stop right here at three thirty," he says. "If I don't see you, you're on your own getting back." She climbs out and shuts the door so softly that the latch doesn't catch. He reaches over, reopens it, and gives it a good jerk. The impact rattles the windowpane.

He drives by Tesco and picks up Teresa's order, throwing a few sacks of ice into the coolers with the frozen goods. Then he calls Marek to see if he's available. His old friend answers, but he and Inga are watching their grandchildren for the weekend. So Bogdan parks the van near Plac Szczepanski and walks through snow-blanketed Planty to Bunkier Café. It's the one where he had his first drink all those years ago, on the day he got out of jail to await trial. He thinks of that day now as among the most important of his life, when he began to honor the small pleasures to which he will never be entitled: a cold beer after a long dry spell, a pretzel with mustard, an evening with friends. He visits this café almost every time he comes to Krakow.

Today, the canopy is covered with snow. The plastic drop panels are down, but because they're transparent, he can watch people stroll by. The tall dishwater blonde comes to take his order. She's the same one who served him that day in the fall of 2009, which means she's been working at the café for about seven years, if not longer. Since he averages a couple of trips to Krakow a month and nearly always drinks a beer here, she's waited on him countless times. Yet if she recognizes him, there's no evidence of it. She lays the menu down on the table and is about to turn away when he says, "I don't need the menu. I'll just have a large beer."

"Tyskie?"

"Pilsner Urquell."

While he drinks, he thinks about what happened back there on the road. The tractor driver and his girlfriend or wife, or whoever she was, weren't doing anything wrong. They had as much right to the road as he did. He understands why he slammed the horn— anger at Elena's strange behavior—but he can't fathom why he allowed himself to vent when he was behind the wheel of an automobile. He believes there are a handful of mistakes he is not allowed to make. Reckless driving is number one. Taking too much of anything for himself, be it food, drink, or space on a sofa, is number two. Cruelty to animals is number three.

It's a while before he notices that today, almost everyone who passes the café is heading in the same direction—toward Plac Szczepanski, near where the van is parked—and many of them are carrying flags. When the waitress brings his check, he asks if something special is going on there this afternoon.

She lays his change on the table. "Some kind of demonstration," she says.

"For or against?"

She looks at him as if he's yet another nuisance in a day filled with them. "Excuse me?"

"I meant are they demonstrating for something or against it?"

"What difference would it make?" she says, then picks up his empty beer glass and carries it inside.

The demonstration is definitely against something: the new government, which has fired numerous people at state television and radio, revamped the constitutional court to prevent rulings it opposes, and released those Walesa documents that may or may not be genuine. The crowd is a fraction of the fifty-five thousand that will be reported in Warsaw, but the square is still packed, hardly enough room to move, and it seems as if almost everyone has a flag or two, the Polish banner waving alongside the EU's. When he gets there, the speaker on the raised platform is shouting that this is not about finding scapegoats; there's been too much of that already. This is about maintaining twenty-seven years' worth of progress. "We've got to rush to meet the challenge." He illustrates by jogging in place.

As if by prior agreement, everyone else begins to do the same. Before he knows it, Bogdan is doing it himself, bouncing on the balls of his feet, like he's at one of those idiotic exercise classes his sister attends between packs of cigarettes. Somebody hands him an EU flag, which he begins to wave with all the others. The last time the country saw large-scale protests, he kept his head down. He sympathized with the protesters but figured he had too much to lose to get caught in their midst. Since he lost everything anyhow, he figures now, he might as well have acted on principle. Though he's unaware of it, a film crew is a short distance away, behind him and to his right. Later this evening, back in Zakopane, he will spot himself on independent television. It will be a fleeting glimpse, just a second or two, but seeing himself there among the other protesters will evoke an emotion last felt so long ago that he cannot properly identify it.

The woman next to him is bouncing up and down too, puffing hard. She's about his age, maybe a little older, and she looks at him and shouts, "My knees are about to give out. I've got arthritis."

"My bladder's full," he hollers, the repeated impact with cobblestones making the synapses fire an alert. "I drank a beer."

Continuing to run in place, she points toward Planty. "There's a bathroom over there. Not far."

"I know. I used to live here."

"And now?"

"Zakopane."

"Zakopane," she gasps. "It's beautiful."

She's a nice woman, with gray hair that was probably once brunette. She's wearing Nikes, as if she came prepared to exert herself on behalf of the cause.

It's the kind of day when the rules of decorum seem not to apply, when who you are and who you might like to be don't seem so far apart. "Are you married?" he hollers.

"Married?" Playfully, she digs her elbow into his ribs. "Listen to you. Making a move on an old woman." She gulps air. She probably ought to take a break. "The answer's yes," she wheezes. "My husband's at home in his wheelchair. What about you?"

"My ex-wife's at home with her girlfriend."

She stops for a moment to catch her breath, so he does too.

"What your ex-wife's doing?" she says. "That's exactly the kind of freedom these new bastards want to rob us of. You're so good to be here."

She locks her arm with his, and together they bounce up and down a few more times. Then he detaches himself and takes off toward the bathroom, still waving his EU flag. He makes it with seconds to spare.

BECAUSE OF the demonstration, traffic around the Old Town is a nightmare. It's after four when he pulls up in front of the Ukrainian consulate. To his relief, Elena is not there. The demonstration acted as a mood elevator, and her sullen presence could only spoil the vibe. He switches the van's audio over to Bluetooth, whips his phone out, and scrolls through iTunes until he finds what he's looking for: Willi Boskovsky and the Vienna Philharmonic. He pulls away from the curb to the opening strains of "Blue Danube."

When he glances into his mirror, he sees Elena running after him, shouting and waving. "Shit," he sighs. He stops and sits there waiting.

The woman who opens the door is a different person than the one he deposited a few hours ago. Her face has more color than he's seen before, which he initially puts down to her recent exertion. But it's more than that: he can tell as soon as she climbs in.

She's smiling.

"Thank you. Oh, thank you for waiting," she says. "I don't think they'd let me spend the night at the consulate. Do you?"

"I doubt it," he says.

"No, certainly not. They have rules. Rules everywhere you look. Some good, some bad, but lots and lots of rules."

There's no traffic on the street right now, and he still has his foot on the clutch. For a moment, he entertains the possibility that she might be bipolar. Then he notices the bottle protruding from her purse. Elena has had herself a few drinks.

He looks into the mirror again, then pulls into the street. "So," he says, "I guess whatever business you needed to take care of went well?"

"Oh, it went very well," she says. "I thought it wouldn't, that this is why they made me come in person. But I was wrong. It was opposite. She's alive. My daughter," she exults, "is *alive*."

Teresa has just finished her entree, a saddle of rabbit with buckwheat, walnuts, and carrot puree, when she looks out the window. It's an oddity of contemporary Zakopane that its most elegant new restaurant stands right across Krupowki from a peasant kitsch place—the kind of establishment where hams and farm implements hang on the walls and a spitted pig roasts perpetually. For a moment, she can't believe her eyes. "Hey," she tells Roman. "Quick. Take a look." She points across the street.

He hasn't got his glasses on, so there's nothing to do but squint. "Is that Bogdan?"

"It sure is. Do you see who's with him?"

"It's not Elena, is it?"

"It most assuredly is." She watches the door close behind her brother, who politely held it open for his companion.

Their waiter is just passing, so she taps his arm, and when he turns to her with ill-masked annoyance, she orders herself a Pour Moi and, for her companion, a double Ballantine's.

Roman watches the waiter walk away, then looks at her and laughs. "You didn't think maybe you ought to wait and see if I wanted something different? Since you're paying, I might've preferred a twenty-year-old single malt."

"I knew you'd ask for Scotch," she says, "and it's the only one I can remember the name of right now."

"What's our hurry?"

No one, not even Roman, knows how her brother's fate troubles her. Such a sweet man, he never did anybody any harm until his business losses dragged him down. She would have helped. All he needed to do was ask. He's been alone for years, and his marriage was not good. "I want to celebrate," she says, "before he turns back into a pumpkin."

IN THE venue on the far side of Krupowki, the tables are wooden slabs balanced on sawed-off stumps. A folk ensemble is playing up front, but the place is full this evening, and you can't hear the music very well over the raised voices. Behind Elena, mounted in the corner, there's a flat-screen TV. The businessman running for the American presidency must have insulted somebody again. He's pointing a finger at the camera and snarling.

Their waiter is decked out in embroidered woolen pants and a sheepskin vest, a halberd suspended from his sash. Bogdan orders them each a big mug of *herbata po goralsku*—tea the mountain way, laced with vodka.

After all this time, it feels strange and wonderful to be together with a woman in a bar. For years, he assumed it would never happen again, that he shouldn't even let himself hope for it, that it was about as likely as the reappearance of the powdered *oranzada* he loved as a child.

When their drinks come, he props his elbows on the table and leans forward. "So tell me," he says. "You promised."

The glow that graced her face back in Krakow has dimmed a bit, but it's not entirely gone. "I don't know do you really want to hear it. It's not pretty."

"I do. And by the way, my story's not pretty either."

"I know. You went to jail."

"How'd you find that out?"

She shrugs and mentions the name of another waitress at the pension. "She told me, but it don't matter. I've seen worse places than prison."

Strictly speaking, so has he. But the evening's not about him. "Go on," he says. "Please."

Her husband was a mechanic. He worked a long time for someone else. They saved. One day he opened his own shop. Their son worked with him, and before long they'd built a solid clientele. They could fix any car: Russian, Japanese, German, it didn't matter. If they couldn't buy the parts, they'd invent them. She once walked in there and found an enormous green thing suspended from the post-lift. It looked like a tank.

"An American Ford Galaxy," she says. "Made in the 1970s. Nobody ever saw such a vehicle in Luhansk. I asked him who it belonged to, and he said it was owned by a Polish man who love America's things and was driving in this terrible car from Warsaw through Belarus, Ukraine, Georgia, Turkey, then back up through Bulgaria and Romania, taking pictures of people and landmarks in all those countries. This was before the war came, but I still thought what he was doing was stupid. That car was old and unusual, and if it hadn't been for my husband, probably can't nobody fix it."

Unfortunately, while her husband loved working on cars and would get excited talking about throttle linkages, their son took no pleasure in his job at the garage. He couldn't figure out what to do with himself. Nobody would pay you for doing what he loved, which was to sit on his bed and watch YouTube videos. As far as she could tell, it didn't necessarily matter what the videos were. She got hold of his computer once and went through his recent browsing history, and she found all sorts of items: sure, he watched a little pornography, and that bothered her, but he didn't have a girlfriend, and that's what boys do. He watched a lot of music videos, too, terrible-sounding stuff by loud bands that jumped around a lot onstage, shrouded in smoke of various colors. He watched cartoon clips. His favorite seemed to be about a ghost called Casper.

"Can you imagine that? Cartoons are for children, and somebody invents one that stars a ghost?"

In the summer of 2012, when Ukraine and Poland cohosted the Euro Cup, he went to see one of the matches in Donetsk, and though he said he'd be back that night, he wasn't. They didn't see him again for two days, during which she was frantic. The match had been played against the British team, and everyone knew their fans' reputation for rowdy behavior. Serhiy was a mild-mannered boy, but maybe after Ukraine lost, he'd said the wrong thing at the wrong time.

It seems ludicrous now, some of the things she worried about. He met a few people at the football match, and they went out afterward for drinks. Donetsk was twice the size of Luhansk, it had all kinds of clubs. He spent the first night carousing in one after another, and somebody let him crash on their sofa. The next morning, he was too hungover to go home, worried about facing his parents, so he stayed and did it again. He should've been worried too, because when he returned after missing two days' work, her husband was livid. He was a big man, much larger than Serhiy. He'd been drinking that night, which unfortunately was how he'd always dealt with his worries. She was on her knees in the bedroom praying when she heard the door open. The next thing she knew, there was a loud crash.

"It sounded like a gun," she said. "Like today when the tractor driver threw something on our car."

Her husband had hurled the son he adored against the wall.

The picture of her grandfather saluting General Zhukov in Berlin was dislodged, the glass shattering when the frame smacked the floor. She ran into the living room and found him straddling Serhiy, hitting his face hard, alternating hands while their son did his best to shield himself.

"The next day," she said, "rather than go to work at the garage, Serhiy decides he'll join the army. I begged him not to, because he hadn't been conscripted. But he told me he can't never work for his father again."

Listening to her story is like watching an impending train wreck in one of those old American Westerns. The camera cuts from one locomotive to the other and back again, and the audience knows they're bound for destruction. The engineer in one of them is dead, slumped over the throttle with an arrowhead in his heart. You can't do a thing in the world but wait for the crash.

"So off he goes to the army," she says. "People do it. Everybody in my family. My grandfather, my father. All my uncles. Every one of them lived to be old. But Serhiy don't. The war comes. And Serhiy goes."

You can't let a statement like that glide by without posing the obvious question. If the person you're talking to chooses not to answer, it's her business. Then you honor the silence. "What happened to your son?" he asks.

She says a missile hit the armored vehicle he was riding in. "Some say it was the separatists, some say it was the Russians." She shrugs, her eyes dry as stones. "Me, I say once it's shot, a missile's got its own mind. It took the top off his vehicle, and the ammunition they were carrying blew up. Everybody else burned to death, but Serhiy was thrown into the air. He caught on some kind of high-voltage wire. And for days they let him hang there. You may've seen the picture. It's on YouTube too. At last my boy got his own video."

His eyes look away from her, at the TV set she saw when they walked in. Until now, the only people she's told about her son were officials of one sort or another: border police, embassy personnel. At the refugee center in Warsaw, where others had their own troubles, some perhaps as bad as hers or even worse, nobody passed them around. Why she's chosen to tell this particular man, she doesn't know. Maybe because after she shared the good news about her daughter, he cared enough to ask how she came to be where she is. He told her he'd heard her footsteps every night. He knew what that kind of walking meant.

But now he's embarrassed. Confronting another's grief is almost always embarrassing, because you know something about them that you shouldn't. Whether they've told you themselves is beside the point. It's as if their skin has been peeled away, revealing their internal organs, their bowels full of decaying matter.

The thing is, he did see the photo: it was in *Gazeta Wyborcza*, on the front page, if he recalls correctly, the soldier draped over the power cables, his pants bunched at his ankles, his shirt and jacket hanging over his head and shoulders, his bloated corpse gleaming as if lit from inside. He remembers thinking that if that had been his son, he could not have faced another day.

Is the loss of one child balanced by the discovery that the other is still alive, that if things go well, she'll join her mother here or someplace else? A conductor for Ukrainian Rail, she was trapped in Debaltseve when the Russian-sponsored insurgency gained control. For more than a year, Elena told him on the drive back, she'd received no news of her despite repeatedly contacting the embassy. Then last night, they called and asked her to go to the Krakow consulate. She thought she'd be told her daughter was lost too. Instead, she learned she's been hospitalized in Mariupol. God knows how she's suffered, but she's alive.

He can't look away from her forever. "And your husband," he asks, "what happened to him?"

She says that one day after the fighting started, some men came to the garage and told him they needed his help. They knew he could fix anything, and they wanted him to repair some military equipment. One of them was a man her husband had known all his life, an ethnic Russian. He'd worked on this man's car; they got along. "This was after we lost our Serhiy," she says. "Did these people know it? I think not. They didn't tell who he was when they showed the picture on TV. They didn't put his name in the paper either. It was like he was everybody, but because he was everybody, he was also nobody.

"Would they have asked my husband this question if they knew who that was they'd seen hanging off the wire? Maybe yes, maybe no. But if no, it would've been because my husband was a big man, with a big wrench in his hand. It would've been because they were scared he would hurt them rather than being scared they would hurt him. And they would've been right, because for a man his size, he could move fast, and he hit that man whose car he worked on, he hit him hard across the head with that big wrench. He split this man's head open. He wasn't going to drive that car for a while.

"The other men, they left carrying their friend. I know they did, because my husband called and told me. And he told me he might not see me again, that when it got dark and he closed the shop and started for home, something might happen. And he said if it did, I had to leave, and that if it didn't, both of us would have to leave now anyway, that we should have left weeks ago. He said for me to call our daughter and tell her we need to go, so I did what he advised, though I already knew what our daughter would say: that she couldn't, because she had her own life, her own guy, and he couldn't leave because, like Serhiy, he'd gone to the army.

"In his life, my husband was wrong about many things, and I must admit that after what happened to Serhiy, I had made up my mind to leave him. I told myself that when things get normal again, I'm gonna sit down with him and explain my reasons, so it wouldn't be sneaky, it would just be what it was. But unfortunately, he was not wrong about the last thing he ever told me. I never did see him again, not alive I didn't. Somebody shot him before he walked a block.

"For a long time, the only thing I could think of to be glad for was that he never knew I was planning to desert him. But now I'm glad our daughter is alive. And I'm glad you asked me to tell you what you called my 'story.' I never knew a story could kill nobody, but sometimes it seemed like mine would kill me." She finishes her spiked tea. "That's what I was trying to walk away from," she says, "on all those nights when I made your ceiling sigh. But I guess we can't walk away from our story, can we? We can't do nothing but tell it."

He signals their waiter for another round. Then, without giving himself time to think it over, he begins to tell her his.

TERESA OWNS a small villa, and for a good while now, she's been living there with Roman, granting him, as he likes to joke, provisional permanent residence. It's only a block from the older of her two Zakopane pensions, the one where her brother stays.

It's snowing when she and Roman start home. Bogdan is still in the farm kitsch place with Elena. There's only one way out— through the front door—and they haven't taken it.

When she and Roman reach her villa, she tells him to go on inside, that she needs to continue down the street and check on a few things in the office. He offers to accompany her, but she says that's not necessary, and he doesn't protest. She's got him trained.

Their situation, vis-à-vis each other, is satisfactory. This has been a surprising development. A decade ago, she hired him to wash dishes.

At the pension, she finds a few guests sitting near the fireplace, having drinks and swapping lies about their prowess on the slopes. She has firm rules: no alcohol downstairs after ten o'clock, which has come and gone. As she passes, she glances at her watch. They're clearing out before she unlocks the office.

It's at the foot of the stairs. She goes inside and sits down at her desk but leaves the lamps off. Otherwise, a strip of light would be visible. She knows it would because she saw it one evening back in the late '90s, and when she entered to turn them out, she found a newly hired waitress at her computer stealing the guests' personal info. You can't be too careful whom you trust.

She trusts Bogdan, and she's come to trust Elena. More importantly, she would entrust Bogdan *to* Elena, though she didn't realize that until this evening, when she saw them together on Krupowki. There's a certain steadiness about the Ukrainian woman; you can see it in the way she handles plates and saucers, cups and glasses. She understands how easy it is to break things.

They don't come back and they don't come back, and it gets later and later. Finally, Teresa hears the front door opening, followed by the sound of soft voices. They linger in the foyer for a moment, then start upstairs. When their footsteps stop, she cracks her door and listens, her forehead pressed against the wood.

Here is what he will always remember:

She pauses on his landing rather than continuing up the stairs toward her room, where he had hoped they would go together. There's a single light here, a wall-mounted lamp that matches those on all the other landings. Three or four years ago, a drunken Latvian grabbed it as he was about to fall, as if something so flimsy could save him, and the light came free, pulling a chunk of wall with it. Bogdan replastered and toggle-bolted it up there. It won't come down again. Because he can think of nothing else to say as they stand there facing each other, and because something needs to be said, he points at the light and tells her that he put it there himself. He tells her about the Latvian, how apologetic he was, how the next morning, as he sat in the dining room, contemplating a breakfast he was too ill to eat, he saw Teresa bearing down on him.

"He was a tough-looking guy," he hears himself tell Elena. "If I'd seen him coming toward me in a dark alley, I would have taken off running. Which is exactly what he did when he saw my sister. He threw his napkin on the table and jumped up so fast his chair went over backward." The last part is made up, invented there on the landing to help both of them through an awkward moment that he now knows will not end the way he'd dared imagine it might. How could you tell the things they've told each other tonight and do anything more than seek the silence of your own room? Nobody in his right mind would think otherwise.

The problem is, there's a serious flaw in the story he's just made up, which should conclude with the big Latvian racing out the dining hall's rear entrance to escape Teresa's wrath. The flaw is that the dining hall has no rear entrance. It's a single long room, with a doorway that leads into the living room, which is where Teresa would have come from. The only other door leads to the kitchen, but the kitchen has no rear entrance either, which Elena knows all too well, since she spends a good part of her days in there and part of her evenings too.

While he's trying to imagine some graceful way out of this narrative conundrum, Elena wraps her arms around him, the top of her head grazing his chin. "Make me love," she says.

In the remains of the Tatra winter comes a flowering. Neither announced nor denied, the shift in his standing with Elena is understood by his sister and Roman, by the desk clerks and cleaning women and the other waitresses, who regard the interloper with rigid smiles. The one who'd told her of Bogdan's term in jail had recognized the potential entanglement from the outset. That was why she had passed on news of his sketchy past. Though he would not suspect it, she'd fancied him herself. He reminds her of her grandfather, perhaps the only other man she's ever known who never behaves like a lout. Overall, she holds a higher opinion of draft horses.

After breakfast, when Bogdan drives departing guests to the station, Elena sometimes rides along. The pension serves only breakfast and supper, and once the kitchen is squared away, she has several hours to herself. They often park the van at the foot of Krupowki and visit the farm stalls. Most days, at least two or three breeders are offering St. Bernard puppies.

He broached the possibility of buying a dog the afternoon his sister picked him up from the correctional facility. She said absolutely not. The codes governing B&Bs require special permits, she told him, and she didn't need the hassle. Still, he loves to stop by the stalls and play with the puppies. At first, the breeders considered him a nuisance, because it quickly became apparent he'd never buy. But over time, their attitude toward the aging man with the ugly mole has softened. As one of them observed to a competitor, "Dogs like him, and that's usually a good sign. Most of my dogs are smarter than I am, and all of yours are smarter than you."

One March morning, when it's unseasonably warm and snowmelt has turned everything soggy, Elena stands watching him as he kneels on a tarp, letting one of the furry creatures slobber on his palm. It seems every boy wants a dog—Serhiy did, but they always told him no—and in certain ways every man is still a boy. She has thought a lot about this lately and is convinced that the obverse is not true. There is none of the girl left in her. There is none left in most women she knows.

Some of Bogdan's boyhood passed when he crushed that dog's skull. Much more of it passed when he panicked and ran back to the car and left that man and his family to die. He didn't know he was carrying that boyhood around with him; this much was clear to her when he told her in the bar about all that had happened. His innocence was touching, it was maddening, it was somehow right and wrong at once that a man could reach the age he must have been when he committed these bad acts and still carry a boy around inside.

He rolls the puppy onto its back and pats its pink belly. "You'll be a big one," he says. He clasps one of its forepaws like he's sealing a business deal. "Look at the size of these paws," he says to no one in particular. "He'd make a great rescue dog."

In the bar, she asked if he prayed to God about what had happened, and he said no, he didn't believe in God. He said it apologetically, as if he feared it would offend. He must have heard her praying at night and would naturally have assumed she was pious, when in truth she was anything but. She prayed because she was scared, the same reason she drank and walked the floor until she fell in upon herself. Now that she knew her daughter was alive, she had quit. When all the addition and subtraction were done, God was still in the red with her.

She'd asked Bogdan what he would say if he ever met the wronged American face to face. He couldn't answer. He could only bow his head. That was when she knew that no matter what he claimed, he believed in the god he didn't pray to. In one way or another, she thought, most people do. Her grandfather was a Communist. He prayed three times a day.

Finally, Bogdan said, "I'll never see him again. I don't even know if he's still alive. His reports no longer appear in the paper. They haven't for years."

"You still ought to know what you would say," she said. "For your own understanding. You couldn't just stare at him. You couldn't run away again."

"What could I say? 'Sorry' is too small a word."

"It may be small, but it's a good place to start."

"Elena?" For the first time, he addressed her by name. "If the man who shot the missile at your son told you he was sorry, what would *you* say?"

"I would say to him that he was some other woman's son. I would say all day long if I have to, and maybe I would have to."

"What good would saying it do?"

"What good not saying it would do when somebody lays his 'sorry' down before you?" She could tell from his facial expression that her Polish had just failed her. Yet she continued. "What good it would do," she said, "to keep an angry air?"

Bogdan quits playing with the dog he can't buy because his sister won't let him. "Well," he says, "we'd better be getting home." When they leave, the puppy tries to follow, but the breeder grabs him by the scruff of the neck.

Driving back to the pension, he asks if she saw the news this morning from Donetsk: Nadezhda Savchenko, the Ukrainian pilot accused in the deaths of two Russian journalists, has been sentenced to twenty-two years. Apparently, the trial was a mockery, the judge taking two days to read the decision, during which time Savchenko periodically broke into Ukrainian folk song and shot her finger at the court.

"No," she says, turning away from him, looking out the window at a group carrying their ski gear toward the lift. "But then I wasn't searching for news either. I already got the only news that matters."

Two days ago, she finally spoke to her daughter. Last year, during the shelling of Debaltseve, she suffered severe shrapnel wounds. Her surgery, the doctors said, lasted fourteen hours. In frigid weather, with poor sanitary conditions and untreated water, she developed viral hepatitis. Her weight dropped to thirty-eight kilos. She's regained some of her strength, but now she has chronic hypertension and elevated blood sugar. Elena says her health will probably never be good again, though she used to be a robust girl.

He rarely mentions the war to her, and when he does, it's usually at night, when they're together in his bed—he has not been inside her room since the time he went to check on her radiator. She comes to him each evening around ten thirty, fully clothed, the nightgown he bought her rolled up and tucked away beneath her sweater.

In the dark, she's different, the stiffly starched daytime persona replaced by something soft. Rather than the explosive, even angry lover he might have expected, she's slow and probing, each move tentative, as if subject to revision. Her voice changes too, its timbre, its texture. Especially when she speaks her own language. Some of it he understands. Some of it he doesn't.

"Will you ever go back?" he asked the other night, after she talked to her daughter. He lay on his back, her head resting on his chest.

"No," she said, "I won't never."

"Not even if the war ends?"

"No. It's not home anymore."

"You must've had friends."

"Some died. Some that didn't might as well have. They won't be alive the same way they were."

A novel and not altogether unpersuasive notion: that there were different ways of being alive, as opposed to different ways of living. He resisted the urge to ask that she expound. It might not sound as viable the second time around.

The other thing he resists is thinking too much about the future. He does not take it as a given that she will keep appearing outside his door, even though it's been happening for several weeks. He regards her company as a gift, one that he does not deserve but will gladly accept as long as it's offered.

On nights when they don't feel like making love, they drink a shot or two of vodka, lie there, and talk. When she asks about Krysia, he answers all her questions. No, he doesn't hate her girlfriend. Yes, they're doing well: he knows that from Marek. They own their own salon now, and from what he's heard, you have to make an appointment a couple of weeks in advance. She asked him about Marek. He suffered a heart attack last year, he told her, and he and Inga have moved to a smaller flat, in a not-so-great building, but whenever he sees them, they seem cheerful. They dote on their grandkids.

Once, she asked him if he'd ever slept with his friend's wife. He said no but that the night he got out of jail to await trial, after having a lot to drink, they'd fooled around while Marek snored in the next room.

"Did you feel evil about it?"

"I felt evil while I was doing it. I think maybe that was part of the pleasure."

"And what about afterward?"

"No, I didn't. I mean, compared to other things I've done, it seemed kind of minor. But I would've hated it if Marek found out."

"What happens when you see this woman now?"

"Sometimes she winks at me. And I wink back."

"That's good," she said. "It's the correct way to behave."

"Why'd you ask me about her?"

"I was curious. The way you talked about her told me."

"Told you what?"

"That there was something about her you valued a lot. How solid she was, like a German monument."

He ran his hand over her shoulders. He'd found supple languor rather than the angularity he'd expected. "Did you ever do anything like that?"

"I did twice. A long time back."

"By twice, you mean two different affairs?"

"No, I mean twice one night. Same man both times. It was worse than what you did. We was not just clowning around. For several hours, we was very serious."

"And then?"

"The sun shined on us. Don't it always?"

He asked if overall her marriage had been a good one.

"Overall? It was not so bad. I knew him since I was four years old. I knew everything about him."

"What was one thing you knew that nobody else did?"

"He brush his teeth with hot water."

"I've never heard of anything like that. Why'd he do it?"

"You know, I never wondered about it till . . . well, till after what happened, which is when you start over the stuff that don't matter to anyone else. His teeth looked nice, but I think he must have had some of those holes in them."

"Cavities?"

"Cavities. And so maybe cold water hurt them. Such a big man, he wasn't scared of much, but he was fearful of the dentist. Not for nothing would he go."

Morning came. *Don't it always?*

She never sets the alarm but wakes without fail at five thirty, puts on her jeans and green sweater, and leaves him to sleep alone for another hour. At breakfast, when she serves him, she behaves like he's nobody special. Maybe he is. Maybe he's not.

He parks the van, and they climb out and start across the slippery parking lot toward the pension. He knows that if he doesn't rush to keep up, she will get ahead of him. Wherever they might be, she walks with greater purpose than he does. She always seems to know exactly where she's going. Whereas he knows only where his next step will fall.

The main street in the Hudson Valley town where Richard has lived since 2012 is lined on both sides by restaurants, cafés, and antique stores—more than twenty of the latter, by his own count, a new one having opened just last week. Lots of people from the city come here on weekends, some of them because they own properties like the one he rents from a young literary agent, some because they can't stand the pace another moment and have to get away for a couple of days or go crazy. There's no hotel in town, but it's the Airbnb capital of New York state. On Fridays and Saturdays, if you haven't made a dinner reservation, you can't get a table anywhere.

There are plenty of choices here for breakfast, which he nearly always eats out. He does this because mornings are still sometimes tough, and though he likes to start his days slowly and does not necessarily want to run into friends from the strange little college where he works, he does want to hear voices, see people moving around. If he eats breakfast at home, it's far too easy to remain there all morning, and if he remains there all morning, he might remain there all day. For this reason, he always requests an eleven o'clock class, but he almost never gets one. The students who are drawn to this particular school are artsy types who love the nightlife and may not go to bed until dawn. Classes before noon don't draw, even if you're as popular as he is.

Today he chooses a café that offers twenty-five or thirty different types of crepes and has a vintage sign motif. Only one table is free, and it's right in front, with a perfect view of the street. His predecessor left behind a copy of the *Times*. After the waiter takes his order, he picks up the paper.

Sipping coffee, he scans the articles about the current presidential campaign, which has become one of the most ludicrous in history, featuring references to penis size and menstruation, along with nude photos of one candidate's spouse. With greater interest, he reads a piece about the new Polish government, whose defense minister has suggested forming paramilitary squads to keep the country safe. These organizations, the minister says, could draw their membership from gun clubs and football "associations"— presumably allowing soccer hooligans to subject the rest of society to the beatings they typically inflict on one another. It sounds like the Brown Shirts. More than twenty-five years of progress have been wiped out in a matter of months, and it's hard not to wonder how Julia would react if she still lived there, whether she would have it in her to fight those battles all over again.

When he turns to the sports section, his attention is grabbed by a small item under "NFL Notes":

> *Nick Major, the former head coach at Central California, has been hired as a consultant by the Baltimore Ravens. Major will work with the offensive coordinator Mike Brown and advise the scouting department. Last year, Major was quarterback coach at the University of Louisville. Previous stops in his coaching career include Texas Tech, where he was offensive coordinator, Northern Iowa, Montana State, New Mexico*

and West Virginia. His only prior NFL experience came in 2013, when he served as tight ends' coach in Cincinnati. In 2009, a season in which he was involved in a sex scandal, Major's Central California team earned the right to play for the national championship, losing to LSU. He was fired the following year after a 4-8 finish.

"Excuse me, sir?"

He looks up to find the waiter hovering over him with his food, so he folds the paper and lays it aside.

ALONG WITH almost everybody else in Fresno, a city that seethed because the *Sun* had blackened its limelit moment, he watched that championship game. He viewed it in the safety of his own living room, with the curtains closed—not because he had much, if anything, to fear but because he was watching it with Maria, who'd seen trash strewn across her yard, found graffiti painted on her car, and just the week before received several death threats. She'd spent the previous couple of nights at his place, sleeping in the bed occupied until recently by Franek.

The game started badly for UCC. They trailed by fourteen at the end of the first quarter, twenty-four at the half. The final score, 45-7, could have been a lot worse had LSU not pulled most of its starters early in the final period. "Well," Maria said from the opposite end of the couch, "so much for a national title, huh? I guess that's my fault too."

A few weeks earlier, they'd watched Nick Major stand behind a podium while flashbulbs popped and the largest press contingent he'd ever faced scribbled furiously as he admitted that the *Sun*'s allegations were true: he'd conducted a "brief but improper relationship" with a woman whose name he never mentioned, and a member of the police department had subjected him to blackmail. His family stood behind him. His wife looked drugged, his son seemed excited to be onstage, and his daughter's face resembled nothing so much as a piece of raw meat. She'd clearly been crying for days. Following Major's brief statement, the athletic director announced that because of the coach's lapse in judgment, he would be suspended for the final two games of the regular season, contests against Air Force and San Jose State that the team stood no chance of losing. They would address the postseason, he said, at the proper time.

Maria was still Maria. True, at the press conference, where Richard hadn't sat next to her but kept his eye on her, she'd swallowed hard every time she'd glanced at Major's daughter. But she'd shown no adverse effects at the arraignments of Joe and Cloris Garcia. There, she'd looked quite pleased, her vilification notwithstanding.

After the game ended, he got up and switched off the TV. "You want another beer?" he asked.

She shook her head. "I don't think so. You don't happen to have any cigarettes, do you?"

"Afraid not. I didn't know you smoked anything except weed."

"Normally, I don't. You wouldn't have any of that, would you?"

"As it so happens," he said, "I do."

He went into the kitchen, opened the drawer where he kept the silverware, and removed one of the joints Franek had had the presence of mind to turn over in the airport parking lot the day he'd flown home. Richard didn't know why he'd held on to them or why he'd hidden them in the same spot where Maria kept her own.

He walked back into the living room and handed her the joint. She lit it and offered it to him.

He declined. "It doesn't agree with me."

"Seems like a lot of things don't."

Until a couple of days ago, he hadn't seen much of her since she'd broken her story. In the aftermath, she'd understandably stayed busy. ESPN had interviewed her several times, her photo had appeared in *Sports Illustrated*, and she'd been quoted in pieces that ran in the *New York Times*, the *Washington Post* and *USA Today*. He'd quoted her himself, in a bland article that made no mention of his own role. She hadn't acknowledged it either, but then, he'd asked her not to.

She brought it up that night, though, after three or four deep drags on the joint. She still hadn't quite disengaged, though she would because she would have to. He'd seen to that.

"You know you're not going to be able to keep doing this, don't you?" she asked.

He considered pretending that he didn't know what "this" was. Maybe she'd choose not to spell it out, thereby saving both of them the embarrassment. On the other hand, why should she feel any embarrassment? She hadn't done anything embarrassing.

"I could probably keep getting by for a while," he said.

"You probably could. But you shouldn't. It's not . . ."

"It's not what, Maria?"

She drew her legs up under her. He thought she was probably the last woman he'd ever make love to, if you could call what they'd done at her place making love, and maybe you could. He'd enjoyed holding her after she fell asleep, the warmth of her body against his own. The next morning, he'd stood at the foot of her bed a long time, looking at her placid face, her red hair spread out on a sky-blue pillow. Then he'd walked into the kitchen, made coffee, and prepared to wreck their chances.

"It's not worthy of you," she said. "You ought to step aside and let somebody do the job right. If it had been strictly up to you, this story might not have gotten told."

"That's true. And then we wouldn't have seen Major's wife and daughter standing up there looking gut-shot, and Cloris Garcia would still be taking care of sick children, and Jacinta Aguilera and her whole family would still be dead."

Before the last words were out of his mouth, he knew that for the rest of his life, however long that slog might take, he'd regret having spoken them. Things should not end the way they would now have to.

She dropped the joint into her beer bottle, put her shoes on, stood up, and grabbed her coat. "I'm going home," she said. "If somebody shoots me in my sleep, better call one of your younger colleagues to come up and write the story. Unless, of course, your paper will agree to ignore it."

THREE MONTHS later, at the age of fifty-one, he took the buyout, joining the ranks of the unemployed.

He had enough money to make it for a good while, so he hired a gardener to look after the lawn, then locked the house and drove away. Normally, he would have given the key to Bob Lyons, but both Bob and Sue were angry at him for letting Franek break Sandy's heart. He did his best to explain, telling them that during his brother-in-law's gall bladder operation, the surgeon had noticed lesions on his liver that turned out to be malignant, and that his son had to go home. But Bob would not be mollified. "If a kid showed up next door, broke your daughter's heart, and then high-tailed it," he said, "you wouldn't give a shit about the whys or wherefores."

When he left, he drove up the coast, with no particular destination in mind. He stopped for one night in Lincoln, Oregon, where they'd rented a cottage near the beach the year Anna started school. Then he found himself in Anacortes and took the ferry to Orcas Island. They'd stayed there for ten days in the summer of 2001. To his surprise, he could not locate the house. Things looked the same, but he knew where nothing was.

He wandered through Idaho and Montana. In Butte, once among the most polluted towns anywhere and home to the world's tallest slag heap, he stumbled across something that piqued his interest: the Butte Academy of Beauty Culture, *Where Students Learn to Earn*. He wrote a travel piece of sorts—gently mocking but not without uplift—that plumbed the incongruities. It ran in the *Guardian* and served as a template.

Over the next couple of years, he drove from one small town to another, staying in motels and B&Bs, eating in diners, seldom remaining anyplace very long, returning home only occasionally and rarely for more than a week. He kept himself busy writing colorful articles. For the *New Yorker*, he wrote a funny one called "The Mores of Moore County" about the dry county in Tennessee where Jack Daniels is distilled. He explored new beer-canning technologies, the use of skimmers in ATMs, the disappearance of independently owned truck stops, Elvis's eating habits. For *Boston Magazine*, he wrote about a fretted instrument shop in his hometown where the owner wore earplugs to muffle the sounds produced by inept guitarists.

It was on a trip to Massachusetts, one of several he made to visit his father before his death, that his old BU classmate Alex Veranakis called and invited him out for a drink. They met in a bar in Framingham, about halfway between his dad's place on the North Shore and Alex's home in Worcester. Each of them could barely recognize the other. Alex, who'd been darkly handsome in college, was bald and rotund, his vast belly making it impossible to tell if he wore a belt or not. Richard still had plenty of hair, but he weighed at least thirty pounds less than he had in school.

The conversation began, as he'd feared it might, with a question about Maria. Did Richard know she'd gotten married? He did, though he pretended not to. By that time, she'd been at the *Post* for eighteen months, and he'd read most if not all of her articles. He knew where she lived, the name of her husband.

"She's done all right, hasn't she?" Alex said.

"She's done better than all right."

"She told me a little bit about her time out there."

"Yeah. Well . . ."

"I'm not trying to butt in. But I know she'd be happy to hear from you if you ever wanted to get in touch. She gives you a lot of credit. That story about the football coach really made her career take off, and she says you handed it to her."

"That's not exactly right."

Alex stirred his drink. He'd ordered something called a Bourbon Daisy. "It's not exactly what I wanted to talk to you about either." He told Richard that, like him, he was quitting the newspaper business. Any day now, the *Morning Journal* would be sold, he said, and he didn't intend to stick around waiting to be let go. He asked if Richard had ever heard of Aarden College.

He had, but he didn't know precisely where it was, just that it was one of those slightly odd schools that artsy misfits used to think of attending back in the late '70s. "Yeah," he said. "Why?"

"Well, they don't have anything resembling a journalism department. They don't have an English department either, or a drama department. They've got something called the Institute of Narrative Arts, which packs all kinds of 'storytelling' under the same colorful umbrella. They once offered a course called 'Transgressive Writing' that wasn't a thing in the world but porn. The school's got three thousand students, and seven hundred of them major in Narration. I shit you not—that's what it'll say on their diplomas. You ever heard of anything like that?"

"I can't say that I did."

"Me either." He said that the director of the Institute had just retired and that he'd been hired to replace her. "The school's got a new president who wants to move in a little more practical direction, so rather than an academic, the board chose me. I'm going to revamp their journalism and mass comm offerings. We'll have courses in media entrepreneurship, blogging, fashion writing, foody writing, music writing, and so on. You see where this is going, right?"

"I'm not sure."

"Sure, you're sure. If I can turn you into a stone, I can kill a lot of birds. Since you started this magazine stuff, you've become versatile. It's pretty damn impressive, the way you've adapted."

The idea that anyone would think he'd adapted to anything was so much at odds with how he saw himself that he downed his Bushmills and signaled for a second. When he recovered the power of speech, he said, "Alex, I don't even have a graduate degree."

Alex laughed. "Richard, they've got people teaching at this school who probably don't even have a high school degree. But here's the thing: most of them are plenty damn accomplished. Journalism and mass comm are wrecks right now, but they've got a poet who won the National Book Award and a social historian who was a finalist for the Pulitzer. Most of the students score high enough to go to Ivy League schools if they wanted, but they don't want to, bless their iconoclastic little hearts. I met a bunch of them when I went there for my interview, and to my surprise, I fucking loved them. There's plenty to be said for hanging around young people when you start to get old."

He said the school didn't operate on the traditional tenure model. It gave faculty four-year contracts, perpetually renewable pending satisfactory performance. The pay wasn't bad, and you got full health and dental coverage as well as membership in a gym. "It also offers tuition to the children of faculty, but of course, that wouldn't pertain in your case. You'd have to fill out an application, but they've given me carte blanche to hire whoever the hell I want to. You wouldn't even need to interview. So what do you say, Richard? Interested?"

He promised to think it over, but initially the idea held scant appeal. He ranked academics somewhere slightly below copy editors and just above the extended news desks that had sprung up in the digital era to rewrite reporters' articles off and on all day.

That night, he woke at three a.m. to the smell of frying fish. His father followed nothing even resembling a schedule. It had probably been that way ever since he was widowed. When he got hungry, he ate. When he got tired, he went to bed, though how much he slept was open to question. All his friends were dead. The only person he saw on a regular basis was the woman who brought him groceries each Friday.

This was the logical end, Richard knew, of the way he himself had been living. Unlike his dad, he had some choice in the matter. He could keep driving around the country, doing freelance work, until his eyesight grew so poor he couldn't drive anymore, or the publications he sold his articles to went out of business, or taste changed even more than it already had, or he grew more and more confused so that he didn't know if it was three a.m. or three p.m. and didn't care either. Or he could accept the offer and see if he couldn't put his time to fruitful use. He still knew a few things that might be worth passing on to younger writers, and they might show him a thing or two themselves.

The next morning, he called Alex and told him he wanted the job. A couple of days later, he began the long drive across country, making the trip west for the final time.

THE HOUSE sold the first day it was on the market. Rather than hold a yard sale, he boxed up a few of Anna's things and a few of Julia's, carried them to UPS, and shipped them to Aarden College, then called the Salvation Army to come get the rest. When it was otherwise empty, he loaded his own stuff, locked the door, and got in the car. He sat in the driveway for a couple of minutes, staring at the house. It hadn't been home for years. It would never be home again. He backed out and drove away, reaching Grand Junction, Colorado, before he finally stopped.

He stayed with the Veranakises while he searched for a place. Since he rose earlier than Alex, he ate breakfast with his wife those first few mornings, and because she was a good conversationalist, he started to look forward to it. But he soon found an old nineteenth-century townhouse near the rail station for a reasonable rent, and then he was on his own once again.

The ease with which he adapted to life as a college instructor came as a pleasant surprise. From the beginning, he felt comfortable in the classroom. The classes were small, limited to twelve students, and they were always conducted around seminar tables. No blackboards, no overhead projectors, none of the things he hadn't liked at BU. Aarden eschewed rank and title, so nobody called anybody "professor." Everyone knew him as Richard.

He came up with catchy titles for classes, like "How to Help a

Story Tell Itself." During the first session, he quoted a Rodney Crowell line about learning to listen to the sound of the sun going down. If they wanted to help the story tell itself, he said, they needed to learn how to listen, especially for those things they never expected to hear, because those were nearly always the most interesting.

He taught them to record the smallest details. He told them how in the fall of '89 he'd noticed several people walking around Warsaw with hoops of twine suspended from their necks. "I didn't know what it meant," he said. "Before I got around to asking anybody, here comes a shipment of toilet paper, which had been unavailable for two months due to the consumer shortages plaguing the country, and suddenly people are leaving stores with twenty or thirty rolls hanging off their bodies. That's what the hoops were for."

Nobody took notes, but everybody took note. In one of the classes he taught his second semester, a twenty-year-old junior wrote a piece about the mysterious disappearance of her high school math teacher in a north Texas town. The most gripping thing he'd read in a good while, it needed only minor revisions, which she performed overnight. The editor he sent it to at the *New Yorker* rejected it with an admiring note and a request to see more, but *Harper's* accepted it. The following year, even before she graduated, she had a book contract. She was the first but not the last of his students to experience that kind of success.

Taking stock, which he did from time to time, he concluded that this was the second-best period of his life. In conversation, he would not have chosen the word "happy" to describe himself, because the awareness of loss that hung over his days was sometimes so heavy that it leadened his legs, as if he'd been outfitted with a set of the ankle weights sprinters wore during training. The word he would have used if he'd been queried by one of his new friends, like the poet he often had drinks with, was "engaged." He'd found something worthwhile to do. Several times a week, he walked into a small room and sat down at a table where he was surrounded by bright, talented young people who were nearly always eager to learn what he knew.

THIS MORNING, after finishing his ham and cheese crepes at the Main Street café, he pays for his breakfast and sets off toward campus. While he walks, he thinks about the note in the *Times* and wonders where Nick Major's daughter is today. She would be twenty-one and must be about to graduate from college. A couple of years ago, he started to check to see what he might learn about her online, but he talked himself out of it. It seems strange now, but for most of his life, he didn't worry that the stories he wrote or helped develop might hurt someone else. The only thing that mattered was whether they were true. He shamed drunken drivers, politicians major and minor, an allergist who sedated his female patients, then removed their clothes and photographed their naked bodies; countless drug dealers, crooked financiers, tax cheats; purveyors of child pornography; wife beaters, child molesters, gangbangers, rapists; even one deranged UCC animal husbandry major who sexually assaulted a sheep. If it pained their wives, husbands, mothers, fathers, sons, or daughters to read about them—well, too bad. Somebody has to do it: he'd never deny that. It just won't be him anymore. He still writes the occasional magazine piece and recently published an article about the saxophonist Charles Lloyd, but he's through inflicting collateral damage.

At the Institute, he stops by the mailroom but finds nothing in his box, so he climbs the stairs to the fourth floor. His is the last office on the back side of the building, overlooking a purple Victorian that was once a brothel but is now home to Global Studies. This used to be a source of amusement, but it's been a while since he heard anyone joke about it. Last fall, one of his best students asked if he'd sign her petition to have the program relocated.

Today, when he reaches the top of the stairs, he sees Jarvis James sitting on the floor outside his office. The young man's dreadlocks hang all the way down his back, and his high cheekbones have always made Richard wonder if he has Native American blood. At present, he's the most accomplished writer in any of Richard's classes, one of the two or three best he's had since he came to work here. He's also one of only about a hundred African American kids on campus. "Can I talk to you a little more about grad school?" he asks.

"Sure. Come on in."

His office furnishings are sparse: a framed California Journalism Award hangs on one wall, and he's got two shelves of books, mostly novels and biographies. On his desk, a MacBook Air, a large monitor, and a printer. Also, positioned so that only he can see them, pictures of Anna and Julia.

Last year, the first time Jarvis paid him a visit, he became the only student who ever leaned over, craned his neck, and examined the photos. He asked if they were his wife and daughter. Richard nodded but offered no information. So Jarvis said, "You lost them, didn't you?"

"Yes. But what makes you say so?"

"I don't know. Just an intuition, I guess. Divorce?"

"No. They were killed in an automobile accident."

"Was it long ago?"

"Two thousand six. It happened in Poland. My wife was Polish, and we had an apartment over there. I actually still own it." Later, he wondered why he'd chosen this particular young man, whom he'd known for exactly two weeks, to open up to. Was it solely because he'd posed a question that nobody else, neither student nor faculty, had? He told him how the wreck occurred, that the weather was terrible and that his wife, who was not the best driver, was behind the wheel because he'd had too much to drink. He told him about the man who'd looked at him through the shattered glass, then turned and left them there in the snow. "I can still see his face," he said. "That's really all he was to me. A face. Sometimes . . ." He stopped, aware that he probably should not continue.

"Please," Jarvis said, "go on."

"Sometimes I wonder if he was real, or if my mind made him up." He pushed his chair back and crossed his legs. "I still miss them, my wife and daughter. I'm past the point of grieving every second of every day, though. You can't do it forever. It would kill you."

"I never have lost anybody," Jarvis said. "Both my parents and both sets of grandparents are still alive, all of them living in Cleveland. Even all my aunts and uncles. That'd surprise the hell out of some of my friends here. They figure I grew up without a father and did a lot of crack in the IC."

"They think you did crack in an intensive-care unit?"

Jarvis laughed. "Inner city."

"Ah. I thought our students were a little more enlightened."

"They're enlightened enough to wish those terrible things hadn't happened to me."

That initial conversation meandered on for thirty minutes, the only unfocused talk among the many they'd had, an icebreaker most students didn't desire or require. From that day forward, when Jarvis came to see him, he had something specific in mind, and his concerns were multifarious. Whether or not to use the semicolon when reporting dialogue. How to represent auditory experiences in prose. When to resort to the one-line paragraph. Who was the greater jazz pianist, Tommy Flanagan or Hank Jones? What were his impressions of Joan Didion, James Baldwin, Ta-Nehesi Coates, Thomas Frank? Was he feeling the Bern?

Today, grad school.

"I don't think I'll be ready for it when I graduate," he says. "I've thought about it a good bit since we talked the last time."

"Well, like I told you, I never went myself because I was offered the kind of job I would have gone to grad school hoping to get. Lots of different roads lead to the same location."

"Speaking of location, Richard, I never have gone anywhere outside the U.S. So what I've been considering is getting a TESOL certificate, then trying to land a job teaching English for a year or two someplace in Europe. My pop thinks it's a great idea, that it would be like when the army stationed him in Germany except I'd have a lot more freedom to do as I pleased. What do you think?"

"I'd tell every young person to do some traveling if the chance arises. Any particular country you've got in mind?"

"No. That's what I was hoping you might advise me about."

Richard tells him he'll probably find more teaching opportunities in Eastern Europe and the Balkans than in countries like Germany and France, that there used to be several English-language schools in Krakow, where he still has some contacts, and that if Jarvis would like it, he could make inquiries on his behalf.

"That'd be great, Richard. I'd really appreciate it. I figure it'd be good for my writing to see someplace else and just good for me as a person."

They talk for a while about the election campaign, then Richard nods at the wall clock and says they'd better get going or they'll be late to class.

The seminar room is at the opposite end of the hallway, and the other students are already sitting at the table when they walk in. The author of the piece scheduled for discussion is one of the stronger writers in this group, a quiet young woman named Lee Ann who comes from the place in Pennsylvania where the novelist John O'Hara was born. So far, everything she's written concerns something happening in Pottsville or nearby, and they've had several good conversations in his office about her fascination with her hometown. This semester, she's written about the descendants of various people who inspired the characters in O'Hara's novel *Appointment in Samarra* and about a union protest against local billionaire brewer Dick Yuengling.

Today's piece describes how a young man she went to school with got high one night, committed a petty crime, was caught and fined and suspended from school, and was then ostracized by all his former friends. Though one of the brightest kids in Pottsville, he never went to college. Instead, having no one to turn to anymore, he got himself into much greater trouble and is now serving three to five years at nearby SCI Frackville.

"The Problem with T. G." has some problems of its own. In previous submissions, she carefully evoked the town, noting the stained bedspreads at the Schuylkill Motor Inn, where so many girls lose their virginity; the faded billboards lining Route 61; the many quaintly named businesses, like the Dirty Dog Self-Serve Pet Wash and Boutique. Her new effort, in contrast, conveys little sense of place. And that's only the beginning.

A student from Long Island named Euniss says, "This house that T. G. broke into and took the laptop from? I can't see it. You say it was on Mahantongo Street and that it was a big house, but that's all. What kind of street is this Mahantongo anyway? A big house on one street might mean one thing, on another the exact opposite. And by the way, what kind of laptop was it?"

The only male in the class besides Jarvis says that we need more information about

T. G.'s family. "Right now, the only thing you tell us is that his mom works at the brewery. But what does she do there? I mean, is she working on the bottling line, is she a receptionist, does she run the whole outfit?"

Over the next half hour, numerous other objections are raised. There's not much praise.

Richard likes to keep an eye on the student whose manuscript is under discussion, checking from time to time for signs of distress: red cheeks, clenched teeth. Lee Ann, a small brunette who wears just a touch of eye shadow, looks fine. She's made a note or two on her own copy and keeps nodding as they offer their observations.

Jarvis is down at the far end of the table, where he always sits. So far, he hasn't said anything, which is unusual. When there's a lull, Richard looks at him and says, "What about it, Jarvis? I don't think we've heard from you yet."

He's slow to respond. He turns and looks out the window, as if for once he has nothing to say. "Well," he eventually replies, turning back to the class, "I do have one question."

Euniss is sitting closest to him. "Let's hear it, Jar," she says. She and others have called him that before, and Richard has heard Jarvis, and others too, call Euniss "Unique." These kids all know one another well, and there's a fair amount of playful banter.

"Is T. G. black?" Jarvis says.

"Does it matter?" Euniss asks.

"Sure, it does."

"Why?"

Jarvis pushes his chair away from the table and stands. He's not quite as tall as Richard, but he's a good six feet, slim and graceful. He turns his back to Euniss and takes three or four steps toward the window, then stops. "If you'd been walking along behind me now," he says over his shoulder, "you *could* think I'm a woman because of my hair, though I'd certainly be a tall one." He turns around and retraces his steps until he's standing over her. "But when you see me coming toward you, you know I'm a man. And that has a certain tendency to alter the dynamic."

There's at least one red face in the room right now, and it belongs to Euniss.

Jarvis sits back down. "I looked this town Pottsville up last night," he says. "It's ninety-six percent white, two-point-five percent African American. From what little we're told, it seemed to me that even before T. G. snatched the laptop, the people in Lee Ann's piece were relating to him like he was black. One of the few specifics we're given is how the mother of a girl at his school acts surprised when she opens the door and he shows up for a party. I think she says something like, 'Yes, can I help you?'

"If he's black, and the writer's chosen not to tell us, I'm curious as to why. But whatever the reason is, I think it's a mistake. If his mother's the only family member mentioned, maybe she's the only one he's got. But if she's not, and the writer mentions her, why not mention his father? And why not say where T. G. lives and what his mother does at the brewery? My point is, he's just a big blank for us to fill in. Think how much we learned about the people who protested at the brewery in Lee Ann's last piece. I still remember the heavyset guy with the scraggly red beard who drove the Chevy pickup and got laid off even though his wife was dying of cancer. I remember he lived in a trailer with green-and-white siding, and his wife painted their name on the mailbox in an artsy scroll.

Whereas I don't know if T. G. is six foot three or three foot six, if he's fat or skinny, whether he walked to school, rode a bike, or crawled. We're told he's smart, and we're told he fucked up, and we're told he went to prison. The same could be said of a couple hundred thousand others."

The class has grown still, and nobody is looking at anyone else.

Attached to the manuscript that lies in front of Richard is his own response to Lee Ann's work. The long opening paragraph says something very similar to what Jarvis just said. He began by telling her he knew far too little about T. G., then referred to the woman's reaction when T. G. came to the party. Was he possibly African American? Had he triggered the woman's prejudice, and was this something the piece needed to explore? Even before he stole the computer, Richard wrote, T. G. seemed something of an outsider, and given his excellent academic record and the fact that he was said to be unfailingly kind, his outsider status was puzzling, as was the paucity of physical description, so much at odds with her previous submissions. Just as Jarvis had, he referenced the laid-off worker from the brewery and cited the detail about his wife's artwork on the mailbox as the kind of thing this piece needed a lot more of.

Before he can voice general agreement with the comments that have so far been offered, Lee Ann raises her hand. Normally, the writer whose manuscript is under discussion doesn't respond until after the critique. But this situation is unusual, and her eyes have a watery glint now, so he calls on her.

She addresses Jarvis but doesn't look at him. "You're right. T. G. is black. That's not his real name, though. We were seeing each other for a while. Why I didn't put that and all those other things in, I don't know. The thing is, it never mattered to me that he was black, though it mattered to my parents. It was my mom who opened the door and said, 'Can I help you.' And then, well, the other stuff happened. So this piece was probably a bad idea. It probably makes it look like I think being black is a medical condition."

Richard wishes he could get up, walk around the table, and put his arm around her.

She manages a smile. "I guess," she says, "that I should stick to writing about white people who live in trailers."

HE OFFERS some general comments about the importance of revision, then tells everyone to pass their critiques to Lee Ann. He hands her his and dismisses the class. He's hoping to speak with her afterward, to assure her that even the best writers fall short on occasion, that it's happened to him countless times, but she's the first one out of the room. There are usually three or four people who want to talk to him, but today only Jarvis lingers.

"I wasn't trying to cause a problem," he says. "I like Lee Ann. She's a good writer and a good person."

"You said almost exactly what I did in my written response, Jarvis."

"Yeah, but when you say it, it's one thing. When I say it, it's another." He shakes his head, and for an instant Richard wishes he could hug him too. "They wanted you to tell me to sit down and shut up, Richard. *I* kind of wanted you to tell me to sit down and shut up."

Richard tucks his class folder under his arm and tells him not to worry, that he's done nothing wrong. Leaving the room, he turns off the lights.

Half the students miss the following class, among them Euniss and Lee Ann. They have a lackluster discussion of a piece about a snowless winter in Minneapolis. Nobody submits any more work. Since there's not enough to talk about, he cancels the final session, tells them to leave their revised portfolios in his faculty mailbox, and says he hopes to see them in another class next year. He sends Lee Ann an e-mail asking her to drop by his office, but she never writes back, and when he spots her on the other side of the quad one afternoon and calls her name, she either doesn't hear or pretends not to and keeps going.

The day after graduation, Alex sends a text asking him to come in. Richard responds, saying why don't they meet for a drink instead. Alex replies that this is "work-related" and asks if he can be there at two.

When Richard walks in, Alex gets up and closes the door. His desk is a mess, just as it must have been during his years at the paper. "Take a seat," he says. "We've got a problem. Have you read your student evaluations?"

He hasn't. The only critical comments he ever receives are that his courses are not the best organized, but even those quibbles are rare. Again and again, students say he's the finest instructor they've had since they came here, and everyone says he treats them with respect and always has time for them. "No, I haven't looked at them yet," he says. "Why?"

Eight of the twelve students in that section have written lengthy accounts of what happened when Lee Ann's final piece came up for discussion, most of them saying that they feel that the student who offered the "inappropriate" or "demeaning" or "embarrassing" or "humiliating" critique was guilty of a microaggression. Most of them say that he received favored treatment all semester and that he and the instructor actually entered the classroom together that day and remained there after everyone else had left. Several of them use the phrase "safe space" to describe what they feel was absent during the session. Three, according to Alex, specifically state that they did not feel comfortable returning to the classroom. One of them—most likely Euniss—said that while the author of the piece refuses to make this charge herself, it seems perfectly obvious to her and others that Richard called on this particular student because they had discussed the submission ahead of time. The student voiced almost exactly what Richard wrote on the manuscript he handed back, even using several of the same examples from previous submissions. That the student he called on happened to be African American, the evaluator said, was offensive in and of itself, as if the instructor wanted to appropriate his race to make a point.

"Bottom line, Richard," Alex says, refusing to look at him, as if to do so would shame them both, "is that yeah, overall, your evaluations are fine. Always have been. Even whoever said you appropriated the black kid's race gives you straight fives on everything except the question about whether or not you fostered a safe learning environment. She—I'm assuming it's a she, since nearly all of them are—she says that when it comes to writing, you know more than everybody else on the faculty put together." He waves his hand around the office. "But Jesus Christ, Richard. Don't you know where we are? This is not the fucking newsroom at the goddamn *L.A. Times.* Every time I turn around these days, some student's hollering about a 'microaggression' or a 'safe space' violation."

A few days from now, one morning when he wakes in a calm, contemplative mood and again replays the encounter, Richard will finally entertain the possibility that precisely because Jarvis is black, he should not have called on him, should have let him sit there silently, remaining—insofar as the only black person in a room full of white people can—an invisible man. He will see how both Lee Ann and Euniss could think he set the class up. After all, he and Jarvis did enter and leave together. Yes, his office hours *are* right before class, and he has often walked into the room with other students who visited him and has often left with whichever student or students remained behind to talk to him. But given the combustible nature of this particular session, the students probably wouldn't recall those other instances.

Maybe the truth is that while there are plenty of new perceptions for him to achieve, he's either too old, too tired, or too damaged to process them. For him, the best means would have been through osmosis, by observing and responding to the experiences of his daughter as she aged and reacted to the changing environment. In the natural order of things, she would have graduated two years ago this spring. By now, she would have shared numerous college experiences with him—this is almost certain, though it's certain too that she would have kept others to herself—and he could have considered them over a solitary drink late at night or discussed them with Julia.

In a few days, he will think back over his conversation with

Alex and wish he had handled it differently. He will not mourn the end result, which will seem inevitable, just how it was arrived at. Mistakes will have been made. And he will have been one of the makers.

Today, Alex's heat elicits only a corresponding rise in Richard's temperature. They may not be back in the newsroom, but he behaves as if they are. "Goddamn it, Alex, I called on him because at a certain point, I always call on everybody who hasn't yet *spoken*. That's the way the fucking class *works*. Besides, he's the sharpest kid in the group and says the smartest stuff."

"It didn't occur to you that maybe because he's black himself, you should have been grateful he was keeping his big mouth shut, since all he was likely to do once he opened it was make trouble?"

"You know what, Alex?" he says. "That's a truly disgusting remark. It truly is. I doubt the Office of Diversity and Inclusion would be favorably impressed."

You can see the anger draining out of his longtime friend's face, just as the smugness left Nick Major's all those years ago when he was asked if he'd ever had a drink at the Golden Palomino.

"Ah, shit, Richard," Alex says. "I'm just trying to hang on till sixty-seven. We don't have a whole lot saved. Can you please . . . can you *please* just try to be a little more careful from now on? Don't go in pursuit of truth without regard to cost. I'm asking for my own good as well as yours. I'm asking for the good of all concerned."

He drops his head again, looking at his cell phone. As if he's received one of the many urgent messages he's been getting every day since joining the busy world of academia, he stands, signaling the end of their meeting.

"There's no problem renewing your contract," he says. "I can't find anybody else that can do everything you do. Not to mention somebody else I respect and admire so much. Unfortunately, the school guidelines don't leave me any choice but to report this snafu to HR. My guess is they'll probably make you go to training."

Richard has risen too and was about to leave. Now he stops. "What kind of training?"

Again, Alex looks at his phone. "You know. One of those sessions where they give you simulated situations and teach you what not to do or say."

"Or think?"

Alex never answers. He stands there staring at his cell, this short, bald little man who's hoping to hang on till sixty-seven.

BY THE time he gets home, the heaviness owns him. Feeling it in his arms and legs, his shoulders and hips, he lies down and falls into a deep, unmedicated sleep. When he wakes, it's nearly midnight. He pours himself the first of many drinks, then turns on his laptop, sits down, and writes a resignation letter to Alex Veranakis and the Aarden College Institute of Narrative Arts, thanking them for giving him the opportunity to teach there for the past four years and wishing them and their students much success in the years ahead. He attaches it to an e-mail and hits *send*, marking the end of another chapter.

One fine Saturday in June, Elena says, "I want to take a hike."

Bogdan is not in great condition. True, he's never smoked, and he drinks much less than he used to, but he's fifty-eight years old and hasn't subjected himself to exercise in a long time. He gets winded climbing stairs. He has corns on both feet, and he's run out of those adhesive pads that provide cushion. His knees are swollen. There are plenty of reasons why he hates the thought of a hike—chief among them the indisputable fact that he's always hated hikes and most other forms of exercise as well—but none of them matter. If she wants to take a hike, they will. If she wanted to go for a swim, they would.

Possibilities abound. The two he thinks she would find most rewarding are Dolina Koscieliska, a valley that lies about seven kilometers west of town, where you find broad meadows that offer stunning views of the nearby peaks, and Morskie Oko. The latter is a mountain lake—the name means "Eye of the Sea"—about thirty-five minutes away by car. You have to park at a jumping-off spot and make a strenuous trek to get a view of the lake itself. He did it once with Krysia, and it nearly killed him, though he wasn't yet forty. He hopes Elena will choose Dolina Koscieliska, but she prefers Morskie Oko. She fixes them a picnic lunch, and he puts it and a large bottle of water and a couple of cans of beer in a backpack, and they climb into the van.

They reach the car park at Lysa Polana before noon. The elevation here is around a thousand meters, so it's already a little cooler than it was in Zakopane. He puts on his windbreaker and suggests she do the same. Then he slips the backpack onto his shoulders, and they set off up the asphalt path. It's wide enough to accommodate horse-drawn carriages, and he wishes he could hitch a ride on each one that creaks past loaded with tourists.

The difference in altitude between their starting point and the lake itself is only about four hundred meters. But the grades are steep, and in no time, he's puffing badly and covered in sweat. He stops a moment to pull off the windbreaker and stuff it into the backpack alongside their lunch. If Elena is perspiring, he sees no evidence. She seldom sweats when they make love, whereas he tends to get soaked. Some of us have cool bodies. Some of us don't.

Along the way, she takes note of various birds, telling him their names in Ukrainian. He's never had the slightest interest in birds, and by now, he feels comfortable enough with her to say so.

"Why this is?" she asks.

"I don't know. They've always just seemed so . . . well, so different from me."

She falls silent, pondering his response. In her opinion, a lot of what's not right in the world at any given time is wrong because somebody somewhere decided that some other creature—very often another human being—is too different for them to relate. When she was housed at the refugee center in Warsaw, she went out one day to buy a sweet roll, and after she placed her order, the woman behind her in line muttered, *"Banderowka."* Seventy-some years ago, Stepan Bandera massacred the Poles, and she's somehow to blame? Never once in her life has she called the Russians names. Not even after she lost her Serhiy.

"Your sister says no dogs?" she says. "You should get yourself a pet bird. Let it teach you how to love it. But don't make it sit all day in a cage. Show it the world from your shoulder. A white cockatoo, maybe."

"You have those in Ukraine?"

"Ukraine is not the moon. At least, it doesn't used to be. In any nice pet store you can buy. Online too."

While he puffs along beside her, his body purging itself through his pores, he thinks that lately she's making many more grammatical mistakes. He considers this a positive sign, as if she feels safe enough with him to let down her linguistic guard. There are still words and phrases, though, that neither of them ever employs. *The future. Next year. Next month. From now on.* About the farthest they ever go is *Tomorrow.*

Tomorrow is far enough. He recalls how it feels to think you have no tomorrows, when the notion that there might be something worth doing the next day would have seemed like a cruel joke. Through a web of shattered glass, he again sees the face of his own Richard Brennan.

THEY REACH the lodge above the lake at a quarter till three, and he plops down at a picnic table on the stone terrace. Below them, Morskie Oko shimmers so brightly he has to shade his eyes. Even lifting his arm is taxing. His feet ache, his back hurts, he's so wet that in no time the brisk air begins to chill him.

Elena seems amused. "You won't be worth much tonight," she observes.

Her resilience never fails to amaze him. Despite all she's lost, she still enjoys a cold beer, dark bread smeared with *smalec*, a few shots of vodka late at night. She loves lying on her back, watching him go down on her. Until he met her, he was not much good at it.

How we find the ones we belong to is a matter of mystery. While for many, this is obvious, it was not always clear to him. He accepted the sanctity of the neighborhood, not to mention national borders. He was born down the street from Krysia, they'd known each other since childhood. It seemed apparent that they belonged together. Yet their marriage was only good for a while, and then it was bad for what felt like forever. Elena's was fine for some years, but then it too went sour. Maybe it would have lasted if they hadn't lost their son; maybe it would have revived if her husband hadn't lost his life. But he suspects not.

Her world has come unmade, throwing her together with him. He shouldn't be glad—it's dangerous and wrong—yet it's hard not to rejoice at his blind good fortune. Maybe happiness is always a zero-sum game. Somebody loses, somebody else gains.

She removes the wax paper from the canapés, pulls the plastic top off the salad, and parcels it out onto two paper plates, giving him a little more than she's kept for herself. She pops the tab on both beers, hands him one, and takes a swallow from hers. He still hasn't moved. She looks at him, intending to ask if he's not hungry or thirsty. He's staring at the lake as if struck by its beauty. But no lake, no matter how pretty, could put that look on the face of a man who dislikes birds.

Between them, there exists a great imbalance. She understands this, though he doesn't. He is puzzled by her, whereas she can read him as easily as the instructions on a can of oven cleaner. He believes he's a bad man, that the difference between bad and good is as clear as the line down the middle of the road. He crossed that line one night, and catastrophe occurred. And now, no matter how long he's driven on the right side, he still feels like he's in the wrong lane. He thinks something big and hard should hit him, when in fact it already did.

She says, "You need to eat your lunch."

"I'm really tired," he says, and he sounds it.

"You are not so tired you can't eat. It don't use much energy or take a lot of brains. If a baby can do it, so can you, though you are not much more than a baby yourself."

At least this makes him look away from the lake. It was about to hypnotize him or do something worse. The vulnerability on display was becoming painful to observe.

"I'm a baby?" he says. "How do you figure that?"

She takes a look around the terrace: there's a family nearby—mother, father, a little girl, and a hyperactive boy wearing a football shirt with the Polish eagle on it. Over at the edge of the terrace, in the shade of a tree, two trekkers nap, using their backpacks for pillows. Otherwise, it's just her and Bogdan.

She leans close to him. "Come the night," she whispers, "you're like momma's little baby. Thirsty to do what a little baby gets to."

THE BENEFICIAL effects of gravity are sometimes overstated. For him, going down is nearly as difficult as coming up. He's huffing less and sweating less, but both calves have caught fire, and every time he takes another step, his corns are like nails being pounded into his feet.

"You are in terrible shape," she says, holding on to his forearm. "What you have been doing for the last few years?"

"I spent one of them in prison."

"You must have sat in a cell the whole time. Don't they have no gym at your jail?"

"They had a few free weights. But just picking myself up was strenuous enough."

"When we get home," she says, "I'm going to have to start walking you around town like a dog. I don't want another man on me to die. Already I lost two."

Those words create buoyancy and lift. So what if he's hurting? Isn't nearly everyone, to one extent or another? Despite his discomfort, this is the nicest day Bogdan has experienced in years. Sometimes it's important to let yourself be dragged. You never know what you might learn along the way. He's with a woman who plans to walk him like a dog.

They round a gentle curve, and the car park comes into view. In a couple of moments, they'll be in the van heading back to Zakopane. Why let pain prevent pleasure? At his age, you never know how much time remains. He could have a stroke and die tomorrow. Tonight, he'll pop some anti-inflammatory medication and do what momma's baby gets to and a few other things the baby can't.

On the first of July, Richard wakes in a Marriott Courtyard a few blocks down Tremont from Boston Common. He has coffee and half of a cinnamon twist at Dunkin' Donuts, then gets his car from the garage and drives up Route 1 to Cedar Park, where he grew up. His father's house sold more than a year ago, and though it's several blocks from downtown, he decides to drive past it. The couple who bought it had a three-year-old and a four-year-old, and he thought—correctly, it turns out—that they would give the place some much-needed attention. It's been repainted warm amber, the steps replaced, the front porch turned into a sunroom that his mother would have loved. After she died, his father quit taking care of the house, which Richard thought he understood at the time but did not. He drives past the old jazz club too. It's been the home of various businesses over the years, none of which lasted long. It's an antique store now. All you can see through the window is junk: broken lamps, old typewriters, soft-drink bottles. He takes a right on Main, passing a CVS that stands where his mom's favorite grocery store used to be. The storage facility is a block away.

Using the code he received via text message, he unlocks his unit and neatly stacks the plastic containers on the highest shelves. This area is called the Highlands, and because the shed is near the base of a hill, he knows without being told that flooding is a possibility.

He still has friends in town. He could walk up onto any number of porches, ring the doorbell, and be invited in. The first time he brought Julia here, he took her to visit his senior English teacher, his baseball coach, and three or four former classmates. Doing something of this nature, it seems to him now, requires confidence that you're meeting on equal ground, that both you and your hosts will have news worth sharing, the majority of it good. He has none, and if he did have some, he would want to keep it to himself and savor it alone. So he drives back into the city and takes a walk through the Common and the Public Garden and considers but rejects the possibility of riding the Green Line over to Fenway to see the Sox. He eats dinner in Chinatown, then returns to the hotel and sleeps eleven hours. When he wakes and remembers where he is, it comes to him that the last couple of nights are the only ones he's spent in Boston since he was twenty-two years old.

TICKETS WERE cheapest on the fourth of July, so that's when he leaves the country, taking a Lufthansa flight to Munich. He drinks some whiskey on the plane and some red wine too, but most of his dinner remains untouched. Somewhere about halfway across the Atlantic, he finally drops off, getting a couple of hours' sleep before landing in Germany.

Unfortunately, there are storms all over Europe. First, the departure board says his connecting flight will be delayed for forty-five minutes. Then it says an hour and a half. Then they take it off the board altogether but put it back twenty minutes later. Most of those waiting at the gate are speaking Polish, and even if they weren't, he would have known where they're from. It's not their clothes, or their faces, or their posture, or any one thing he can put his finger on. It's everything together, the strangeness of the once familiar. If necessary, he'd be content to spend the night here. The seats are by no means uncomfortable, and there's free coffee from a dispenser, several bars at the top of the escalator. So he sits and watches it rain, heavy drops bouncing off the tarmac.

At three forty-five, nearly four hours late, they announce his flight. He goes through the turnstile and boards a bus that delivers him and the other passengers to an RJ, and after sitting on the runaway for another forty minutes, it takes off. The flight is just over an hour in duration, and he's looking out the window when the clouds break. For the first time in nearly ten years, he sees the green, rolling hills of Malopolska.

He's good at judging his distance from the ground, and he can tell when they drop below ten thousand feet. Features on the landscape stop being blobs of color and assume three-dimensional properties. He sees a rocky promontory crowned by an alpine castle, a road winding down the hillside toward the *autostrada*. The plane banks, and the sight slips away. The spoilers extend, the landing gear locks.

ALMOST NOTHING looks like it used to. The airport is three or four times larger now; there are many more planes on the ground, and most are parked at jetways that didn't exist before. The baggage area, once a dingy affair with a single U-shaped conveyor, could be at almost any airport in the U.S. or Western Europe. He checks the information board for LH 1622. Carousel 3. His duffel bag is the second to emerge. He pulls the handle free and extends it, then walks through Customs unmolested.

One thing hasn't changed: in the arrival hall, it's shoulder to shoulder, people holding signs up with the names of those they've come to collect, the same unsavory characters hanging around, looking for a pocket to pick or hoping to find an American who knows no better than to pay a hundred dollars for a ride into the city. He scans the crowd, then feels a tug on his sleeve.

She's still dying her hair—there's not a streak of gray anywhere. It's as black as the blouse she's wearing. She rises onto her toes, just as she used to, so his lips can brush her cheek. "I'm so glad to see you," she says, giving his hand a little squeeze. "You look great, Richard."

In fact, she finds his appearance disturbing. He's far too thin, and his shoulders slope inward as if he's spent a lot of time hugging himself.

"So do you, Monika. But then, you always did. I would have called you," he says, "and told you how late we were going to be. But I don't have a European cell phone anymore, and I don't think my other one works here."

"That's all right. I checked ahead of time, so I knew you'd been delayed. Shall we go?"

Across the street, where once there was nothing but a few trees and bushes, there's now a large parking garage. She's driving a small white BMW. She opens the trunk, and he puts his bag inside.

"You're traveling fairly light," she says. "From what you said, I thought perhaps you planned to stay longer."

"Well, I might. I'm not sure." The truth could embarrass or even alarm: he has no plans beyond the moment. He had planned to fly to Krakow, and now here he is.

On the way into town, she says that since it's nearly six, she thought maybe they would have dinner at their place. Afterward, she can drive him over to his apartment, or perhaps he will stay the night with them and she will take him there in the morning?

"The latter option might be best," he says. "I imagine I'm going to cave in pretty quickly after a meal."

"So that's what we'll do," she says. "Franek will be there with his girlfriend, and Stefan invited Bronek."

"Bronek?"

"Malinowski. The detective."

"Ah."

She casts a sidelong glance. "I hope that was all right?"

"Of course it is," he says, though the prospect is one he doesn't relish. "Is Stefan any better?"

"No. And he's not going to be. I have to warn you, Richard, that he's terribly frail. I'm with him every day, but it still sometimes shocks me when I walk into the room and see how he looks. He's lost every last hair on his body, and he only weighs about forty-five kilos. According to his oncologist, the amount of chemo and radiation he's absorbed through the years would be enough to kill the average person three or four times."

"Well, there's nothing average about Stefan," he says.

"No, there isn't. I can say many things about my husband, and that's definitely one of them. Would you believe he still writes every day? He does it propped up in bed now, rather than in his study. Sometimes I hear him laughing, which tells me he's just completed another sex scene. He behaves as if he's too busy to die."

"With that kind of attitude, he may still beat it."

"No, he won't. The doctor says that at best, hospice is only weeks away. Stefan wanted badly to see you again. And so did I."

The highway that used to be a two-lane blacktop is hardly

recognizable. Multiple lanes go in each direction now, and due to his disorientation, he has only a general sense of where the accident happened. There's probably no piece of ground anywhere on earth, he thinks, that hasn't served as the site of one tragedy or another. Every spot sacred to someone means nothing to a few billion others.

When they reach the city, just before crossing the Vistula, they pass an enormous asymmetrical building made of glass. "What's that?"

"ICE—the new Congress Hall. It hosts conferences, exhibits, concerts. The acoustics are much better than at the Philharmonic."

"Have you performed there?"

"No. I'm sorry to say it opened after my retirement."

"Do you miss the orchestra?"

"I would be lying if I claimed I didn't. What I don't miss is the constant pain. It had become more than I could stand."

"Pain has a way of becoming intolerable after a while, doesn't it?"

"It certainly does."

On the other side of the river, while they wait for the traffic light to change, he says, "I don't think I ever told you how much your calls used to mean to me, Monika. Especially those first couple of years. The sound of your voice was about the only thing I looked forward to. You always cleared your throat before speaking to me. Were you aware of that?"

"I don't believe I was. But I knew you looked forward to the calls, as did I. I wish I could have made more of them. That was a hard time for me too. I don't suppose I need to explain the reasons why?"

"Not really."

"Did he ever discuss other women with you?"

There seems little point in being untruthful. "Just once. It was the night of the wreck."

"When the two of you went to smoke cigars?"

"Yes."

She doesn't say anything for a while. "Well, I'm sure that made you very uncomfortable," she finally observes, "since it's the kind of thing you would never have done yourself. I used to be so terribly jealous of Julia, Richard. It seemed to me that she had everything, that one day she just walked into a café, and there it was waiting for her. I'm not proud of having felt that way, especially given what happened. But I did, and I'm sure she knew it."

"She liked you a lot."

"I know she liked me. I liked her too. But she knew. She had to." She glances at him again. "What about you? Did you know?"

"I'm not sure, Monika. I guess maybe I did."

The traffic begins to move, and she lets out the clutch. "If God were a composer," she says, "he would write like Mahler. A teardrop one minute, a belly laugh the next. Following that, a loud belch."

THEY'RE ALL waiting when he and Monika enter the apartment. The only one of the four he would be able to identify in a police lineup is the policeman himself. Malinowski looks more or less like he did when he visited Richard's hospital room: heavy-lidded eyes, tall, wrinkled forehead, long ears. Franek now has shoulder-length hair and a beard every bit as bushy as his father's used to be. He's wearing Day-Glo orange pants and a tight black long-sleeved tee shirt. His girlfriend is a tall, dark-haired Brazilian named Rafaela who is twice his age, a visiting lecturer in the philosophy department. Richard has stayed in touch with his nephew, and he knew the woman he was involved with was from somewhere else. He just didn't know she was forty.

Still, the greatest surprise of the evening is his brother-in-law's appearance. No amount of preparation could have prevented the shock. In the decade or so since they last saw each other, he has aged half a century. He's sitting in a wheelchair, a small, shrunken creature with no eyebrows who looks like he might disintegrate if you touched him. The only thing left of the old Stefan—and it's not to be discounted—is his sense of humor.

"Rysiu," he says, "don't act so somber. When it comes time to bury me, you'll be one of the pallbearers. You won't have to do much more than lift a finger."

Monika leans down and puts her arms around his neck, kissing his bald head. He clasps her hands with his, and it looks like it took all his strength to do it. As far as Richard can recall, this is the first time he's ever seen them touch each other with affection.

The women disappear into the kitchen, where, unless his nose is badly off, duck is being roasted. Franek asks what he'd like to drink. Whiskey, if there is any. Stefan says, "Of course there is. I like to sniff it from time to time and grow nostalgic." He nods toward the sideboard, and his son pulls out a bottle of Bushmills malt and pours half a glassful. Stefan continues to nurse a cup of tea.

They talk politics for a while. The Law and Justice government, Franek tells him, has enacted various surveillance measures allegedly designed to protect the country against terrorists. They don't require a warrant to read your e-mail or your texts, and they've given themselves permission to listen to everyone's phone calls. "A few days ago, they introduced another bill in the Sejm specifically targeting foreigners," his nephew says, "and while it's being read, a bomb just happens to go off in an empty bus a block or two away. They insult our intelligence day after day."

"You remember when all those refugees drowned in the Aegean?" Stefan asks Richard.

"Sure. Over seven hundred of them."

"That night on TVP, they didn't even mention it. Instead, they ran a segment about a Polish tourist who'd been assaulted in Greece by a Syrian. Public Television looks like it did under the Communists."

Detective Malinowski says he retired a month ago rather than hang around and get fired. They are letting people go left and right, he says. All you have to do is oppose them. They started with the media, firing producers and reporters from the state-run networks. Then they began cleaning house at publicly funded cultural institutions: museums, theaters, and so on. "At the Ministry of Agriculture," he continues, "they even fired the director of a stud farm."

"And as for publishing," Stefan says, "it's gone straight to hell." He leans over and lays a bony hand on Richard's knee. "Being a journalist, you'll want me to back up my statement. So here's hard evidence: my books no longer sell!" When he laughs, his chest rattles.

Franek is deeply involved in the Committee for the Defense of Democracy, and he says there will be a big demonstration the following weekend in Warsaw, which he and Rafaela plan to attend. The last one drew a couple hundred thousand protestors, he says, and the energy was incredible. His uncle would be more than welcome to accompany them.

"I might take you up on that," Richard tells him. "Very little of this is being reported in the American press."

"Of course not," Stefan says. "They've forgotten us. We're yesterday's news."

Richard was right about the main course: roast duck with apples. Monika couldn't know that the last time he had his once-favorite dish was the night of the accident. The thought of eating it makes him queasy, but he doesn't want to be rude, so he fortifies himself with another slug of Bushmills, then lets his nephew pour him a big glass of Malbec.

When he takes the first mouthful of dark meat and dissolving fruit, something startling happens. It's as if his taste buds, so long dormant, erupt. He feels them rising on the surface of his tongue. For a moment, he shuts his eyes, overcome by the sensory onslaught. It's the taste of his life, what's lost and what's left.

He has an extra helping, along with several more glasses of Malbec, saying very little himself, just enjoying the smell of the food, the glow from the wine, the sound of their voices speaking Polish.

Monika keeps an eye on him. When he rises to go to the bathroom, he's unsteady, and for a moment, she fears he might lose his balance and crash to the floor. After they hear the door close, she tells Franek not to pour him more wine.

"Why embarrass him?" Stefan says. His hand quivering, he points at Richard's glass and tells Franek to fill it halfway up with water, then add a little Malbec. "He won't taste the difference," he says.

They needn't have worried: Richard knows he's on the verge of collapse. When he returns, he says that jet lag has overtaken him and that though he's enjoying the company, he'd better go to bed. He shakes hands with Malinowski, gives Rafaela a peck on the cheek, and hugs his nephew.

Monika shows him to his room. He sits down on the side of the bed, starts to lean over and unlace his shoes, then realizes he'd better not risk it. "I'm really drunk," he says.

"Yes, I know." She kneels on the bedside rug and unlaces first one shoe, then the other. She has to tug hard to pull them off, but she manages. Then she helps him lie back on the pillows. She's not strong enough to get his clothes off, and she doesn't want to call Franek. So she covers him with a blanket and tucks his feet in.

"Stay with me a while?" he asks.

"Of course."

She remains there on the side of the bed, hearing Rafaela removing dishes from the table, Bronek bidding everyone goodnight, Franek rolling his father's wheelchair down the hall, past the closed guest-room door and into their own bedroom. At some point, Richard takes her hand in his, and she sits there holding it until his eyes fall shut and his breathing grows shallow.

He sleeps until eight thirty the next morning. He has a shadowy awareness of visiting the bathroom sometime around dawn. But dawn seemed to arrive about three forty-five. So he must be in Krakow. Once he's acceded to that, fragments of the evening return: the image of his brother-in-law shrunken in his wheelchair; his nephew's shaggy mane, so much like the Cowardly Lion; the tall Brazilian woman; the detective who resembles de Gaulle. Monika sitting on the side of the bed, her hand locked in his.

He rises, pulls his shaving kit from the duffel bag, then walks down the hall to the bathroom. His mouth tastes like metal, so he brushes his teeth, rinses, then brushes them again. He splashes cold water on his face.

He finds Monika in the kitchen, making coffee. "How do you feel?" she asks.

"Physically? Like a bowl of microwaved dog shit."

"Well, that's not surprising, is it?"

"No. I drank far too much."

"Have you been doing a lot of that?"

"Over the last month or two, I'm afraid so."

"I had the sense that something unpleasant recently happened."

He sits down at the kitchen table, tells her about the incident at Aarden College, the conversation with Alex, how he went home and resigned.

She pours two cups of coffee, then sits down across from him. "You didn't want to hire a lawyer and fight back?"

"No. I realized there would be more of it ahead and that I was taking up a position somebody more in tune with the times ought to fill. I don't know where I fit anymore. Left and right don't mean what they used to, my profession is more or less on life support— sorry, that was a poor choice of words, but it seems I often choose them poorly these days. Bottom line, Monika? I'm just tired."

"Tired of exactly what, Richard?"

"Just tired." He takes a sip of coffee. "As horrible as my hangover is, though, I'm glad to be here with you. I've missed you. Is Stefan still asleep? Or is he writing?"

"Oh, he's been writing since six a.m. I think he hopes to finish this novel before . . . well, before."

"He and Franek seem to be getting along great these days."

"Stefan quit laughing at him years ago. He treats him with respect, though it may be respect born of envy."

"Because he's young and healthy?"

"Possibly. Franek had a number of girlfriends much younger than Rafaela, and I think maybe Stefan got a little vicarious pleasure from that. I really don't always understand how his mind works. That's one of the reasons I stayed interested all these years. I assumed one day I would get to the bottom of it. But that's not going to happen." She takes a swallow of coffee, then places her cup back on the saucer and asks what he'd like to do today.

He tells her that if she wouldn't mind, he'd like her to drive him over to the apartment, though of course he could also take a taxi. She says not to be silly, she wouldn't dream of letting him do that. She had the place cleaned top to bottom last Friday, she says, and she placed fresh sheets on the bed and left him plenty of water and coffee as well as some beer. She went ahead and turned on the fridge. If he decides on a lengthy stay, she tells him, or perhaps even moves here permanently, he should probably install air conditioning, at least on the lower level. "It's not the hassle it used to be. We had this entire flat vented for central air. But you could just buy a couple of standing units and have someone make openings in your window frames to attach the hoses to. When the weather cools off, you can remove them and replace the wooden blocks that were cut from the frames. It's low-tech, but it works. Bronek did it at his place."

He knows she's trying to find out what his long-term intentions might be, and if he knew what they were, he'd share the information. But he doesn't. He just knows where he wants to go this morning.

He finishes his coffee, takes a shower, and puts on clean clothes. She tells him to leave the dirty ones here, that she'll wash them and bring them by tomorrow or the day after, so he wads them up and leaves them on the bed.

It's nearly noon when she parks in front of his building. She pulls out the keys that she has kept in her pantry all these years. "The door latches became recalcitrant," she says, "so last week, I had a handyman spray them with some type of lubricant, and now they work just fine." She shows him a gray plastic tab that's attached to the ring. "Back in 2012, they installed a keypad by the door. You either type in a code—yours is 8888—or just tap the top of the pad with this tab. The lady in 1A died three years ago, and the couple in number 5 moved to Gdansk last fall. Other than that, I think you will find things pretty much as they were, except that your neighbors and your appliances are ten years older. Would you like me to go up with you, or would you prefer to be alone?"

"If you wouldn't mind," he says, "I think maybe I'll go by myself. Get reacclimated, then run some errands, buy a little food and so forth."

"That's not a problem." From her purse, she pulls a mobile phone. "This is one of those card-operated devices that tourists use. The number is printed on the back, and I put 150 zlotys' worth of service on it. Use it until you buy a better one. I'll leave you be for the rest of the day, but you can call me anytime. I'm free for lunch tomorrow if you feel like it."

He thanks her, and when they embrace, he holds her a little longer than he intended before getting out and removing his bag from the trunk. She waves and drives away. He watches until she reaches the end of the street and turns the corner. Then he walks over to the door. Heart fluttering, he taps the pad. The buzzer sounds. He opens the door, steps inside, and confronts the dark stairs.

"This machine we're going to get costs *how* many zlotys?" Elena asks as the light changes and they roll onto the bridge.

"Forty-five thousand," Bogdan says.

"Mother of God. How many cups of coffee it can make at one time?"

"I don't know. Three or four. It's one of those elaborate ones from Italy, and because our currency's in free fall, it'll probably soon cost even more than it does today. She says we've got to have it, that the other good pensions have them because that's what guests expect. They also expect you to have beer on draft, not in bottles, and you need to have at least three kinds, and one of them has to be a brand they'll recognize if they're from the U.S."

On the other side of the river, she can see the nicer parts of Krakow: old buildings, church spires, the famous castle where all the kings are buried. "I drank an American beer once," she says. "I never will forget its name. Miller's Beer. Terrible. Just yellow water, and the smell reminded me of the time we went camping and my husband pitched our tent where somebody peed."

"It doesn't have to be an American *brand*. Apparently, the

Americans she's got in mind don't like their own beer any more than you do. They just need to recognize it, so that's why we have Heineken along with Lech and Tyskie."

"I drank one of those Heinekens the other night," she says. "It tasted to me about like Miller's."

Maybe because the day is sunny and nice, the traffic is awful. They only make it halfway across the river before they again have to stop.

"I spent one of the worst nights of my life here," he says while they wait.

"Where?"

"Here on this bridge."

"You slept on the bridge? You never said you was homeless."

"I was and I wasn't. This was after my wife and I split up, and I'd moved out of the flat. I was staying at Marek and Inga's, so I had a roof over my head. But I couldn't sleep. I'd wait till they went to bed, and then I'd go out and walk the streets. One rainy night, I ended up on this bridge and stood here forever, looking at the river."

"You were thinking of jumping in?" The traffic begins to move again, and they roll off the bridge and onto a broad street with a grassy median and plenty of trees.

"I don't know. I guess maybe it did cross my mind." He reaches over and lays his hand on her knee. "I'm glad I didn't, though."

She places her hand on top of his, but this is all she will do to indulge his self-dramatization. "Yes," she says, "me too. It's not that far down, and the fall probably would not have killed you, or even knocked you out. And as soon as you knew you were drowning, you would have started to swim anyway. You could do that in a pool." With her free hand, she gestures at the tall buildings they're passing. "If a person plans to kill himself, he should jump from one of those. You know why?"

"Why?"

"Because that sidewalk over there don't believe in second chances."

WHAT'S IN a place?

In this one, to start with, there's the white wardrobe. It stands in the hallway and is the first thing Richard sees when he opens the door. It was bought at Ikea in the summer of 2005 and is not nearly as nice as the one it replaced, which belonged to Julia's parents and before that her grandparents. The older one had ornate wood carvings on both doors, but it got invaded by powderpost beetles, and because they were gone for most of each year and Stefan and Monika never opened it when they stopped by to check on things, no one discovered the damage until it was too late. Some men came and hauled it away. Next to the wardrobe, there's a coat rack, a spindly one that has been there as long as he can remember.

He sets his bag down, bends, and pulls off his shoes. He opens the wardrobe and puts them inside, then pulls out his leather slippers, which were bought from a vendor beneath the Hala Targowa overpass thirteen or fourteen years ago. They're now the color of a well-worn catcher's mitt. He puts them on and steps into the living room.

There's the leather sofa that replaced the Communist-era daybed Julia's parents used to sleep on so that she and Stefan could each have a room, a nearly unimaginable luxury for a Polish child in the '60s and '70s. Her father, a history professor who died the year before Richard met her, did his work over there at the round dining table, trying to figure out how to convey some version of the truth without losing his job and having to leave the country. Pictures of him and her mother stand on the nearby sideboard, pictures of various family members like her maternal grandfather, who died at Monte Cassino. Below that, behind glass doors, a set of blue-and-white Boleslawiec stoneware: a large teapot, a smaller one, matching cups and saucers. In the liquor cabinet, a ten-year-old bottle of Bushmills, unopened and ready for use. Two Bordeauxs, both from 2003; a Montepulciano; two bottles of prosecco. He steps over to the big bookcase and runs his finger along the spines of books that he brought here, read, and left behind.

Next, the bedroom, with the familiar brown curtains that failed to prevent the sun from waking him at four a.m. The photos on the wall: the three of them negotiating rapids in the Truckee River, all wearing orange life jackets, Anna at the bow with a canary-yellow cap; Julia leaning over to cut a chocolate birthday cake with the number 4 in white icing; Richard shirtless on the back steps in Fresno, Anna with red baby cheeks perched on his knee.

He walks into the downstairs bath, where there's an oversized shower they installed in 2002 so that he would no longer have to fold himself into the small bathtub. The kitchen, with a framed poster advertising the 1998 Krakow Summer Jazz Festival headlined by Branford Marsalis.

He climbs the staircase to the attic, ducking at exactly the right moment to avoid banging his head. He steps into the room where first his wife and then his daughter slept. Several British editions of Harry Potter remain on the shelves. A pink jacket hangs in the closet. He hears someone moving around on the other side of the wall, sees a rectangle of the purest blue through one of the skylights.

He returns to the living room and takes a seat in his old armchair, removes his slippers, and places his feet on the coffee table. He leans back and within a moment is sound asleep.

BOGDAN LETS her out in front of the Ukrainian Consulate. Her daughter has no passport and no means of obtaining her birth certificate, but fortunately, Elena brought the original with her when she left their former home. Someone at the consulate—from what she's said, a man about her age, who he suspects is taken with her—promised to expedite her application. She says they told her to plan on being there for an hour. She promises to text when she's finished.

He drives to the freight office where the espresso machine is waiting. Having it delivered to Zakopane would have cost another seven hundred zlotys. If you're willing to spend forty-five thousand buying the damn thing, it seems to him, you shouldn't balk at dropping another few hundred to have it brought to your door. But his sister's mind works differently from his, which is why her business is a big success and his was an abject failure. He arrives at such judgments now without rancor or bitterness. It's just how things are. They could be many times worse, and anyway, picking the machine up will give him a chance to see Marek and Inga and let them meet Elena while saving her from a solitary bus trip to the consulate and back.

Two guys load the heavy box into the back of the van, and he hands each of them a ten-zloty tip. He still hasn't heard from Elena, so he gets into the van and drives around for a little while, enjoying being back in his hometown. He passes Galeria Kazimierz, the site of the grocery store where he once woke up drunk on the floor. He wonders what happened to the young assistant manager who fired him, whether he moved up in the chain or is still unlocking the doors at six a.m. and wearing the same green tie. He drives past one of his and Marek's old stores, the one where the judge who sentenced him to prison got cheated. What happened to her? As strange as it might sound, from time to time he thinks of her fondly. She saw him at one of his better moments, when he did what was right, and at one of his worst, when he admitted committing despicable acts. That she remembered him when he appeared in her courtroom remains a source of amazement these many years later. Just as he gave her back the sum she'd been cheated of, she gave him something too: the chance to write *Paid* on at least one delinquent debt.

Finally, he receives the text from Elena saying she's finished. He pulls into the parking lot at Hala Targowa and calls Marek.

"Ready, Bogdan?" his old friend asks.

"I still haven't picked her up, but I'm about to. So why don't you wait fifteen minutes before you leave?"

"Sounds good. We're looking forward to meeting your lady friend."

"See you at the café," he says, then pulls into traffic.

RICHARD IS not sure how long he slept, but the angle of the sunlight streaming in through the window would suggest it's past two p.m. This is not something he has to think about, just as he did not have to think about when to duck as he started up the stairs to the bedroom in the attic. It's the kind of thing you know when you've lived someplace long enough. And he has been living here for years, even though he last set foot within these walls ages ago.

His neck hurts, and his head does too, which is not surprising given how much he drank last night and how little he's slept over the past forty-eight hours. In addition, he's damp all over. It's a hot day, and there's no air conditioning. Monika is probably right: if he plans to stay, he should install it. And maybe, he thinks as he rises and works the kinks out of his shoulders, staying is what he should do. Go to the demonstration in Warsaw with Franek and Rafaela, start talking to people and working on a piece about where the country is right now. One thing he knows, because he knows Poles: as dissatisfaction grows, a breaking point will come, and stories will demand to be told.

Tomorrow, he will go to the cemetery. He intended to do it today, but his stomach is growling, and there's no food in the apartment. The food court at Galeria Kazimierz never had anything fit to eat and probably still doesn't, just stuff like McDonald's and KFC. It's a fifteen-minute walk to the Old Town and another five or ten to his favorite café, the place where he met Julia. He decides to go there. He wants to see it again anyway.

He locks the apartment and sets off, taking the most direct route, as opposed to the lengthier one along the Vistula that they used to prefer. This requires him to walk up an ugly street named Blich, where the buildings are still covered in soot. The balconies on the top floor are level with the tracks, and he used to wonder how anybody could sleep in those flats, with trains clattering by all day and all night.

He turns the corner onto Kopernika, walking past the Church of St. Nicholas. Up ahead, he can see Planty. He waits for a tram to pass, then crosses the street and enters the shady park, where he follows the contours of the old moat, passing the fortified outpost known as the Barbican and opposite it, on his left, the Florian Gate. Bikers pedal by in each direction, young women push baby carriages, older ones lounge on benches in groups of two or three, drunks snooze beneath the chestnuts or sip from bottles and cans. It's all so familiar, as if he never left.

MAREK AND Inga are the first to reach the café. They came on a street car. Though Bogdan doesn't know it, they no longer own an automobile. Since his heart attack, Marek hasn't worked a day. They live off his disability payments, the salary Inga draws as a ticket clerk at Polish Rail, and the money she's able to earn cleaning people's flats on Saturdays. They never go to cafés anymore, and they even discussed the possibility of making an excuse again today, or letting only Marek go. Neither of them, though, wants to miss a chance to meet Bogdan's new companion. Earlier, Marek remarked that they had better meet her now, since odds were the relationship wouldn't last. "Poor Bogdan," he said. "He just doesn't seem to have what women are looking for." Inga didn't contradict him, though there's more to Bogdan than her husband suspects.

They seat themselves at a table in the nonsmoking section. They agreed ahead of time that even though their friend will surely try to pay their check, and they will have to let him, neither of them will order anything except a cup of tea.

A waitress comes over and slaps two menus on the table. She's tall, a dishwater blonde with such a miserable expression that Inga takes note of it. "I wonder what's wrong with her?" she says. "She looks like she couldn't smile if you paid her."

"She waited on us a few times when I came here with Bogdan," Marek says, examining the menu. "She always looks like that. She's just extremely sullen. I'm surprised they didn't fire her years ago."

Inga watches her disappear inside. She's a big-boned young woman, not so different physically from Inga herself at that age. She isn't wearing a wedding ring, so she's obviously single, whereas Inga married Marek at the age of nineteen and gave birth twice before she was twenty-three. Back then, they had as little as they have now, and then things changed, and for a while they had a lot more. She knows they will never have more again. If anything, they might soon have even less. But at no point in her life has Inga ever shown the world such an unhappy face.

She reaches under the table and squeezes Marek's knee. "All things considered," she says, "we've had a wonderful ride, haven't we?"

Marek closes the menu and lays it on the table. "Yes, we have," he says. "Do you think I could order milk with my tea? It's only an extra fifty groszy."

BECAUSE THERE'S a forty-five-thousand-zloty espresso machine in the back of the van, Bogdan decides to park at a guarded lot on Karmelicka, two or three blocks from the café. His friends are already seated when they arrive. He makes the introductions, and they seat themselves, and the waitress he hoped they would not be served by appears and throws down two more menus.

They talk for a while about the reason for his and Elena's trip to Krakow, the expensive coffee machine, her visit to the consulate. On the phone, he gave Marek a heads-up about the deaths of her husband and son, her daughter's health and immigration issues. He would have put it all in an e-mail, where he could have elaborated, but Marek almost never checks his e-mail anymore, and Bogdan thinks he knows why: they can no longer afford to pay for the Internet. Odds are, when Marek does check it, he's at a public computer in the library. Though Inga is still robust, his longtime friend has turned into a frail little man who looks a lot older than fifty-eight. He still has his hair, but it's nearly white now, and his skin has that translucent quality you find in the elderly. If there's a positive in all of this, it's that his facial scars have eroded along with everything else. They are no more than thin white lines, hardly visible.

He orders coffee, and Elena has a glass of red wine. It pleases him to see how easily the two women are talking. He hears Inga telling Elena about a trip to Ukraine that she and her family took when she was a girl. "We only went as far as Lviv," she says, giving the city its Ukrainian name rather than calling it "Lwow" like most Poles would.

Marek tells him about their grandson, a burgeoning football star who, like the great Robert Lewandowski, once scored five goals in a single match. "Since my heart attack," he says, "I'm supposed to avoid getting overly excited. I told him, 'Mietek, if you're not careful, sooner or later you are going to kill your poor grandpa.'"

Neither of them is aware of the tall man in jeans and a white long-sleeved shirt when he steps into the café. Bogdan has his back to the entrance. Marek would be able to see him if he looked in that direction, but he's caught up in his grandson's exploits. Inga would also be able to see him if she looked that way, but she's giving all her attention to Elena, to whom she has taken an immediate liking. The only one who notices him is Elena herself. She happens to glance at the entrance. He's staring at her. When their gazes meet, he smiles and looks away, as if to make it clear that he's just searching for a vacant table.

There aren't many. A moment or two later, he sits down at the one next to theirs, positioning his chair so that he can observe people strolling by in the park.

THE WAITRESS, of course, has a name—two of them. The one she was born with is Bozena, which means both "happy" and "blessed by God." She likes neither the sound of the name nor its dual implications. "Happy" she sometimes is and sometimes isn't, like most people. "Blessed by God" she is not. Her father drank himself to death, and her mother worked herself to death taking care of four children. The name she uses in her professional life is Carlotta. As far as she knows, it means nothing at all. She likes how it sounds.

Bozena/Carlotta is an actress. She's appeared in a couple of films—a peasant woman drawing water from a well, a hooker working a street corner—but most of her parts have come in theaters in Krakow and Katowice. She's never had a leading role, though she did once play Dunyasha in *The Cherry Orchard*. People like Marek and Bogdan assume she's been here nonstop for many years, but that's not true. The café is owned and run by a friend, and thus far, he's always been able to give her hours when she needs them. She works here only when she has no work that matters, and the absence of it is one source of unhappiness. She sometimes wonders if she won't be waiting tables off and on for the rest of her life. That's another.

She grabs a menu and heads toward the tall man who just sat down next to the two older couples. He's an American, she decides. In a job like this, you get good at spotting them. She's about to lay the menu down and walk away when he provides the first surprise of a mundane day, addressing her in flawless Polish. "When," he asks, "did the café get these new chairs?"

You hear a lot of pickup lines from men his age, which is the major reason she puts on a stiff face when she approaches a table where one of them is sitting. Even if they are with their wives, they'll often return by themselves and come on to her. She knows, without ever being told, that it's the kind of thing her father used to do. He treated himself to several drinks and then tried to treat himself to something more.

She's not unobservant. These chairs and tables have been at the café since the day she first worked here. "They've been around," she says, "as long as I have. And that's quite a few years."

It's as if he's looking at her but not seeing her—that's how she will put it later, when she tells a friend about him. The thought that he isn't really seeing her is something new. The other men who have come on with lines like his were looking right through her clothes as if they possessed x-ray vision. Which is an altogether different way of not being seen.

"I met my wife here," he tells her. He nods at the next table, where the two older couples are sitting. "Right there. That's why I asked. But back then, the chairs were different. They had rawhide seats, and they were rickety as hell. You never knew what might happen when you sat down in one of them. I haven't been here for a long time."

She seldom engages the patrons, not even women with small children, the ones all the other waitresses and waiters *ooh* and coo over, hoping to increase their tips. But she has yet to move away from this man, though two young guys just sat down at a table in the corner and are waiting for menus. "When did you meet her?" she asks.

"Nineteen eighty-nine." He smiles. "Here and yet not here. But it was closer to here than anyplace else." As if he understands that such reflections have the potential to unsettle her, he glances at the menu. "No Zywiec now," he says. "Just Tyskie and Pilsner Ur-quell. I believe I'll have the latter. And a burger and fries. I might want a second beer pretty quickly, so keep an eye on me, if you wouldn't mind." He hands her the menu and smiles again, and she goes off to place the order, then carries menus to the two guys who recently entered.

When she returns to the bar, the pilsner is waiting, so she stands it on a serving tray and carries it to his table. He's watching something in Planty and at first doesn't react when she places it before him. Just as she's about to walk away, he says, "Thank you. It used to take forever."

ELENA IS the only one at the table who pays him any mind. He looks, she thinks, like a man with nowhere to go. A moment or two later, she revises her assessment. What he really looks like is a man who has already seen everything worth seeing. Or at least thinks he has, which amounts to the same thing.

It hasn't been long since she felt like that herself. What kept her going through the motions at the refugee center and, later, when Teresa hired her to wait tables, was the possibility, slim though it seemed, of seeing her daughter again. And then she found out that she was alive, and this led her to go to the restaurant with Bogdan, and then to his room, and now she sees him every day, and in a matter of months, she and Leysa will be reunited. She hopes this man has one good thing to look forward to. One is all you need. More than one is icing.

Marek starts telling a story about how he bought a car in Germany in 1992 and drove it to a shop near the Polish border. "I had them completely disassemble it," he says, "and ship it over the border as 'used auto parts,' which had a much lower tariff. On this side, I paid another shop to reassemble it. I saved a huge amount."

"Yes," Bogdan says, "but what happened later?"

"Well, they didn't get all the bolts completely tight, maybe because they put some in the wrong holes."

"And?"

Elena can tell that they've been through this routine many times. Little boys talking about little boys' toys.

Marek laughs. "And one day I went out to get in it, and it was lying on the ground. The chassis had come loose from the wheels. But that didn't happen for several months. Until then, it was a wonderful car."

The two couples talk a while longer, then Bogdan takes a look at his watch and tells Elena that as much as he hates it, they'd better be going. The traffic will be at least as bad as it was earlier, if not worse. He signals for the check. When the sullen waitress arrives with it, Marek and Inga mount the obligatory protest, but he tells them not to be silly, that today, the privilege is his.

Though Richard is watching the activity in Planty, he has been listening to the conversation at the next table, where so long ago a happy accident occurred that altered his life. It's a habit, listening to others—an essential habit for a writer of any ilk. You can learn all sorts of things that way, and if ninety-eight percent of it is inconsequential, there's always the other two percent. This is what he often told his students, back when he still had them. "That two percent could be worth everything. It could give you the beginning of your story. Or, if you've already got most of a story written, it could lead you to your ending. Or it could provide you with the single detail that could energize the entire narrative. At any given moment, you never know what might be laid on your table. As a writer—or, for that matter, as a human being—sometimes your main job is simply to be receptive."

He has freely given that advice, but it's been a long time since he took it himself. He's felt so little investment in his surroundings for so long that he stopped paying attention as he once did.

Today, he has already learned that the older of the two women belongs with the little white-haired man with faint scars on his face. The woman who keeps mangling Polish grammar is with the man whose back is turned to Richard. His best guess would be that she's Ukrainian. Given what's going on in that country, most likely a refugee. The Poles resist taking them if they're from the Middle East, but about a year ago, the *New York Times* reported that over three hundred thousand Ukrainians had arrived here since the conflict began. A great many have been granted temporary work permits. Suffering, apparently, has been assigned its hierarchies too.

The two men and the older woman have known one another forever. They've made numerous allusions to a shared past, but they speak with greater detail than they would if they were only talking among themselves. The Ukrainian woman, if that's what she is, and the man whose face he can't see are a more recent pair. This is a get-acquainted encounter, a chance for the other couple to meet their old friend's new interest. A café is, after all, a place where people often greet others for the first time. *Let's meet at Bunkier Café. Three o'clock. Would that be okay? You know the place I mean, the one in Planty that's attached to the art gallery?* Those are the exact words once spoken to him, over a phone line that both he and the speaker assumed was tapped. The majority of these meetings lead nowhere or, at most, to casual relationships. Every now and then, things follow a different course, as they did for him and Julia. Deeper attachments get formed, the kind that can survive anything, including death.

The older woman and the little white-haired man will almost certainly remain together forever. This is Poland, where divorce is still rare, no matter how rocky a marriage might be, and theirs doesn't sound troubled. They have children and grandchildren, and they see them all on a regular basis. Their extended family probably visits the cemetery together on All Saints' Day, they attend Christmas Eve mass together at St. Mary's, and they open presents together on Christmas morning.

In the natural course of things, one day, either the man or the woman will not wake up. If you were going to place a bet based on their physical appearances, you would place it on the man, who looks as if he's withering from the inside out. His skin is pale and flaky-looking, as if it's been sprinkled with white powder, and when he gets excited, he grows breathless. But then again, you never know. As healthy as she looks, the woman could go first. One of them will bury the other at Rakowicki, and eventually, the other will follow.

The second pair has embarked on a new adventure. The Ukrainian woman looks eight or ten years younger than the other woman. Mid- to late forties. If she's here as a refugee or even as a guest worker, it's probably because leaving was her only option. And if that's true, it's possible she left no one behind. Maybe she lost her husband in the war. Maybe she lost others as well.

He can't see how old the man with his back to him is, but his thin gray hair and lifelong friendship with the first pair would indicate late fifties. There aren't many single men in Poland in their fifties. It's a country where people marry young. About the only men who don't are the ones with such fatal flaws—alcoholism chief among them—that nobody will have them. But this man doesn't sound like a big drinker, and out of the corner of his eye, Richard can see the coffee cup standing near his right hand. He's not even having a beer or a glass of wine, perhaps because he's driving.

It's likely that at one time, the man whose face he can't see had a wife. It's not impossible that their marriage ended in divorce, but the odds are against it. Maybe he lost her to breast cancer. Or uterine cancer. Or ovarian cancer. Or heart attack. Or deep-vein thrombosis after a twenty-two-hour flight from Melbourne. Or any number of other diseases that kill thousands of women every day.

Maybe he lost her in an accident.

Maybe she's not the only one he lost.

Maybe he lost everything and everybody but the people at that table.

The man whose face he can't see has a calm voice, a steady voice, resonant without being loud. He sounds affable. He laughs when a good line demands it, pokes gentle fun from time to time at his male friend. They've been buddies forever, after all, and he wants him to meet this woman who has stepped into his life. He wants his friends to become hers.

Whatever loss he suffered, this man, whose name Richard doesn't know, whose face he can't see, found the means to overcome it. It could not have been easy, and there's no telling how long it took, how often he felt as if his body were a great leaden weight, how many nights he lay awake staring at the ceiling, how many mornings he woke and thought, *Why bother?* Luck may have lent a hand, as luck does more often than some of us want to admit, but the choice to accept it was strictly up to him. Now, here he sits where Richard once sat, with a woman he probably didn't know existed this time last year. They've seized that space and made it theirs.

Certain endings should be resisted. Others had better be embraced with all the grace you can muster.

As the people at the next table are leaving, Richard looks over his shoulder and gets a glimpse of the face that he couldn't see until now. The guy is around his age, maybe a little older, and thoroughly unremarkable.

WHEN THE waitress returns with his food, she discovers that he has moved to the table where the two older couples were sitting, transferring their cups and glasses to his own and wiping their table off so that there's no extra mess for her to clean up. He asks if she could bring him another beer and some ketchup. She grabs a bottle of Heinz from a nearby table, slaps it against her palm, sets it before him, and goes to the bar to order another pilsner.

The burger is cooked just the way Richard used to love them, seared on the surface but still juicy inside. The French fries are crisp, the pickles sour. He can't even recall the last time he ate a hamburger and fries, nor can he recall the last time he was this hungry. When he's finished with his meal and the second beer, he considers ordering one more but rules it out and beckons for the check.

It comes to forty-four zlotys. He pulls out two one-hundred-zloty notes, places them in the leather check holder, and hands it to her.

"I'm sorry," she says. "I don't understand. Would you like me to break the other hundred as well? I don't know if they will let me do that."

"No, it's all for you."

"But it's too much."

"The service was great," he says. "And in the end, I got to sit where I hoped to all along. Things worked out for me today." He smiles, tells her good-bye, and walks away before she can protest.

For the next week or so, each time she reports for work, she will expect to find him there, ready to try one form of flattery or another, just like so many of the other aging men she's served. But he won't return tomorrow, or the day after that, or next week, or next month. After a while, she will forget his face, though she will always remember the extravagant tip.

He takes a circuitous route back, wandering the streets near the market square for an hour or more, then making his way down to the ancient Jewish Quarter. Once dark and seedy, this area is now lined with bars and restaurants, which are starting to fill up with young people, nearly all of them speaking Polish. He hears rap blasting from one pub, alt country from another. He strolls around there for a while longer, getting himself reoriented. Then, without giving it too much thought, he heads for the river.

In the fall of '89, he and Julia walked along the Vistula nearly every evening right around this time. After they bought Stefan's share of her parents' place and began coming here with Anna, the three of them took the walk together. They did it almost every day. The nice thing about a river is that while the water may be a little lower or a little higher, it's otherwise the same, looking just how it used to. This evening, the only thing he sees that surprises him is a new bridge for bikers and pedestrians, a graceful, arcing construction that reminds him of the Zakim Bridge in Boston.

On the way to their building, he drops by the grocery store in Galeria Kazimierz, picking up a couple of rolls for breakfast along with a package of butter, some cheese, and a carton of orange juice. He'll worry about laying in more substantial supplies tomorrow.

The apartment, he discovers, is stifling, as he should have known it would be. He opens the windows in the living room and bedroom, carries the food and the juice into the kitchen and stores them there, then sends Monika a text, asking if she's still available for lunch and if he could drop by their place beforehand and see Stefan—assuming, of course, that it wouldn't disrupt his writing.

She responds immediately: *Yes to lunch and Stefan says he wants to see you every day for the rest of his life. Come over around noon.*

He steps back into the living room, opens the liquor cabinet, and breaks the seal on the Bushmills. After pouring himself a nice-sized drink, he carries it to the coffee table and sets it down. The stereo stands on the lowest bookshelf, a point of contention, he recalls, between him and Julia. Who puts a stereo that close to the floor? She won, he lost. It's a small, basic unit, a Panasonic with detachable speakers that can't do all they were designed to because they stand side by side. To his surprise, it comes on when he flips the switch. It's tuned to a rock station, probably from the time when Franek hid here to keep from being sent away to Fresno. He turns off the radio and punches the CD button. The tray hesitates, then slides out.

The discs are lined up on the shelf next to the speakers. They're all copies that he burned and brought here over many years. They have labels, but they're not alphabetized, though they once were. It takes him a while to find the one he's looking for. He slides it in, sits down in his old armchair, and takes a swallow of the Bushmills as Ella caresses the first lines, inviting him to listen to her tale of woe.

EVERYBODY'S GOT a tale of woe, though some are worse than others. He let his tale turn into a tail instead. Some days he didn't know if he was dragging it around or if it was dragging him. Most often, it was the latter. It dragged him to the ground and all but buried him.

She soon glides into "Day Dream," written by the great Duke Ellington with John Latouche and Billy Strayhorn. Who was John Latouche? The same lyricist who wrote "Taking a Chance on Love." Friend of various luminaries, all more famous than he was. Gore Vidal, Leonard Bernstein, Jane Bowles. These kinds of facts matter. He shared them with Anna, as his father once shared them with him.

About halfway through the disc, he leans over and changes the mode to continuous play. Ella sings the same songs again and again, just as she did the day he and Anna decorated the Christmas tree all those years ago, right here in Krakow, right over there in that corner. Outside, it grows dark. He rises and turns on the lights. On the way back to his chair, he pours himself another drink, smaller than the first.

The apartment hasn't cooled off, and it's not going to anytime soon. The hottest time at the top of the Bauhaus is between midnight and two a.m. The sun turns the roof into a griddle, and the heat is slow to dissipate. Until he installs AC, it's going to be like this. It would make sense to go take a cold shower. But he's reluctant to leave his chair. Some of the sadness that plagued his nights and days has lifted. For the first time in years, he feels at home.

Acknowledgments

As always, my deepest debt is to my wife, Ewa Hryniewicz-Yarbrough, who has been my first and most astute reader now for thirty-three years, and to my daughters, Antonina Parris and Lena Yarbrough. My agent, Sloan Harris, remains the finest champion any writer ever had. Greg Michalson, who along with Fred Ramey launched my first novel eighteen years ago, did a magnificent job editing the book, and my gratitude to him and Unbridled Books knows no limit. Thanks to Maria Koundoura, Robert Sabal, Michaele Whelan, and Emerson College for the sabbatical that allowed me to finish the novel in Krakow, where I started it, and to my colleagues in the Department of Writing, Literature, and Publishing at Emerson College and also those at the Sewanee Writers' Conference for their friendship and support. Special thanks to Pablo Medina and Pamela Painter. My thanks also to all my friends in Krakow and Warsaw, especially those in the Komitet Obrony Demokracji, for welcoming this American into their midst. Tim Judah's superb nonfiction book *In Wartime: Stories from Ukraine* was an invaluable source of information about that tragic conflict, as were the *Guardian* and the *New York Times*.

JOANNA GROMEK

STEVE YARBROUGH is the author of ten previous books for which he's received numerous awards, including the Mississippi Institute of Arts and Letters Award for Fiction, the California Book Award, the Richard Wright and the Robert Penn Warren Awards, etc. He has also been a PEN/Faulkner finalist. His work has been published in several foreign languages, including Dutch, Japanese and Polish, and in a number of other countries. Yarbrough currently teaches at Emerson College and lives in Stoneham, MA with his wife Ewa.

The son of Mississippi Delta cotton farmers, Steve is an aficionado of jazz and bluegrass music, which he plays on guitar, mandolin and banjo, often after midnight.